1994

a novel of politics

by Jack Miller

White Tiger Press
Portland, Oregon
©2019

This book is dedicated to my students, whose curiosity, dedication, and outrage have always driven me to explain what I know about politics as clearly as I possibly can.

"People who claim to know jackrabbits will tell you they are primarily motivated by Fear, Stupidity, and Craziness. But I have spent enough time in jack rabbit country to know that most of them lead pretty dull lives; they are bored with their daily routines: eat, fuck, sleep, hop around a bush now and then... No wonder some of them drift over the line into cheap thrills once in a while; there has to be a powerful adrenalin rush in crouching by the side of a road, waiting for the next set of headlights to come along, then streaking out of the bushes with split-second timing and making it across to the other side just inches in front of the speeding front wheels."

— Hunter S. Thompson, *Fear and Loathing on the Campaign Trail '72*

"Power is not an institution, and not a structure; neither is it a certain strength we are endowed with; it is the name that one attributes to a complex strategical situation in a particular society."

— Michel Foucault, The History of Sexuality

PART 1
THREE SCORES DOWN

We are not going down. Only it seems like they are. The wheels of the plane just left the ground, but the takeoff feels tenuous, the aircraft moving too slowly to maintain flight. The cabin lights flick off and on, and the plane rattles loudly, shuddering like a harpooned whale as it muscles skyward through a driving rain.

Melissa Carnes glances at the stewardess sitting placidly in the forward jump seat. No reaction, but what does that airhead know? Probably so used to dodgy takeoffs that she can't recognize a tragedy in the making.

The plane dips left, thrusting Mel against the window, and even though it rights itself immediately and continues climbing, she can't help the feeling of dread she has.

Come on, Carnes. Pull it together. We are NOT going down. It's a true statement, but it feels like a lie, a half-truth at best. She's managed enough of those over the years to know how it works. Technically the plane continues to ascend, but it can't possibly last. It's a blatant falsehood to maintain that it will. They're simply not moving fast enough to make it through such a fierce downpour. The nose jolts downwards suddenly, then eases back up, the plane laboring valiantly, but it's a baby bird kicked out of the nest too soon. They will be going down before long. That's the hidden truth, the one no one wants to admit.

Mel hunches forward, clenching her knees tightly. She slides her glasses to the top of her head, stares out the window feeling helpless, trying to breathe steadily as the ground disappears and the plane gets swallowed up by the clouds, the universe empty except for the wing lights flashing against blackness and droplets sizzling on the window. The shuddering continues, the interior creaking and groaning like the plane is missing half its rivets. The rest of the passengers seem to think this is normal, nobody looking around in fear or grabbing their seatmate's forearm for reassurance. Mel holds herself in check, doesn't want to be the one to start a chain reaction of panic.

A line from *Airplane* pops into her head. *Looks like I picked the wrong week to quit sniffing glue.* She smiles meekly at the memory—she saw *Airplane* in high school, with her father for a date—but then the plane bucks hard half a dozen times, and Mel's mouth goes dry. Her heartbeat is weak but way too fast, her hands sweating, her eyeballs tight and dry, the hiss of compressed air and the roar of the engines slicing through her tightening eardrums. She's never had a panic attack, but this sure as shit feels like one coming on.

She takes a deep breath, tries to forget that 65% of all plane crashes happen within 5 minutes of takeoff or landing, one of many unhelpful stats Mel has learned over the years. A life in politics dumps all kinds of unnerving facts into your brain, though there's also a fair share of countervailing data that could make you feel less bad if you were so inclined. It's far more dangerous on the highway than in the sky, for one thing. Mel clicks through the stats in her mind: over 40,000 automobile deaths last year, compared to under 1,000 flight fatalities. Plus, 34% of passengers survive fatal accidents involving 10+ people. The facts don't calm Mel in the slightest. A thousand dead is a lot of people, a 1-in-3 chance of survival not exactly the most reassuring of odds.

She drops her glasses back to her nose, pulls out the safety information card for the first time since childhood, when she made a habit of familiarizing herself with emergency procedures whenever her family flew anywhere. She remembers her mother chiding her for it. "They haven't changed any since last time, Boo boo." The memory tightens her chest, makes her long for her mother's casual attitude towards danger. She tries to feel less alarmed as she studies the diagram of the Boeing 727-200, notes that the front hatch is her nearest emergency exit. That's just three rows away. The inflatable slide is also an emergency floatation device. She fights back a growing sense of dread, tells herself she's just having a bad morning, she's not going to die on the 6:42 from Omaha.

She folds and stores the card, dries her hands on her skirt, piles on the reassurance by noting that she's been on far more dangerous flights, statistically speaking—prop jobs flying out of tiny airports even the locals haven't heard of, charter flights on corporate jets of questionable reliability, maintained by mechanics nursing grudges against the uppercrust who fly around the world in sleek comfort, isolated from the grimy, coughing masses. These "general aviation" flights, as the government calls them, are over 5 times more likely to produce fatalities than commercial airline flights, contributing the bulk of that 1,000 dead, taking out half a dozen or a dozen people at a time

1994

with little or no press mention, unfamous businessmen mourned only by their accountants, obscure politicians and their staff on bullshit junkets, the occasional rock star that most people end up assuming died from a heroin overdose. Mel remembers the exact numbers — 25.4 fatalities per million flight hours in general aviation compared to 4.5 for airliners, a 1 in 4.7 million chance of dying on the average commercial flight, roughly 1 in a million for general aviation. She's known these facts for years — she briefly staffed a Congressman on an FAA oversight committee — which is why she's rarely worried about crashing, even under the most statistically treacherous conditions. 1 in a million never seemed all that risky.

We are not going down, she repeats to herself. She pushes her glasses back up her nose. *You're being ridiculous.*

It shouldn't take a shrink to tell her why she's so worked up today. She's never been fired before, never even worried about it, yet it's entirely possible she loses her job on the other end of this flight — a highly coveted position she loves and kicks ass at. She tells herself this would be an odd way to do it, sending her a first-class ticket on short notice just to deliver the news in person. Cliff Barker could've simply called her at her motel last night, told her to pack up and get out, her final check is in the mail. Instead, he sent a ticket by special messenger, no indication of why he wants her back in D.C., just a note telling her to head to the office straight from the airport. There's no agenda for the meeting, not even a specific time, just the number of an anonymous conference room on the second floor. It struck Mel as exceedingly Kafkaesque, but this is the way Barker operates sometimes, his idea of a management style to throw random acts of disruption at his staff to cover for his own wide-ranging anxiety. He's exactly the kind of prick who'd use precious committee funds for a first-class ticket, only to fire the poor schmuck at the other end. His treatment of women at the DNC is particularly random, nervous and sweaty at times, stern and tyrannical at others, no obvious reason for the difference except he's an insecure asshole who quit drinking and smoking at the wrong phase of life. Mel's glad she spends most of her time in the field and doesn't have to see Barker much except between campaigns, when all the strategists are back at DNC headquarters waiting for a new assignment, trying to dry out in anticipation of the extra-hard boozing that's coming with the next campaign.

Mel has been relatively abstemious over the past few months, Bob Kerrey's crew in Nebraska unusually buckled down and no mini-bar in her motel room. HQ is in a dry county or some bullshit like that, no bars within easy range for whatever reason. It feels like she was sent away to Mormon summer camp for misbehaving at school. She's not particularly sad to be leaving that scene behind, though she has come to like and respect the candidate, and the race seemed to be going pretty well. She flatters herself that's because of her, knows it probably is. Lack of confidence has never been Mel's problem. Not that success guarantees she's not being fired. She could've pissed off the wrong person. That's probably it.

Whatever awaits in D.C., Mel has to assume she's off the Kerrey gig for one reason or another, though it's also possible that Barker just wants an in-person report from the field. He's old school, doesn't believe the polls—doesn't understand them is probably closer to the truth. The 50-somethings who clog the upper echelons of the Democratic Party still think in terms of caucus meetings and ward bosses, glance only in passing at the data printouts Mel and her generation of pols rely on. The old boys prefer to operate face-to-face, working out differences over Scotch and cigars, staring down rivals through a thick haze of smoke, analog to the core. Hard as it is for Mel to believe, it really still operates that way, 1994 closer to 1900 than it is to a new millennium. Mel has no idea how her party holds Congress with the outdated way most campaigns are still run. Well, they probably won't after November 8th. Not exactly consolation.

So of course it's both particular and generalized anxiety that has Mel on edge this morning. Doesn't take a Georgetown shrink to tell her that. Her job's in jeopardy, and her party's looking at a drubbing all over the map this cycle. Even if Kerrey holds his seat, the Senate's on thin ice, the House almost guaranteed to flip. A fucking Republican wave. Mel supposes she'd have to live through one eventually, though there was always that secret hope that the Dems could maintain a permanent majority, as though the word *permanent* has any place in politics.

Mel takes another deep breath as the plane labors through the onslaught of rain, the elements fighting desperately to knock this intruder back to the ground. How can this fragile metal tube possibly defeat Mother Nature?

The deep breath fails to reduce the mounting panic, succeeds only in making Mel think of cigarettes. She desperately wants a smoke. Her last one was #3 for the day, just outside the terminal. She should've had one more in the Delta smoking lounge before boarding, didn't think she'd have to endure this stress along with 3 1/2 smoke-free hours. She remembers when you could still light up on flights, the ban going into effect only 5 years ago. Her habit wasn't as strong back then, and she rarely smoked on a plane. It did seem a bit rude to the non-smokers—she's always agreed that smoking on a plane, even in the designated smoking section, was a bit like peeing in a pool—but just knowing she could do it in the past makes her yen for it that much stronger now. You could make an argument that it's more like medicine than an addiction in a situation like this. Critics called cigarettes a drug—well, every drug has a necessary and proper use. If this isn't the time and place for a cigarette, when is? Mel has heard California is inching towards legalizing "medical marijuana." If that makes sense, couldn't she declare an emergency need for medical nicotine and light up right here, right now? They let people facing firing squads have a last cigarette—why not her?

She takes yet another deep breath, lingers on the exhale. *Out with the bad air.* She wants to believe the danger has passed, but the cabin lights flick off and on again, and the plane banks hard to the right, pushing Mel against the shoulder of her seatmate, a typical wide-body Southwestern businessman, complete with 10-gallon hat, bolo tie, crocodile boots, and an oversized Cornhuskers belt buckle—the kind of cliché central casting would put in the adjacent seat to round out Mel's distress if her life were a movie. Sometimes it seems like it is.

"You all right there, little lady?"

Little lady? For Christsakes! People really talk like that? Maybe this is a movie. But is it *Airplane* or *Airport*? That's the million-dollar question.

Mel offers a forced smile in response, pulls a quote from her vast reservoir. *"There has to be a more dignified mode of transportation."* She does a half-decent Molly Ringwald, adds a slight eye roll to make the comedy more obvious. She hopes she seems blasé, not unhinged.

"Excuse me?" The Cornhusker looks down at Mel with what seems like genuine concern, brown eyes sparkling with tenderness and brotherly love.

Oh, Jeez, he's one of those churchy types, she thinks. Could things get any worse? Mel flashes a quick, apologetic smile, though it's possible this makes her come across as even more terrified than before.

"You sure you're alright? You look a little…" He searches for the right word, probably worried about further agitating his distressed seatmate.

"Bedraggled?" Mel offers this before she can consider a better response. What she should've said was, "I'm fine, thanks for asking."

The man's eyes become even more tender as he studies Mel, his face betraying a battle to say the right thing here. He clearly doesn't want to agree, but Mel knows bedraggled would be the right word even if she weren't on the edge of a panic attack. She ran a comb through her hair this morning after a quick shower, but that's the extent of her beauty regimen. No make-up, no curling iron, no effort whatsoever. She doesn't want to be put-together at all for her encounter with Barker. Some women think they have to look and sound perfect all the time to impress their superiors, but in Mel's experience, it's better to be as rough-edged as possible. She tried the look-nice/play-nice approach when she started out in politics, discovered quickly that she gained exactly zero recognition for it. To the old boys' network, it signaled obedience and irrelevance, invited sexual advances but gained no professional respect. She adapted quickly, started throwing elbows, never let herself doubt she could stare down any asshole in the business. It's served her well for the most part, but she knows she can come across as unkempt in circumstances where that's not to her advantage.

"I was thinking *nervous*," the seatmate says. He gives Mel a hopeful smile. "It *is* a mite bumpy."

"I'm fine. Really I am." She forces another smile, knows it looks as false as her statement. Even a robot could tell she's not fine.

"Turbulence makes me nervous too," he says, but he's clearly lying. He looks like he could fall from 35,000 feet, bounce a few times, and walk away singing *Amazing Grace*.

The plane dips again, and the cabin lights flick off and on once more. She notices a few other first-class passengers are glancing around with concern now, but the stewardess remains Buddha-like up front, inspecting the polish on her nails and smiling vacantly. Bird brain! We're fucking desperate here!

"Uh, this is your captain speaking. Just want to give you a little update on this turbulence we're experiencing. We'll be heading through a rough patch here for a few more minutes. Stay buckled up and hang tight. We'll be up and out of this and clear sailing pretty soon."

Is exactly what the captain would say if the situation were completely out of control, Mel says to herself. Remain calm. Don't panic the passengers with the ugly truth. They'll either pull out of it, or 66% of them will die. No use spreading unnecessary terror.

Mel's not usually a disaster visualizer, but her jaw clenches as she pictures quiet mayhem in the cockpit—dials spinning, the stick unresponsive, the pilot and co-pilot pale and sweaty. A quote from *Airport* flies into her brain when she really needs another line from *Airplane*. *Hold on, we're going for broke!* They survive the re-entry in that one, right? It's only a movie, though. Even in disaster flicks, nearly everybody lives—not so much in reality. 66% likelihood of *not* surviving.

Mel's stomach drops with another shudder of the fuselage, her body flooding with every unhelpful chemical in the book, nudging her that much closer to a genuine panic attack. She turns to the window, closes her eyes against the flashing of the wing lights, her breath shallow, her hands and feet ice cold.

We. Are NOT. Going. Down. What a goddamned lie.

Mel tries to remember when she loved to fly, when a flight somewhere was an adventure-in-the-making, a life-changing experience waiting at the other end, or even in the next seat, when a Sony Walkman and a fresh novel was all she needed to occupy herself for a day of travel, when tomato juice seemed like an exotic beverage and the idea of emerging into a jetway somewhere different, hundreds or thousands of miles away, was among the most romantic feelings possible. That began to erode when she started working campaigns, and now all she feels is anxiety and annoyance whenever they're delayed on the tarmac before takeoff, or a stranger's elbow vies with hers for possession of the armrest, or the stewardess is out of Diet Coke by the time she reaches Mel's row. Or, as it's doing now, the plane feels like it can't possibly do anything but crash.

At best, flying these days is another low-grade hassle to be borne stoically—a visit to the gynecologist or dentist—and a time to work, to study polls and news clippings, to draft strategy memos and plan ad buys for radio markets no one a hundred miles away even knows about. Not that Mel planned to do any of that this morning. Waiting for her cab this morning, she decided to give work a rest for once. She was sure Barker was calling her in for the duration, not looking for an in-person status report. Bob Kerrey's fate come election day almost certainly rests with someone else now, probably that fuckwit Daniels. Good luck with that. She brought all her belongings—she's not going back to that piece-of-shit motel again either way—checked everything, briefcase and all. She boarded the plane empty-handed except for her complimentary copy of *USA Today*, trying to feel like she's free, not useless.

The plane finally pops out of the clouds and settles into its cruising altitude, the turbulence gone in an instant like the captain promised. Mel opens her eyes, takes as quiet of a deep breath as she can, tries not to appear as though she just survived a harrowing experience. She blinks at the bright sky, turns to smile at her seatmate—*nothing to worry about, right?*—furtively checks her pulse. Heart rate elevated but slowing. She unfolds her paper with slightly shaky hands, wishing again for a cigarette, a celebratory one in this case. She peels off the first two sections of the paper, tucks them in the seatback pocket. Usually she'd pore over the news, then work through the business section to make sure there's nothing going on in the economy she should know about, but she needs to escape reality for a while, for any number of reasons. Most women would probably turn to the lifestyle section, but Mel's refuge is Sports, football in particular — pro, not college. She scans the NFL standings and injury reports first, looks over the early line for next week's game, then digs into the commentary. The Chargers are the only undefeated team left in the league after a last-second game-winning field goal to beat the Raiders, who were favored by 3 1/2 points but drop to 1-3 after a shocking loss at home. The Chargers? Seriously? With Stan Humphries under center? *That can't last*, Mel thinks, though the *USA Today* pundits are already talking Super Bowl. Idiots.

There's a short piece about the 3-1 Browns leading in the AFC East. The Browns have been Mel's team since childhood, a terminally heartbreaking form of loyalty for her and roughly 1 million other Ohioans. The anonymous writer has some cautiously optimistic things to say about Coach Belichick and QB Vinny Testaverde, but there's the usual wait-for-them-to-blow-it disclaimer in the final paragraph, noting how the Browns started 5-2 the previous season before limping to a 7-9 finish. Mel wishes she could be pissed at the negative coverage, but it's fair enough after four years below .500 and a string of heartbreaking playoff losses for 10 years before that. She'd like to think the Cleveland Curse could be broken this year, but that's even less likely than the Democrats holding the House — roughly the odds of rolling two Snake Eyes in a row, in Mel's opinion.

Her hulking seatmate catches Mel lingering over the NFL page.

"You a football fan, little lady?"

Again with the *little lady*?

"Browns fan," Mel notes dryly.

"That's not exactly the same thing, now is it?" He chuckles in a way that actually makes Mel chuckle too. "No offense," he adds with a warm grin.

"They've got a 3-and-1 start this year," Mel says. She hates that she sounds so defensive about it. "I smell a division championship," she adds, trying to sound more sure. "Maybe even conference."

"Uh huh. Could be. Huskers are 4-and-0h." He taps the Cornhuskers buckle with a thick finger. "'Nother national championship comin', I just know it. Played on the '70 and '71 championship teams myself."

1994

"Let me guess," Mel says. She doesn't want to engage—she could really use a nap after that takeoff—but she can't help it. Pegging people's sports abilities is one of her odd forms of ESP. "Offensive line. Left guard, if I'm not mistaken."

"That's 100 percent correct, little lady. How'd you know?"

"I have a knack." Mel allows herself a sly smile, folds her paper closed and turns slightly in her seat, signaling a willingness to talk to her seatmate. This is not her typical M.O., but this is not a typical morning either. She's got a kind of survivor's high even though all she really survived was her own irrational panic.

"You're not a sports writer, now are you?" He sounds impressed. "I hear some women're breaking into that racket.' Bout damn time, if you ask me. Equality's a long time comin' for too many folks in too many ways."

"Nope, not a sports writer." Mel lets the commentary pass without remark, but she smiles more cordially. Something about this guy makes her feel oddly at ease. Normally this is exactly the kind of person who would piss her off just for being alive, bulging over the armrest into her personal space and forcing conversation on her with his saccharine evangelical grin, but there's a genuine warmth to him that gets through to Mel. Plus he seems to be a friend of gender equality, a nice surprise. Is it possible he's not the standard-issue Great Plains Republican he looks like? Nebraska *is* an oddball place—she's learned that over the past few months.

"Don't tell me, then," he says, rubbing his meaty hands together like he's about to offer Mel a great deal on prime Nebraska grassland. "Lemma guess. Early morning flight to D.C. You're wearing a grey pinstripe lady suit, conservative black heels, expensive wire-frame glasses. No wedding band or engagement ring. Above average in the looks department. You gotta be one a them lobbyist types. Am I right?"

"Close." Mel is impressed and offended in equal measure, but she can't seem to muster any anger at the implicit sexism in his analysis. The fact is, what she does is only a few clicks from lobby work, and there's definitely something disarming about this guy. She knows she looks like hell, especially after that takeoff, but he gives her credit for *above average in the looks department* with such a matter-of-fact tone it doesn't sound like a come-on. "*Really* close. But nope, not a lobbyist."

"Secretary of Health and Human Services, then." He says it with a broad grin and put-on assurance. "Donna something-or-other."

"Getting colder," Mel says, but she's impressed that he knows one of the three women in Clinton's cabinet. Donna Shalala. He's probably a lobbyist himself, National Beef Association would be her guess.

"Well you're not Janet Reno, that much I know. Wait, you're not Diane Sawyer, are you?" He widens his eyes. "Come on now! You are! No way." He looks around comically, as though he simply has to tell someone else who he's sitting next to.

Mel feels herself beginning to blush just before she thinks to feel affronted. She's been told before that she bears a striking resemblance to a *young* Diane Sawyer, but Sawyer must be in her late-40s by now. Does she look that worn down today? She feels a good 20 years older than her age sometimes, and Sawyer does look fantastic on TV, but it's an insulting stretch for a 29 year-old to be mistaken for a middle-aged woman. Mel hates that she thinks in those terms—it galls her how much women are judged by their appearance—but the thoughts fly through her mind unbidden, her own unconscious sexism stronger than she'd like to admit.

"Nope, not Diane Sawyer." Mel still can't dredge up any anger. There's something about this guy that's drawing her in. He reminds her of exactly nobody she likes or respects, except for maybe Bill Clinton. That could be it. He's got that same kind of close-up charisma, the big friendly face, the air of a man who knows a lot about a great many things, wisdom and tolerance belied by his hillbilly get-up and cracker accent.

"I give up, then. I'm usually pretty good at this too, but you've got me stumped."

"I'm a campaign strategist, a perfectly anonymous behind the scenes kind of person."

"And you were in Nebraska for..." He raises his eyebrows.

"I'm running Bob Kerrey's Senate re-election."

"Impressive."

"At least I was until this morning," Mel adds. "I'm headed back to D.C. for a meeting at DNC headquarters. I'm not exactly sure what's waiting for me there. And I'm not exactly sure I care."

"And why's that?"

"High politics is an ugly game. I've spent my whole adult life down in the mud. I'm not sure how much more I can take."

This is far more than Mel would normally say to a seatmate—to anyone—but she can't seem to stop herself. Before she knows it, she's unloading to this stranger, telling him about her mother's unsuccessful battle with cancer and how she's struggled ever since to live up to her dying words, the obstacles and frustrations of a woman in politics—"In *any* top profession"—the denial and subterfuge that make up the bulk of her existence, even the parade of short-term boyfriends who've never amounted to much.

1994

"I mean, what the hell do I think I'm *accomplishing* with my life?"

It's not until the plane banks to begin its final approach into National that Mel halts her outpouring. What the fuck? She really must've needed to talk this out. *Probably time to find a new therapist*, she thinks.

"Wow. Whew. Sorry to unload all that on you," she says over the landing announcement.

"Don't you worry none there, Diane." She never gave her name, and he called her Diane the whole flight, a ruse she played along with, as though he really was sitting next to the famous lady journalist unloading the tale of personal and professional woes.

"I really appreciate you listening so patiently. I don't know what came over me." This is not the kind of thing Mel is used to saying to anyone. None of it is.

"Well, good luck to ya, Diane," he says when they part in the terminal. "I'll be praying for you. I gather from what you've been sayin' that you probably don't believe in God, but He believes in you, whether you want Him to or not. *I* believe in you, that much you can count on. You're an extraordinary young woman, even if you're havin' a hard time seein' it right now. I think your mama'd be proud."

"I hope so." Mel sounds — and feels — unconvinced. That's the whole problem, in a nutshell. *Would* her mother be proud? She's been dead nearly 15 years now, leaving exactly 0.0% chance for Mel to ever find out.

"You need to *know* it, little lady. She would. I'm sure of it."

Mel has no idea who this guy is — he never gave his name either — but she chokes up at their parting, as though a lifelong friend is headed off to war and she might never see him again. It's been a long time since someone she wasn't paying listened this closely to her troubles and doubts, a long time since she's let anybody, paid or unpaid, hear them.

"And good luck to the Browns too," he says over his shoulder, a playful grin on his face. "Something tells me they're gonna need it even more than you."

She remembers that remark 6 weeks later, when the Browns are still running hot at 7-2, a game ahead of the 6-3 Steelers.

"Hah!" she says at the memory, not sure what she means exactly, but pleased to recall her kind Cornhusker from a previous life. She wishes she'd gotten his name.

# # # # #

395 is shut down for some reason, so the cab takes Mel along the south side of the Mall. She sees the big monuments and historic buildings all the time, and she's long since lost her awe at the majesty of D.C., especially with what she knows about how politics really goes down. But today – with her guts recently spilled on the plane – seeing the Lincoln Memorial and all the rest, the flocks of tourists marveling at the grandeur, reminds her of the first time she visited D.C., back in '76 with her parents, their big East Coast tour for the Bicentennial, her father making every landmark an excuse for a mini history lesson, her mother taking deep breaths of the cherry-blossom-scented air and reminiscing about the March on Washington.

"It wasn't just black people," she said, eyes glittering at the memory. "It was a march for jobs and justice, things that concern every American, black *and* white. Brown, yellow, and red too." Somehow her mother could make these sweeping racial references sound not-so-awkward, which wasn't the case with her father.

"The White House was built largely by slave labor," he said, his tone mixing white guilt with admiration for the valiant men in chains who built the symbol of their own oppression

"Always a good reminder of how far we still have to go," her mother said, rescuing Mel's father from saying something even more cringe-worthy. Only 11 years old at the time, but Mel was in the full fervor of adolescent rebellion – against her father, at least. Her mother was – and always would be – perfect.

"That's true, Eleanor. Very true." Her father nodded and took his wife's hand. "One step at a time, right?"

"Only maybe pick up the pace a bit," she said, smirking and letting go of her husband's hand to dash ahead in the direction of the Capitol Building. A crack in the sidewalk tripped her up, and she sprawled onto the concrete, skinning her hands and knees, but when Mel and her father rushed up to see if she was okay, she was laughing. "Guess that's what happens when you try to run before you can walk." She got up and wiped her bleeding hands on her denim cutoffs. "Not that a little blood should ever stop us from charging forward. What's that Thomas Jefferson quote, Boo boo? The tree of revolution?"

Mel recited dutifully, pleased, as always, to back up her mother's life lessons. "The tree of liberty must be refreshed from time to time with the blood of patriots and tyrants."

"Exactly. The blood has to stay fresh. We can't ever let it scab over, or the forces of reaction win the battle for our nation's soul." This last remark was a clear dig at Mel's father, whose own interests lay squarely in the desiccated past, his expertise petering out with the election of Millard Fillmore.

The memory tightens Mel's chest, carries her unbidden into thoughts about her mother's funeral 3 1/2 years later, generally an off-limits corner of her mind. What the hell has her dredging this stuff up today? She cranks down the window, lights her 4th cigarette since landing, tries but fails to push away the image of her 15-year-old self, sitting stone-faced as people she knew and didn't know shed quiet tears over her mother. The funeral was unforgettable, a parade of speakers – Mel thinks it must've taken hours to complete – each of the eulogies more inspiring and heart-wrenching than the last, stories of her mother in college organizing the women on campus to protest the earlier curfew than the men had, her outrage at the inequality and her determination to end it way ahead of the college protests that became fadish a decade after Eleanor had done her difficult work, going sorority to sorority, patiently explaining why the difference of an hour mattered so much. Others told stories of a young community organizer in the wilds of southeast Ohio in '61 and '62, working 18- and 20-hour days to chip away at rural poverty, or the anti-nuke activist chained to a fence at a government facility, or the dedicated feminist joined by a handful of local mothers and a smattering of college students to cheer on Shirley Chisholm when she came through Wooster in '72. And on and on.

They told Mel more stories at the reception afterwards, standing with wine glasses in hand as they poured memories into the daughter they assumed would carry the torch, the girl who looked so much like Eleanor had when she was young, tall and fierce, eyes burning with the will to build a better world one brick at a time. Some of them said this flat-out to her face – at her mother's goddamned funeral! – "You look exactly like your mother when she was in college" and "I'm sure we'll see you do even greater things in the future." No pressure.

What they didn't know was Mel's eyes burned mostly from the effort of not crying. She shed not a single tear as she listened, hardly blinking, taking in every anecdote and tribute, the litany of praise canonizing her mother once and for all. She didn't want to miss anything – she worried that if she started crying, she might never stop – but it became a habit, not crying over her mother, a habit that strengthened over the years. She's still tall, obviously, but not quite as fierce – she's even a touch hunched over at times, diminishing her imposing height – and these days, when her eyes burn, it's with frustration at yet another idiocy or sexist remark, not with the will to build a better world. She's given up on that, embraced what all the men who've come before her in this field have, that progress is measured in millimeters, not miles – or even yards – that ideals must often be set aside for any mote of advantage over those who advance opposing goals. She's adjusted her expectations – an excellent euphemism – telling herself whenever doubts surface that this is the real world, where victory has to stand in for higher purpose, where data printouts and strategy memos are more important than principles and values, where your only choice is to pick the right side and advance its cause at all costs, even if that makes it feel like narrow ambition has supplanted the grand aspiration to make the world a better place.

Every once in a while – why does today have to be one of those days? – she reproaches herself for failing so spectacularly to follow in her mother's footsteps as everybody expected. Even her father – the moderate, the gradualist, the disappointment himself – expected it. Her mother has such a powerful legacy that Mel has to suppress it with utter ruthlessness to keep it from crushing her. That's another habit she has, burying the fact that she's her mother's daughter, ignoring the whispers at the back of her mind that she's wasting her life and her talent doing what she does. Even acknowledging that the whisper exists is heresy.

She has to admit she's been a heretic more and more lately, questioning her motives for staying the course with the career she choose when she entered college. Did she really know what she was doing at age 18? It felt like it at the time, and most of the time since, but seriously? She had it together enough back then to map out a sensible career for herself? Maybe more than now, is the likelihood that tortures her in these moments of uncertainty. She remembers with perfect clarity what it felt like to have no doubts about going into political communications, and she craves a return to that feeling. Her last therapist told her she was seeking a false sense of security in a mythologized past – "Were you really that much more self-assured as a younger person?" – but what if she was actually just smarter and more focused back then and her anxieties now are only a result of moral flabbiness and burnout? Shouldn't she stay the course rather than accepting that the past decade has been a colossal waste of time and energy?

"Hey lady!" It's the cabbie, an angry-looking middle-aged black man. Mel feels the predictable pang of guilt for even thinking about the man's race. He has ample reason to be angry, a working-class man in post-Reagan America – whether he's black or white is irrelevant. Now here comes some privileged politico zoning out in his cab, maybe costing him another quick fare because of the delay. He's right to be impatient with her. "Snap out of it. We're here."

"Yeah, sorry. Thanks." Mel grinds out her cigarette, flaps a $20 bill at the cabbie, tells him to keep the change, then bustles away with too many unhelpful thoughts crowding her brain.

The cabbie calls out again, more sympathetic this time. "Hey lady! Don't forget your bags." He gestures at the open trunk, lifts out her suitcase and briefcase with a semi-genuine grin.

The irony is almost too much to take. Of course she can't forget her baggage, and if she ever does, someone or something is sure to come along and remind her of it. *Christ! Who has these kinds of thoughts?* This is why she always quits therapy after a few months. No one should be saying this kind of shit to themselves. It's even less helpful than simply burying your emotions and plodding on through a fog of denial.

# # # # #

The conference room feels all too familiar, a depressing realization for Mel. It's a generic workspace entirely devoid of humanity, one of hundreds Mel has occupied over the past decade. The walls are light blue yet unsoothing in the fluorescent glare, the floor tiled in off-white with swirls of grey and green, vertical blinds over the windows, open but hogging most of the midday sun. There's a rectangular brown table, a dozen chairs upholstered in thick-woven beige fabric, a pinholed U.S. map tacked to one wall, blank whiteboard on another, TV-VCR combo on a rolling cart playing C-SPAN.

Mel sits at the far end of the table, feet planted, leaning forward and smoking a fresh Parliament. She looks like a weary baseball manager mulling over a bullpen move. The smoke, so soothing at times, does little to calm her as she watches the smug pie face of Newt Gingrich, speaking from the Capitol steps only a few blocks away.

— *For all those who are tired of negative attack smear campaigns. For all those who have asked political parties to get together and be a responsible team. For all those who have said we have to deal in a positive way with the challenges of America's future...*

Mel could be anywhere — Trenton, Jacksonville, Bakersfield, Boise, any of the dozen Columbuses she's been through. She used to keep a map of all the cities and towns where she stayed overnight, an acne-scarred America she left in her last apartment, the '70s studio she lived in after college, before she started making good money and moved to a pre-war building in Dupont Circle. It hardly matters that she's at the Democratic National Headquarters, only about a 45 minute walk from home. That's a raw geographic fact, nothing more. The word *home* is utterly meaningless when there's only 6 weeks til election day. She's never spent September or October in her apartment, can barely remember from her college days what Dupont Circle looks like in early autumn. She's not even sure she pictures her bedroom accurately. Is the TV at the foot of the bed like she thinks, or angled in the corner? Is she still using that dark-green cotton duvet, or did she switch to the charcoal flannel her father gave her for Christmas last year? Does she really have a Cindy Sherman print hanging on the wall, or is that something she transposed from an upscale hotel she stayed in once?

Not that it matters. It's almost certain she'll spend tonight in a hotel somewhere, upscale or otherwise, and the next 40-or-so nights after that – call it the odds the average NFL kicker makes a 25-yard field goal, pretty much a guarantee. It is possible Cliff Barker called her here to fire her, and it's possible the kick gets blocked or the snap fumbled, but neither is likely. Mel was worried earlier, but now that she's here, she knows Barker has a different plan. She sees a brand-new cardboard box on a chair in the corner marked "PORTER," her new assignment no doubt.

She should've known it all along. However much Barker resents her for her youth and her lack of a penis, the fact is, he needs all his best people in the field or his ass is grass. He's probably going down no matter what – he's at the exact right pay grade to take the fall for a bad cycle – but he has to at least look like he's trying or he won't be able to land a cushy consulting job once the DNC scapegoats him out. Mel explores the idea of feeling sorry for Barker. Even if it is a wave election no one at the DNC could possibly stop, someone has to be blamed. That's an iron law of politics – a fall guy must always be found so no one suspects systemic rot. It's sure as shit not going to be the new Chairman of the DNC, not this time around. It might actually be his fault – it's explicitly his mandate to hold and expand the party's base of power – but he's too young and too high up to take the fall. Firing him would be admitting that the future of the Democratic Party has been placed in the wrong hands. Even if it's true – *especially* if it's true – you can't admit that. No, someone a step or two down has to be sacrificed. Barker stands beneath the falling safe, and he probably knows it, knows too that an anvil or a piano takes him out if he evades the safe.

Maybe Barker deserves some sympathy, but Mel can't manage to dredge it up. What's coming November 8th may not be his fault, but he's a certified asshole under the best of conditions, so fuck him. Mel's job right now is to keep herself from getting dragged down with him.

1994

Oh yeah, and to try to make the drubbing they have coming as little bad as possible. That too.

Barker drifts in while Mel's lighting a new cigarette off the tip of the previous one. He studiously ignores Mel, perches on the far edge of the table and glares at the TV, crosses his arms and tries to look annoyed and wise at the same time. It's a signature expression, a mask to hide anxiety and burnout, or so Mel has always thought. Barker wears the expected costume – white shirt and blue tie, pleated khakis, oxblood loafers – but he's dumpy and rumpled, eternally slouchy, exhibits the body language of a man who's actually as sad and hopeless as he should be, stuck at deputy national strategist at age 54 and looking down the barrel of a Republican tsunami.

—We were asked as recently as this morning, why are we here? Why not just run against the Clinton administration and its collapsing public support? And in the spirit of total honesty, I have to say, when you watch them collapse this badly, it is tempting.

"I hate that weasely shitbag." Mel flicks her old cigarette at the TV. It bounces off the screen with a spray of sparks and drops to the floor.

Barker considers the cigarette with a frown, steps over to crush the glowing tip with his toe.

"Get used to him," he says. "He's going to be the next Speaker of the House. Thank you Hillary Goddamn Clinton."

Mel blows a cloud of smoke at Barker. "You're gonna blame the First Lady for that haughty piece of shit? Nice, Barker. You're a real team player. Go Team Patriarchy."

"She botched the healthcare thing, and this is what we get." Barker squats with a groan and picks up the dead butt, twisted like a question mark. He wags it at Mel. "Newt Gingrich is an ambitious motherfucker, and he smells blood. Blood that Hillary dumped in the water with that ridiculous tome of a healthcare plan of hers. A Hillary Goddamn Disaster."

Mel says nothing in response – what counter-argument is there? She opens her briefcase, squints through the smoke of her own cigarette to peer inside, as though there's something important she needs to find. The truth is, she just doesn't want to look at Barker. She's pissed that she has to concur with his assessment, double pissed that it stretches the sisterhood that much thinner. Barker doesn't have to feel bad about every male Democrat who fucks up. Why should she take it so personally that the First Lady whiffed on her first swing at a policy homer? And why did Big Bill let her take the lead on something every Democratic president since Harry Truman has coveted? It's his deal with the devil, is the conventional wisdom. Probably about right. The bullshit Hillary put up with during the campaign justified her pick of the litter, even if was a colossal mistake.

Barker drops to a chair still holding the mangled butt. He places it in the ashtray ruefully—an ex-smoker missing the good old days—scratches the side of his nose, shakes his head as he watches the speech, giving Mel no indication what the point of this might be. Is she supposed to be watching this speech for a reason, or is it just what happens to be on C-SPAN at the moment?

—*Think of America as a giant family of 260 million people, of extraordinarily diverse backgrounds, riding in a huge car down the highway, trying to pursue happiness and seek the American dream.*

Mel scissors her cigarette and looks away, scans the room with disgust, exhales another burst of smoke across Barker's face. Let the son-of-a-bitch remember what he's missing. She looks out the window, tries to tune out the surroundings and smoke placidly until Barker decides to tell her what's going on. *Empty your mind, Carnes,* she tells herself, but she can't forget that she's spent her entire adult life in rooms just like this, watching grown-up frat boys like Newt Gingrich on C-SPAN and CNN, plotting how to get them elected or defeated, which task depending only on party affiliation, not any real relationship to what Mel believes in, where she wants the country to go, what's right and what's wrong. Maybe she should just quit, flick another cigarette at the TV and simply walk out. *Fuck you, Barker, and fuck all this shit.*

What would her mother say about that? Good riddance, probably. To the cigarettes as much as the job, Boo boo. Don't you remember that your mother died of cancer?

Mel brushes tobacco crumbs from her lap, spins her lighter on the table, tries to convince herself that it really is time to quit—the cigarettes for sure, if not the whole shitshow of politics. She's not an 18-year-old waif anymore, so why keep up the habit? All it does these days is make her hair brittle and her skin spongy. Otherwise she might not look so bad, even by America's ridiculous beauty standard. She looks like Diane Sawyer, for fuck's sake, or close enough, even if it is present-day Sawyer, not the version closer to Mel's actual age, back when she first joined *60 Minutes*.

Mel takes a deep drag and looks back at the TV, reminds herself that it's the existence of men like Newt Gingrich that keeps her going in this job, and the keeping going keeps her burning through pack after pack of Parliaments. Politics is a shitty enough endeavor for any human being. For a woman in the '90s—a decade when they're supposed to be treated like equals, for fuck's sake!—it's an exquisite

1994

hell of immeasurable despair. Without her Parliaments, she wouldn't be able to take it.

Her anger flares at the thought of a Republican-controlled Congress. Much as she hates what it might take, she has to do whatever she can to stop that from happening. She might not be able to make the world a better place, but she can stop it from getting worse. *That* might be within her grasp.

—And then a tire blew out because the welfare state failed so totally, and it's so clear we have to replace it with an opportunity society. And with three blowouts, the American family car began to have a terrible ride, and people were anxiety-ridden…

"Contract with America my ass," Mel mutters. "Hypocritical peckerwood."

Barker ignores the remark, blinks at the TV, thinking God-knows-what, maybe just wondering when he can sneak off to the men's room to masturbate—or sneak a cigarette is more likely.

"Look, forget about this." Barker jumps up, snaps off the TV, strides to the corner and yanks open the PORTER box. He tosses an accordion file towards Mel. It hits the table with a sharp slap, slides a few inches. Mel takes a casual drag, pretends not to see the folder. "There's a Senate race we need you to win for us." Barker cracks his knuckles. "Forget about Newt Gingrich and the lost cause of our House majority and focus on that."

"I'm already winning you a Senate race." Mel says this matter-of-factly, but she knows that no, she's not—not anymore, at least. Her position with Kerrey is in the hands of someone else, some dumpy white guy like Barker, a loyal time-server who hopefully won't fuck up the lead she worked so hard to build. And why, exactly, should she care? Did she believe in Bob Kerrey any more than she ever believed in any candidate, or is she just annoyed that the DNC brass thinks it owns her?

Barker looks uncomfortable for a second, then turns to the map and considers it ruefully. "We need to move some pieces around the board. Wilhelm thinks Nebraska's in the bag. Ohio, on the other hand…" He glances pointedly at the folder.

"Nothing's ever in the bag," Mel says. She's calm for the moment, but she feels the familiar anger building." You think Kerrey's sailing to victory? You have no idea what's going on out there. You can't yank me now. We've barely got an eight-point lead. That's right on the margin of error. You know what a margin of error is, right?"

"Don't blame me. It's not my call."

"Don't shoot the messenger, huh? Fuck that, Barker. I hate messengers."

Mel glares at Barker with disdain, borrowing a look she's seen men give other men innumerable times. It's an animal challenge, nothing more, the outcome a function of determination more than anything. This is just men locking horns or thumping their chest, a wordless fight to establish dominance. Women can do it too, though in Mel's experience, they rarely try. Probably because they rarely win. Mel, however, wins all the time, at least lately, her premature wrinkles and a smoldering cigarette giving her an edge, a lack of make-up and unkempt hair further adding to her power. She does what she can to be prepared for these showdowns, goes into potentially contentious meetings looking disheveled and harried like she does now. The average 29-year-old woman, washed, coiffed, and carefully made-up, wouldn't stand a chance against an asshole like Barker in a conventional staring contest. Even a beta-male has enough pride to hold on against a pretty-ish woman trying to take a stand. Just look rough, don't move, don't blink, and you carry the moment, whether your position is actually stronger or not.

Mel feels her glasses sliding glacially down her nose, fights the urge to scratch the itch on her cheek, reminds herself what a useless piece of shit Barker is, tries to remember what they're staring down about. Not that it matters. Once engaged, thinking about the issue at hand is sure to bring defeat. Fortitude is all that matters. Mel has a deep reserve, even at the most fragile moments in her life.

Barker breaks first. "Just take a look, wouldja? Kyle Porter. Son-in-law of a former Ohio governor. Good-looking guy. A touch raw, sure, but, well…" He shrugs, scratches his nose again, smiles wanly. He looks like an anguished Pop Warner coach struggling to buck up his puny misfits in the face of another 42-0 blowout.

Mel grinds out her cigarette, unclasps and opens the flap with exaggerated slowness while Barker nods encouragement. *This can't be good*, she says to herself, the tiny thrill of victory draining away as she remembers what this is all about—some new dickweed to get elected with just 6 weeks on the clock. She pulls out the stack of file folders, spreads them in front of her like she's preparing a card trick, looks for the latest poll results. May as well find out the bad news right off the bat. She flips open the folder, glances at the tracking poll graph. Holy fuck, seriously?

"Eighteen points! He's down by 18 points? You've got to be kidding me."

1994

"Turn him around, Mel." Barker wipes his sweaty hands on his pants, lifts the cardboard box onto the table with a muted grunt. "Win the election, keep the seat, help safeguard our Senate majority. A grateful party awaits your victory."

"You're fucking kidding, right? Eighteen points? With 6 weeks to the election? How the hell am I supposed to turn *that* around?"

"You're a miracle worker, Carnes. That's what everybody says."

"Everybody?"

"Like it or not, that's your reputation, and right now, we need a miracle worker in Ohio. Oh, wait. You're from there, aren't you?"

"You know perfectly well I'm from Ohio, asshole."

"Oh, right, sure. How could I forget?"

Mel narrows her eyes, wonders for a second if Barker is bullshitting her. He's got the dry humor thing down, she'll admit that much, but she often catches him on a piece of honest-to-God sincerity too. Another weakness.

"Yeah, well, bonus points for the local connection," Barker says.

"*Bonus points*? It's gonna take more than gold stars from the goddamned teacher to overcome an 18-point deficit. Where'd you get this bozo anyway?" Mel glares in outrage at the graph, the line for her guy drifting downward from June to September, bottoming out a week ago at 31% to the Republican's 49%. She knows a bit about the opponent—Dick Musgrove, sitting lieutenant governor, founder of a regional telecom company that got bought out for a hefty sum before he went into politics—a generic Republican fatcat but exactly what the American public seems to want this cycle, a businessman-turned-politician allegedly bringing the drive and efficiency of the private sector to government service. Fucking idiots.

Mel tries not to feel defeated already, only half listens to Barker explain how Porter stole the nomination, took them all by surprise getting into the race in the first place, a rich entrepreneur with zero political experience edging out the Cuyahoga County Commissioner the ODP had its eye on.

"So we're working with Grade B meat here, is what you're telling me." Mel pages quickly through the latest newspaper clippings, headlines shuttering past her eyes, Porter's optimistic smile and thick wavy hair the only bright spot she can see. He certainly looks the part of a self-made-man turned Senate candidate, running against—what?— a turtle-man with beady eyes and flabby cheeks. In a straight-up battle of faces, their guy would win, hands down. So there's that much at least. It's not nothing, she knows. Porter's got a kind of Clintonian sparkle in his eye too.

"Despite the father-in-law, his roots in the party are pretty shallow," Barker admits, "but he's got good name recognition on the private-sector side of the ledger. Porter Legal Services. Something like 150 offices in the Midwest and upper Southeast. New York too. And still expanding. Maybe you've seen his TV commercials?"

"Good name recognition, and he's 18 points down to some no-neck lieutenant governor?"

"Something about Ohioans distrusting lawyers, I guess it is," Barker says. "*Negative perception of candidate's chosen field of endeavor*, is how Shep put it."

"So we've got name recognition, and that's our *weakness*? Jesus piss-ant, Barker, what am I supposed to do with this mess?" Mel shoves the files away in disgust and rummages through her briefcase.

"Cigarettes are right there," Barker says after watching her dig around for a few seconds. He points forlornly at the pack.

Mel lights up, exhales with relish, the angst briefly melting from her face. "Let me get this straight," she says with clinical calmness. There's no sense drowning in outrage. She has a job to do. The harder it is, the more she has to stay focused on the task, the more rewarding it'll be when she wins. "Our guy's a newbie to politics, minimal connections with local party orgs, distrusted for the exact reason he's well known, and he's running in what looks like a Republican wave."

"And." Barker cracks the lid again, reaches furtively into the box, ease out a plastic-coated report like he's sneaking a cookie.

"There's another *and*?"

Barker hands the report to Mel with a pained smile. He almost looks apologetic. "He's got a slow start staffing up. He had a solid organization running up to the primary, which is partly how he got past our guy, but he dismissed most of his campaign staff immediately after winning the nomination, manager and all. It's all in Shep's report."

Mel glares at the generic title, *Preliminary Analysis of the Kyle Porter Senate Campaign* by USA Data Services. She opens to page one, scans the executive summary. "*While his new team was still getting organized in August,*" Mel reads aloud, "*the Republican mounted a radio and television campaign in the Cleveland media market, an indispensable segment of our base, and made significant inroads there, as the post-Labor Day polling shows. See Appendix C for a detailed breakdown of the latest results.*" Mel helicopters the report across the table. "Appendix fucking C? Sweet baby Jesus, Barker, is it April first, or am I just imagining that this is all a cruel prank?"

"There's more," Barker says. He retrieves the report, opens to a back page, turns it to face Mel.

"What am I looking at here?" Mel barks, but the header is clear. Campaign Staff List.

"Alex Tremont is campaign manager," Barker says. He sounds genuinely sorry. "Porter hired him just before Labor Day. Wilhelm tried to object. He wanted to send out Paul Begala—this is a crucial goddamned race, as everyone knows—but Porter insisted. Tremont is a friend of his father-in-law, or some stupid shit like that."

Mel's mood collapses. An 18-point deficit she could accept, but this is too much. In a world of sexist male pigs, Alex Tremont is one of the worst. You might think a gay guy would sympathize with the plight of women, but not Alex. Doesn't like to sleep with women, doesn't like to work with them, and he's not afraid to show it. He seems to think that being gay makes him immune to charges of discrimination, which it pretty much does, among Democrats at least. Plus, he's as old-school as they get, and not in a good way. Out of touch with modern campaigning, he still seems to get work at the highest levels. This is the hardest part to swallow.

Barker tries on an encouraging smile, but it only makes it look like he has gas. "Wilhelm did get Tremont to take on Shep Blumenthal as his pollster, so you've got that going for you."

"And I suppose David's the genius who insisted on sending me in as a second wave of kamikazes?"

"The Chairman thinks very highly of you." Mel notices more than a touch of sourness in Barker's voice." As do I."

"Well, that makes me feel just fantastic. Validation from a couple of privileged white males. Just what I've always wanted." Her sarcasm is genuine, but she has to admit that her actions over the past decade give credence to what she just said. If she's not seeking validation from the old-boys' network, what *is* she doing? It's the one thing all of her therapists have agreed on, that she's dedicated to obliterating her mother's memory by seeking success among the very people her mother was always trying to overcome—career politicians, the Establishment, the Man. She never believed them, but it gets harder all the time to deny that they're right.

Barker checks his watch, eases the box in Mel's direction, tries on another version of a hopeful expression, but now he's like a father watching a kid with his fly down botching his lines in the school play." You're on a 3:30 flight to Cleveland. Porter's got a rally in Lorain tomorrow, just outside Cleveland, not far from his HQ. Struggling blue-collar town. The perfect place for a reset."

Mel stares hard at Barker, the cigarette smoldering in the corner of her mouth. "You don't really think I can do this, do you?"

"It's politics, Carnes. Anything can happen in 6 weeks. If you win this one, you'll be an even bigger hero than you already are. Could be on your way to a major position on Clinton's re-election campaign. Something national, close to the top. Assistant Campaign Manager. Deputy Chief Strategist. Something along those lines. You know how Wilhelm favors you younger guys." Barker scrunches his face, struggles not to look too bitter. "Sorry, gals."

"Gals?"

"You know what I mean. No offense, okay? You've got a career out ahead of you, and this is a real opportunity here."

"Opportunity? You've got the brass balls to call this," Mel shoves the box back at Barker, "an opportunity?"

Barker's anger flares up. "A hopeless situation like Porter's in? Hell yes, it's an opportunity. Think of what happens if you win. If you even get close." Barker slides the box back towards Mel, keeps his hands at the back as though he expects Mel to shove it back again. Mel goes into stare-down mode again.

"We got you a hotel near HQ," Barker says, his bitterness escalating. "Four star, office nook, mini bar, the whole nine yards. Usual compensation plus hazard pay for the late deployment, full expenses. Per diem to keep the paperwork down. Ninety-five a day's the rate at this pay grade."

"Generous."

"Don't be snide, Carnes. It *is* generous. Ridiculously so, if you ask me. You're what, 31, 32 years old? That's a chunk of change for someone your age, especially in this economy."

"Twenty-nine." Mel wishes she didn't feel the need to say it.

"Well there you go, then." Whatever that means. Barker is trying his best not to look jealous, without much success, Mel thinks.

She breaks down. Money talks, bullshit walks, right? This may be bullshit, but the money can't be denied. Besides, what else would she do? Slink back to her apartment and start reading that Camille Paglia book she's had on her nightstand for 3 years? Find a new therapist to help her beat back a premature mid-life crisis? Cruise the D.C. bars for one-night stands? Join a gym, quit smoking, and get her life on track with a career that's healthier and more sane? There's only one path to take here, and she knows it.

Mel draws the box closer, to Barker's obvious relief, the image of a Navy PT boat gliding upstream into the jungle popping into her mind as she does it. The voice-over is an automatic response, Martin Sheen's gravelly narration a familiar companion to treacherous turning points in her life. *When I was here, I wanted to be there. When I was there, all I could think about was getting back into the jungle.* It's true. Whenever she has down time, she paces her apartment like a caged animal, waiting for a new assignment, jonesing for the adrenaline of a campaign, the smoke-filled rooms like this one, hashing out strategy, pitting her mind against the vagaries of the American electorate.

Mel yanks off the top of the box, sends it spiraling across the room. She loves throwing things, especially when there's no risk of breaking something. Inside there's a stack of video cassette tapes, more newspaper clippings, campaign credentials, even a roadmap of Ohio.

She lights another cigarette, tosses the folders and Shep's report in with the rest of it.

"I took the mission," Mel says with her best Captain Willard impersonation. "What the hell else was I gonna do? But I really didn't know what I'd do when I found him."

Barker's brow crinkles. He's obviously not familiar with the quote.

Mel draws fiercely on her cigarette. *"Apocalypse Now,* dimwit. Greatest movie ever."

"Whatever you need to get charged up." Barker reaches down the table, takes one of Mel's Parliaments without asking. Mel reflexively flicks her lighter, watches Barker's face melt in relief. His plods across the room to turn the TV back on, steps back and smokes placidly as they both watch.

—But isn't that what America is about? The right to dream these kind of heroic dreams.

"We have to hold the Senate, Mel, or their vicious, backward-looking agenda sails through Congress and veto be damned."

Mel watches the crowd cheer, fights the temptation to flick her cigarette at the screen again, squints at Gingrich like he's there in the room and they're about to draw pistols for a duel.

—We are in the business of reestablishing the right to pursue happiness, and the reality of the American dream, for every child born in this country…

Mel feels a surge of adrenaline, or maybe it's just the nicotine. Whatever it is, it's getting the job done, firing her up for the challenge of bringing this Kyle Porter shithead back from the dead. She a junky and she knows it—politics, the endless duel with Republicans, the challenge of winning the unwinnable. She's been hooked for nearly 20 years, ever since she led that strike of the safety patrol in 6th grade because the principal made them stay in their posts for a full half hour, well past the time when there were any students to usher across the street. She got suspended for that one, but her mother fought the principal, won not just a reinstatement without a note in her school record but an apology from the school board for violating her First

Amendment right to assemble peaceably to redress grievances. Her first lesson in insurgent politics, the moral codified by her mother. "A short-term loss means nothing as long as you never give up," she said. That's been a guiding principle for Mel ever since, even as she's drifted further and further from her mother's ideals.

Barker is saying something, but Mel's not listening.

"Just win it, Carnes. Don't think about *not* winning it, okay. We don't expect a victory, not exactly, but we *need* one. Very much so. Work your ass off, but be comforted by the thought that a relatively close defeat won't hurt you personally. While a blowout, on the other hand..." He tries to look stern, mostly succeeds.

Mel ignores Barker, keeps her eyes trained on the TV screen, wallows in her hatred for Newt Fucking Gingrich and his crowd of self-serving ass hats. In the end, the politics does motivate her, however stupid and futile that might be. She wants Porter to win, even if he doesn't deserve it. With a weak-kneed sack of shit in the White House, a Democratic Senate is the nation's only hope — if there even is any hope.

— America is the most revolutionary experiment in human history. We truly believe that we are endowed by our creator, that our rights come from God, and not from the government or the state...

Mel gives in to temptation, flicks her cigarette at the screen again. She pushes her glasses up her nose, grabs the box, and marches off to lend her talent and energy to yet another white male champion of all that's not Republicanism.

"We are *not* going down," she says under her breath as she strides down the hall with a renewed sense of purpose. It's not until she's standing by the elevator that she realizes this is exactly what she told herself on the plane earlier today. *Well, it was true then...*

# # # # #

Another taxi ride, another airplane, a pleasant surprise that the flight to Cleveland is virtually empty. The takeoff is smooth, Mel's terror from earlier in the day forgotten. *1 in 4.7 million chance of a crash*, she thinks briefly, chiding herself for getting so worked up this morning.

She's in coach this time, but she has the row to herself and a renewed sense of purpose, her briefcase bulging with files like usual, work to be done and no time to lose, 6 weeks to the day, and an 18-point deficit to overcome. Is it a winnable challenge, or is she doomed from the start? She thinks of *The Bad News Bears*, a favorite of her and her mother's, reminds herself the team came a long way but still lost the championship game by 1 run. A favorite Walter Mathau quote comes to mind. *Listen, Lupus, you didn't come into this life just to sit around on a dugout bench, did ya? Now get your ass out there and do the best you can.* "And if the best you can isn't enough, do even better," her mother whispered to her right afterwards, that knowing smile on her lips and the box of popcorn held out to Mel.

She pushes away thoughts of her mother — *No more of that shit today, OK Carnes?* — spreads out the Porter materials on the tray tables on either side of her and digs into the ugly news. First she makes a thorough study of Appendix C. It's always best to know the worst of it before anything else. The crosstabs paint a pretty clear picture of a candidate doing poorly among traditional Democratic constituencies — union members, minorities, young college-educated voters, the unemployed. Porter's not actually *losing* among any of these groups, but he's drastically underperforming. You know it's bad when a Republican isn't being blown out among Africa Americans, and Musgrove's got solid numbers there, especially younger suburban blacks. When a Democrat can't get 80 or 90 percent of the black vote, he's doomed. That's axiomatic.

Mel runs her finger along the numbers, shaking her head in disbelief. Porter tops out at 67% among African Americans with a college degree, an odd group for a forty-something white lawyer to do well with, though maybe they're the ones in the best position to see through Musgrove's bullshit. She turns the page, sees that the gap among traditionally Republican-leaning groups is predictably large — 21 points behind with older voters, almost the same with non-union whites, nearly double that with people making the median income or greater, nearly 70 points among people who identify Christian values as their most important issue.

Oddly, the number for suburban, college-educated, married white women doesn't look so bad, the one ray of sunshine. What is it about this group that isn't repulsed by Porter? Is it his good looks? Do they not distrust lawyers as much as other people? Do they see this Contract with America for the empty rhetoric that it is?

Mel should be able to tell. She could very well be in this sub-group herself. In a parallel universe, that's exactly what she is, a professional woman living in the Columbus suburbs, 2.3 kids, a husband in finance, or maybe a tenured professor at Ohio State. Her father would love that. She can picture him in the living room, smiling and hugging the grandkids, waving her and her husband out the door for a weeknight dinner date. Grandpa Mike building a swing set in the backyard and staying for dinner, arguing politics with her Reaganite husband, playing endless games of Life and Monopoly with the kids. Grandpa Mike taking the kids for the weekend while Mel and her husband fly to Florida for a much-needed getaway, regaling the kids with stories of Mel as a girl, the safety patrol strike, her tumultuous tenure as student-council president, the time in high school when she ran her science teacher's unsuccessful campaign for Wooster City Council. They listen in awe, hug grandpa tightly, pepper Mel with questions when their parents get back from their trip. *Did you really organize a walkout at your high school to protest Apartheid?* They can't possibly believe that their mother was once so political.

Mel tears herself away from the fantasy, reminds herself how little time she has to get up to speed on the ins and outs of this race. She slaps the report closed, turns to the clipping pile. She picks up a piece about the primary from the *Cleveland Plain Dealer*.

Close Race To Succeed A
Retiring Democratic Senator
By Thom Reynolds

PARMA, OHIO, APRIL 28— Kyle Porter, who is running to fill the Senate seat being vacated by three-term Democratic Senator Howard M. Metzenbaum, worked his way through a shopping center, shaking hands in the final days before Tuesday's primary election.

The layer-turned-entrepreneur, who founded a regional chain of low-cost legal clinics, repeatedly introduced himself to the shoppers, but he is so well known from the steady stream of television ads in Ohio for Porter Legal Services that most people he meets seem to be familiar with him already.

A typical response came after he greeted Marvin Unger, a 70-year-old retired pipe-fitter who looked unmoved by the candidate's disarming smile and warm handshake. "I'm voting for Boyle," Mr. Unger said to Mr. Porter, referring to Mr. Porter's main rival for the Democratic nomination, Mary Boyle. "She's not rich like you."

Score one for Mrs. Boyle and her ad blitz, which has suddenly given shape to this down-to-the-wire election with the clarity of a bumper sticker: "The Senate doesn't need any more millionaire lawyers," she says in her latest radio and television ads. "What it needs is more moms."

The Senate race here is being closely watched in Washington as one of a handful that together could potentially save the Democrats' imperiled majority this fall. Like voters in other states, people in Ohio are anxious about crime and health care. They express a deep

1994

cynicism toward Washington and a profound dissatisfaction with government, and have approved term limits for their elected officials.

With so few issues dividing them in their respective primaries, the Democratic and Republican Senate candidates are trying to distinguish themselves by claiming to be the most ordinary candidate.

Mrs. Boyle's "Mom versus Millionaire" advertisement, which is being broadcast statewide, deliberately echoes the successful 1992 Senate campaign of Patty Murray in Washington State, who converted a legislator's dismissal of her as "just a mom in tennis shoes" into a winning campaign slogan. Mrs. Boyle, the mother of four and a popular three-term Cuyahoga County Commissioner, has sought advice from Senator Murray as she seeks to become one of only a handful of women in the United States Senate.

The article comes to an end there, the rest of the clipping missing from the packet. Not that reading more will tell her much. She knows Porter won the primary, but she can see why he's having problems.

Mel looks at the byline again, dredges up Thom Reynolds from her memories of '92. He gave Clinton some pretty sympathetic coverage, if she remembers correctly. Cute too, in a rumpled, high-school sports star who managed to grow up a little but still thinks about the past all the time kind of way. *Cleveland Plain Dealer*. Mel checks the press contact list, sees that Reynolds is still the *Plain Dealer's* guy on the politics beat. That's good. He's a friendly, or at least a potential friendly. They'll need sympathetic coverage from as many in-state rags as possible. Mel makes a note to seek out Reynolds, use her wiles to keep him from more unflattering coverage like that snarky anecdote about the pipe-fitter who shook Porter's hand but pledged support for his opponent. That's the kind of writing Mel tries to steer the scribblers away from when she can, the subtle negativity that can sour voters on a candidate even more effectively than a dozen attack ads from the other camp.

The next clipping mentions that Musgrove's campaign is being run by Howard Kane. Goddammit, really? Howard "The Shark" Kane. Mel has never run against The Shark, but he's a legend in the business, the kind of opponent everyone dreads. Brilliant, ruthless, utterly amoral. One of the best in the business, if not *the* best.

A real prick, too, Mel reminds herself, a true-blue asshole of the worst kind. Back in '90, he raped a friend of hers from college, a speechwriter working for him on the California gubernatorial race. The son-of-a-bitch got away with it in a he-said/she-said situation, and the woman quit politics and went to nursing school, last Mel heard.

Mel originally got the story from another DNC strategist who worked the other side of the race against Kane, a smug little prep-school asshole who remained studiously neutral as he told Mel the story. "Kane says he didn't do it, she says he did." He sipped his gin-and-tonic as Mel fumed, pounding the bar with both fists.

"What the fuck, Orton? Nicky gets raped by some piece-of-shit Republican, and that's what you have to say about it?"

"Innocent until proven guilty, right?"

Mel controlled her urge to grind out her cigarette on the back of Orton's hand, rose and walked out without paying for her drinks. Goddamned old-boys' network, circling the wagons around one of its own, even a scumbag from the other side who raped somebody. That's how it went, forever and always, even now.

Mel never spoke to Orton again, but she heard the same story—and the same blithe dismissal of guilt—from a bunch of other people, including some college friends of hers and Nicky's who should've been more incensed, out of loyalty to a friend if nothing else. Even the ones who used the word *rape* without qualification—some called it *date rape*, as though that made a difference, others said *alleged rape*, taking the same presumption-of-innocence tack as Orton—were quick to note that there wasn't anything you could do about it, so what good did it do anybody to dwell or get outraged?

"You think Nicky can just decide not to *dwell on it*?" Mel came close to delivering a few punches, did throw her drink in the face of one particularly haughty little asshole who said, "Look, you play with fire, you get burned, right? Everybody knows who and what Howard Kane is. Just don't ever get left alone with him, when it's his word against yours. Simple as that." Simple, sure. Just don't ever be a victim.

Mel threw her drink with glee. "I'm a drink-thrower, fuckface. Just don't ever get within 3 feet of me, or you're asking for it." She told herself later—sitting alone in a different bar, fuming—to keep her fury focused on the one who really deserved it, not waste her energy hating the endless parade of apologists who would always be there to shield the villains. It was too draining to maintain outrage at half the world. "Stay focused on the real evil," her mother told her once. "The world's full of distractions, Boo boo. Both the shiny things and the easy targets of outrage. You have to keep your eye on the prize."

Mel stuck to it, vowed that if she ever ran across the so-called Shark at any point, she'd castrate him—literally if possible, metaphorically if necessary. Mel pounds the armrest remembering what Kane did to Nicky Simmons, and who knows how many other women exactly like her. She was writing speeches for the future governor of California one day, an emotional wreck the next, and all because of Howard Kane.

Mel knows she just found her true motivation for the race. The hell with New Gingrich and the Senate majority, Cliff Barker and the DNC, Kyle Porter, David Wilhelm, Bill and Hillary, and everybody else. She'll come back from 18 points down and humiliate Howard Kane and Dick Musgrove, and if she comes across a way to ruin Kane in the process, she'll seize the opportunity, even if it means losing the election. Whatever it takes, she'll do it.

Mel calls up an image of Kane's face to sharpen her hatred, pictures the slicked-back hair, the beady eyes set deep in his face, the Mephisthophelean goatee. She's throwing mental darts at the image when she remembers her first encounter with the son-of-a-bitch, back in college. Jesus, that's right. He gave a guest lecture to one of her classes in political management, and she hated him even then, before she knew.

"Politics is about winning," was the first thing he said. The slight Texas drawl lent the statement a certain air of poetry. "No one who forgets that lasts long in my job."

He paused to let this sink in, scanned the class slowly as he paced the front of the room in jeans and cowboy boots, blue cotton dress shirt open at the collar — the only thing missing was the ten-gallon hat — waiting for some idealistic idiot to dispute his claim. Only there weren't any idealistic students there to defy him. George Washington University's Political Communications program wasn't a place where idealists went. Those dweebs were all over in PoliSci, the Congressional hopefuls, the self-aggrandizing jerks who saw themselves on the Supreme Court some day, the Reaganite Young Republicans sure they would ultimately occupy a governor's chair or run a legislative office as chief of staff, or work in important positions in State or Defense. The PoliCom majors were the people who would get them there, the strategists and pollsters and campaign managers of the future. While the idealistic ones were reading de Tocqueville and John Stuart Mill, *The Federalist Papers* and Madison's *Notes of Debates in the Federal Convention*, the PoliCom students were taking classes in campaign advertising, data analysis, grassroots organizing. Kane was guest lecturing in PC 432: Advanced Campaign Strategy, a course that covered everything from micro-targeting demographic groups to stump-speech writing. The title of Kane's guest lecture was "The Three Essential Keys to Electoral Victory." No one expected a civics lesson or a call to higher principles.

Kane broke the silence at last, repeated his maxim. "Politics is about winning. And once you've won, the next thing you do is win again. Then again. And again. Because that's the only way to get something done in American politics. You have to not only win elections, you have to *keep* winning them. The getting something done, the enacting your agenda and changing people's lives—that's for the politicians." He said *politicians* with an obvious sneer of disdain. "The type of people that *my* type of people put into office. For political professionals such as myself, and for some of you someday, winning is all there is. Ever. Doing good—that's what someone else does with your victories. That's why you bring them their victories, like a mother bird feeding her young. Without the nourishment of victory, the politician starves, and whatever good he might've done dies with him."

Mel could tell that Kane loved this part, the moment after he likened politicians to innocent, hungry birds and himself to the caring but ruthless mother bird. He was there to tell them the truth, not inspire them to a higher calling in public service. The pens were going a mile a minute, the 25 or so juniors and seniors in the room hunched over their notebooks, capturing every syllable of Kane's wisdom.

"If you're interested in doing good, you should close your notebook and head on out, save yourself an hour of your life. Don't be embarrassed. I won't be insulted. The world needs do-gooders—I won't ever say it doesn't—but I'm here today to talk about winning a political campaign, not making the world a better place." Again the sneer of disdain. Kane scanned the room a second time to see if anyone would raise an objection. Mel figured he usually spoke to political science classes—GWU's Political Communication program was the only one of its kind at the time—where he was sure to run into some tall Midwestern presidential hopeful ready to stake out the moral high ground and call out the ugly cynicism of Kane's enterprise. No one in Mel's class took the bait. No hands went up. No notebooks were closed in self-righteous indignation. When the silence had gone on for maybe a full minute, Kane nodded his head, leaned back against the desk.

"Good. Okay. Nobody has any illusions. Let me start by telling you a little about myself. I've been in politics for over three decades, since Harry Truman was president. Yup, that far back. I've worked on everything from city council to Congressional and gubernatorial campaigns. Never had the honor of running a presidential campaign— not yet, but I'll get there. Could be '88, could be '92. I already work in The Show—Senate mostly these days—but presidential is the World Series. I'm patient. So far, my record as chief campaign strategist or campaign manager is 15-and-14, a batting average of .517. Amazing for professional baseball, even more amazing, believe it or not, for politics. One of the best. But enough about me. What you're here to learn about is winning a political campaign. I'll repeat myself yet again. *Politics is about winning.*"

Kane removed a package of Marlboro's from his shirt pocket, tapped out a cigarette, continued speaking while he lit up. "One of the toughest things about any campaign is keeping your candidate squarely focused on that fundamental truth. Sometimes your biggest obstacle in politics is the politicians themselves. I'm completely serious. This is something you should know about politicians and never forget. The vast majority of them want to do something good for the world. Believe it or not, that's why they go into politics." Kane exhaled, nodding sagely, his face saying, *Yeah, that's what motivates those stupid fucks. Can you believe it?*

"Surprising, isn't it? But that's why they subject themselves and their families to all the bullshit that comes with running for office. Because they *care*. They want to think about policy. They want to talk about values and progress. They want to fix what's wrong with the country and make the world a better place. Sometimes they get so wrapped up in all that do-gooder mumbo-jumbo that they forget that you have to win elections — and keep on winning them — if you want to accomplish any of that stuff. I'll repeat this point. In politics, only the winners get to make a difference. The losers go back to defending criminals, or selling cars, or running a chain of funeral homes or pest control businesses, whatever stupid shit they were doing in the private sector. Without victory, someone else gets to decide what's good. Someone else gets to make the future."

He took a deep drag, exhaled with obvious relish, narrowed his eyes and peered through the smoke at the classroom of acolytes eating up his wisdom. "Here's another surprising thing. Winning elections doesn't come naturally to most politicians. Winning elections — that's what the professionals are for. If politicians were good at winning elections, they wouldn't need people like me." He thrust out his chest in pride, or tried to anyway. His taut beer gut led the way instead, and to Mel, if no one else in the room, he seemed comical suddenly, an insecure wreck pretending to be tough and cynical. She kept writing down what he said, but her awe disappeared, just as it would for every confident-seeming man she'd come across over the ensuing decade. They all revealed their inner loser eventually, usually sooner rather than later. The more they bloviated, the more obvious to Mel how deeply they feared exposure as a terrified, unconfident child. She saw it all the time.

"So how do you win a political campaign? The most crucial factor is information—possessing it, using it correctly, controlling its flow. Write down that one word and underline it three times: Information."

Kane stopped and nodded as 25 pens scratched out the word, hands bearing down on paper as everyone obeyed his command. Information. Always a bit of a rebel, Mel put a box around it instead of underlining it three times as everyone else did.

"The next crucial factor is expertise. You need to know how to acquire reliable information, how to utilize that information effectively, how to control its flow through your own campaign as much as through the news media. And just as importantly—no, *more* importantly—you need access to other people who know how to do these things, because you can never do it all yourself. You have to be good at everything—I mean that—but you also have to surround yourself with people who are even better than you at particular tasks. You need a top-notch speechwriter, a top-notch pollster, a top-notch strategist, the smoothest press secretary you can find, the most organized chief of staff. Hell, you even need the best secretaries, the best coffee-fetching interns. Politics is a team sport, people. Write that down too."

Kane smiled as the class frantically wrote down everything he said. He paused to let them catch up.

"The third crucial factor, you won't be surprised to hear, is money. But I mention money *last*, not first, because money in politics, as everywhere, is simply a means to an end. Without money, you can't buy the information and expertise you need to win. Without money, the most you'll have—and this is only in the very best of cases, so you should never enter a campaign expecting to have this—the most you'll have is ideas and charisma, and that's not nearly enough to win in politics. Not today, not ever. So yes, you need the very best fundraisers too, and it helps to have a candidate with deep pockets, but don't ever think that money buys you victory. It's the *sine qua non* of victory, but even if you've got a ten-to-one margin in fundraising over your opponent, you still have to know how to use that money to buy the information and expertise that win elections."

Kane paused again, scanned the room with satisfaction, let the pens catch up once more.

"Everything else is just strategy. I can give you some basic tips on strategy, but this is where the real art of campaigning comes in. You have to make up your strategy as you go along. That's what all that information, expertise, and money is for—to develop and deploy a winning strategy—but exactly what that strategy is will always be

1994

contextual and highly dynamic. It'll be vastly different from campaign to campaign, from week to week sometimes, so even if you're a master at the high-level stuff, like I am, you still have to study the situation like a motherfucker." Kane turned to the professor. "Can I say 'motherfucker' in a college classroom?"

The students laughed for the first time. The professor smiled.

"I think you just did. Twice." The students laughed again.

At the meet-and-greet afterwards, Mel overheard a fellow student ask Kane why he was a Republican. "Do you honestly think the Republican agenda is better than the Democratic agenda?"

Kane chortled like an amused Texas oil baron, put his hand on the guy's shoulder and said, "Son, being a Republican is the only way you can be utterly ruthless. People value that in a Republican. They expect it. It smacks of competitiveness, frontiersmanship, results. Republican candidates, they'll let you do pretty much whatever you want as long as you get 'em a win. Democrats, not so much. Democrats *want* to be ruthless, but they have to tiptoe around it, look like they care about the little guy, about principles and civility. You run the campaign of a Republican, and you don't have to take off the gloves at any point because the gloves are always off, right from the get-go."

Kane turned to the professor. "Chalfont, why the hell are you a *Democrat*? Never made sense to me, you being such a cold-blooded prick and all." Kane's tone was admiring, as though he'd just said, *You're about the most wonderful human being I've ever come across.*

Mel remembers being appalled when the professor, whom she'd always admired for his liberal principles as much as his practical brilliance, admitted he wasn't really a Democrat — not in his bones. He said the Democratic Party was no more of a natural home to him than the Buffalo Bills were to O.J. Simpson. He was a Democrat because he'd gotten caught up in the Free Speech Movement at Berkeley — "the chicks were just simply amazing" — then he was drafted by the Democrats after college, and they never traded him. He worked for Democratic candidates because they kept paying him, and he knew how to mobilize and motivate their constituencies. "If I'd ever been in a country club before I turned 25, I could've been a helluva Republican," he said, clinking his glass with Kane as though they'd just made a sweet deal to drill for oil on the last plot of fertile land on the last Indian reservation.

And so another idol fell, eventually leading Mel to stop seeking role models in the first place, at least among men. They were all self-serving dickweeds, the principled-seeming ones worse in the end than the blatantly mercenary.

Mel remembers watching Kane drape his arm over the professor's shoulder—both of them obviously pretty drunk at that point—grinning at the admission. "It's not too late, my friend. You're always welcome in the Party of Lincoln."

"Thanks, Kane. The Party of Jefferson, sadly, wouldn't touch you with a 10-foot pole. He's right about the ruthlessness thing," the prof confided as the group of student admirers leaned in closer—all males, Mel noticed. "That's one of our built-in disadvantages. Hasn't stopped us from controlling Congress for the past 30 years, but it makes the climb a bit steeper."

Mel walked away, not sure if she was disgusted or not. A touch disillusioned maybe, but that was hardly a new feeling. The process had started freshman year, her intro to political communications class making it abundantly clear that style would always trump substance in terms of swaying the public. She accepted the necessity of such a cynical operating principle—*To get anything done in politics, you have to win first*, she told herself all the time, not realizing she was paraphrasing what she would hear Kane say 3 years later—and now that she was this far into the program, she understood pretty clearly what she was getting into with her chosen profession. Most of her classmates would've gladly taken a job with either party after graduation, worked their asses off to elect any candidate who paid. Mel always assumed she'd go Democratic, but she knew she was prepping to be a gun-for-hire—that much was more clear now than ever. If she was good at it—and she already suspected that she was, top 10% at the very least—the Republicans might make her a lucrative offer. Would she balk, simply out of principle?

Mel never had to find out. Professor Chalfont helped get her a job that summer doing mid-level staff work at the DNC—an actual paying job, not an internship—and her career as a Democrat was locked in.

Thinking back on it now, Mel wonders if she wouldn't have been happier working for the other side. At least she wouldn't have had to be terminally disappointed, watching the men she helped get elected do little or nothing to advance a progressive agenda. She wouldn't expect a Republican to do any good in the first place, so she could just walk away after election day and never check the paper see if anything had come of her efforts. If the RNC had hired her instead…

Mel pulls off her glasses, rubs her eyes to erase the memories and doubts. *There's no place for ifs in the life you've chosen*, she says to herself. Besides, you probably would've had to work under Kane at some point if you'd gone red instead of blue. However sexist a lot the Dems were, at least they weren't rapists—not literally, anyway. Not a very inspiring motto—We're not actual rapists like the other guys—but it was enough for Mel at this point in her life. And whether it was enough or not, it's where she found herself at the moment, jetting to Ohio to face down Kane from 18 points behind. She lets the thought of overcoming such a massive deficit charge her up for what lay ahead.

"I'm gunning for you, you fucking asshole," Mel whispers to the empty window seat, imagining Kane sitting there to hear it. "I'm going to win, and when I do, I'm going to grind out my victory cigarette on your forehead."

"Excuse me, miss." Mel pivots to the stewardess, wondering how loud she was. "Please close your tray tables and buckle your seatbelt. We'll be landing shortly."

WEDNESDAY, SEPTEMBER 28TH
6:12AM

Mel stands in the mirror-lined "vanity nook" of her ridiculous hotel bathroom—the entire suite is *Miami Vice* meets Rust Belt glam, gold paint and marble veneer all over the place—the mirrors showing an infinite regression of faces, ears, backs of her head, an endless reminder of exactly how much she looks like shit. She's been up most of the night, so it's no wonder. She did get a bit of sleep—more like a series of restless power naps starting around 1am—before bolting out of bed just after 4 and rummaging through her suitcase for the video tape of Porter's legal clinic ads. She went to bed without watching any—there was too much other material to absorb before bothering with it—but her 4am brain got the message through that she needed to see the impression that Ohio already had of her candidate. There was only so much the hard data could tell her, so she passed on a few extra hours of fitful sleep to immerse herself in the visuals.

She took a quick, tepid shower—she couldn't quite force herself to go full *Apocalypse Now* and run the water all-out cold—made coffee in her room, slid in the tape, and spent half an hour engrossed and appalled. The production quality was good, no doubt about that—at least after the first few, which dated from the early-'80s. By '85, the ads were slick, national quality, Porter smooth and confident in his role as lawyer-spokesman.

In her favorite one, Porter strolls down the marble steps of a neo-classical courthouse building, jacket draped over his shoulder with a hooked finger, that natural politician's smile beaming expertise and common caring at the same time. *Millions of Americans are so intimidated by our legal system, they don't get a lawyer even when they need one.* Cut to a strip mall storefront. *At Porter Legal services, we make getting an experienced lawyer as easy as coming to one of our convenient offices.*

In another one, Porter strolls through a law office fit for John Houseman—wood paneling everywhere, leather-bound books from floor to ceiling—holding a tome as he strolls to the bookshelf. *Somewhere in all these dusty law books, a great idea got lost.* He slides the book in place and turns to the camera with a self-assured grin. *The idea that law is for people, and people should be able to afford it. At Porter Legal Services, we take the fear out of legal fees.* He leans casually against a desk, picks up another book. *You can discuss your problem with a Porter lawyer for just twenty dollars, and for cases like divorce, bankruptcy, wills, and accidents, we tell you our fee up front.* He marks the book with a bookmark and closes it gently, almost lovingly. *I'm Kyle Porter, founder of Porter Legal Services. Your port in a storm since 1982.*

"*Your port in a storm since 1982?*" Mel says aloud to the TV. She controls her urge to flick her cigarette at the screen, just barely. "You gotta be kidding me."

When she's done, she pops in the tape for the Democratic primary debate, hoping to see the same acting skills on display, but in that setting, Porter seems robotic, saying exactly what an elitist lawyer would say in those moments when he most needs to let some humanity show. In response to a question about Michael Fay, the Singapore caning case, he starts out fine, but then gives Mel a truly cringe-worthy moment.

—*I believe that the sentence they have over there in Singapore is inhumane. Obviously here in Dayton, if you were caught spray-painting cars, caning would not be your punishment. Um, on the other hand, I think people have to be accountable for their actions. We expect visitors here to play by our rules, and Singapore's deciding that this young man over there is going to have to play by their rules.*

The journalist asking the next question pretty much rolls his eyes at that one—Mel knows how he feels—before asking Porter's view on a Texas inmate facing the death penalty without review by a federal court. Porter's answer is even more lofty and lawyer-like.

—*I have always supported full habeas corpus review by the federal courts, and while I support the death penalty for heinous crimes, and I don't believe my opponents do, I have never supported limiting in any way the rights of judicial review of people committed of capital crimes.*

Mel sees some potential in Porter, but he has to learn how to sound more like a human being and less like an uptight law-school professor with conservative sympathies. Maybe he scooped up some of the law-and-order vote in the primary with that kind of talk, but he's running against a Republican now, not a crop of squishy liberals. Porter can't outflank Musgrove on bread-and-butter Republican issues, not without giving up more votes to depressed turnout than he gains from peeling away moderates.

Mel pauses the tape, scrawls a new answer for the capital punishment question on a yellow legal pad. Some states have adopted execution as the punishment for certain heinous crimes, she writes, but we have to be extremely careful when allowing the use of this most extreme of punishments. Full review by impartial sentencing boards, as some states already have, is necessary so that we, as a society, can be absolutely sure we're not putting innocent people to death. She wonders how hard it'll be to turn Porter in this direction. Some candidates are more pliable than others. Porter looks like an actor playing a Senate candidate, but how amenable will he be when presented with a new script? She'll find out soon enough.

Mel starts the tape again, watches Porter get out-clumsied by his Democratic opponents. No wonder he dismissed his campaign staff after he won the primary. He breezed past those clods by a safe margin, and with absolutely zero political experience. He probably thought he could win the general with the same combination of tough rhetoric and casual self-confidence. *These self-made millionaires are all the same,* Mel says to herself. They figure the same approach that made them rich would make them successful in politics.

Done with her 2-hour crash course in Porter's strengths and weaknesses on the TV front, Mel stands at the bathroom mirror, says Porter's tagline out loud to her scowling mirror face. *"Your port in a storm since 1982.* Jesus God." She ties up her hair and considers her reflection, plans how to mold herself into a semblance of the bold leader she needs to be this morning. Her first address to the troops, important for so many reasons, not the least of which is the clock running down fast, every day of the next 6 weeks crucial to closing that 18-point gap.

She catches herself staring blankly at the mirror, no idea how long she's been standing there, asleep on her feet. It happens sometimes. She bends around the doorframe to peer at the digital clock. Shit, 7:05 already. She makes a monster face at the infinite mirror, lets her hair down, brushes it out with a few quick strokes and dusts on some make-up in a futile effort to look well-rested. However disheveled she lets herself appear among superiors, to keep them from writing her off as a bimbo—God, she hates that word but catches herself using it from time to time—she always tries to present herself to the troops as a well-put-together professional woman, at least in the early days. "First impressions matter, Boo boo," her mother used to say. It's one of the few pieces of advice both parents endorsed with equal strength.

Mel remembers her first day of high school. Her mother was already sick, closer to the end than Mel wanted to admit, her hair gone and her wrists so horribly thin. "Every day is the first day of the rest of your life," she said to Mel, "but some days are more first than others."

She smiled brightly, the warmth of her eyes undiminished by the cancer. "Today you announce to your peers that you're a powerful presence in this new institution. By your very attendance, you're going to make the school a better place, and by extension, the whole state. The whole nation. None of this *malaise* crap. Right?"

Mel couldn't help smiling. She loved it when her mother was mock-grandiose. There was always a kernel of true grandiosity behind it, an unwavering belief that even a teenage Ohio girl could help right the world's wrongs and usher in a new era of fairness and equality. What would her mother say if she could see Mel now?

Mel smacks her palm with the brush—hard, so it stings. Why is she thinking about her mother so much lately? A disruptive trendline she has to reverse. She wipes a lone tear from the corner of her eye, makes another monster face, more earnestly this time—*Come on, Carnes, get your mind right!*—forces herself to concentrate on the task at hand. She brushes her hair ferociously, mentally scans the outfits available in her suitcase, tries to resist the conclusion that she looks like shit and won't be able to do anything about it—not on 2 hours of sleep. It sucks to show up on Day 1 looking like she's been going full-tilt for a month already, but it can't be helped. A man could waltz in looking like he just got rescued from a desert island, but not a woman. Not if she wants respect from her underlings. Add it to the list of inequalities.

She pushes away that thought as well, tells herself not to let a nascent feminist rage distract her at a time like this. She'll drink it away later, maybe get into a yelling match with some unsuspecting middle-aged businessman who offers to buy her a martini. For now, she has to run through her rally speech a few more times to guarantee it has the proper force. She checks the clock again. 7:32. Goddammit! She has to leave plenty of time to get her presentation ready, to find a Kinko's so she can print out transparencies. She reminds herself to call HQ at 8, to verify that they have an overhead projector and a screen. She could simply pass out memos and reports, but she finds it more effective to shine the numbers big and bright, to slap a canvas screen when she wants to make a point about a particularly telling cluster of data.

It's doubly important today, with a manager like Alex Tremont. He's a ground-game guy, Mel knows that. She's never worked with him directly, but she's heard him lecture too, knows that he's wary of any strategy aimed at trying to sway people one way or the other.

"Are there persuadable voters?" he asked the students in her senior seminar in campaign management. Mel almost raised her hand to say, *Yes. Obviously.* She was cocky by that point, the top of her class by a wide margin. Everyone said she was headed for great things, sooner rather than later. But there was something about Tremont that told her not to answer him, that he was a rhetorical question asker, one of the many know-it-alls her professors brought in for guest lectures.

"Of course," Tremont said after a long pause. "A few. But not many. Not enough to swing an election. Note this and note this well, young hopefuls. The only way to win a political campaign is to get more of your people to the polls than the other guy. That's not just obvious math, it's foundational strategy. Grassroots organizing. Voter mobilization. Election day logistics. *Those* are the things that win elections in this country."

There's some truth in this old-school way of doing things, but not enough, certainly not to get over an 18-point hump. She wonders how receptive Tremont will be to her poll-based analysis, to her overall strategy. The crosstabs don't lie—Porter is in dire straits with key Democratic constituencies—but there's a path out of this disaster. She sees it clearly after poring through the files from the DNC. She can win this one. It took her all night to convince herself of that, but she's confident now, grateful that David Wilhelm gave her this opportunity to prove herself under the most difficult circumstances. But if she's going to win, she has to have Tremont backing her—or at least get him out of her way. If she can't win him over, she'll execute a palace coup. She's done it before.

She tosses down the brush, ties her hair up hastily, washes away the lack of sleep and the awkward makeup job, starts again with a different foundation and a light swirl of rouge, thicker mascara. She puts on a scoop-neck, semi-tight mid-length dress and redoes her hair in a well-crafted bun. Tremont might be gay, but the staffers—mostly male, from the names on the org chart—probably aren't. Whatever age they are, political nerds generally have a soft spot for the hot librarian type. Mel wouldn't normally call herself *hot* – she's too thick around the middle, too soft at the neck for that—but she knows there's something about a certain hairdo and wire-frame glasses, with a dress like this, that conveys smoldering sex goddess to the prep-school boy-men who staff most campaigns. They picture her taking off her glasses and slowly letting down her hair, quoting de Tocqueville as she slips out of her dress. It pains her to deploy femininity this way, but she'll wield every weapon in her arsenal to achieve success. If she can't prosper in her chosen field—a man's world if ever there was one—she can't hope to advance the cause of gender equality. Or so she tells herself at moments like this, when she's guiltily prepping to use her looks in such a primitive and blatant manner. *Disheveled for the Cliff Barkers of the world, sexy librarian for the interns and volunteers.* It's a formula that's worked well over the years, and she's not about to abandon it now — not for some abstract principle, not when there's so much turning this shit around to do.

# # # # #

Tremont is hostile and snippy when Mel steps into his office at precisely 9am. "Melissa Carnes," he says with his nasally Wisconsin accent, just the tiniest touch of the classic gay lisp. The combination is highly comical, but the look on his face is pure disdain. He gives Mel a wary up-and-down, a displeased butcher on the verge of refusing a questionable shipment of meat. "I knew things were bad, but I didn't think they were *this* bad."

Mel squints through the smoke of her cigarette, lets Tremont feel her looking him up and down in return. He's repulsive — flabby and pale like most pols, thinning hair swirled artlessly over a bald spot he's the only one in denial about, pants too loose, suspenders too tight, obvious coffee stain on his tie. She exhales, watches the smoke drift towards Tremont, pushes her glasses up her nose, stokes up her anger. "What the fuck is that supposed to mean?"

Tremont eases a toothpick into the corner of his mouth. "Everybody knows who you are, Carnes. You call yourself a strategist, but you're just a gussied-up pollster who's managed to catch the eye some well-placed people. Hardly impressive."

"*Gussied-up*? What kind of sexist crap is that?"

Tremont ignores her. "You were not asked for. I'm sure you know that. I'm required to give you an office. Part of our deal with the Devil. The DNC, I mean. We get their money, we have to take their BS. One of the girls carved you a space. So just go." Tremont flutters his hand at the door. "And stay out of my way."

Mel tenses all over, controls the urge to explain the situation, to point out that they moved her over here from another crucial race in Nebraska because she was winning there, and they need a win here too. She could list her accomplishments, her nearly perfect win-loss record, her rapid elevation up the party hierarchy, but that's exactly what Tremont wants, an underling reciting her resume to impress the boss. That plays into the narrative that he's in charge here, and Mel won't allow Tremont to see himself that way — not after his petty opening gambit. He's an obstacle, pure and simple. She thought that might be the case coming in this morning, and Tremont didn't have the artfulness to conceal it, which gives the advantage to Mel. It saves her time trying to figure out how he really feels.

45

It's clear what she has to do, the strategy unfolding in obvious sequence. First she has to cow Tremont, then win over the staff—make them *her* staff—then charm the candidate. Easy as 1-2-3.

Mel lets the silence prolong, sits without being asked and lights a new cigarette from the tip of her old one. "Let's get one thing straight, *Alex*. You're a colossal failure here. Whatever you've done in the past— whatever connections got you this job—you are screwing this up big time. Things *are* this bad, and I'm here to do whatever's possible to *un*-bad them. You can either back me up, or you can get the fuck out of my way, but you cannot stop me from busting my ass to win this thing. You got that?"

"You are way out of line, Carnes. There's not a line anywhere near where you are is how way out of line you are."

"I don't give a fuck how out of line I am. I'm here to win this election, and that's what I intend to do. If you don't like it, pick up the phone and call David Wilhelm, and see what he says." Mel yanks the phone from its cradle, wags it at Tremont.

"David Wilhelm isn't my boss. Kyle Porter is."

Mel slams the phone down, squares her shoulders. "Would you rather take it up with him, then? I assume *he* wants to win too. Are you really sure he'll favor your stodgy bullshit over my approach?"

This is a calculated risk, escalating to a *Let Daddy decide* so quickly. Mel hasn't even met Porter, has no idea what he thinks of Tremont and his old-school ways. Porter's father-in-law is an ex-governor, probably how Tremont made the connection—he's tight with the Ohio old-boys' network. Porter might be steeped in the same kind of approach. It used to work just fine. But Porter is young, clearly ambitious. Mel bets that in a head-to-head duel of strategy, her approach beats Tremont's in Porter's eyes.

Tremont sighs, worries the toothpick across his mouth. "Listen Carnes. You know as well as I do that you don't win elections by convincing people to vote for you. Maybe you can win a few so-called undecideds. But that's hardly ever enough. You win elections by *not* alienating the people who might vote for you, and working your ass off to get them to the polls come election day. That's your time-tested recipe for victory."

"*Time-tested recipe for victory*? That's what you call what you're doing here? You're 18 points down in late-September, and there's a storm cloud of Republican horseshit about to rain down on the whole country. You need to get your head out of your ass and take a good hard look at what reality presents you with today. *Today*, Alex. Not 1972. Not 1982. Not even 1992. Can you do that for me?"

"I'm not sure who you think you're talking to, *Miz* Carnes. I'm the campaign manager here. You work for me. Or did you not realize where you fit in the pecking order?" Tremont raises his hand above his head. "Campaign manager." He drops his hand down to eye level. "Strategist."

Mel ignores this, senses that Tremont is weakening. If he's already summoning the official pecking order, he's all but beaten. She eases back, crosses her legs, adopts a posture more appropriate for a situation where they're already in complete agreement. "Listen. We don't have any time to waste. We've got 6 weeks minus a day to turn a debacle-in-the-making into something that won't embarrass everyone involved. Eighteen points! What the fuck have you been doing?" Mel sits forward, plants her feet on the ground, jabs her cigarette at Tremont. "I'm serious, Alex. What have you done in a month on the job that gives you the right to call yourself the boss around here?"

Mel watches Tremont deflate. She didn't think he'd be able to hold his bravado together very long. He's old and tired, capable of only the most surface resistance to her onslaught. If he had more energy, more fortitude, the campaign might not be in such disarray. Tremont sighs, lean forward heavily. He tries to explain that he hasn't been sitting on his hands, that he's doing everything a campaign manager can.

Mel doesn't believe him, doesn't think Tremont can do anything but follow his stale ground-game formula. The org chart and expenditure records show a campaign heavy on grassroots organizing—door-knocking, lawn sign distribution, community relations staff—light on campaign rallies, even lighter on advertising and content expertise. There's one speech writer, a young guy named Colin Burke who at least has a Yale pedigree, one local press assistant—a volunteer—a deputy campaign manager nominally in charge of focus groups and media strategy—also a volunteer—another deputy for organizational outreach, whatever the hell that is. No communications director, no press secretary, no media expertise of any kind. Tremont would've done without a strategist entirely if the DNC hadn't insisted.

Mel smokes placidly, watches Tremont continue justifying himself. He claims he's been getting pushback from Porter over any change he does suggest. "You don't think I want him to be more aggressive? You're wrong. He just won't do it."

"Does he not realize that his numbers don't just spell defeat, they spell embarrassment? He's looking at complete humiliation here. He loses a decently close race, even by 6 or 8 points, he runs again in 2 or 4 years, takes another stab at Senate, maybe governor. If he goes down by 18 points, he's done in politics before he's even gotten started."

Tremont spits his toothpick in the trashcan, replaces it immediately with a new one. "He doesn't." He swallows hard, looks like he's wondering whether to say what he's about to say. "He doesn't like polls. Won't look at them."

"That's fucking retarded." Mel can't believe it. "And you let him get away with that?"

"What the hell could I do? Tie him down and pry open his eyes? He thinks polls make a politician too self-conscious. It's some shit his father-in-law told him."

"Are you fucking kidding me?"

"He's the candidate. He calls the shots."

"Really, Alex? *He's* the candidate? That's your line? That's how you position yourself with this newbie? He's a rookie. Green to the core. I don't care who his father-in-law is. He has no idea what he's doing. It's your job to *tell* him what he wants. And now that you've fucked that up, it's *my* job to tell you and him both. How the holy hell have you let things sink this far? It's like you don't even care if he gets destroyed by this dipshit lieutenant governor."

"What the hell could I do?" Tremont sounds pathetic, completely defeated. At least he's aware of how badly he's failing.

"You explain to him what polls are. They're the scoreboard. They're your bank balance. They're you're goddamned AIDS test. You're not going to look at that when it comes in the mail? Then you're an idiot. You put it differently, of course, but Jesus H. Christ! He won't look at polls? I can't remember the last time I heard something so fucking retarded. Probably never."

Tremont opens his mouth to reply, slumps back in his chair, looks like he just barely stopped himself from saying, *I know, I know, I know.*

Mel softens a touch, realizes she's won this battle. It's time to show some mercy, to turn the conversation forward. "I know you've always been a ground-game guy, Alex, but we can't grind this one out to the finish line. Not with this lawyers-are-assholes attitude dragging us down, and a Republican tsunami bearing down full speed. It's the 4th quarter here, and we're 3 scores down. It's time to pass the ball. That's why Wilhelm sent me here. You run the ball, I pass it."

Mel softens her tone further. "We need to work together. I know what you can do with a get-out-the-vote effort. We'll need that. Absolutely. But we need movement in the polls too, or we're doomed, even with a five-star ground game. Musgrove's got soft support up and down the crosstabs, and there's more than enough undies to put us over the top if we get a good chunk of them. It'll be close, and it won't be easy, but we can win this one. I know we can."

1994

"Fine. We'll try it your way." Tremont clearly hates himself at this moment, and Mel makes sure not to gloat. These old turds are stupendously sensitive. "But let's wait a few days to broach a major change, OK? We've got a speech this afternoon at the Lorain Labor Temple, then dinner with some AFL brass tonight at Morton's. Why don't you take a couple of days to settle in here, watch Porter give his stump speech and work some bigwigs, get a feel for his approach, a feel for the race. Then we can re-evaluate. OK?"

Mel exhales with extra drama, drops her butt in a coffee cup on Tremont's desk. "Unacceptable. Read my lips, Alex. We. Cannot. Wait." Mel glances out the window of the office, eyes the staff like a predator sizing up her prey. It's time to meet the underlings, fire up the troops, get this beast turned in the right direction. "I've got some internal polling I want to go over with the staff," she says. "You're welcome to listen too, if you're interested."

Mel stands, tries to hide her distaste as Tremont pushes himself slowly from his chair. *Out of touch, out of shape, and out of ideas,* she says to herself. She tamps down what might be a surge of pity. She can't get soft on Tremont now, or he might find the strength to push back. She completely castrated him here, but he's an old war horse. Unless he quits outright, Mel knows she'll have to keep putting him in his place, day after day. That's *her* ground game for the duration.

She lets Tremont open the door for her, call a few times for everyone's attention. The room quiets slowly, the tension palpable. The staff obviously heard mommy and daddy fighting, and they're embarrassed, unsure what's about to happen. Mel doesn't care. It's good for them to know there's a power struggle going on at the top, that there's someone around who's serious about turning this shit around. Let these folks see that the new boss-lady means business.

"So, we've got a new strategist," Tremont says with exactly zero emotion. "Sent out from the DNC to help us win. This is Melissa Carnes. She wants to talk to you for a few minutes about." He glances at Mel. "About her ideas."

The room is dead silent now, not even a single telephone ringing. Mel can sense that morale is pathetically low. The 18-point deficit must weigh heavily on everyone. They're mostly volunteers and underpaid support staff, true believers and Porter groupies. Mel has been in this room before, knows how fervently trubies need reassurance, even in the best of times. Politics is a team sport, and she's the new coach, her guys way down in a win-or-go-home situation, 3 scores behind in the 4th quarter and the game clock ticking implacably. She thinks back to Buffalo's amazing comeback in the 1993 wildcard game—trailing 35-3 in the 3rd quarter, they won 41-38 in overtime, led by a backup quarterback no less. Mel wonders what Marv Levy said in the locker room at halftime. She needs to give her team the same kind of confidence boost, remind them it's not over til it's over and she knows they can do it. *Now go out there and turn this son-of-a-bitch around!*

Mel is pumped up, but she starts calmly, intending to build to a crescendo rather than rant and yell from the outset. "Thanks, Alex. I'm glad to be onboard." Mel smiles brightly, makes eye contact around the room. "I'm going to meet you all individually throughout the next couple of days, but I wanted to start off by laying out for the whole team where we are in the race, and more importantly, where we're going."

She signals Cindy, the secretary she spoke with earlier. Cindy points to the overhead projector, gives a thumbs-up, begins wrestling open a folding screen.

"We've got our first round of high-quality internal polling," Mel says. "I'm sure that you've all seen the latest public poll from the *Columbus Dispatch* that shows us 18 points down, 49 to 31. I won't lie to you. That's bad. Extremely bad."

She lays her first transparency on the projector, strolls to the screen while the women begin reading the data and the men look her up and down. She's used to this, doesn't take it personally, wonders only what they're thinking, whether it breaks towards *Who's this hot chick with the overhead projector?* or *Who does this frumpy bitch think she is, coming in here to tell us how to run our campaign?* What she wouldn't give for a quick glance at a focus-group summary for this crowd.

"Our data shows the same deficit, but the numbers we have — this is proprietary information, so none of this leaves the room — our numbers have a more granular breakdown, and the picture they reveal is less hopeless."

Mel stands in front of the screen, rows of data striping across her body. She can sense the desire for her to say something inspiring, to give them hope that all is not lost. "For one thing, undecided stands at 15 percent. We get all these undies, we're nearly in the lead." Mel sees some eyes begin to sparkle, worries that she shouldn't have led with that point. They're not going to get every undie, not even close — not with the way Porter is doing among key groups, not with a third-party candidate to sop up latent dissatisfaction, not with Howard Kane running Musgrove's campaign.

"But I'm not here to blow sunshine up your ass. Porter's in trouble. We have to admit that to ourselves. The crosstabs paint a pretty clear picture of a candidate underperforming among traditional Democratic voters." Mel scans the room, sees a grossly unrepresentative collection of Ohioans—not a black person in sight, precious few women, no one over 45, hardly anybody with a trace of blue-collar sensibility. Any precinct or census tract that looks anything like this is already safe territory for Republicans. What do these people understand about the Democratic base?

"The good news is, there's plenty of room to move here." She steps aside and smacks the screen to emphasize the row of union members broken down by age. "Our guy is way underperforming with blue-collar workers, especially here and here." Mel stabs the screen, scans the room again to make sure they're following along. Everyone listens intently. She can feel the power of their hope, the undercurrent of desperation. She's the savior from D.C., the brilliant new strategist sent in to rescue the situation. The expectation is almost too much to take, but it's one of the reasons Mel loves this job. Every campaign she joins needs her talent to survive, craves the kind of analysis and guidance that she and only she can provide.

"It shouldn't be too hard to break off a chunk of Musgrove's support," she continues, "particularly at the higher age range." Mel spends five minutes explaining how they'll do this with a combination of issue and character ads, TV, radio, and print, a new stump speech, an intensified schedule of appearances by the candidate.

Tremont makes a point of retreating to his office to show his displeasure. He doesn't go quietly. Mel controls the urge to roll her eyes at his childishness. She doesn't yet know who's loyal to Tremont and who's just as fed up as she is.

Mel gets back to the data, building to her Win One for the Gipper moment from a solid foundation of facts. "Musgrove's pro-NAFTA, anti-public school tenure, a corporate sleazebag who's been in trouble with the S.E.C. We'll paste him with everything. And let's not forget that he's even richer and more out of touch than our guy, whose parents are bona fide immigrants who ran a small haberdashery that put their son through law school. It's the classic American success story. So we're also going to tell our guy's humble story much better than we've been doing." Mel watches a few heads nod, knows that she's winning loyalty here—saying "much better than we've been doing" implicates her in their past screw-ups even though she wasn't around. It's a team-player move, a leader attitude.

"We'll start there and see how much we can move the needle. By the middle of next week, we'll have a good idea of how soft Musgrove's support is among our traditional constituencies, how many of those undies we can pull our way. For now, I want each and every one of you to start thinking about this campaign like it's a war."

Mel clasps her hands behind her back, assumes her *Patton* opening monologue pose, slips into her George C. Scott impersonation. *"And I want you to remember that no bastard ever won a war by dying for his country."* She pauses, tries not to smile. *"He won it by making the other poor dumb bastard die for his country."*

There's some laughter, a bit of it nervous, some clearly relieved that the new boss-lady has a lighter side. Mel wonders if anyone realizes who she's impersonating. She sees a few looks of awe, not a single snide expression or furtive whisper to a neighbor. She presses on confidently, channeling Patton. *"Americans, traditionally, love to fight. All real Americans love the sting of battle. When you were kids, you all admired the champion marble shooter, the fastest runner, the big-league ball players, the Olympic gold-medal winners. Americans love a winner and will not tolerate a loser. Americans play to win all the time."*

Mel allows a grin to creep onto her lips, letting the room in on the joke.

"There's another thing I want you to remember. I don't want to get any messages saying that we're holding our position. We're not holding anything. Let the other guy do that. We are advancing constantly." She smiles wider now—the next line always brings her to the edge of laughter. *"We're gonna kick the hell out of him all the time, and we're gonna go through him like crap through a goose!"*

Mel claps her hands, finishes in a mixture of her own voice and Patton's. "Okay, then. Let's go out and win this thing."

The staff claps lustily, and Mel feels her chest swell, her fingers tingle. It's always deeply satisfying to win over the staff, to sense that everyone is coming together under a common purpose. She did it. The troops have been rallied, and they're ready to follow her into battle.

She collects her transparencies, passes out memos, introduces herself personally to the various men—it's all men—who'll be working directly below her. She makes a point of introducing herself to all the women too, secretaries and low-level interns, each and every one of them. She grabs Colin Burke, Porter's speechwriter, hands him a three-page script.

"Here's a redraft of Porter's stump speech that works in the stuff I just talked about. Polish it up and get it back to me by noon. We'll go over it first, then take it to Porter. I want a chance to review the new direction with him before he hits the podium today."

"You got it, Ms. Carnes." Burke is fired up, Mel can tell. He looks almost exactly like William Hurt in *Body Heat*, down to the moustache

1994

and butt chin, but he lacks the smarmy charm, seems like he might actually be a nice guy.

"Call me Mel, OK?"

"Sure thing, Mel." He leans closer, glances around the room, speaks semi-conspiratorially. "It's good to have you onboard. Things have been a little—what's the best word?—*lethargic* around here for a few weeks. No offense to Mr. Tremont, but he never gave us a speech like you just did. Folks seem pretty roused."

"Thanks for saying that, Colin. Now take my clumsy speech." She thwacks the script with the back of her hand. "And make it gold."

"Will do."

Mel studies the room again, basks in the glow of purposeful bustle. She notices Tremont glaring at her through his office window, arms folded over his chest, the ubiquitous toothpick worrying back and forth across his mouth. It doesn't take a genius to know he's pissed, that he's summoning her back to his office without summoning her. Here it comes, Power Struggle Part 2. She nods to acknowledge the summons, takes her time rummaging her briefcase for cigarettes, lights up and strolls to his door.

"I saw you talking to Colin Burke out there. You're not having him rewrite the stump speech by any chance, are you?"

"Goddamned right I am. I read that speech on the plane yesterday. It's pure unadulterated garbage. It's well-written, sure. Burke's got talent, that's clear, but..."

The door flies open, and there's Kyle Porter in the flesh. He looks exactly like he does on TV. He's tall and lean, chiseled jaw, perfectly styled light brown hair, wavy with the slightest brushstrokes of grey imparting a subtle dignity. He has the look and bearing of a just-ripened Kennedy brother, more of a Bobby than a Jack or an Edward, which is perfect. Exactly what the times call for, the most charming and serious of the Kennedy boys, reincarnated as a heartland entrepreneur.

Porter flashes his smile at Mel, his eyes crinkling with warmth and empathy. Mel feels like he's thinking only of her, that she's the most important person in the world at that moment. Amazing. Perfect. What raw material.

"I heard our new strategist just got here," Porter says. He beams even more brightly, reaches out his hand. "Kyle Porter."

"Yes, I know." Mel gives Porter her firmest handshake, keeps her eyes locked on his. The first candidate contact is all-important. She has to project strength, certainty, expertise, but at the same time she has to make him comfortable, let him feel like he's in charge. "I've seen your television commercials. You're just as handsome in person."

"Why, thank you." He lingers over the handshake. He may be a rookie, but he's got the warmth-inducing politician handshake mastered. "I'm not sure that's an asset in politics, though."

"Oh, no, it is," Mel says. "No one wants to admit it, but it is. What's *not* an asset." Porter seems like a no-nonsense type, so she'll dive right in to business, keep the moment flowing her direction so Tremont can't weasel in and start undermining. "Sorry, but I'll give you the bad news first." Mel takes back her hand, pushes her glasses up her nose. "What's not an asset, unfortunately, is being a lawyer."

"I thought most of Congress were lawyers."

"They are. Most assuredly, sir. Wall-to-wall lawyers. What I should've said was, *known for being a lawyer.* Whatever else you could potentially be to the people of Ohio, to most of them, you're that TV lawyer with the strip-mall clinics. An excellent business. A real public service, bringing affordable legal expertise to the people who generally can't afford it. But, as my colleague Greg Blumenthal puts it. He's our pollster. Top-notch guy. The best. Everyone calls him Shep. As Shep puts it, the research shows a, quote, *negative perception of candidate's chosen field of endeavor*, unquote. That, Mr. Porter, is the main obstacle to your candidacy right now."

"Kyle. Please, call me Kyle."

"Okay, Kyle. I hope you don't mind me being blunt here, but we don't have much time, and it's important to get this campaign moving in the right direction. You're 18 points down, which is a large but not insurmountable deficit."

"Eighteen points down? Really? I haven't been looking at the polls. Alex here tells me not to worry about them. My father-in-law says the same thing. He's a former governor, if you didn't know that already." He deepens his voice, imitating, she assumes, Governor Travis. "*Paying too much attention to polls makes a politician worry about all the wrong things.*"

Mel shoots Tremont an *Oh really?* look. "I would agree that paying *too much* attention to polls is never a good idea," she says. "But it's important to know where you stand, from a purely strategic point of view. If you're riding a lead, you spend your time focused on not making unforced errors. If you're as far behind as you are, you know it's time for some big changes. Talk to the voters in a different way. Switch up advertising strategy. Hit the trail a little more aggressively. Take some calculated risks."

"If I really am that far behind, all that makes sense." Porter sits on the leather couch, crosses his legs. Mel is impressed by how casually he's taking this. Maybe he doesn't realize how bad 18 points behind is. "Tell me what you have in mind, Miss Carnes."

Mel pulls out her memo folder, hands a page to Porter. "If I'm going to call you Kyle, you have to call me Mel. Here's a summary of the strategy I've devised, based on a close reading of the data. Our own proprietary polls and focus groups, demographic and economic statistics from the government, past voting behavior and public-opinion trendlines, that sort of thing. The good news is, we've got a pretty clear strategic path forward."

Porter glances at the sheet, hums noncommittally.

"That's just the broad strokes, of course. I've got our staff working on the details." Porter follows Mel's glance out the window, where they see the kind of purposeful bustle that was notably lacking this morning. She hopes Porter notices the difference. "Colin's working on a redraft of your stump speech, which we'll launch at today's rally in Lorain. Here's my rough draft." She hands him a stack of note cards. "Give it a practice read."

Porter complies without hesitation, recites his lines like a practiced actor, just as she hoped. *He's definitely got potential*, Mel says to herself. She gives him a few tone suggestions here and there, nods encouragingly whenever he looks up for approval, claps lightly when he's done. "Excellent work, Kyle. And that's just the rough draft. Colin's working his magic as we speak. It'll be much better when he's through with it."

"It sounds pretty good to me. I don't see how Colin could improve it much."

"That's what a top-notch speechwriter does, Kyle. He takes the merely good and makes it soar. I'm excited to see what he comes up with. I'm sure the audience in Lorain, and the public at large, will be suitably inspired."

"You're very upbeat, Miss Carnes. I mean, Mel. Yet I'm 18 points down, you say." Porter turns somber. It's clear he had some idea how badly he was doing but pushed it to the back of his mind. The pain of confronting his denial registers only as a slight crinkling of the eyes. "Do you really think I can win?"

"I wouldn't be here if I didn't think so," Mel answers without a moment of hesitation. It's important to project confidence to the candidate. It helps that it's true. "It won't be easy, I'll admit that much, but this race is yours to win, Mr. Senator."

Tremont pointedly checks his watch. "We need to get rolling, sir. I'd like you to stop off at a few shopping centers on the way out of town. Speeches and ads are important, of course." He scowls at Mel behind

Porter's back, all but sticks out his tongue at her. "But there's a lot to be gained by good old-fashioned retail politics. Shaking hands and kissing babies." Tremont tries to match Mel's cheerful tone, but he sounds unconvinced himself. Mel wonders if he's putting Porter through this shopping-center tour as a sly penance for his falling in love with Mel so easily. She wouldn't put it past him.

Tremont guides Porter to the campaign van, makes sure he gets in the back with him, forcing Mel to sit up front and turn around awkwardly to talk as they drive. She knows she should've stayed behind at HQ, bucking up and guiding the staff, kept her appointment with Colin Burke to go over the stump speech, but it's more important to prevent Tremont from undermining her with the candidate. She knows he's mightily pissed at how forcefully she's taken over, that he might be slow to respond but he hasn't given up yet. Not by a long shot. This idiotic shopping-center tour is proof of that.

Tremont is a plodder, both as a strategist and as a boss, but Mel is sure he's working on ways to push her aside, even if it means torpedoing Porter's chances of winning. Pride and loyalty are more important to these old-school types than winning. Mel knows that's true even if she doesn't understand it. How the hell has Tremont survived in this game so long without adapting to the changing times, without winning more often than he does? The answer, she suspects, is that he's a master at managing his contacts. He gives his unconditional loyalty, and he gets it in return. It's the only kind of exchange his type understands, the only kind he's capable of commanding. Mel gives hard work, brilliance, victory, and she expects praise and promotion in return, obedience to her strategic scripting, recognition that she knows better than these old farts how to win elections in today's environment. That's the kind of exchange that makes sense. She's loyal to the party, but she demonstrates that loyalty by striving for victory, always and forever, not by glad-handing the old-boys' network like Tremont and his ilk.

Not that they would trust her if she tried. They'll tolerate women—most of them more cordially than Alex Tremont—but they still don't fully trust them. Even New Democrats like David Wilhelm and George Stephanopoulos are still sexists, duplicating in subtle, unconscious ways the chauvinistic behaviors they excoriate in others. Mel vows to win this election and show them all how well a woman understands politics in the '90s, how much they're giving up by passing over women for important jobs. She's part of the advance guard here, establishing a beachhead for a future wave of women to command top positions in the political system, both behind and in front of the cameras.

1994

That's the real Big Picture here, something her mother could be genuinely proud of, if she'd lived to see her daughter become an adult. It's the first time in a while that Mel feels confident that she's living up to her mother's legacy, that she's able to fulfill the expectations that have hovered over her like a ghost for the past 15 years.

# # # # #

The crowd is a modest size, scattered unevenly around the hall, sitting politely on folding metal chairs and talking quietly among themselves, maybe a hundred people total in a room that would hold 3 times that number. It's mostly men, mostly white, mostly middle-aged, but there are a few tough-looking women in their 30s, some men in their 20s, a smattering of black faces. Pretty typical for a working-class town in the Rust Belt in 1994.

A half-dozen reporters stand to the side near the front, shooting the shit. The press corps seems thin for a Senate race this late in the cycle, a bad sign for Porter. There can't be many pros who think Porter's got a snowball's chance, and anyone with a choice is apt to be somewhere else where there's more action, down in the 10th district, for instance, where Kucinich is making a good run at a Democratic pick-up, or over in the 14th, where Sawyer is fighting off a strong challenge in a typically solid Cleveland suburb. Political journalists, in Mel's experience, are in it primarily for the thrill, the daily hope that something ugly or amazing will happen—usually ugly—the steady undertone of anxiety and expectation associated with any high-stakes endeavor the junk that keeps them waiting around through all the empty, weary hours. Senate races are generally more interesting than House, but it can't be much fun watching Musgrove grind down Porter. Nobody but a die-hard fan enjoys a blowout.

Mel sizes up the group. All but one of the reporters are men, a familiar ratio. Women are rare in all corners of politics, from candidates to scribblers, secretaries the only exception. Mel spends her life in a cloud of testosterone and dick jokes, elbowing her way through a mob of paunchy, pale-skinned trolls like the coven here. This particular collection ranges in height from about 5'4" to just over 6', but that's the biggest differentiating trait. Otherwise they're more or less the same—the clothes wrinkled, the eyes bloodshot and surrounded by bags, the telltale slouch of a sub-species that stands too much and exercises too little.

They laugh in unison, all but the lone woman—Kate Winkler, *Washington Post*, who offers a thin smile, somewhere between a long-suffering mom and a Catholic school nun about to smash some knuckles. Mel knows how she feels. You want to call out these sexists assholes— many of whom have the gall to think of themselves as feminists, or at least friends of the cause—but the constant flow of occasions to do so is overwhelming, the effort counterproductive in any case. They'll just call her uptight, claim whatever stupid shit they said is only a joke, no harm done. Of course not, not to *them*, which is the only criteria they ever apply. *I wouldn't mind if you made fun of* my *genitalia*, one of these fuckwits actually said to her once. No, but would he mind if she took that cigarette and ground it out on his eyeball?

Kate breaks away from the group to talk to some of the union guys, pen scratching quickly on pad. Mel wonders what they're telling her. Another one drifts to the back of the hall, leans against the wall and scribbles some notes on a pad, probably writing his article already, before the event's even under way. Lazy fuck. He's *Akron Beacon-Journal*, if Mel's not mistaken. Marvin Blakely. He covered '92 as well. In fact, they all look familiar, a 2-year gap between her visits here not changing much. That's good, in a way. Mel doesn't have time to relearn the landscape in every detail, build media relationships from the ground up. It was smart to send in a native, someone who's worked an Ohio campaign in the past couple of cycles. Tip O'Neill was right. *All politics* is *local*.

A creepy Christian-looking guy materializes at her side, painfully young, awkward in his new off-the-rack suit, bug eyes and black plastic-frame glasses, pencil-thin neck, prominent Adam's apple. He looks vaguely familiar. "Hey." He looks at Mel hopefully.

"Yes?" Mel notices his *Porter for U.S. Senate* button, figures he was a face in the crowd at HQ, someone she hasn't had a chance to meet one-on-one yet.

"I'm Carlton Schooley." He thrusts out his hand. "Your new deputy chief strategist."

Mel shakes quickly, looks him up and down with pointed distaste. "Oh yeah. And what were you yesterday?"

Schooley is undaunted, his voice mercilessly cheerful. "Assistant deputy campaign manager."

"What the hell is that?" Sounds like a bullshit title to make the interns feel less insignificant.

"Honestly, I never quite figured it out. Kind of an all-around assistant, is what it seemed like. I did some scheduling, some press clipping, double-checked the expenditure reports, got to do some work on position papers. That was my favorite part. I organized a fundraiser at the Ashland Elks. We pulled in 5 thou on that one."

"Impressive," Mel says. She hopes the kid doesn't think she means it. "And now you're my *what* again?"

"Deputy chief strategist, ma'am."

Ma'am? Jesus, kill me now.

"Mr. Tremont says I'm supposed to listen and learn. Do whatever you ask me to do."

"And report back to him, I suppose?" A spy. Is Tremont that insecure?

"He never said anything about that." Mel believes him. Schooley doesn't look capable of duplicity or espionage. He looks, in fact, exactly like a Mormon missionary. Grey suit, white shirt, crisply knotted tie, close-cropped hair, exuberant eyes.

"And what qualifications do you possess to be a deputy chief strategist, Carlton Schooley?"

"I was graduated magna cum laude from Ohio State, double major in political science and psychology, class of '94." He says this with a mixture of hope and despair, as though Mel is sure to think his hard-earned honors are worthless. "I interned with a state senator my junior year," he adds, trying for a brighter tone. "Wasn't very exciting, but I learned a lot about how lobbyists work."

"Then what're you doing in campaign? You flame out as a lobbyist already?"

"I never got into it. Too much having to know everybody's name and story, what their kids are up to and what sports they care about, that kind of thing. *Relationship management*, they called it." Mel can hear the suppressed air quotes. "It's not at all like I imagined it."

"Uh huh."

"I spent the summer looking around for a campaign to work on. Seemed like a more exciting side of politics."

"Right. And let me guess. Your dad knows Alex Tremont, and he got you the job here?"

"My mom, actually. She's co-chair of the Medina County DP."

"All right, then." Mel rests a hand on Schooley's shoulder. He seems like a good kid if a bit of a momma's boy, probably won't be too much of a nuisance if she keeps him occupied, lets him watch and learn. She's never had a mentee before. Could be fun. "We'll talk about your job later. Right now, it's time to feed the lions."

"Lions?"

"The press." Mel narrows her eyes at the press guys, joking collegially in their closed circle. "If we don't keep them fed, they'll eat *us*, and we don't want that, now do we?"

"No, ma'am."

"Let's cut it with the *ma'am* crap, OK?"

"Yes, um. Yes, Ms. Carnes."

"Just Mel, if you don't mind."

"All right." Schooley looks at Mel eagerly, squaring himself up to take on the press.

"Good," she says with a pat on his shoulder. "Now, stay here. Watch and listen, but don't move. Got it?"

"Yes." Mel can tell he swallows a reflexive *ma'am*, looks like he wishes he had a notebook to write everything down. He strikes her as a dedicated note-taker, probably still has all his perfectly organized notes from every class he took in college. "Don't move," he says obediently. "Just watch and listen. Got it."

"Excellent." Mel slides casually over to the journalists, catches Kate Winkler's eye and nods her back to the scrum, a brief moment of sympathy passing between their carefully composed faces.

"Why, if it isn't Melissa Carnes." That's Jared Block, *New York Times*. "I thought you were in Nebraska with Kerrey."

"Very sharp, Jay. Do you know everything about everybody?"

"Usually. So is this a quick visit home, or you with Porter now?"

Mel remembers her *Porter for U.S. Senate* button, pulls it out of her briefcase and shows it around.

"New chief strategist?" Jared asks.

"That's right. I'm here to help get Kyle Porter into the U.S. Senate."

"Oh yeah?" That's Chris Garvey, *Columbus Dispatch,* another guy she remembers from Clinton '92. He's hard to forget, with his Colombo hat and trench coat and signature five o'clock shadow, like he's an actor playing a journalist in a schlocky political thriller. "And how you gonna do that?"

"More votes than the other guy," Mel shoots back with a grin. She clips the button to her dress, watches the reporters watching her, their eyes drawn to her cleavage. Mel can feel the warmth coming off these men, the subtle shifting of their bodies as hormones spread out and start to take over. She knows they like the hot librarian type too. Every 30-something white guy in politics does, whether he's lobby, campaign, or press. The press guys are less vulnerable than the others—they meet more women, probably—but they're still guys. A little cleavage goes a long way, even in this supposedly post-chauvinist age. 1994? Hell, it might as well be 1964.

"Polls look pretty bad for you." Garvey again. "We've got him 18-points down. I have it from Musgrove's in-house pollster that it's more like 20. Kane's calling it an elephant stampede."

1994

"Howard Kane can kiss my lily white ass." Mel grins. "That's off-the-record, by the way. He knows it's true, but I don't want to see that in print."

"What *can* we print?" That's Kate Winkler, impatient for some action.

Akron rejoins the group. Mel pushes her glasses up her nose, reads the press badges. "Akron, Columbus, Dayton, Times, Wapo. What's that? Youngstown? And Lorain, of course." Mel mimes looking under a nearby chair. "That's all? Why so thin today? Where's Cleveland and Cinci? Toledo? I thought I saw *Wall Street* on the press list too. And no *Chicago Tribune*?"

"They're with Musgrove," Jared says. "Columbus Chamber of Commerce luncheon. Economic policy speech, or so they said."

"We got stuck here." That's Marvin Blakely.

"We rotate and share notes," Dayton offers. "Not that you guys have been doing much. We've all mostly been on Musgrove for the past few weeks."

"That's changing," Mel says. "As of today. Hey, if I called a presser on Friday, would everyone come, you think? You and all the others?" Mel hates how much she sounds like a girl desperate for a prom date, but that's how you have to play the press corps in situations like this — slightly anxious, or they think you're taking them for granted. A mob of scribblers, even a small one, will turn combative at the slightest perceived arrogance.

Jared flips through his datebook. "Looks like Musgrove's dark on Friday, so sure, I don't see why not?"

"What about CNN?" Mel asks. "They have a team in-country?"

"'Course. Just one for the whole state, though. Probably with one of the House races today."

"Sixth district, I'd bet," Kate offers. "That's a hot one. Cremeans is fighting for his life against Strickland. Could be a badly needed pick-up for you guys. I get over there once in a while. Looks to be a brawl down to the wire."

"Not like this turkey," Blakely puts in.

Mel beams at the reporters, pushes her glasses up her nose. "Yeah, well, strap in boys. It's about to get a lot more exciting. I promise you that." Mel checks her watch, glances behind her at the door concealing Porter and Tremont, hopefully Colin Burke too. They're supposed to be going over the new speech.

"How about that statement?" Jared isn't one to let a press agent of any rank get away without something on the record.

"Of course. That's why I'm here."

The notepads and tape recorders come out. It's show time.

Mel lays it out for them, explains how they're shifting the focus to Musgrove's record, his policies, his special-interest leanings. "The guy's in favor of NAFTA, which, as I'm sure you know, is unpopular among union voters, and Ohio's got a lot of union voters." Mel tries not to grimace at the half-empty room. Or is it half-full? Either way, it's a bad sign for a Democrat to pull such a thin crowd to a union hall in the state's 10th largest city.

Mel continues, ticks off Musgrove's offenses on her fingers. "He's against increasing the minimum wage, he's against long-overdue infrastructure spending, he's against tenure for public school teachers and a much-needed expansion of job retraining programs. He's against pretty much anything that helps regular, salt-of-the-earth Ohioans." She attacks Musgrove for his wealth, ties him special interests and sleazy lobbying methods, mentions his history of problems with the S.E.C.

"Kyle Porter, on the other hand, he understands and cares about the regular people of Ohio. These folks here in Lorain, and in cities and towns just like it all over the state. He's been fighting for their legal rights, for fairness, his whole adult life, and he's going to take that fighting spirit to the U.S. Senate. We need more good men like Kyle Porter in the halls of power. Speaking of..." Mel checks her watch again. "Should be about time for the man himself. Always a pleasure, guys." She pushes her glasses up, turns away. "See anyone at the bar at Morton's later?" she says over her shoulder. "Around 10? First round's on me."

Mel strides past Schooley, who falls in behind her. She glances back and notes that the hall is maybe two-thirds full now. Not bad. She slides into the back room where Porter is huddled with Colin Burke, going over a few last-minute wording changes. Tremont slouches pathetically in the background, obviously displeased but keeping it to himself.

Mel claps her hands together, tells Porter it's time for the real thing. She sizes him up, realizes something's wrong. "I think for today, a full suit isn't quite the right thing." She undoes Porter's tie and ruffles his hair, tells him to take off his jacket and roll his sleeves to mid forearm.

"I'm not sure about that," Porter says. "Won't it look like I'm pandering."

"No one's going to think you're pandering, Kyle." Mel circles behind him, slides the jacket from his shoulders. Porter offers no resistance. "The only thing they'll do is feel — not *think*, but feel — that you're a man who actually works for a living, like they do."

1994

Mel tosses the jacket to Schooley, worries she might've unwittingly insulted her candidate by implying that he doesn't actually work for a living. "It'll help them open their minds to what you have to say," she continues quickly. "And that's why you're here today. To tell these good people how you're going to serve *them* in the United States Senate, and why they can entrust you with the most precious commodity in a democratic society. Their vote."

Porter takes a deep breath. He seems like he's inspired. He rolls up his sleeves as instructed, stretches out his face muscles like an actor preparing for the stage, takes another deep breath. "Okay, then. Let's get this show on the road."

FRIDAY, SEPTEMBER 30TH
7:19AM

Another hotel breakfast. Another featureless dining room filled with wet-haired businessmen. Another morning of her life given over to the task of getting a man what he wants — in this case, a seat in the U.S. Senate.

Mel sips her coffee, tries to will away the dark mood. What is she doing here, using up her time and talent for the good of some entitled white male who'll be just fine, win or lose? It's for the party, too, she reminds herself, but is that any better? It's supposed to be, but she doesn't feel it right now.

She takes off her glasses, lays her head on Shep's focus group report, closes her eyes and imagines she's just another suburban housewife up at 7am to make breakfast and pack the kids off to school. Her husband is faceless, his back to her as he pours himself a cup of coffee. *We're doing dinner with the Robinsons tonight,* he says. She wishes he would turn around, smile at her, reveal his identity, but her fantasies are always incomplete, the kids forever in the other room making noise, the husband perpetually facing away, pouring coffee or fixing a flat tire or mowing the lawn off into the sunset. Her first therapist told her it means she doesn't really want a life like that, not deep down, that she doesn't even know what she wishes for herself. It sounded like bullshit at the time, but she sees more and more that a normal family life does lay the opposite direction from where she's always been headed. *Our deepest truth is revealed by our actions, not our desires,* another therapist told her, just a couple of years ago. She felt the truth of that pretty powerfully, realized her choices did demonstrate a clear ambivalence about having a family of her own, but she had to dump that guy a few sessions later when he laid his hand on her knee at the end of a session. Fucking men. What sensible person could blame her for being hesitant about settling down, bringing more innocents into a world like this?

Mel opens her eyes, lifts a head heavy with existential gloom, slides her glasses back on and opens the report. Work is the cure for all despair. Work and success. She notes happily that yesterday's focus group responded positively to her new messaging, that the attacks on Musgrove weren't off-putting and the child-of-immigrants TV spot drew both surprise and sympathy. "Huh, I figured he was born rich," said a 29 year-old African American mother of three from Garfield Heights.

Mel reads carefully, highlights comments here and there that she wants Porter to see. He was cautiously receptive to bringing his parents' story into the campaign, but Mel can tell he's worried about making them look bad. He should be pleased to see the focus group with a positive response to the tale of humble origins and good old-fashioned American grit. "With parents like that, I'm sure he's a good man." 62 year-old white union member from Tallmadge. Mel is certainly pleased.

There are other indications that they can chip away at the negative perceptions created by Porter's legal service ads. She talked him into taking them off the air for the duration, a much harder task than it should've been. "It sends a mixed message," Mel said, trying the gentle approach when she wanted to say, *Are you running for Senate or trying to make even more money, you stupid fuck?* "Voters see you selling your legal service, and they wonder how committed you are to serving the public." *And they're reminded that you're a lawyer, and they hate lawyers.* But she doesn't say that, tries not even thinking it lest it pop out of her mouth. She's had tendencies in the past to make ill-advised comments to the face of her candidate, a tendency she's corrected, for the most part anyway.

"It's not good to get as much public exposure as I can?" Porter said.

"It is, but not like that. You're running for a U.S. Senate seat. When voters see you running a business at the same time, it undermines the message we're trying to convey. If you were a Republican, you could get away with it. I'd still advise against it, but it wouldn't hurt as much. Not fair, I know, but that's the way it is. You need to shore up your Democratic base, and that means presenting yourself as a Man of the People, not a wealthy lawyer." *And that slogan sucks, too,* she wanted to add but obviously never would.

Porter relented, but she could see it bothered him. Shep's report should keep him from changing his mind. "Candidate management is everything," she remembers one of her professors saying. She never forgets it, has yet to meet a politician who didn't need constant management. "Politicians are a cross between toddlers and teenagers," the prof said to back up his point. "Unsteady and vain, impulse-driven and insecure." Entirely true in Mel's decade of experience.

Mel closes the report, notices a man standing at her table. She has no idea how long he's been there, watching her mark up the report, possibly muttering to herself. He has a mop of black wavy hair, press credentials hanging around his neck, white shirt untucked, tie askew already, or *still*—he looks like he might've been up all night, or slept in his clothes. His jeans are in relatively good condition, nice fit around the legs. She looks down, frowns at his sensible brown shoes. Embarrassingly sensible for such a young guy, in Mel's opinion.

She reads the name on his press badge. "Thom Reynolds." She pronounces Thom with a th-sound, like Thong with an M instead of NG. "*Cleveland Plain Dealer.*"

"It's Tom, with a hard-T," Thom corrects.

"Short for Thomas?"

"Nope. Just plain Tom."

"It's spelled T-H-O-M, though, right?"

"That's right."

"Thom," Mel says, using the th-sound again.

"Tom."

"Thom."

"*Tom.*"

"I guess we'll have to agree to disagree," Mel says.

"It's *my* name," Thom says. "*You* can't agree to disagree when there's a right way and a wrong way to say it."

"But it *is* spelled T-H-O-M? I'm correct about that?"

"Yes."

"And that's what your parents named you? Not Thomas, and when you got your first byline you decided to go by Thom?" She uses the th-sound again.

"Tom."

"I just don't know that I buy it," Mel says.

"No one's asking you to *buy it*, just to pronounce it correctly." Thom is clearly frustrated. Mel can tell he's forgotten why he approached her in the first place. "So you're saying it's Tom?" Mel asks. "Like T-O-M?"

"Exactly."

"No, I think I like Thom better."

"I don't care if you like it better. It's not my name." Thom is quietly raging at this point.

"You sound like you could use a cup of coffee, Thom. Why don't you sit down, and let's talk about this Senate race."

Thom takes a deep breath, pulls out the chair, sits warily. He gets out his notebook, looks to Mel like he's resetting to professional mode. She has the upper hand, though, that much is obvious. Thom has to know it too after she unbalanced him over such a trivial matter as how to pronounce his name.

"You know, on second thought," Mel says, pushing her chair back. "Let's take a walk. I always think better when I'm moving." She heads to the lobby without waiting to see if Thom follows. There's a chance he'll give up and write a nasty piece about Porter after the way she just treated him, but they could scarcely do any worse than they already are, so it's worth the risk. She's gotten shit for this from other strategists—the keep-reporters-happy crowd that buys a lot of drinks and guffaws at every puerile joke—but she finds that friendlies respond better to rough treatment. It makes them feel less like a pass-through for press releases and more like real reporters. Unless she's completely mistaken, Thom Reynolds is a friendly, so this is exactly the right way to play their opening encounter. Plus, it's fun to slice down to size such a good-looking guy.

Thom rushes to catch up, arrives at Mel's side with a mischievous grin. "You like to play games, huh?" He begins writing quickly in his notebook, reads what he's writing as he scribbles it down. "*Hostile reception from Mr. Porter's new pollster, Melissa Carnes, indicating a level of desperation well-suited to the current situation.*"

"Chief strategist," Mel says. "Shep Blumenthal's our pollster." She pushes through the revolving door, waits for Thom to join her. "Which way? You have a preference?"

"Doesn't matter to me," Thom says.

"Let's go left, then." Mel offers her most genuine smile. "It's usually the better way."

"Can I assume this is on the record?" Thom asks as they set off at a leisurely pace. Mel is normally a power walker, but she already did half an hour on the treadmill this morning, and it's a perfect Ohio autumn day, clear and mid-60s, no wind, so she gives in to her urge to stroll rather than stride.

"Until I say otherwise, sure. On the record. What've you got, Thom?" She emphasizes the th-sound. He seems unfazed this time.

"Whether you're the pollster or not, I'm sure you realize how far down your guy is. An *Akron Beacon Journal* poll from a month ago had Musgrove up by 13 points. A more recent one from *The Columbus Dispatch* puts the margin at 18. *It's starting to look like an elephant stampede.* That's a quote from Howard Kane, Musgrove's campaign manager."

"*Elephant stampede*? Come on, Thom. You're not printing that drivel, are you?"

"It's a pretty accurate characterization, wouldn't you say?" Thom flips through his notebook. "I've got a guy at the Akron University Institute of Applied Politics who says, and I quote, *Historically, Ohio is a state of close races, so in theory Porter has a chance to catch up, but this is already looking like a Republican wave. Even some more experienced and better-qualified Democrats are in trouble.*"

"Kind of a clunky quote," Mel says. "What else you got?"

"Dr. Chris Farnsworth at the University of Cincinnati Political Science department says, *Mr. Musgrove could still lose, but he'd have to put his foot in his mouth and twist it.*"

"That's a little livelier, but still pretty lame."

"Care to comment?" Thom says.

Mel stops, turns to face Thom, pushes her glasses up her nose. "Here's the thing. People know Porter, but they don't know Musgrove. Not yet. Starting yesterday, at the rally you missed. Where were you, by the way? The rest of the old boys' network was there."

"Musgrove speech to the Columbus Chamber of Commerce."

"Ah. Of course. Well, while you were chasing after Howard Kane, lapping up his self-serving metaphors, Mr. Porter was at the Labor Temple in Lorain explaining to the workers of this state the many ways a candidate like Musgrove is bad for people like them. Bad for the state of Ohio."

"So Porter's going on the attack?"

"We're widening the focus to highlight Musgrove's record, which you in the press have sadly done little to expose. His business activities, his public statements, his record as lieutenant governor. He supports NAFTA and promises to block any increase in the minimum wage, which has already eroded nearly 10% in purchasing power since it was last raised in '91." Mel starts ticking things off on her fingers, well-practiced at her list already. "He's against infrastructure spending, tenure for public school teachers, job retraining programs. He's against pretty much anything that helps regular people, people he knows nothing about. And why would he? He's a super-rich guy who spends his time figuring out ways to circumvent the kind of common-sense regulations designed to prevent him and his cronies from leveraging their wealth unfairly into even more personal gain."

Thom writes furiously. "That's quite a mouthful."

Mel continues undeterred. "He's open about his desire to gut telecom regulations, a clear case of both self-interest and special interests driving his policy. He's got a checkered lobbying record with the F.C.C. *and* a history of problems with the S.E.C. Rich guy problems."

1994

"And yet he's got a commanding lead with less than 6 weeks til election day."

Mel pushes up her glasses once more, starts walking again. "He may be ahead right now, but he's a bleeder. Classic case. And believe me, we know how to make him bleed."

"Okay." Thom finishes writing, trots to catch up.

"And that's it. We're off-the-record now." Energized by a job well done, Mel speeds into her usual power-walk stride, pulls out her cigarettes and lights up.

"Seriously, that's all I get?"

"Seriously. Break it up into a few paragraphs. There's plenty of substance there." Mel blows a cloud of smoke across Thom's face, speeds up a bit more. "I'll get you the text of his speech from yesterday, if you want to pretend you were there. It's quotable from start to finish. I'm particularly fond of the story he tells about his parents working long hours to run a small haberdashery so they could put him through college and law school. You'll love it."

"Thanks." Thom slides his notebook into his pocket, seems a bit stressed by Mel's pace. "Can we do background?" he asks. He's trying hard not to pant. "Unattributed? Or are we done here?"

Mel hits Thom with her most inviting smile, hates herself briefly for using even the tiniest hint of feminine wiles. "I like you, Thom." She slows imperceptibly. She admits to herself that she *does* like him. She finds his rumpled boyish thing charming instead of pathetic. He's got the look of a high-school star athlete gone slightly to seed, just the type she's attracted to — humanized by being slightly out of shape but still lithe and strong, comfortable in his body in a way non-athletic people never are. There's a loose swing to his arms that Mel finds alluring. Even the sensible brown shoes make her happy for some ridiculous reason.

"Sure, let's do some background. What do you want to know?"

"You're kind of a hotshot with the DNC." Thom pulls out his notebook again, flips through the pages. "Product of George Washington's prestigious Political Communications department, class of '86. Interned with the DNC and John Glenn's re-election campaign, worked as a deputy press assistant from '87 to '88, DNC again. Helped win a close House race in New Jersey in '88 as deputy communications director, worked a must-win Senate race in Iowa in '90 for Tom Harkin, deputy chief strategist. Served briefly on Harkin's legislative staff in '91 before joining his short-lived presidential campaign, then moved over to the Clinton camp as chief strategist to the Ohio chairman. Chief strategist for three special elections in '93 and early-'94, 2-and-1 record, including an important win in the California 17th last June to keep Leon Panetta's seat for the Dems. Your recent record is particularly impressive given the way things are breaking towards the GOP these days…"

"Is there a question here, or are you just trying to butter me up?"

"Maybe a little butter. It's too early to start boozing. Anyway, my point is, you're a pretty valuable asset for the Democratic Party. Young, savvy, experienced, excellent win-loss ratio. Almost unbelievable, in fact. If you're here, when Democrats need help in any number of key races across the map, the DNC must think this is winnable. Either that, or you pissed off someone important, and they're throwing you to the wolves."

"I still don't hear a question."

"Right. Do you honestly think Porter can pull this out? Eighteen points down with less than 6 weeks to go? Musgrove's got to be a serious bleeder for you to even get close. Is this mission impossible, or is Melissa Carnes here to produce a long-shot win?"

"That's the longest goddamned question I've ever heard, Thom. And the simple answer is: Yes."

"Yes to what?"

"Yes, it's mission impossible *or* I'm here to produce a long-shot win."

"Come on, we're off-the-record here. For real, do you think you can win this one?"

"I have a question for you first. How do you know all that about me? You're not a creepy stalker, are you?"

"I did my homework. It's basic journalism, Ms. Carnes. Crucial Senate race looking like a blowout. Major staff addition near the top with a 6 weeks to go. I wanted to know who we're dealing with here at the helm of Porter's ship."

"And you found out all that stuff by yourself? In only 2 days?"

"We have an excellent research staff at the *Plain Dealer*. Excellent and highly underutilized. I answered your question. Now answer mine. Can you win?"

"This is background, right? You're not going to attribute this to an *unknown source inside the Porter campaign*, are you?"

"Completely background. I'm not even writing this stuff down." Thom flutters his notebook, makes a show of pocketing it, holds out his empty hands like a two-bit magician working a 10-year-old's birthday party.

Mel notices they're nearing Porter HQ. She slows her pace, flicks away her cigarette, pushes her glasses up again. "OK. Honestly, yes, it's mission impossible, or it could easily look that way. Eighteen points is pretty far down. But yes, we can win. I *intend* for us to win, and we're already heading that direction."

"You really think you have a shot at this?"

"We—are—going—to—win."

"Did you just do an LBJ impersonation there?"

"Nope."

"Yes you did."

Mel stops, glances pointedly at the *Porter for U.S. Senate* signs plastering the storefront window in front of her. She timed their arrival perfectly.

"Thanks for the great walk, Thom." She emphasizes the th-sound. "I assume I'll see you at the presser this afternoon." Mel pushes through the door, forces herself not to look back. *That went perfectly*, she tells herself. Her sense of job pride slams into the wall of Alex Tremont.

"You do *not* call a press conference without my approval!" he yells from the open doorway of his office. He's clearly been waiting there for Mel to arrive. Heads turn as he marches through the bullpen. She stays where she is, pulls out her pack of Parliaments, bides her time by lighting up. She thought he'd wait until she got to his office to blow up about this. If he wants to have this out in front of the whole staff, that's fine by her. Maybe he thinks he has something to gain by doing it this way, or maybe he simply can't control himself.

"If you want my job, be man enough to say so."

"Man enough? *Man* enough, Alex?

"You know what I mean."

"I know you're a cock-sucking sexist pig. That's what I know."

"Cock-sucking? Are you gay-bashing me, Carnes?"

"No more than you're woman-bashing me, asshole. Look Tremont, I don't want your job." She blows smoke in his face. "Campaign manager. That's too stuffy a title for me. Schmoozing union leaders and organizing fundraisers, making sure checks get signed and phones are answered, folding chairs rented for rallies and volunteers sent out to knock on doors. That's boring to me. Necessary, yes, but it's not what I do."

Mel says this for the staff. People are pretending not to listen, but they obviously can't ignore a fight in their midst. She wants them all to know she values what they do for the team, however tedious or trivial. "The campaign manager has to do all kinds of stuff I wouldn't want the responsibility for," she adds.

"And with that responsibility comes power." Tremont is obviously forcing himself to calm down. "For example, the power to call, or not call, a press conference for our candidate. Scheduling is entirely my purview, Carnes. You want something to happen, for *strategic* reasons, you run it past me. Got it?"

Mel knows Tremont is right, but she won't say it out loud, certainly not in front of the whole staff. Women in positions of power can show no weakness, no contrition, no regret. At the tiniest crack in her self-assurance, a woman in her job is doomed to constant second-guessing and undermining by men. *They* can make mistakes all day long without losing their bosses' confidence, but as soon as a woman makes even the tiniest mistake, it's all over. She has to strut around with 10 times the self-assurance of any man, and even then, she's one stumble away from falling completely. Add it to the list of the world's many iniquities.

Instead of admitting her mistake, Mel goes on the offensive. "I'll tell you what I want. I want *you* to do *your* job, so we can all work together as a team to win this one. I called a presser today without running it by you because you've been a sloth this month. There's no goddamned good reason we're 18 points down. That's on you. Every fucking bit of it. *On you*! Are you completely burned out or what? Would you even have gotten to my request in time for me to pull this thing together?" Mel grinds out her half-smoked cigarette in an empty ashtray on a nearby desk, crosses her arms and stares hard at Tremont. "Do you still have what it takes to win? Because things are gonna move fast over the next 5 weeks, and for *strategic* reasons, I'm gonna need you to keep up. Got it?"

Mel feels the tension in the room ratchet up. However much the staff might share her disdain for Tremont, there's a pecking order in place, and she's openly challenging the boss.

"Don't let it happen again, all right?" Tremont pokes his finger towards Mel.

He's such a weakling, Mel says to herself. Backing down so fast, and so publicly. She's almost embarrassed for him. "Do your job, and let me do mine," she spits out. "And we'll be fine."

# # # # #

Mel peeks into the ballroom, likes the crowd of press she sees, notes with satisfaction that CNN is setting up. All the Cleveland stations have a camera crew on hand. There's a station from Columbus as well, another from Cincinnati, even Dayton, a bunch of radio people newly added to the press list just this morning testing field recorders for sound level.

1994

Mel goes to the makeshift green room to check on Porter, adjusts his tie like a loving wife. "Nice crowd of reporters out there," she says. "This is our big moment. The campaign starts right here, right now. Everything else that's happened up to this day is prologue."

Mel looks into Porter's eyes, sees that he doesn't need any more bucking up. He's ready to go. He must feel bolstered by his practice session earlier. He nailed every question, said exactly what Mel told him to say, looked both tough and comfortable, worked in every oblique shot at Musgrove and all the folksy anecdotes she drilled him on. She loves a malleable candidate.

Mel smoothes the front of her dress, checks the lay of her bun in the mirror, pushes her glasses up and heads to the podium. She speaks quickly—she's never been completely comfortable doing press secretary tasks, not at this large of a scale—thanks everybody for coming, lays out the ground rules, then introduces Porter and steps aside. She drifts along the side wall to the back of the room, 50 feet from the podium, way behind the line of TV cameras. She likes to watch pressers and debates from as far away as possible. It gives her the critical distance the viewing audience will have, keeps her from getting caught up in the emotion of the room, which rarely if ever comes across on the screen, definitely doesn't come across in the written accounts. She'd watch on a TV monitor in a different part of the building if any of the crews had set one up.

She lights a Parliament and listens to Porter read his opening statement, another nice piece of writing by Colin Burke. He beams his perfect smile and offers to take questions, scans through the raised hands to find her guy—a friendly at the *Cincinnati Enquirer*—just the way she told him. It's deeply satisfying to see her candidate behaving so well.

"Dan Barnaby, *Cincinnati Enquirer*. This is the first time you're running for public office, Mr. Porter. What prepares you to be a U.S. Senator, and why should the voters of Ohio believe you'd do a better job of representing them than Mr. Musgrove?"

"That's an excellent question Dan. I understand that I'm entering politics at a high level. Much higher than most people do. I understand that, and I take it very seriously. I wouldn't be running for this Senate seat if I didn't think I had an awful lot to contribute for the people of Ohio. My entire professional life has been dedicated to making the legal system more responsive to the needs of regular citizens. That's why I started my business. By founding a chain of legal clinics that are open on weekends and at night, and making fees affordable for the kind of people normally denied top-flight legal expertise, I think I've gone a long way towards making government more responsive to the needs of the people. Now, we all know how many entrenched interests there are in Washington, that the power brokers there don't always pay attention to the folks they're supposed to be serving. As a man who's experienced at navigating the labyrinthine passageways of our legal system, I'm well-prepared to fight those entrenched interests and make government similarly responsive to the needs of *all* the people, not just the wealthy few."

Mel holds herself back from applauding. *That's only one*, she reminds herself. She knows tougher questions are coming.

"A Friday presser smacks of desperation." Mel turns slowly at the intrusion, sees Howard Kane leaning against the wall 4 feet away, stroking his goatee, eyes locked on the podium. He looks exactly the same as the last time Mel saw him, dark eyes pressed deep in his face, hair slicked tightly against his skull, beard rustling beneath meaty fingers. "No one watches the news or cares about politics on Friday evening," he adds, playing up his Texas drawl. He doesn't bother to keep his voice down but continues looking forward, as though he's talking to himself.

"Sunday papers, Kane," Mel whispers sharply. She hates herself for saying anything, and this wasn't even a particularly smart retort. She wants only to narrow her eyes and blast lasers at Kane until he slinks away in shame. Nothing will be served by engaging him over tactics. Ideally, she'd put out her cigarette in his left eye and knee him in the nuts, then walk away calmly and start a new life in some other field, but that's obviously not happening. Second best is pure silence, ice out the Neanderthal piece-of-shit and destroy him later, plant a brick of cocaine in the glove compartment of his rental car, or hire a hacker to sneak kiddie porn onto his laptop, then call in the feds. *Hey, that's not a bad idea*, she thinks.

"Oh, right," Kane says after a thoughtful pause. He slides over, almost shoulder-to-shoulder, lowers his voice slightly. "Because that's the secret sauce in every political campaign. Sunday papers. Goddammit! Why didn't I think of that?"

"It's not like the old days, grandpa. They have this new-fangled thing they call videotape." Mel gestures at the line of TV cameras. She started this. She may as well make a decent case for herself. "Means they can play clips of this whenever they want. A Friday presser feeds the boob-tube for a week."

"Oh, come on. Friday's where the news cycle goes to die, videotape or not. Just admit it. You wouldn't have been able get the whole press corps up here for your little dog-and-pony show unless the real star of this race, the guy everyone knows is Ohio's next Senator, if *he* weren't off the field today. Your relaunch party, or whatever this is, is both desperate and pathetic."

"You can't rattle me. I know what kind of slimy scumbag you are."

"Why so crude, Miz Carnes? I know my guy's up by 20 points, but there's no need to make it so personal."

"You're a rapist, Kane. A low-life, piece-of-shit rapist." Mel says this as tonelessly as possible, the need to keep quiet helping her stay controlled. She keeps her real anger at Kane buried deep, lets herself appear outraged just to make him think he's got the upper hand.

"Gimme a break. That's bullshit and you know it."

"I know you fucked my friend against her will."

"Christ, are you serious? You're dredging up that shit? I'll let you in on a little hard reality. You can say No before sex. You can even say No during. But you can't say No after the fact."

"Fuck you. You get that line out of rapist advice pamphlet? She said No the whole way through, and you didn't listen, dickbrain."

"That's what *she* says. I never heard No until afterwards. Weeks afterwards."

"*He said, she said.* That's how you fuckers always get away with it. How many others have there been? I know it's more than one. Shit-sticks like you think they can do whatever they want, to anyone they fucking want. How many lives have you ruined, Kane? Be honest for once in your lying sack-of-shit life." Mel checks herself. She's starting to feel genuine outrage here, starting to get loud enough that some of the reporters might hear.

"Look Carnes. Just cut the crap, OK? This is displaced anger, nothing else. My guy's whipping your guy's ass, and it hurts. I know the feeling. I've been on your side too. We all have. You get a turkey once in a while, and you're screwed. Nothing you can do about it. I'd feel sorry for you if it didn't come with the job. Deal with it or get out."

"First of all, I just got here, and I'm turning this shit around. You watch." Mel jabs her finger in Porter's direction. He's talking about how hard his parents had to work to put him through college, just the way Mel rehearsed him. "Second, this is not *displaced* anger. I hate your twisted-up, acid-filled guts. This is personal, and I will cut your balls off."

Kane remains impassive. "I know you don't want my advice, but here it is. Never make it personal. Let's say you have a legitimate reason to hate me. Let's say additionally that you think Musgrove would be a disastrous Senator, that a Republican majority in Congress will destroy the nation. So what? What's any of that got to do with winning a political campaign? When it comes right down to it, that's all you and I are here for, right? So do yourself a favor and keep your emotions out of it."

"Spoken like a person with zero feelings about anything, including fucking a woman who doesn't want to be fucked by a pencil-dick like you."

Kane smirks at that one. "Very nice. I'd fire my speech writer if I were you. It's clearly a waste of money."

"Compliment accepted."

They stand in silence for a minute, watching the action. Jared Block fights for attention, asks Porter how he squares his calls for campaign finance reform with the kind of money he's taken from political action committees. "Isn't it hypocritical of you to promise limits on campaign contributions when you're the recipient of so much special-interest money yourself?"

Mel tenses up. This is a crucial moment, a tricky bit of politicking.

"If I'm going to fight entrenched interests, I have to get elected," Porter says with the perfect mixture of feistiness and sincerity, just like Mel coached him. "The idea isn't to fall down on your spear and die. The idea is to win so you get to be one of the decision-makers, one of the people who can right the wrongs and change the unfair rules." She notices Kane nodding agreement. "My opponent doesn't even think about campaign finance reform. He thinks big money in politics is just fine. Which makes a certain kind of perverse sense. He's a rich man, a multi-millionaire with multi-millionaire friends. Of course he thinks big money in politics is fine. If I'm going to change the system, I have to win this election. If I don't—if my opponent gets this Senate seat— the cause of fairness in elections, the cause of rights for working people, the cause of common sense regulations on greedy businessmen and influence peddlers. All these important causes, causes that I care deeply about, all of them will be sidelined for the special interests and inside dealing of the wealthy elite who've run things for far too long."

Mel crosses her arms in satisfaction, forgets about Kane smirking next to her for a second. Porter is handling the press exactly the way she hoped. He consistently sticks to the talking points she laid out for him, maintains just the right demeanor—a combination of leading man charm and preparedness on the issues, with a new mixture of empathy for the little guy and feisty bootstrap combativeness. Not a touch of the robotic lawyer, none of the emotional distance of a rich guy without the same problems as most voters. *He's a natural actor*, she thinks. *All he needed was a better director.* Mel feels a surge of confidence. The only reason he's 18 points down is his inexperience as a campaigner and a lack of hustle and strategic thinking on the part of Alex Tremont.

Oh, yeah, and the Republican wave. There's that. Mel tries to put that out of her mind. She can't do anything about the larger political forces potentially dooming Porter's campaign. All she can do is manage Porter so his inexperience isn't a liability and keep Alex Tremont sidelined so she can make the best use of Porter's talent and the remaining time.

Kane leans into Mel's ear, whispers hotly. "Look, Carnes. I don't care if you hate my guts. In fact, it helps me a great deal if you're all emotional all the time. That's why there aren't more women in this game. You're too emotional. Your little hand-wringing friend? She was never gonna make it in politics. I opened her giant Bambi eyes to that, and the thanks I get is some bullshit rape charge no one but you and a few woe-is-women losers took seriously."

Mel turns to Kane with true hatred in her eyes, but she lets the bait dangle without snapping at it. Kane is right that she's shouldn't get emotional. The more she hates his guts, the more she has to force herself to forget about it so she can do her job with a clear mind. If she lets him rev up her feminist anger, she'll get distracted from the task at hand. "What're you doing here, anyway?" she asks impassively.

Kane smirks. "Due diligence, Miz Carnes. We're up by 20, but I'm not about to get soft. As the mighty Buddha once said, *It ain't over til it's over*. Until I hear Porter's concession speech on TV, I'm coming at you as hard as I know how. And that's mighty hard. Ask your little friend, what's-her-name."

Mel forces herself to stay calm. She'll yell and punch her pillow later, when it's just her and her hotel room. For now, she can't let Kane get a rise out of her again. It was a mistake to do it once. Hard as steel, cold as ice. That's what she needs to be right now.

"You're gonna need every bit of your A-game, asshole," she says in her normal tone. "And I'm still gonna win. Porter's the real thing, and your guy's just another garden-variety rich boy. I've beaten his type before, and I'll beat him every time."

"It's a tough cycle for your side," Kane says calmly. He almost sounds collegial, sympathizing with Mel's uphill battle. "Under different circumstances, I'd be more worried about my guy's weaknesses, especially with an opponent like you. You're good, I'll admit it. Solid record for a newbie. Very impressive. I wouldn't mind having a savvy datahead like you on my team. But there's a Republican revolution on its way, and we both know it. Makes your climb outta this hole ten times as hard."

They listen to the guy from CNN asking about Porter's thoughts on President Clinton's failed health-care reform effort.

"Well, anyway." Kane holds out his hand. "Good luck. It's just politics after all. Doesn't mean anything, right?"

Mel glares at Kane's hand like it's smeared with dog shit. "Get out of my presser, you slimy fuck."

Kane drops his hand. "Fine. Have it your way. I'll be seeing you around, *Miz* Carnes. And good luck. I really mean that."

Mel hates to admit it, but it sounds like he does.

# # # # #

Mel lies on the bed panting. She spent 5 minutes punching her pillow, and now she feels giddy and drained, her equanimity returning slowly. She gets up, clanks through the mini-bar, takes two bottles of Clan Campbell Scotch over to the bed and flips on CNN.

The news is predictably annoying. A panel of mid-level pundits rehashes yesterday's House vote to ban lobbyists from buying meals and entertainment for members of Congress. The debate is lackluster, the shots back and forth glancing, no real damage done to either side. It is Friday night, Mel reminds herself. The A-listers are off somewhere else, trading on their cable celebrity, saying the exact things to each other over cocktails they'd be saying if they were on the air right now, sparring to stay in shape for the Sunday-morning shows. Mel has been to those cocktail parties, often wished she had a remote control with her to mute the volume.

She rips open the tiny bottle, slugs down the Clan Campbell, flips over to ESPN. Jesus, the sports news is even worse, a genuine shitshow. Not only is Major League Baseball still on strike, the NHL owners look like they're ready to follow through on their threatened lockout, starting tomorrow. ESPN has a CNN-like panel discussing the repercussions of the strike and the lockout, the records missed, the all-but-certain cancellation of the World Series for the first time in 90 years, how labor disturbances threaten to destroy sports fans' confidence and enjoyment.

— Is this the beginning of the end for American sports?

Jesus Christ, just shut the fuck up! Mel clicks through the channels, restlessly seeking something to take her mind off politics, settles on Nickelodeon to watch a rerun of *Clarissa Explains it All*, but even here she can't escape politics. Clarissa and Sam get arrested for protesting against animal testing at a local company.

1994

She nips at her second Clan Campbell, mutes the TV on Clarissa and Sam arguing about whose parents to call from the police station. Speaking of calling parents...she eyes the telephone warily. She's been in Ohio 4 days already and hasn't called her father. She can't put it off much longer or it'll get worse each day, more awkward to make excuses, a bigger heap of guilt to swallow when she does eventually call. She snatches the handset, punches in the numbers before she can talk herself out of it.

"Hello?" Her father sounds groggy.

Shit, it's past ten. Was he asleep already? At 10:25? Really? Is he that old?

"Hi, dad. It's Mel."

"Mel? You okay sweetie? It's late. You're not in jail, are you?"

"It's only 10:30, dad. I'd hardly call that late. And no, I'm not in jail." You get hauled in once for underage drinking and every late-night phone call is a bail-out plea. Jesus! "I'm in Cleveland. Same difference, I suppose. Ha ha."

"Cleveland? How long have you been in town?"

Here it is, the first jab of guilt-mongering. This is why she should've called sooner. It's also why she never wants to call in the first place.

"Just since Tuesday. Tuesday night. I'm working a campaign. Kyle Porter for U.S. Senate?" She says it like she's reading a campaign button on someone's jacket, an acquaintance she didn't know was a Democrat. *Really? That guy? I never would've guessed.*

"Porter?" Her father sounds just as incredulous. "You poor gal. He's getting his butt kicked. At least that's how it looks in the paper."

"Yeah. Well. That's why I'm here. Got the call from David Wilhelm himself." Why is she always name-dropping with her own father? "That's Clinton's campaign manager. DNC Chair now."

"I know who the hell David Wilhelm is, Mel."

"Anyway, we need to save the Senate majority, blah blah blah. So here I am. Back in Ohio." She sings a snatch of Neil Young. *"Tin soldiers and Nixon coming. We're finally on our own."* She can practically see the forced tolerance on her father's face.

"When are you coming down for a visit?" Right on cue, guilt-mongering, phase 2. "It's Sunday tomorrow. You have the day off? We can do a Sunday supper, like the old days."

"Sorry, dad, I can't. Things are pretty crazy around here. We're 18 points down. I have to whip things into shape. Fast. I don't know when I'll be able to make it out there. We might have a rally in Wooster sometime. Then again, maybe not. Depends on a lot of factors. Time. Resources. Internal polling. Campaigns are highly fluid, especially ones like this, where you're so far down." Mel can hear all the things her father's not saying, loud and clear.

"Anyway. I'll do what I can. I just wanted to call, let you know I'm here. You might see my name in the paper this weekend." *And I didn't want you to find out that way*, she doesn't say, but she knows he hears it. "You know, official quotes from the campaign. I do a lot of talking to the press these days. On the record. They like to use names when they can." She's way over-explaining, but that's how these calls go. If she can keep up a running patter, she won't have to live through the awkward silences, the guilt-inducing *Ahems*, the feeling that she's letting her father down, that she's a bad daughter, a bad person.

Eventually she runs out of steam, has to pause for a breath.

"You're only an hour away, Mel. You can't take half a day to drive down here for lunch?" He doesn't offer to drive to Cleveland and visit her. Mel could point this out, but that's not how it works. He does the guilt-mongering, she plays defense. It would be way less horrible to meet in a neutral location, like a U.S.-Soviet summit in Iceland, but Mel doesn't want to get embroiled in trying to talk her father into doing things differently. This reluctance, she knows, is how old patterns reproduce themselves endlessly, but she's powerless to change her ways. She visits her father's house when she can—the house she grew up in, why can't she put it that way?—but he never comes to see her. She supposes that's the way she wants it to. She can control the visits, the timing, the duration. If he ever came to see her in D.C., he might stay at her apartment, for days. If he drove to Cleveland, he might get a hotel room, stay the night so he could drink over lunch, then she'd be stuck with him for an indeterminate amount of time. No, it's better this way.

"Maybe I can, dad. I'll see what I can do. Like I said, it's crazy here. There's a million things to do. A lot of ground to make up in 5 weeks. I'll call again when I have a better idea of my schedule."

"Okay, sweetie." That's the worst guilt-mongering of all, the disappointed acceptance. "You know where I live. Ha ha."

"Thanks, dad. I knew you'd understand. I'll make it down there as soon as I can, I promise. As soon as possible. Very soon." Now she's over-doing it. The more vigorously she makes promises to her father, the harder they are to keep and the uglier it gets when she fails to follow through. *Just say Good-bye and hang up the phone, Mel.*

There's a long silence. Mel writhes, forces herself not to say more until her father speaks.

"Okay. You do what you can, honey. I'm here."

1994

"All right, dad. Bye, then." Mel hangs up, relieved that Nancy never came up. That's about the only thing that went right.

She clanks through the mini-bar again, downgrades to Jack Daniels, flips over to ESPN2, a reliable source of mindless second-tier sports. Oh thank God, it's a snowboarding competition in Calgary. She cracks open both bottles of Jack Daniels, glugs them into a plastic cup, rests it on her chest and takes a deep breath.

It's technically a day off for Mel—the DNC scrupulously abides by federal overtime rules, on paper at least—but there's no way she's skipping work with so little time until the election. None of the principals gets freedom this close to the polls opening. Shep's running a focus group in a back room, Tremont's working the phones for money, even Colin Burke came in to keep polishing up the new stump speech, Carlton Schooley doing unpaid overtime to provide him with a sounding board. Porter is spending the day with his family, but Mel arranged a small press escort in exchange for promises of a warm-hearted human interest story in next week's Sunday papers. If the candidate and everyone else has to work today, so does she. Besides, what would she do with 2 days of free time? Drink alone in her room? Watch CNN and get depressed? Go shopping? Read a book? Ridiculous.

She sits at her desk typing furiously, a cigarette smoldering in the ashtray as she pounds the keys. She drafts a series of radio ads, rewrites big chunks of the debate-prep manual, slams out a long strategy memo for the policy team. Hah! The *team* is Carlton Schooley and Rich Lowry, another kid in his 20s thin on experience, probably a nephew of Tremont's. She has to admit they do a pretty good job though. Lowry has an M.A. in Sociology from Harvard, and his white papers are well-crafted and thoroughly researched. Not that it matters much. Campaign white papers are the biggest waste of trees imaginable. A handful of interest group leaders pay careful attention to the one or two they care about, and a few of the scribblers skim through for quotes to use in their longer pieces, but that's the extent of it. The TV and radio jocks never get past the executive summary, just attention to policy detail to help them think up questions for the next presser. Mel reminds herself to go over the new Page 1s Schooley passed along yesterday, make sure they push reporters in the right direction. She wants as much focus as possible on areas where Musgrove is weak in the middle—NAFTA, unions, public education, workplace safety regulations, financial regulations, all the uncaring rich guy problems he's saddled with.

She Xs out the entire executive summary for their new white paper on crime policy, writes notes in the margin. *Downplay community policing, that's a GOP strength. Play up the human side: halfway house reform, mental health funding, etc. We want questions from the press about how we'll help people, reduce recidivism, not beef up the police state. New title also. Something less sterile. Imagine the title in a newspaper article and try not to make us sound like 2nd-rate Repubs with warmed-over ideas.*

She sits at her desk, smoking and working like any other day, occasionally stopping to listen to the volunteers in the bullpen making calls, chattering about the Ohio State game playing muted on one of the office TVs. The Buckeyes are 3-1 so far this year, ranked 20th and looking pretty mediocre. Not that Mel cares. College football has never moved her. The players aren't smart or vicious enough for her taste, especially the linebackers, the talent too spread around in any case, and the one-foot-in-bounds rule for complete passes utterly asinine in her opinion.

There's a light cheer as the Bucks score a TD. Mel closes her door and stands in front of the whiteboard, arms crossed over her chest, cigarette smoldering in the corner of her mouth as she peers skeptically at what she's written over the past 3 days. She has a sense there's something missing. They're pushing hard on Musgrove's weaknesses on economic issues and class allegiance, bringing out Porter's humble and caring sides, targeting the groups they're underperforming with, but there's something she's still not getting at...Mel can't put her finger on it. There's more there to exploit, she knows there is. She just can't see it yet.

She goes back to her desk, glugs down the rest of her Diet Coke, bends mercilessly to the task of uncovering every strategic advantage her guy might have. She does knock off earlier than usual—just after 5—leaves a pile of unfinished work on her desk and drags Schooley, Burke, and Shep to the Gold Lantern Lounge, the bar next to her hotel, a decently dive-y place that seems not to attract politicos and serves half decent food along with appropriately cheap drinks. She wishes she knew someone outside politics to hang out with, to drink away the empty hours of Saturday evening. She doesn't want to talk about the election tonight but knows the only way to avoid it is to drink alone in her room, where she could deaden her mind with mini-bar whiskey and ESPN, which sounds even worse. She needs the company right now, and that means paying the price of shop talk.

She brings up the Browns' prospects this year to avoid the inevitable. "I can't remember the last time they had a 3-and-1 start," Mel says, "and they've got the 2-and-2 Jets tomorrow, at home. I'm calling it 21-10 Browns."

"They started last year with 3 wins," Schooley notes quietly. "Went 5-and-2, then imploded, like always."

"I know, I know, but the defense is looking strong, and Testaverde seems to've gotten in stride. I think Belichick's finally turning the Browns around."

"Speaking of turning things around, I feel like that's what you're doing for Porter." Colin raises his glass to Mel. "Here's to you, Mel."

Mel watches Colin, Schooley, and Shep clink glasses. She cups both hands around her drink to block them from clinking hers. "Let's not jinx it, okay. We've got a long way to go, and we don't have any polling yet to know if our new approach is having an impact."

"It is too early to know anything for sure," Shep says, "but the focus group today points in the right direction." Shep takes off his glasses, polishes them with a bar napkin. He's a saggy middle-aged Jewish guy, frumpy in all the lovable ways, but he tends to make noises in his throat that disturb Mel. He's got those half-plastic/half-wire glasses that remind her of Kevin Costner in *JFK*. Not that he's got a Kevin Costner bone in his body, but he carries around the intensity Costner showed in *JFK*, a let's-get-to-the-bottom-of-this-nonsense pluck that Mel doesn't usually associate with pollsters, a generally mole-like crew in her experience. She's heard that everyone loves Shep, and after only a few meetings with him, she sees why.

"Porter seems re-energized," Schooley says. "He was great at the presser yesterday." Mel knows already that her new sidekick loves to use jargon like *presser* and *undies*. She was wrong about the notebook. He never writes anything down, must have a steel trap for a memory. He's green but super smart, never needs to hear something twice to get it completely. Maybe Tremont actually did her a favor lashing him to her side.

"He was rock solid," Shep says. "Hit all the talking points on policy, got in all the shots on Musgrove, did his new Man of the People routine pretty nicely." Shep sneaks in a clink on Mel's glass. "That's all your doing, Mel. No one but you. You should be proud of yourself." Shep crinkles his eyes, looks like he's celebrating his daughter's graduation at the top of her law-school class.

Mel rides out more praise, tries not the play Devil's advocate like she usually does, point out the pile of downsides they face. Porter's way down with the clock running out fast. He's never run for office

1994

before, and it's obviously a Republican wave this year. Clinton's coming to town for a rally in a few weeks, but with approval ratings in the low-40s, that might be more of a drag than a help. Et cetera et cetera. But Mel doesn't raise any of these valid points. Why not let these kids feel good about the race for one Saturday night?

She gulps down her drink, waves the bartender over for another. Did she just think of 2 men less than a decade younger than her as *kids*? Shep's in his early-50s, but Colin Burke and Carlton Schooley are barely out of college. They seem so fresh-faced and optimistic, it's hard for Mel not to feel old by comparison. She tries to remember when she felt the same way about politics. When did she get so disillusioned? It must've happened so slowly she didn't notice when she hit the tipping point. She hates Howard Kane's guts, but she knows he's right. Politics doesn't mean anything. It's just wins and losses on a stat sheet, same as the NFL. If the Browns implode again, if Porter gets his ass kicked by Musgrove, if the G.O.P. takes over Congress—what does any of it really matter?

Burke and Schooley head out around 7. They probably have girlfriends to meet, or at least friends their own age to keep drinking with. Shep lingers for one more quiet whiskey, then leaves Mel alone with her thoughts. She orders a beer and a Cobb salad, settles in to watch college football on the muted TVs—it's better than nothing. She's about to head upstairs for TV with the volume on when Thom Reynolds comes in. *Waltzes in is more like it*, Mel says to herself, watching him approach with a grin on his face.

"Looking for me?" she says. She knows she's drunk, but it's the pleasant kind—for now at least. She's glad for the surprise company, feels uncharacteristically voluble. She wants to share things—her history, her ideas, her pet peeves. *Be careful here, Carnes*, she reminds herself. *You're never off the clock with these vultures.*

"Only the finest," Thom says, whatever that means. He orders a whiskey for himself and one for Mel, leans on the bar, blinks his baby blues. "Tell me something about yourself that no one on the Porter campaign knows."

"That's very forward of you, Thom." She smirks at her own joke, continuing to pronounce his name with a th-sound.

Thom ignores the bait. "I'm a reporter," he says. "It's instinct to be forward."

"Not exactly a professional question, though, is it?" The drinks arrive. "Put that on my tab, Sam," Mel says.

"You know his name's Pete, not Sam, right?" Thom looks dead serious, but he winks.

"Did you really just wink at me?"

Thom sips his whiskey. "So, come on. Tell me something about yourself. Any fact. Doesn't have to be a deep, dark secret. This is off-the-record, in case you're worried. Not even deep background. Just two human beings talking to each other on a Saturday night."

Very charming, Mel thinks, reminds herself to be careful nonetheless.

"I was born on election day," she says somberly. "So maybe I was destined to go into politics." She swirls her whiskey, stares at its soothing brown texture, takes a sip. "Hell of a destiny."

Thom waits. Should she tell him the year? Fuck it, who cares if he knows she's staring down that barrel at 30? How old is *he*? He could be anywhere from mid-20s to mid-30s, even a well-preserved 40 or 41. She wouldn't be surprised if he was 22, except he's covering the U.S. Senate race for one of Ohio's largest newspapers. Child prodigy politics reporter? Perhaps.

"Oh yeah?" Thom prods. "What year?"

"64."

"LBJ," he says. "I knew you were doing an LBJ impersonation yesterday. Do another one."

Mel shakes out her shoulders, drops her jaw, channels her favorite and most disappointing president. "This administration today. Here and now. Declares unconditional war on poverty in America. It will not be a short or easy struggle. No single weapon or strategy will suffice. But we shall not rest until that war is won. The richest nation on earth can afford to win it. We cannot afford to lose it." Mel swallows the rest of her drink. "Last great president we had."

"Tragic," Thom puts in. He knocks back his drink as well, catches the bartender's attention, swirls his hand over their empty glasses.

"Tragic as a motherfucker," Mel says. "War on Poverty. Voting Rights Act. Goddamned Great Society. Medicaid. Affirmative action. Equal Opportunity Employment Commission."

"Vietnam, though," Thom adds. He sounds slightly apologetic, as though he hates to burst Mel's bubble.

"Piece of shit little war. Got away from him and ruined everything. If it weren't for Vietnam, they'd be carving his face on Mount Rushmore." The drinks arrive. Mel takes a bigger sip than she intends, feels her drunk going from pleasant to mendacious. "Fucking Kennedy, ineffectual pretty boy turned martyr, and Johnson just had to do him one better at every turn. *We are going to win.*"

Thom grins, lifts his new drink in toast to the tragedy of LBJ.

"Let us carry forward the plans and programs of John Fitzgerald Kennedy," Mel says, her LBJ half-hearted now, more than a touch of anger in it. "Not because of our sorrow or sympathy, but because they are right." She shakes her head ruefully, sips her drink, feels maudlin about to tag out mendacity if she doesn't do something about it.

"Tell me," she says. "Did Porter seem like a new candidate to you yesterday, or what?" *No, for God's sake*, Mel scolds herself. *Do not talk about politics, especially not your own race.*

"I don't know about *new candidate*, but he was more aggressive about attacking Musgrove, that's for sure."

"And," Mel prompts. She wants to stop but can't help herself. She could look on the dark side when Schooley, Colin, and Shep were around, but she needs reassurance suddenly, a bit of praise from an outside observer.

"And?" Thom looks puzzled.

"And, he also seemed more…" Mel looks at Thom hopefully.

"He seemed more?" Thom shrugs. "I dunno. More relaxed? More sure-footed?"

"How about more down-to-earth? More like a Man of the People?" Mel knows she's being too unsubtle here. She wants coverage of Porter to start downplaying his rich-lawyer status and start playing up his humble origins and his parents' American Dream story, but she can't push that narrative too obviously. She shouldn't talk about her candidate when she's this drunk. Jesus, she didn't even want talk politics at all tonight.

"He did tell that story about his parents' haberdashery shop," Thom admits. "I hadn't heard that one before."

"You probably had no idea his parents were immigrants, did you?"

"Not until you sent me that copy of his stump speech, no."

"Well okay, then. There's your new candidate. Your *winning* candidate." Mel looks deeply into Thom's eyes, notices how insanely blue they are. She makes a snap decision. "I've got something off-the-record to say. Very off the record."

"OK. This is all off-the-record anyway, but sure, go ahead."

"Come up to my room and have sex with me." Mel cocks her head, wags her eyebrows up and down like a Marx Brother. Why did she do that? *Jesus, just be normal*, she tells herself.

Thom chuckles, sips his whiskey.

"I'm serious," Mel says. "Uncomplicated campaign sex. No strings attached. Whaddya say, fly boy? You down?"

Thom shoots his drink back. "You're serious?"

"Serious as a..." Mel stops herself from saying *case of AIDS*. That's definitely not a winning strategy here. "Yeah, 100% serious."

"Okay, sure. Why not? Who doesn't love uncomplicated campaign sex. Right?"

# # # # #

"What's the strangest place you've ever masturbated?"

"What?" Mel has her back to Thom. She stares blankly at the digital clock—it's still only 2:18am—hoping this wasn't a stupid idea. It was fun, that's for sure, but that's how campaign sex starts out— uncomplicated, like she promises. It can be wild and uninhibited, sometimes outright kinky. The men she picks for these liaisons tend to run with the hot librarian scenario in highly personal ways, take Mel on a ride through their individual version of the fantasy. She's had her glasses tossed away and her dress torn off in shreds, been licked from the toes upward, spanked with leather-bound books, which is better than it sounds. She's been put through every position in the porn catalogue, though the most common by far is reverse cowgirl. She'd love to put together a focus group to figure out the source of that trend.

She finds it strange that it wasn't like that with Thom. Something about the whole encounter struck her as highly normal, an oddly disturbing description for first-time sex, especially the campaign variety. They undressed themselves, kissed for a bit, fondled in all the right places, did it missionary style for a while, then he rolled her on top, and they finished that way, more or less simultaneously. It was a good orgasm. Not great but not lame, probably well above average for the amount of alcohol in her system.

Thom repeats his question. "I said, What's the strangest place you've ever masturbated?"

Mel rolls on her back, lays her hand on Thom's chest. It's oddly hairless, muscular like she imagined but completely smooth, almost feminine. She wonders if he shaves it.

"I heard you. I'm just wondering where this comes from."

"It's a straightforward question."

"I have a question for you. Why are you still wearing your socks? Do you always do that, or is this a special treat just for me?"

They look down at the white tube socks bunched around Thom's ankles. He bicycles his legs, yanks off the socks and balls them together, tosses the ball deftly through the open bathroom door and out of sight. It sounds like it went straight into the bathtub. There's the high-school athlete Mel suspected.

1994

"Let me venture an educated guess here." Mel flips on her stomach, rests her chin on her hands, blinks into Thom's baby blues. "You played baseball in high school."

"I did."

"Wait, there's more." She rests her finger on his lips. "You were star of the team, but you weren't quite good enough to get a scholarship to college, so you were a walk-on freshman year, played doggedly through graduation. You majored in journalism instead of geology like the other baseball players because you knew a pro career wasn't in the cards. You took some PoliSci classes because you were interested and ended up getting sucked into political reporting after graduation."

She removes her finger and kisses Thom lightly, straddles his hips and looks down with a grin. "Close? Right on the nose? I'm generally pretty good at this."

"You do this with all your uncomplicated campaign-sex hook-ups?"

"Yes I do. Keeps the mind sharp." Mel taps her temple. "So? How right am I? Entirely? Mostly?"

Thom hooks his hands behind his neck. "Remarkably close but wrong on several important counts. I played football and basketball in high school as well as baseball."

"But you were a star player on the baseball team, weren't you? I could tell from your throw."

"I was indeed, but I *was* good enough to get a scholarship. O.U. Bobcats, center fielder, batted seventh sophomore year, .275 average, moved up to third by junior year, hit .305. I broke my leg senior year winter break in a non-sports-related incident, and that was the end of my baseball career."

"So sad," Mel says without sounding the least bit sad.

"I never took a single political science class, and I didn't major in journalism."

"Okay, wait. Back-up guess. Communications."

"Goddamn. That's right. It's what all the scholarship athletes majored in."

"Of course."

"I learned enough to get a job writing sports for the *Toledo Blade* right out of college."

"Ah, the amazing, highly-regarded *Toledo Blade*. Baseball coach hooked you up with that one, right? Otherwise, you would've ended up a bartender in Athens."

"Actually, it was the athletic director, if you must know. But yes, I'm sure I would've been a loser if it weren't for him. I wasn't even trying to get a job. I thought I could rehab my leg, get back in fighting shape, take a shot at the minor leagues, see if I had what it took for The Show. I never did get good enough again to make it back."

"This story is so sad, it's killing me." Mel clutches her hands over her heart, pouts cinematically.

"Jesus, you are cold."

Mel drops down to hug Thom's neck, fires off a Bull Durham quote with an extra thick helping of Southern accent. "Listen, sweetheart, you shouldn't listen to what a woman says when she's in the throes of passion. They say the darndest things."

"Wait, no, I got it. *Bull Durham*. 1988. Oscar nomination for best screenplay."

"Oboy, we got ourselves a sports-movie fanatic."

"Indeed. Throw me a line, I'll name it."

"Post-coital Sports-Movie Quotes for 200, huh? Okay. Lemme think." Mel rolls off Thom, taps a Parliament from the pack on the nightstand, crinkles her eyes in thought while she lights up. Thom props on an elbow, hums the *Jeopardy!* theme

"Okay. I got one. Wait a minute. Let me get in character." Mel jumps out of bed, stands with her feet planted shoulder-width apart, little caring how ridiculous she must look, pretending to be a high-school basketball coach while stark naked in a Cleveland hotel. She fights down a smirk at the thought of it, summons her best Gene Hackman. *"If you put your effort and concentration into playing to your potential, to be the best that you can be, I don't care what the scoreboard says at the end of the game. In my book, we're gonna be winners."*

"Come on, that's too easy. Gene Hackman. *Hoosiers*. 1986. Best goddamned basketball movie of all time. Post-Coital et cetera for 300."

Mel takes a long drag on her cigarette, paces as she thinks, Thom watching her with a crooked smile on his face.

"Alright. This is a little tougher. *It's their rink, it's their ice, and it's their fuckin' town. But tonight we got our fans with us!*"

"*Rink* kind of gives it away. There's only one hockey movie worth a damn. *Slapshot*, 1976 or 77, can't remember exactly. Paul Newman at his best, if you ask me. Post-Coital for 400."

"We got a champion on our hands here people." Mel jumps on the bed, bounces up and down while she thinks. She wants to fool Thom at least once. Oh yeah, that's a good one. Mel can't do a Charles Durning, so she delivers it straight. *"This is national TV. So don't pick your noses or scratch your nuts."*

Thom narrows his eyes, looks up at Mel standing above him with hands on hips. She's sure he can't get this one. "I repeat. *This is national TV. So don't pick your noses or scratch your nuts.*"

"I heard you, but that's a tough one. It's got the sound of a parody. It's not *Caddyshack*. I know all the lines in that one. Could be *Major League*, but I think that's too obvious. Lemme see. National TV. *Don't pick your noses*. It's a team sport. Football? Baseball? Football? Uh. No, I got it. *North Dallas Forty*. Nice one. One of my all-time favorites. Pretty obscure line, though."

"Goddamn. You are good." Mel returns to straddling Thom's pelvis. "Let's go for 500, Alex."

"For a clean sweep then." The perfect line pops into Mel's head. She doesn't care if Thom gets it. She loves doing a De Niro impersonation, any De Niro impersonation—*Taxi Driver, Deer Hunter, The King of Comedy, Midnight Run, Goodfellas, Angel Heart*, she has a giant catalogue. She leans forward on her palms, her breasts dangling on Thom's chest. Maybe a bit of distraction will get her a win here.

"I'm gonna make him suffer. I'm gonna make his mother wish she never had him, make him into dog meat. He's a nice kid, a pretty kid, too. I mean, I dunno. I dunno if I should fuck 'im or if I should fight 'im."

Thom grins broadly. "That's too easy for 500. Jake La Motta. *Raging Bull*, 1980. Oscar win for De Niro. You do a solid impersonation, by the way."

"Thanks. I work on it to fill the long, lonely hours." Mel flattens herself against Thom's chest, nibbles his ear. "By the way, a very impressive performance, Mr. Washed Up Athlete Turned Political Journalist. But you never answered my question about the socks. Habit or special treat just for me?"

"I'll confess that I tend to leave my socks on in the colder weather. I find it distracting when my feet get cold. And you never answered *my* question, Ms. Carnes. What's the strangest place you've ever masturbated?"

Mel hoists herself up. "Call me Mel. At least here in my room. Outside, I'm still Ms. Carnes." She begins to move her hips slowly across Thom's pelvis, feels his erection stirring.

"Uh huh. And I suppose I need to keep this little liaison from the other guys in the press pool?"

"Only if you want it to keep happening. Your choice. I'm not one to muzzle the press. It's the cornerstone of our democracy, after all. Isn't that what you guys are always saying? Now let's shut up and go again, OK? All this sports-movie talk has me revved up."

Mel sits behind a mound of files, writing a new TV spot with Porter in a hardhat, empathizing with construction workers about the state of the economy. Mel loves that she can go straight at the issues with visuals like this. Porter's a gem of a candidate, has the look and demeanor to pull off any costume, a Democratic answer to Ronald Reagan. Put Musgrove in a hardhat and he'd look like a poseur, an awkward businessman itching to get back to his cushy office, Michael Dukakis in a tank.

Shep Blumenthal comes in, his face unreadable. "I've got the latest tracks," he says flatly.

"And?" Mel keeps typing.

"There's good, there's bad. Take a look." Shep slaps the plastic binder on the desk, eases into a chair and stares at the scrawl on the whiteboard while Mel scans the data. There's fairly good news as far as forward movement goes. The deficit is down to 11 points, and they're underperforming among a few key groups much less egregiously. Of course, even with pretty astounding progress for a single week, they're still 11 points down, 47-36, and as Mel explains to Carlton Schooley, who drifts through Mel's door whenever someone leaves it open, they could actually be down by as much as 19 if the sample overstates Porter's position and understates Musgrove's at the high end of the margin of error, always a possibility.

"So we might actually be moving in the *wrong* direction," Mel says.

"But the last poll had us down by 18 points, and this one's 11," Schooley says. He sounds like Mel told him she ran over his dog.

"The last batch could've been off by as much as 8 points in the opposite direction," Shep puts in. "So maybe we were only 10 points down before, and now we're 19."

Schooley looks confused, reminds them that the new poll from *Columbus Dispatch* printed that morning showed the gap at 10, 48-38.

"Correct," Shep says. "And that gives us a bit more confidence that 10 or 11 down is where the race actually stands right now, but *that* poll could be off as well. It's not likely, statistically speaking, for two errors to align like that, but it's also not highly *unlikely* either."

"What? Really?" Schooley's mood sags noticeably. He slumps into a chair as Shep jumps up and heads out, rolling his eyes. He has no patience for data illiteracy. Mel usually doesn't either—most of the time she'd hustle an annoyance like this out the door and get back to the mountain of work she has—but she likes Schooley. He's smart and tireless, handles everything she gives him, asks questions because he wants to know the answers, not like most men she knows, who ask almost no questions, and when they do, they barely listen and cut her off to finish her thought, always looking to show how smart they are. He's also a genuinely sweet guy and obviously loyal to his girlfriend, a sweet little Ohio girl he proudly introduces around whenever she comes into the office, which is pretty often already in Mel's single week. Mel isn't used to working with men who aren't on the make at all times, who seem genuinely interested in learning from her, who love politics but still seem to have a moral core.

"Did you really never learn this stuff in college?" she asks.

"I didn't. I swear. We didn't do much with polls except see them in the paper. I never had a prof who explained margins of error or statistical likelihood. Seriously. Tell me how it's possible that we're moving in the wrong direction when the polls look like they've tightened by 7 or 8 points."

"Polls as a single number are highly deceptive," Mel says. She explains that news outlets present polls as though they're a precise score, and a lot of people, even political scientists and a certain breed of campaign pro, take that at face value, but even the best polls come with a margin of error of +/- 4%, some higher. "That makes polls much fuzzier than most people think. Imagine you asked someone what the score of the Browns game was at halftime, and they said, *The Browns are up by a touchdown. Or maybe it's tied. Or they're down by a field goal.* That would be absurd for a football game, but it's the reality of polls. The fools out there reading the newspaper can forget it, but *we* can't."

Mel can tell Schooley still doesn't get it. She goes to the whiteboard, erases a square of space in the middle of mostly illegible brainstorming, writes *Musgrove 48 Porter 38*. "Here's the *Dispatch* results from this morning. Based on the size of their sample, the margin of error is plus-or-minus 4 percent at the 99 percent confidence level. And that error applies to *both* candidates." Mel writes 44-52 under Musgrove, 34-42 under Porter. "So this apparent spread of 10 points leaves open the possibility that the two candidates are actually only 2 points apart, or separated by as much as 18, or anywhere in between."

"That's insane," Schooley says.

"In a way, yes. Statistically, it's most likely that the separation is somewhere between 8 and 12 points, but there's a roughly 10% chance that it's as high as 14 or as low as 6. That's about as likely as rolling a 5 with two dice, and that happens pretty frequently, right? So this result." She circles *Musgrove 48 Porter 38*. "Might mean we're making significant progress, or losing ground, or maybe there really hasn't been any change at all. And I haven't even mentioned Harris, that pro-life single-issue dipshit who's pulling in 6% in Shep's tracking, much less the 10 or 11% undecided. Those are both complete X factors. Harris could stick it out all the way, maybe tick up a few points if Musgrove isn't definitive enough on abortion, or he could drop out any second and most if not all of his supporters go to Musgrove. And obviously that chunk of undies could go either way, and in fact, many of them might not vote at all, especially in a mid-term year."

"How are polls useful, then?" Schooley sounds completely dejected.

"Public polls really aren't." Mel balls up Schooley's copy of the *Dispatch* and stuffs it in the trashcan, pushing it down as far as she can for added emphasis. "Noise for the masses that's mostly garbage to us. The real problem with these public polls is that we don't get any data breakdown. We don't know how we're doing with women versus men or union members versus non-union, minorities, older voters, people with median incomes. We have to wait for our own polling." She picks up Shep's report, holding it almost lovingly before handing it to her deputy. "Very expensive but essential. It's all in the crosstabs. That's the useful data, the gold dust in the pile of dirt."

Schooley opens the report tentatively, glances at the numbers but doesn't even pretend to know what he's looking at.

Mel explains that the crosstabs have a similar margin of error to the poll as whole, but not much more if the overall sample is even decent sized, +/- 5% for the way Shep does his surveys. "So there's still fuzziness, but the results for these sub-groups cross referenced against other sub-groups are generally much farther apart, so there's clarity even within the uncertainty."

"*Clarity within the uncertainty,*" Schooley repeats. "That's pretty Orwellian, Mel."

"No, come on, let me show you." Mel leans over Schooley's shoulder, points down to a row of figures. "So, look here. Porter's doing way better than last time with women 35 to 65 who earn below the median income. His improvement is 16 points with this group. That's way outside the margin of error. Maybe we're only 11 points improved with them, or maybe we're actually 21. Either way, we know we're starting to do something right with these women, who typically care more than other groups about the future of the economy as opposed to the current state. The hopes and dreams of their kids and grandkids, right? Our ads and speeches have been speaking to that much more over the past week, and these numbers tell us it's probably working. So we stick with that messaging." She flips the page, stabs a line midway down. "Same thing with white union members, 18 to 35 and 35 to 45 years old. Big improvements in both columns. Not so much at the higher age levels, where undie is still ridiculously high. So we're not resonating with the older, diehard Democrats even though we've got all the usual endorsements. The question is, why not?" She flips again. "Movement among black voters, also slim. See how gains all along here are at or close to the margin of error, so we have to assume no movement."

"Alright. That makes sense, I suppose." Schooley pages through the crosstabs.

Mel circles her desk, drops into her chair. "So the question is, why are we getting more poor women, and younger and middle-aged union guys, but not older union guys and African Americans?" She lights a cigarette, looks up at the ceiling, as though the answer is written there. "One thing is pretty obvious. We're not saying anything to minorities. I've seen this problem before. White Democrats have a tendency to take minority voters for granted. How could the black community ever go Republican, is the way they think about it."

"But Mr. Porter has 65 percent of all black voters," Schooley says. He places his finger on the number for emphasis, looks at Mel like he just discovered the Northwest Passage.

"Right, and that's not nearly enough to make up the deficit with white voters. We need 80 percent, minimum." Mel leans across the desk, takes the report from Schooley's hands, squints over the top of her glasses at the array of numbers. "Worse than the black votes Musgrove's getting, which isn't much, is the black undies."

Schooley smirks at the phrase. "Do you really have to say *black undies*?"

"You think that's funny?" Mel barks. "Almost 30 percent undecided." She looks like she's about to burn a hole in the report with her cigarette. "I've never seen undie so high for a key group. A number like that indicates a serious enthusiasm gap among minorities, and that impacts turnout in a major way." Mel spirals the report against the whiteboard, pulls deeply on her cigarette. "If this were a presidential year," she continues a bit more calmly, smoke curling out her nostrils, "we could count on most of them coming home on election day. Not in a mid-term year, and especially not with a Democratic president hovering in the mid-40s for approval. In the end, even if we get close to 90 percent of the black voters who *do* vote, if those undies mostly turn out to be non-voters, we're doomed."

"So?" Schooley looks at Mel hopefully, as though Shep's data is all she needs to make their problems go away.

"So, I need to figure out how we can make Porter more appealing to minorities, and I need to hope that Tremont and his get-out-the-vote operation is as reliable as it usually is. We start by sending Porter into predominantly black parts of the state. Tomorrow and the rest of the week. We get him into a black church this Sunday, somewhere high-profile, and we march him through black neighborhoods as much as possible, show he's not afraid of walking through the ghetto like a lot of minorities think rich white people are. Then maybe, just maybe, we start cutting into those black undies."

"Isn't that a bit mercenary?" Schooley says. "Not to mention pandering?"

"Maybe it is, Mr. Magna Cum Laude, but that's how you do political strategy in the 1990s. That's why we pay Shep and his ilk big money for their data, and that's why I make big money for my expertise."

# # # # #

Mel crunches over limestone gravel to the front of the Porter residence, wishing *mansion* weren't the only way to describe this ridiculous place. There's no other word for it, a sprawling brick Tudor complete with gated entrance, circular driveway, and porte-cochere. It's just past dusk, but she thinks she sees a horse paddock out back, nestled against wooded hills. *Man of the People, my ass.* And she was stupid enough to let those writers tag along with Porter over the weekend. Big mistake. She can only imagine how much those *warm-hearted human interest pieces* are going to set back her effort to recast her candidate in a more sympathetic light. She was so desperate to get things moving in the right direction that she pushed a strategy before having all the facts. *Rookie mistake, Carnes*, she said to herself as the taxi rolled up the driveway.

Stepping out of the car, Mel imagined herself hijacked into the mansion scene of *North by Northwest*, and as she paid the driver, she unconsciously muttered a favorite Cary Grant line. *"We'll throw the book at 'em. Kidnapping and assault. With a gun and a bourbon and a sports car. We'll get 'em, alright."*

"Excuse me, ma'am?"

1994

"Nothing. Just talking to myself."

Approaching the broad wooden front door—a Hollywood set designer's creation if Mel ever saw one—she recites another nugget from the legendary Roger Thornhill. *"In the world of advertising, there's no such thing as a lie. There's only expedient exaggeration."* Politics, advertising—how similar they are. *Not that that's news to anybody,* Mel says to herself. The casual cynicism of the American electorate makes her *expedient exaggerations* that much trickier to pull off—trickier, but not impossible. Far from it. Most people, in her experience, are highly guarded about campaign advertising, but deep down, they want to believe the hopeful lies they hear. *My guy can bring your job back* or *This terrible decline in* <u>fill in most hated, inevitable trend</u> *will be reversed if you elect* <u>fill in name of whoever you're working for this cycle</u>.

All you have to do is tell those lies in a way that aligns with the denial people are already practicing on themselves every day. "We're being outcompeted by the goddamned Japanese and Germans," and "Affirmative action hands what few good jobs are left to a bunch of lazy blacks." She's heard these exact words in focus groups, coming from the mouths of men who want nothing more than the right to have the same job that ground their dad and their uncles into a hunched-over nub. *No dumbfuck, the reason you're chronically unemployed is your failure to stay relevant in an economy that's changing fast because of automation and the predictable shift in capital investment to low-wage/low-regulation economies, neither of which any politician can do anything about, if they even know those are the problems in the first place. What you need is government investment that creates new opportunities, and public funding for training programs that'll help you take advantage of them.* You can pass along that message—if you're a Democrat, and that's the message you're stuck with—but you need to do it as an aside, sort of whispered out the corner of the campaign's mouth, let it sink in subconsciously, while more straightforwardly, you play to the reflexive fears and hatreds that your target audience carries around, like these emotions are their most prized possessions. *Don't tell me not to be afraid. Don't tell me not to hate the people I hate.* Okay, shitbird, fine, good, go ahead. And while you're at it, don't forget that my opponent hates *you* and everything you stand for.

The need for such constant subterfuge would be disgusting if it weren't so universal. Mel knows the same things work on her—not in politics, where she's trained to see through it, but everywhere else. What are these $350 shoes she's wearing but a hollow promise of empowerment? What's the pack of Parliaments nestled in her briefcase but one giant lie about the serenity a cigarette break brings. Serenity, sure—the serenity of the grave.

Mel shakes her head, tries to clear her mind of unhelpful thoughts, looks around wondering if she'll be able to smoke inside or if she should have a quick cigarette out here before announcing her arrival. She checks her watch, presses the bell—predictable Bach chiming—refocuses on the mission at hand. She's here to huddle with the candidate for their first full-on strategy session, not to commiserate about the feckless nature of the American electorate. She prepared a scaled-down version of the crosstabs, highlighting Porter's current strengths and weaknesses, and she's ready with her pep talk about the importance of taking poll numbers seriously. It's almost exactly the opposite of what she said to Carlton Schooley. There won't be any mention of fuzziness or margins of error for crosstab correlations. She'll willfully mischaracterize polls as the election scoreboard, playing up exactly what she knows is misleading about it.

That's the way you have to talk to candidates. *You don't ignore the scoreboard in the last quarter of the championship game, right?* is something like what she'll say. She also has a list of bullet points for the next phase of the campaign, a draft script for a new commercial Shep and his aide Carl agree should appeal to minorities more, and a small pep talk to make sure the candidate doesn't lose heart at how far down he still is. The problem with having a miracle-worker reputation, Mel has learned, is people expect miracles, and they expect them fast. A bump of 7 or 8 points, if that's what they really got, *is* miraculous, but Porter might focus instead on the remaining gap, which is still quite large. Plus, they probably just picked up the easy points, the low-hanging fruit that Tremont's laxity left ungrabbed. Every point from here on out is going to be increasingly harder to put on the board.

The door opens, and Mel is confronted by an honest-to-god butler—or so she thinks. She realizes her mistake when he turns and bellows into the foyer. "Charlie! There's some kind of solicitor here!" Mel realizes this must be a relative—brother-in-law would be her guess, dressed up for a gala evening. Unless this is how the Porters dress for dinner. Looking at the house—the two-story paneled foyer, lavishly decorated, in no way betrays the outside impression—it wouldn't surprise her if tuxes and gowns were required at the Porters' evening meal.

"Actually, I'm with the campaign," Mel says. She points to her *Porter for U.S. Senate* button as proof.

"Oh, sure. Of course," says the brother-in-law, or whoever he is. "Come on in. Charlie's in the study. No idea where Kyle's at. Getting dressed, I hope. We've got this fundraiser at the club tonight. Charity, not politics. Leukemia, a very noble cause. Curing it, of course, not having it. Not that I think politics isn't a worthy endeavor. We're a political family, you know. Born and reared on the hustings, harvesting donations day and night for twenty years. Fun stuff. Always fun, stealing from the rich to give to the other rich." He's walking backwards as he talks, an overdressed tour guide who never takes a breath. Mel follows him inside, trying not to let her expression betray how bizarre this whole scene is, the Hollywood version of an old-money mansion, the not-butler brother-in-law and his weird rant, the fact that she has to come out here at all instead of meeting her candidate at the office. She hates getting pulled into the domestic life of politicians. It's always a touch creepy, though not usually this much.

"Don't be frightened by Big Daddy. He's not half as mean as he looks." The brother-in-law turns and scowls fiercely at an oil painting of Governor Travis when he was still in office, presiding ominously over the back of the foyer. "Grrrr. Stay back, old man. Back, I say. Back."

Bonkers, Mel thinks.

The brother-in-law throws open the study door and calls inside. "Campaign people, Charlie!" He gestures Mel inside with florid excess, an obvious parody of the butler Mel originally took him for. Does he get that mistake all the time?

"Thank you," Mel says, wishing she hadn't. It's not like this guy has made her feel welcome in any way.

He ignores Mel, yells into the study again. "I'll tell Kyle she's here!" The yelling is completely unnecessary, Mel thinks. He heads for the stairs. "Ta, campaign lady," he says with an odd flutter of the hand.

Lady? At least it's better than *campaign girl*.

Mel steps inside the so-called study, looks across the expanse of room — plush Oriental rug, classic drawing-room furniture, tall oak bookshelves lined with leather-bound books, practically a stage set for the study of a well-born family, or the library of a tony law firm. It looks oddly familiar. Mel wonders if this is where Porter shot one of his commercials, the one where he's practically caressing law books. *Somewhere in all these dusty law books, a great idea got lost. The idea that law is for people, and people should be able to afford it.* "Afford" isn't the word she would use for anything she sees.

The room is deadly quiet, its sole occupant sitting behind an antique writing desk at the far end, ignoring the newcomer to read what looks to Mel like a government file of some kind.

Mel takes the opportunity to study Charlotte Travis-Porter, aka Charlie. She's dressed to match her brother, lavender gown that must cost $3,000, a swoop of perfect blonde hair, high cheekbones, piercing blue eyes, the kind of aquiline nose that every heroine of every 19th century novel has. *Meryl Streep plays her in the movie,* Mel thinks. She hopes Charlotte is more *Out of Africa* than *Postcards from the Edge.* Maybe a touch of *Sophie's Choice*? Probably not. It strikes Mel that the mansion came to Porter as a Travis property. He made a bucket of money with his low-cost legal clinics, but the house smacks of old money. Old *political* money at that, the absolutely worst kind.

Mel sits on the couch, resists the urge to cough to make her presence known. Charlotte couldn't not have heard her brother's bellowing. She's either immersed in something important, or she's asserting her superiority by ignoring the interloper from the plebeian campaign staff. Either way, Mel knows to wait it out, let Charlotte set the tone for their meeting. Or maybe she'll simply ignore Mel until Porter shows up, display her disdain for the whole messy operation of running for office.

A candidate's wife is always tricky. Some of them love the sting of battle, demand to know everything about the campaign, pore over the latest polling like they know what they're looking at, pace the floor throwing out ideas like their movie impression of a campaign strategist. The worst you get from those is a raft of unusable suggestions, easily ignored, but you have to play along, a waste of time and energy. Others pretend a kind of benign ignorance of *man's business,* looking Mel over curiously as though wondering what kind of woman wants anything to do with the nasty world of politics. Some of them go even further and openly display their hatred for electioneering. That type makes no secret of her wish that her husband will lose so she doesn't have to be a Senator or governor's wife. It does seem a pretty terrible fate. There's one thing Mel will never do, and that's marry a politician.

Mel wonders which type Charlotte is. She comes from a political family, obviously, but which direction did that push her? Other, more practical questions come to mind. Is she willing to make campaign appearances? How well-spoken is she? Can she handle the press? Mel wonders if she wants to be called Charlie, or maybe that's reserved for family. She'll start with *Mrs. Travis-Porter,* force herself not to smirk at the ridiculous hyphenation. Why not simply keep your own name instead of creating this false impression of independence? The husband doesn't hyphenate, so how is hyphenating any better than simply taking his last name? It's the kind of purely symbolic show that's doomed that generation of women to disappointing the cause of feminism, or so Mel thinks. If she ever gets married, she's keeping her own name, and if her husband-to-be doesn't like it, that's a pretty clear signal that she shouldn't be marrying him.

Mel is about to go down the rabbit-hole of envisioning her future husband when Charlotte rises from her chair, crosses the room briskly, and shuts the door to the foyer with the air of someone who wants privacy.

"Ms. Carnes, I presume." Her tone gives Mel no clue how she feels about all of this.

"Call me Mel, please." Mel rises, holds out her hand. "It's very nice to meet you Mrs. Travis-Porter."

"Likewise." Charlotte shakes quickly but firmly, gestures Mel back to the couch, takes a seat across the coffee table. She looks Mel up and down with the eye of someone buying a horse. Whatever judgment she makes, she makes it quickly. "I'd like to have a word with you before my husband comes down. I assume I can count on your discretion?"

This sounds oddly conspiratorial, and Mel is at a loss how to respond. Her instinct is to avoid any kind of unsolicited confidence. "If this is about the campaign, perhaps we should wait until Mr. Porter is present." *And if it's not, let's skip it, OK?*

"My husband knows all about this," Charlotte says. "So there's no need for him to participate in our discussion. It's a highly sensitive matter of utmost importance to his campaign, but he's best left out of it at this point." This sounds highly rehearsed to Mel. She's intrigued but also worried, doubts she'll like what she's about to hear. "I've looked into your background, and I feel that you can be trusted. You're a professional, Ms. Carnes. That much is clear from your record. Your loyalty to my husband, at least until November 8th, is taken for granted, so I know that what I'm about to reveal to you will remain strictly confidential."

Oh Jesus. Something awful is coming, Mel thinks.

Charlotte rises, retrieves a padded envelope from the desk, holds it out like a brick of plastic explosive. "This is a DEA surveillance tape. A copy, obviously. I shouldn't have it, and neither should you." She hands it to Mel, sits again, smooths her lap. "*No one* is supposed to have it, but the fact that it exists represents an existential threat to my husband's campaign. I want you to be prepared for Musgrove's people to leak it to the press."

Mel sets the package on the coffee table, tries to remain calm. "A DEA surveillance tape of..." She knows it's not Musgrove smoking crack. It's obviously something Porter did. The goddamned DEA? They're dead. Even if they weren't already a dozen points down, they'd be dead. Fuckin'-A. She never would've pegged Porter for dirty.

101

Charlotte glances at her watch, a slim, jewel-studded affair. Mel suddenly hates Charlotte, hates Porter, hates everything about politics. It's a new twist on an old feeling. She's never had an honest-to-God scandal on her hands. *Well, it's a new experience*, she says to herself. *It was bound to happen eventually.* Small consolation.

"You should watch it yourself," Charlotte says. "Whether you show it to Mr. Tremont is your call. I trust him as well, but he's not the man to handle this kind of situation. How *you* handle it is entirely up to you. It's a question of strategy, and I wouldn't presume to tell you how to do your job."

Lovely. Charlotte hands her a time-bomb but doesn't presume to tell her how to diffuse it.

"And what, exactly, *is* the situation?"

Charlotte smooths her lap again, explains with clinical detachment. Back in 1986, the DEA snagged Porter in an undercover money laundering operation focused on profitable cash-intensive businesses like Porter's legal service clinics. Hoping to interdict the financial pathways of cocaine networks in the U.S., a special task force set up a wide-ranging sting operation, code name White Shadow. Undercover agents posed as drug-cartel reps seeking new channels to cleanse the millions of dollars a week they were bringing in.

"Without any evidence that Kyle was involved — he was completely uninvolved, I can assure you — they set out to snare him in their trap. They wanted to make a few high-profile take-downs to scare off the cartels' new recruits. They figured going after someone who was already well known on television was a good play." Mel is amazed at how unruffled Charlotte is as she says this. There's not a trace of anger, no indication that what Charlotte really wants to say is, *Those bastards went after my husband for no goddamned good reason!* It has been almost a decade, but the absence of even the tiniest bit of rancor stuns Mel. Must be what happens when you grow up a politician's daughter. Everything bad is just one more thing to spin, nothing to get worked up about.

"I'm assuming he took the money," Mel says, "or you wouldn't be telling me this. How has this not come out sooner?"

"Charges were never filed, and White Shadow was shut down over entrapment concerns. The whole thing was poorly-conceived from the start." Charlotte explains that her father got wind of the operation from friends in the DEA, and he convinced the head of the task force to bring in Porter and his lawyers to see the tape at the same time the U.S. Attorney got his copy. Porter's lawyers convinced the judge to throw out the charges before the tape could be entered into the public record.

"He ordered the surveillance tapes sealed and a gag placed on the investigators to prevent them from tarnishing my husband's reputation. Fighting this would've destroyed his business even if they couldn't make the charges stick."

"Can I assume the entrapment is obvious on tape?" Mel worries that she already knows the answer.

"That, unfortunately, is not the case," Charlotte says, the first trace of emotion entering her voice. "That's why I'm giving it to you now, so you're prepared in case the tape comes out. The DEA is full of Republicans who aren't beyond leaking something like this for political purposes. We have to assume Musgrove's people will get it eventually. Howard Kane may even have a copy already, and he's just waiting for the perfect moment to drop it. Now that Kyle's climbing in the polls, it's likely that he'll act relatively soon."

"And what, exactly, do you expect me to do?" Mel doesn't anticipate a useful answer, and it hardly matters. She's already forming an idea — a crazy, far-fetched long-shot of an idea, but her fingers tingle at the audacity of it.

"If I could answer that question," Charlotte says primly, "I'd be doing it myself." Obviously. Charlotte's not the helpless, hapless political wife — quite the contrary. If she doesn't know how to handle this, it might, in fact, be unhandleable.

Yet Mel knows what she's going to do — is she really? Holy shit, she is, but she feels she needs to offer token resistance. "It seems that what you're asking me to do borders on the unethical. It might even be illegal."

"What I'm asking you to do is prevent a needless scandal from destroying my husband's chances of becoming a United States Senator. That *is* your job, isn't it? To get him elected and help stop the Republicans from taking over Congress?"

The women stare hard at each other. It's no different than Mel's stare-down with Cliff Barker, except Charlotte seems far more secure, doesn't flutter her eyelids or fidget uncomfortably. She's a rock, in fact, and Mel quickly determines that there's no winning this one. "Yes, I suppose it is," she says.

"I wouldn't entrust this to you, Ms. Carnes, if I didn't think you were completely reliable. David Wilhelm assures me that you're the very best. If there's anyone who can get us through this, it's you, is what he said. Is he right about that?"

Mel can't help but be impressed. Charlotte is a true political warhorse, appealing to Mel's sense of pride, her party loyalty. She's obviously used to maneuvering people into doing what she wants. Mel has never run into this kind of political wife. She wonders if this is what Hillary's like.

Charlotte rises, a strained smile coming onto her lips, the effort of maintaining her composure in the face of—what did she call it? An *existential threat*?—beginning to show. "I'll let my husband know you're here. There's no need to discuss this with him. Whatever you came to talk about this evening, that's all you need to address. Is that clear, Ms. Carnes?"

Mel slides the tape into her briefcase, offers nothing else by way of answer. Charlotte can talk to her like she's the hired help, but Mel doesn't have to respond that way.

# # # # #

Mel rushes through her sit-down with Porter. He seems impatient as well, either because he'd rather be at a charity fundraiser glad-handing people who might also donate to his campaign, or he knows that Mel knows about his indiscretion, and he doesn't want to linger in her presence. She spares him the polling lecture, quickly hits the bullet points on the next phase of her strategy, heads straight to her hotel to watch the tape.

It's as bad as she fears. There's Porter in a gritty black-and-white shot that reminds her of the ABSCAM footage that took down all those Congressmen back in the early-'80s. He looks like a criminal before he even does anything, huddled in a hotel suite with two Hispanic men in tight suits, slicked-back hair, gold chains and clunky watches. Do drug lords really look like that, Mel wonders, or is that how undercover agents dress up to present a convincing picture?

Used to seeing Porter in his own highly-polished TV ads, Mel doesn't recognize him at first. She watches intently, wondering if they can simply stonewall and counterpunch their way through this one, deny it's Porter, accuse Musgrove of making up the whole thing, decry mud-slinging and negative campaigning and demand that the press stick to the issues the voters care about. The angle makes it hard to be sure if it really is Porter. It looks like the camera is hidden in the overhead light fixture, the fish-eye lens distorting the scene just enough to support plausible deniability.

Yet Mel knows that's a doomed strategy. Charlotte must've thought that same thing and rejected it as well, or she never would've risked giving Mel the tape. Howard Kane will eat them alive for a month if all they can do is deny that Porter's the man on the tape. For every denial, there'll be another airing of the tape, closer scrutiny by the press, anonymous sources inside the DEA confirming Porter as the man on the tape, a constant bleed-out on the way to a 30-point defeat. No, she knows that her idea is better — it probably won't work either, but it's the only chance they have.

> PORTER. Go over that part again. I'm not clear
> how I'm safe from scrutiny here.
>
> AGENT #1. You've got a cash intensive
> business. Lots of walk-ins, right?
>
> AGENT #2. See, that's perfect. It's easy to
> pad the records, increase your cash
> deposits. With all those outlets, you can
> spread the money around, avoid any
> suspicion by the banks.
>
> AGENT #1. We bring you the money, you wash it
> clean, bring it back to us. Minus your cut,
> of course.
>
> AGENT #2. Twenty percent. You're looking at a
> mill, mill-five every month if we can do
> this in the volume we're proposing.

Mel watches in horror as Porter lets the feds talk him into accepting. She sees why his lawyers could plead entrapment. Porter raises every possible objection, looks like he's on the verge of saying *No* several different times, but the agents wheedle and cajole until he agrees. It's a classic case of inducement. But an election isn't a court of law. Voters don't know what inducement means and probably wouldn't care if they did. What matters is Porter's eventual *Yes*. It doesn't take an experienced strategist to know how screwed they'll be if this tape surfaces.

"Fuck me," Mel mutters when Porter gives in and shakes the agents' hands.

She watches a second time, stopping herself from saying, *You stupid fuck, just say No!* every five seconds. She ejects the tape, turns it over in her hands, then calls Tremont at home. "We've got a situation. A serious problem."

"What is it?" Tremont sounds annoyed.

"Meet me at the office as soon as you can."

"Right now? Is that really necessary?"

"It is," Mel says firmly.

"It's *that* serious, huh?" Tremont sounds mildly alarmed now, but he shows up at HQ 45 minutes later looking the way he always does, slovenly but unhurried, sleepy-eyed and unstressed, a man who could give a shit if his candidate faces a major crisis. He's seen it before, survived it or not, c'est la vie. Mel wonders if it's a good idea to show him the tape, knows she's mostly doing it just to torture him. She could, and should, take care of this herself, without any interference by Tremont, but she wants him to suffer alongside her, if that's even possible.

Mel plays him the tape, watches him watching, notes the gradual change in his posture as Porter tangles himself in the web.

"Fuck me," Tremont says when the tape is done. He slumps back in his chair.

"Exactly what I said."

"And Musgrove's got this?"

"Unconfirmed, but we have to assume they either have it already and they're sitting on it for now, or they'll get it eventually." Mel wonders why Tremont doesn't ask how she got the tape. Then again, she never asked Porter's wife where she got her copy, or why she waited until now to alert the campaign. The mere existence of the tape renders certain questions moot.

"We're sunk, then." Tremont almost sounds relived, as though this absolves him of any need to hustle — or feel bad about not hustling.

"Not necessarily. I have an idea. It's kind of a crazy Hail Mary, but it's all we've got."

"OK. What is it?" Tremont sits forward as thought he's genuinely interested. Maybe he's never had a scandal like this either, and it's exciting to him as well.

"I'm reluctant to tell you." Mel ejects the tape, makes a show of sliding it into her briefcase. "Maybe you don't need to know."

"Carnes, goddammit! If you're planning something nefarious, you'd better goddamned tell me. I mean it."

Mel hesitates, wonders which way to go here. Why shield Tremont? She's going to do it whether he green lights it or not. Why not implicate him as well as herself?

"We make a new tape," she says. "Or more precisely, an expanded version of this tape." Mel stops to gauge Tremont's reaction. He looks like he doesn't get it. She explains that she has a guy in New York, an underground filmmaker who's done some commercial work for her in the past. He's fast and cheap, highly discrete. Political work pays his bills, lets him keep up his boho lifestyle, but he's embarrassed by it, keeps it under wraps among his artsy friends. She can rely on him to keep it a secret.

"Keep *what* a secret?" Tremont asks. "What do you mean by *an expanded version*?"

1994

"We'll reshoot the entire tape, only with extra dialogue that changes the story. I haven't got it all worked out yet, but I'm thinking that the agents tell Porter what they're up to. They're undercover agents, they're trying to track down the trail of money from the streets back to Columbia, they need his help to get connected with the bosses. We flip the whole thing around, make it look like he's doing them a favor. They're asking him to aid the operation, and that's what he agrees to. The handshake deputizes Porter, signs him up as a undercover agent. *We need your help. You're a high-profile businessman. The Columbians will never suspect you're a DEA plant.* That sort of thing. I haven't written it yet, but that's the basic idea."

Tremont's face is drained of all expression. "I'm speechless, Carnes. You're serious about this?"

"A hundred-and-ten percent."

"Unbelievable." Tremont widens his eyes, nearly swallows his toothpick.

"Look," Mel says. "This tape surfaces, it's going to hurt, no matter what we do. Some people are going to see Porter in a shady situation and automatically turn against him. But we can flip the narrative and claim — with outrage — that Musgrove's people cut up the tape to make Porter look like a criminal when in fact he's a hero. He took a big personal risk to aid a major government investigation. We don't brag, of course. We're just outraged that Musgrove would stoop to such a low blow."

"You're insane."

Mel is undeterred. "We'll lose ground when the tape first hits. If we weren't down so far, we could try to just stop the bleeding. Deny it's him. The footage is poor quality. There's plausible deniability. But we're already way down. We can't afford any distractions, the slightest hint of a scandal. I know it's risky, but we stand to gain among people who buy that Musgrove's the dirty one here. Willfully taking this out of context to smear his opponent. What a scumbag, right? Tell me it's not brilliant."

Tremont shakes his head, leans far back in his chair and hooks his hands behind his neck. Mel thinks he's relenting. "This takes spin to a whole new level. I'm impressed, Carnes. Disgusted but impressed. It's brilliant, sure. It'll never work, but it's genius in its own twisted way."

"It *will* work. Look. The tape is super low-fi, shot from a weird angle with a fish-eye lens. My guy in New York can duplicate the shot exactly, get some actors who look just like Porter and the feds, make sure their hair and costumes are identical." Mel grows more confident as she talks. She's convincing herself as much as Tremont here, working herself up to actually follow through on this crazy idea.

"I'll write a new script, make sure it has all the original dialogue, verbatim, plus everything else we need to flip the story. We release our tape right after Musgrove releases his, go on the offensive, tear down the weasely son-of-a-bitch for butchering the tape to malign a man volunteering for a dangerous assignment to aid his government."

"That's insane, Carnes. Completely fucking insane. You are not going to do this. And don't ask me *Why not?* either. I can see you getting ready. Just forget about it."

"Why not?" Mel says, smirking.

"It's just a goddamned political campaign, that's why not. You really want to go to jail over that?"

"That's your problem," Mel shoots back. "You haven't got any skin in the game. *It's just a political campaign*? Maybe that's true, but if you're that casual about it, no wonder we're getting our asses kicked so badly."

"It hardly matters what I've done or not done. Porter's poison. If we were up by 10 points right now, we'd still be doomed. Jesus, Carnes. Did you see the same tape I saw? How is an *expanded version* of that going to do anything? We're fucked and you know it. There's no Hail Mary pass here."

"You watch, Alex. I'll pull this off and bring down that sleazy motherfucker Howard Kane. It'll work. I know it will."

1994

PART 2
ON THE ROPES

THE NEXT TWO WEEKS FLY PAST in a blur of scandal-mongering and crisis management, punching and counter-punching to get back in the fight, then in a desperate effort just to stay in it. Sometimes it's a rope-a-dope, taking body blows to wear out the opponent with the hope of bursting out in a late round with reserve energy to land a knockout, and sometimes it's simply being on the ropes, getting pummeled and trying to say upright, hoping to go the distance and sneak in enough punches to eke out a split decision. Mel spends the whole time knowing Porter could go down for the count any second. Even when they rally with a couple of sharp jabs to the face and look to be maybe taking control, Musgrove rears back and lands a nose-crunching roundhouse. They get a standing eight count, shake it off, stagger into another flurry of body blows. There's no bell, no minute in the corner to sponge off and have a Burgess Meredith moment. *You can do this, Rock! Goddammit, you got the power! The body, get the body! You got him goin'!*

Mel has always worked tirelessly on campaigns but never did the hours fly past so maniacally, so urgently. It's fight-or-flight 24-7, wearing her down, doubling her liquor and cigarette consumption, stripping away her emotional veneer one layer at a time until she ends up in a bar fight she's pretty sure she started, except she can't remember. And even then, she can't quit. She soldiers on into oblivion.

It starts pre-dawn on Wednesday, exactly 34 days til the polls open. An eternity in campaign time. Mel gives the front section of the *USA Today* a quick glance and spends half an hour on CNN, then she's in a cab to the airport to catch an early flight to New York. She's exhausted and depressed from a sleepless night going over the tape again and again, making sure she has an exact transcript, brainstorming additions to fit the new storyline.

She struggled to make the new dialogue plausible, to maintain continuity, to find a way to show as clearly as voters need to be shown that Porter was signing up to help out, that he's the good guy here, not a money laundering scumbag. For this to work, the version Kane has — Mel reminds herself not to forget that it's the *real* version — needs to come across as obviously butchered, a cleverly edited *fraud* that paints a drastically misleading picture when seen in its full context. A few of the exchanges are particularly challenging to work around.

> PORTER. What about my taxes? That's income to me, every deposit, every dime. Not just my cut, but the money I sneak back out to you.
>
> AGENT #2. What, you don't have accountants who know how to shelter you?
>
> PORTER. That's a lot of sheltering. A lot. And people to pull it off. So I'm exposed in two directions.
>
> AGENT #1. You negotiating with us here, or what? You want a bigger cut? We can go 25%, no higher.
>
> PORTER. That's a start. But I'd also need a way to increase my write-offs. Business expenses, preferably also cash. At this point, it's starting to look extremely complicated. There's too many exposure points. I don't know, gentlemen. I'm not sure there's a deal for me here.
>
> AGENT #1. Just wait a minute there, amigo. We can work somethin' out. I'm sure we can.

Why didn't he walk out right then? Did he really need the extra money? Mel sometimes wonders why rich people do sleazy things to get even richer, but as soon as she asks herself, she knows the answer. It's human nature. Greed and insecurity. He probably felt inadequate in the face of his wife's family money. There's also *thanatos*, and simple boredom. She's amazed sometimes by the mistakes politicians make out of sheer boredom, the irresistible impulse to make life more exciting. Not that she's seen anything as fatal as this. *Goddamn you, Kyle Porter! And you too Cliff Barker, for getting me into this.*

Mel rewound, checked her transcript. It's self-destructive thrill-seeking, plain and simple, Porter's attempts at pushback all part of the rush. He doesn't take his objections and leave because it gets him hard being in that room, struggling with drug lords trying to reel him in a like a sportfish. Or maybe Porter knew what he was doing all along. The consummate lawyer, he might've suspected a sting and knew if he played it right, he could wiggle out on inducement, which is exactly what happened. Is that what he was up to? Mel cuts off her speculation. It hardly matters if Porter was being greedy or clever or thrill-seeking. He obviously didn't imagine he'd be running for office someday. Then, when it came time to throw his hat in the ring, he did what? Conveniently forgot about this episode in his life? Thought it wouldn't matter? Believed someone would come rescue him if it came out?

1994

Whatever it was, Mel *is* coming to rescue him. Or at least she's trying. Can she actually pull it off? It struck her more than once as she watched and re-watched how impossible it might be, fitting her desired storyline into the pre-existing material. She was constantly worried it wouldn't matter anyway, that no amount of damage control could rescue Porter from defeat if there was even a whiff of impropriety around his already struggling campaign. Would enough people believe Porter was a hero, not a crook, even if she could piece together a plausible script?

The ethical question caught her out a couple of times as well. Why was she risking this kind of fraud for a mere campaign, for the furtherance of a privileged white man who already had way more than he deserved out of life? The party? The country? That's all bullshit, and Mel knows it. There's only one reason: Kane. Beating Kane — *humiliating* Kane — that's all that matters. She has to eviscerate him and knows by the end of the night that she is in fact willing to do anything to pull out an upset victory here. It kills her that Kane probably won't give a shit. *It's just politics after all. Doesn't mean anything, right?* He believes that as much as Tremont does — Mel's sure of it — so why risk her reputation, her career, if her nemesis won't even care?

She almost said *Fuck it!* half a dozen times, picked up the phone to cancel her flight to New York, but then she thought of a perfect bit of dialogue, got a renewed sense of purpose, reminded herself that victory is all that matters, whether Kane cares or not. She knows also that this is the kind of thing that makes legends. Riding into Brooklyn from LaGuardia, she imagines the story circulating as a rumor, pictures herself hearing it third-hand a few years from now, some young pol in a bar bragging about the time a strategist he worked with made a bogus surveillance tape to push back against a scandal.

She arrives at Ernie's studio sticky and drained, nursing what feels like the onset of a nasty cold. He's sympathetic until she explains what she has in mind.

"Impossible. How are we supposed to match the shot exactly?"

"I don't know, Ernie. You're the expert. You tell me."

"Can't be done." He folds his arms over his chest and gives Mel a long-suffering-older-brother look. *Sorry sis, can't bail you out of trouble this time.*

"That's bullshit, Ernie. Maybe *you* can't do it, but that doesn't mean it can't be done." Mel has never met an artsy type who didn't have a massive ego.

"Okay, maybe not *impossible*. But really fucking hard. Not to mention tedious, if it needs to match exactly, which I'm gathering it does."

"Yes, exactly." Mel can sense Ernie relenting. "A hundred percent exactly."

"And you need this when?"

"End of the day."

"Gimme a goddamned break! End of the day? Definitely impossible."

"Tomorrow at the latest."

"Come on, Mel. You're asking a lot here."

Mel removes a crisp manila envelope from her briefcase, passes it to Ernie. He peeks inside, counts the money with the tips of his fingers, eyebrows going up as it becomes obvious how much this is worth to Mel. This is completely off-the-books, obviously, a pure cash transaction. It's a good thing Mel had the foresight to start a crisis management fund as soon as she hit Cleveland. She drained it for this trip, $30,000. "That's all I've got right now. I can make it another 20 large if you give me a few days to rustle up the rest. You know I'm good for it."

"Fifty grand for a day's work. You really need this, huh?"

"I do. And I know you're the man for the job." Mel blows her nose loudly, plays up the sick foundling angle. Not that it's necessary. She can tell Ernie's onboard — he was already leaning that way before she forked over the cash. Massive egos and perpetually hungry for money — that's every artsy type under the sun.

Now it's just a matter of making it flawless. Ernie starts working the phone to rustle up a cast and crew while Mel puts the finishing touches on the script.

"Hey Frankie, you wanna earn five hundred bucks today?…Uh huh, top secret project, and you gotta get to my studio in like an hour, ready for a long day…Yeah, pizza's on me, no problem. And whiskey when we wrap."

Mel smiles as Ernie throws around what must seem like big money. It's just before noon by the time they're all there, three actors, a cameraman, a soundman, a lighting guy, and two hair/makeup/costume girls. Ernie offers only minimal context for the task at hand, introduces Mel by a fake name and reiterates the top-secret nature of the project. Smirks from the bohos, but Mel has only the most remote fear of a leak. None of them looks like the type who follows politics, certainly not at a level where they'd pay attention to a political scandal in Ohio.

1994

Mel's cold gets worse throughout the afternoon. She coughs and shivers through the shoot, but it gives her immense satisfaction to see Ernie and his guys bring her words to life. If writing TV commercials was fun, it was smoking pot and drinking whiskey fun. This is heroin fun. Not that she knows what heroin actually feels like, but this must be close. She's hacking up phlegm, but she's never felt so elated. She catches herself standing there with a shit-eating grin and her hand on her cheek like some dumb-ass junky. *Is this how movie writers feel?* She wonders if she should give up politics and write screenplays. She has plenty of great stories, knows she can concoct plenty more. This right here would make an awesome scene in a movie, the desperate strategist filming a fraudulent DEA surveillance tape in a makeshift Brooklyn sound stage. *Anything to Win,* she'd call it.

It turns out to be easier than it seemed. Static shot, consistent light, minimal movement by the actors, extremely simple hair and costumes. The hardest part is matching the graininess of the footage. Ernie's cameraman spends 45 minutes cycling through different filter combinations to get it just right, but once he does, it's a set-it-and-forget-it situation. Meanwhile, Ernie rehearses the actors, places a monitor so they can watch the original tape and their own scene simultaneously, runs them through her script a dozen times before the first take, correcting body language and gently nudging them away from a personal interpretation of the characters.

"Exactly like it is on the tape, guys, not one tiny bit different. You're robots today. Just be the ball."

Mel hopes it looks as good on tape as it does in the room, that the final cut really does match the original footage. She deflates as they roll the first take, certain there's no way their product can align as precisely as it has to for this to work. Then she looks over Ernie's shoulder at the main monitor, imagining this is exactly how it looked to the agents in the next room watching Porter take the bait, and she's sold. *This is going to work,* she tells herself. *This is goddamned brilliant! Screw Hollywood. This is real-life fantasy-making, right here.* Something far beyond expedient exaggeration.

"When can I have a copy?" Mel asks Ernie when he decides the 7th take is exactly right.

"Right now, if you want," he says. "Can't cut it up—you know?—or it won't play like a surveillance tape. It's gotta be one continuous shot. I think we nailed it. " Ernie pops the tape out of the camera. "Just need to run that take onto a fresh tape, and you're all set. Half hour."

"Make me 5 copies. Needless to say, none of this ever happened, right?" Saying this makes Mel feel like she's actually a character in a movie. She wishes she had the right quote to ice the cake, remembers a line from *Goodfellas* that's roughly suitable. She shakes out her shoulders and squints her eyes, channels Robert De Niro. *"And hey, I'm proud of you. You took your first pinch like a man and you learn two great things in your life. Look at me. Never rat on your friends and always keep your mouth shut."*

"That *Godfather 2*?"

"*Goodfellas*," Mel corrects.

While Ernie prepares her copies, Mel checks in with Schooley. There's a message from Gary, her oppo research guy back in D.C. Mel wants to linger in her feeling of elation, but she calls Gary right away in case he's got something important.

"Turns out Musgrove's got an ex-wife in his distant past," Gary says. Mel can tell he's exited.

"Uh huh. Anything good?"

"Ugly divorce, apparently, just before he hit it big with his company, so the ex-Mrs. M didn't get much in the way of a settlement. I'd imagine she's more than a little pissed about that, given how rich Musgrove is now. Lives in Chicago. You want me to fly out, follow up in person, see if she's got any dirt she's willing to pass along?"

Mel considers it. She's worn out—it'd be nice to catch a day of rest here in New York, holed up at a fancy hotel in Midtown, hot baths and plush robes—but she knows she has to do this herself, and right away. Digging up dirt is one thing, pulling it out of an actual human being quite another. She'd like to entrust it to Gary, but she knows it's on her, however miserable it'll be to travel again today.

So she's back on an airplane two hours later, the 7:15 flight to O'Hare. She lands at 8:58 Chicago time, grabs an Italian sausage sandwich in the concourse, checks into the airport Hilton. A scalding hot bath and two mini-bar Scotches is all she gets for medicine, but she's asleep by 10:30, the earliest she's been to bed since middle school.

1994

Thursday, October 6th
-33 to Election Day

The cab leaves Mel outside a brick duplex, nicely maintained but indistinguishable from the other duplexes running for blocks in every direction. It's a decent part of town, but nothing more than decent. For the one-time wife of a multi-millionaire running for U.S. Senate, it's pretty depressing.

Mel reminds herself to play it slowly here, let the resentment build naturally. Linda Musgrove can't feel like Mel is trying to exploit her pain and anger, but Mel has to do exactly that, let the pain and anger grow until Mel seems like a savior, not a snoop.

She checks her press credentials, applies Chapstick, dabs her nose with a Kleenex. The cold seems to be getting better already, but she feels weaker than she'd like, hollowed out from the DayQuil she took this morning. She hopes her pink nose and puffy eyes humanize her, show a woman dedicated to the truth, nothing more. She's picked a scab like this before, both blown it and pulled it off. The idea of getting embroiled in an ugly political brawl is fascinating to some people, repellent to others. If Linda hasn't come forward yet, Mel has to assume she's the latter. It's delicate work getting that type to tell their story to the press.

The doorbell works, a gentle chime with a lingering note, a cheery sound that promises a pleasant visitor, not a lying politco looking for dirt on her opponent. The door opens, and there's Linda Musgrove née Abernathy. It means something that she kept her taken name even after the divorce. Mel knows that's common among women of that generation. So is an odd loyalty to the scumbag who cheated on her, or ignored her, or couldn't control his anger problem — whatever broke up the marriage.

"Yes? Can I help you?" Linda has an open face, an efficient bob haircut, the clothes of a mid-level secretary. She's medium height, pretty in the way of every mid-level secretary Mel has ever met, the prettiness of make-up deftly applied, teeth well-maintained, good posture and a warm smile. In short, completely forgettable.

"Hi. Linda Musgrove? I'm Mary Baker, *Wall Street Journal*." Mel produces her badge, waits for Linda to give it a thorough inspection.

"I wondered when you people would get here. Come on in." She turns and leads Mel down a narrow hall. "You'll have to forgive me, I'm getting ready for work." Shit, of course. Mel scolds herself for failing to think of this, blames the cold for such sloppiness. Somehow she counted on having all morning with Linda, sitting over cup after cup of herbal tea and letting the story wend slowly from Linda's mind. Mel assumes there's a story, can't believe there's *not* a story. Whether or not it does her any good remains to be seen.

"I'm sorry to disturb you on a work day."

"No, not a problem. I'll just call in, tell my boss I'll be a few hours late. You want some tea? Looks like you've got a cold going there."

Mel perks up. Linda has something to say, and she's not playing coy. In fact, it looks like she's trying to ingratiate herself with Mel. *I wondered when you people would get here.* Linda's been waiting to tell her story. Mel's fingers begin to tingle. There might be something really good here.

Linda sits Mel in the smallish living room—furniture tightly packed but the style tasteful, the knick-knacks not excessive or tacky—a not-unpleasant place to sit while Linda goes to the kitchen to make tea and phone her boss. She takes her time, goes up the narrow back stairs at one point, leaving Mel to speculate about the nature of the intel she has. She bets it's something financial, hopes it's an obviously corrupt or illegal act rather than some complex scheme to defraud investors or evade obscure regulations. It's known that Musgrove has run afoul of the S.E.C. and flirted with violations of the Federal Elections Campaign Act, that he probably has offshore accounts hiding money from the I.R.S. None of it seems to hurt him much. Republican voters can easily forgive offenses of that sort, often find them appealing in fact—goddamned government harassing a man just trying to earn a buck, is how the reasoning goes. Mel doesn't understand that attitude, particularly among the evangelicals and blue-color Southern whites who have about as much in common with Musgrove's ilk as they do with Jesse Jackson. Linda may think she has a bombshell when it's some complicated maneuver to squeeze a few extra bucks at the margins of legality, a waste of Mel's time coming here. Amateurs usually overestimate how damaging their story can be, forget how much bullshit they themselves forgive for the politicians they support. Mel's done it for Bill Clinton, that's for sure.

Mel itches for a cigarette, looks around for an ashtray as a signal that it's acceptable here. It's getting harder and harder to smoke in the

1994

civilian world, non-smokers testier than ever, many of them affronted by even the suggestion that someone might want to light up in their presence. There's no ashtray, which makes Mel yen for a smoke that much more. Maybe it's in a drawer somewhere, or Linda has her guests use a coffee mug or a saucer, but Mel rejects the idea of asking. She doesn't want to insult her host. Even bringing up cigarettes could make Linda snippy, and Mel needs her to be as comfortable and trusting as possible. Maybe she actually has something good on Musgrove. Mel sneezes, tells herself she shouldn't be smoking anyway when she's nursing a cold, wishes she'd had a quick butt outside before ringing the bell.

Linda comes in with two mugs and a file folder, sets one of the mugs in front of Mel, curls into a wingback armchair and cradles her tea, the folder tucked away at her side. She looks like she's settling in for a long heart-to-heart. Mel's fingers tingle again at the sight of the manila folder peeking out beneath Linda's arm. This might actually be good.

"Thanks for waiting," Linda says, as though Mel is doing her the favor here.

"Not a problem. I appreciate you taking time out of your work day to answer my questions."

Only Mel never has to ask any questions. Linda starts right in, tells her story calmly, tonelessly, as though she's relating what someone else told her, a hand-me-down tale about a friend-of-a-friend-of-a-friend that she's passing on as a cautionary tale, one woman to another. Linda is so unemotional that it takes Mel a minute to catch on that this is a true horror story of domestic abuse, 2 years of beatings, repeated threats to kill her if she went to the police or told anybody, the occasional rape thrown in when Musgrove was feeling particularly brutal.

Mel sits in shock as the tale unfolds, Linda circling back to add details after her initial synopsis. The horror is unbelievable, Musgrove an absolute monster. Though Mel is sickened by what she hears, she finds herself amazed, even a bit appalled, at how businesslike Linda is, how organized in her presentation. The first few minutes was the executive summary. Then came the detailed breakdown, graphic descriptions that make Mel's skin crawl, her body tensing as Linda takes her blow by blow through one horrendous episode after another. It's not until she's done with this segment of her report that Linda brings out the photos, Appendix A, "Visual Evidence of the Accusation." Mel almost breaks down as Linda places them slowly on the coffee table, each as terrible as the last, 25 pictures spanning 2 years of merciless abuse. Mel blows her nose, dabs at her eyes with a tissue as though it's just the cold making her tear up, watches Linda deal out the photos without a single tear herself, with barely a trace of emotion in her voice as she notes the date of each one.

Mel has to keep reminding herself not to ask Linda why she didn't go to the police despite Musgrove's threats, or just get out. It's a natural reaction to think that's what *you* would've done, but Mel knows she has absolutely no way of understanding what Linda went through. The level of fear that must accompany such horrific abuse is completely unfathomable. Would she have gotten out after the first time, or kept making excuses, unable to act on her deepest instincts for self-preservation? Mel wishes she could be sure she would've done what she believes she would've done, but her doubts mount as Linda's exposition continues. She imagines herself paralyzed by terror the way Linda must've been.

Linda seems to have dealt with the psychological trauma somehow — years of therapy, Mel suspects — her ability to relate the tale in graphic detail both impressive and mystifying to Mel. If Mel had gone through something like this, even just one episode… — she doesn't know how she'd be coping with it. Not as calmly as this, she suspects. Mel gets more visibly outraged when she even hears about someone getting beaten or raped. Linda probably does too, the impassive veneer limited to her own case, a protective shell to keep herself going when it would be so easy to collapse in powerlessness and despair.

Despite her shock and horror that anyone could be such a monster, Mel's professional instincts begin to kick in as Linda gathers the photos back into her folder. Obviously aware of Mel's surprise at her own sang froid, Linda concludes by saying, "Of course, this all happened years ago. It's a period in my life that I've put behind me."

It's the perfect ending if you're rooting for Linda as a survivor, but not what a strategist dedicated to bringing down Musgrove wants to hear. Mel can't help thinking that Linda will have to display more emotion for this to play well on the morning talk shows. She hates herself for having that thought, but that's the reality here. Unless Linda can convey this horror story effectively, Musgrove won't suffer the consequences of his actions the way he should. He shouldn't just lose an election. He should rot in jail for the rest of his life, the miserable sack of shit. But nothing will come of this if Mel and Linda don't work it correctly. Mel can already picture a smug defense attorney cross-examining Linda, shredding her for being so dispassionate about what happened to her. *I'm having a hard time believing this was as horrible for you as you say it was, Ms. Musgrove,* and the men on the jury nod in agreement. *What a fucking world we live in,* Mel says to herself.

Linda leaves the room, taking the photos with her, calls over her shoulder to ask if Mel wants more tea.

"No, I'm fine, thanks." She blows her nose, her mind racing to figure out how to handle this bombshell. Mel reminds herself not to feel too exuberant over a fellow woman's misery, but she's almost giddy at how thoroughly and completely this is going to destroy Howard Kane. She means *Musgrove.* Kane too, but it's not about him anymore. Musgrove is beyond monstrous, the top villain in that crew of low-life motherfuckers. This is going to kill him with suburban women, the Jesus crowd too — that's the one that'll really hurt.

What a race, Mel says to herself. My guy caught on tape agreeing to launder money for drug lords, the other guy with a brutalized wife in his past. Not that there's any comparison. If Porter looks sleazy on that DEA tape, those photos Linda has paint a picture of pure evil. Her guy's suddenly the lesser-of-two — way lesser. Fucking politics. It gives you whiplash sometimes.

Linda returns with a fresh tea for herself, curls back in the chair and blinks her tearless green eyes at Mel. "Well, where do we go from here, Miss Baker?"

Mel blows her nose to cover a surge of anger that Linda can be so dispassionate about this, reminds herself that's exactly how she needs to be as well. If she's going to destroy Musgrove and Kane with this, she can't let her judgment get clouded by emotion. She'll scream and howl at the horrifying male-dominated universe later, when she's alone with her mini-bar. For now, she has to remain calm and professional.

"First of all, let me express my sincerest sympathies for the horror you've had to endure, Ms. Musgrove. As a woman, as a human being, I'm appalled." Mel, however, sounds as clinically detached now as Linda. "As a journalist, I'm interested in only one thing. Exposing the truth so those who deserve punishment receive it in the full measure they deserve." Mel is annoyed that she repeated the word *deserve.* She wants to sound entirely professional here, a high-level journalist capable of handling such a big story.

"I understand the delicacy of this," Linda offers. She sounds like a colleague, not the victim. She smiles helpfully at Mel. "I know it's important that I do this right. I've seen too many men get away with worse to be naïve enough to think that Dick's automatically going to suffer for this."

Worse? Mel has never seen worse. She knows it's out there, but she's never encountered it personally. She blows her nose again to cover the return of moist eyes, figures Linda's just using a figure of speech. Unless she's worked at a women's shelter, she couldn't possibly have seen worse.

Mel smiles wanly. "I should tell you up front that I can't pay you for your story. Even the photos. The *Journal* doesn't operate that way. It would impugn our integrity. But I want to make sure you're compensated somehow." She tells Linda she knows she didn't fare well in the divorce settlement. Mel sees the resentment surface when she brings this up.

"I'm not looking for money, Miss Baker. I just want the truth finally told. I'm sure you understand that."

Mel checks her impulse to ask why she hasn't come forward before, reminds herself that Linda probably lives in a constant state of low-grade terror, PTSD from 2 years at the mercy of that animal. If she seems unusually robotic about it, that's her own business and entirely understandable.

"Absolutely." Mel leans across the coffee table, rests her hand on Linda's knee. "This must be exceedingly difficult for you. I appreciate your bravery. I also want to make sure you don't have to undergo any more unnecessary pain. If you're willing — if you're able — to appear on television and tell your story, I know that television stations aren't as, ahem, aren't as old-fashioned as the *Journal* about paying for stories."

"I'm not in this for the money, Miss Baker," Linda repeats fiercely.

Mel pulls back her hand, hopes she's not blowing it here. "I believe you. Absolutely." Mel dabs her runny nose, licks her lips. Goddamned cold, clouding her thinking. "I just want to make sure you're properly compensated for the time this may take up. There's no compensating for the pain you've suffered, but you shouldn't have to undergo any more hardship as a result of bringing this forward."

"I understand that, and I thank you for your concern, but I wouldn't want to profit from something like this. Letting the truth be known after all these years is compensation enough."

Mel finds Linda's use of the word *profit* unusual, but it's not until later that she thinks back on this conversation and puts together the signs. She leaves with a solemn promise to Linda that this will be more than a minor story carried by just one newspaper, hoping Linda doesn't wonder later why there's never an article by Mary Baker in the *Wall Street Journal*.

She has only one concern, getting this into the news cycle before Kane releases the DEA tape. She'd like to start on offense here, watch

Kane struggle with a scandal. It's perfect, if it plays out that way, the best-case scenario for dealing with her own looming nightmare. Musgrove, under the blackest of clouds, releases what Mel is now able to show is a selectively edited videotape, clearly intended to distract from his own gargantuan misdeed. It'll be ugly for both sides, sure— Mel knows that even if some people believe her tape, others will still think Porter's hiding something—but if Linda's story goes public first, the fallout is sure to hurt Musgrove more than Porter, and in all the cross-currents, her fake tape might not get scrutinized as closely as it otherwise would.

# # # # #

Mel flies back to Cleveland feeling hopeful. She lets herself relax and dwell on the accomplishments of the past 36 hours, doesn't even try to use the 50-minute flight to get work done. She stares out the window at the flat vastness of Indiana and western Ohio, downs another shot of DayQuil as Lake Erie comes into view, skips the bank of payphones in Hopkins International to get a cab back to her hotel. She'll check in with Schooley while she's running a hot bath, tell him she'll be in first thing in the morning, ask him to work with Colin on Porter's opening statement for tomorrow's debate at the League of Women Voters.

She makes a few other calls first, puts the Columbus, Cleveland, and Cincinnati TV stations onto Linda's story as she promised, phones anonymous tips to Jared Block and Kate Winkler, the cold doing all she needs by way of disguising her voice. She considers putting Thom Reynolds on the case as well but decides against it. It's better to let local TV and national newspapers have first dibs, then watch as the Ohio papers join the feeding frenzy for round 2. She's about to call the office when the phone rings.

"Carnes." It's Howard Kane, his Texas drawl unmistakable. "You'll never guess what I just watched?"

Oh fuck. Mel flops on the bed, her fantasy of beating Kane to the punch destroyed with that single sentence.

"You there, Carnes?"

"Yeah. I'm listening. I'm just trying to imagine what kind of twisted midget porn you're talking about, you sick fuck."

"Oh, it's waaay better than that. Maybe you've seen it yourself. Picture a seedy hotel room, two Latin gentlemen making a pitch to a certain Senate candidate of the Democratic persuasion. An agreement, a handshake. Any of this sound familiar?"

Mel's pulse is racing. She never expected Kane to give her notice that he has the tape, but apparently he couldn't resist the temptation to gloat in advance. She sees a decent way out here, Kane's foolish need to rub it in giving her an opening to head this off at the pass. If she can sell Kane on her flipped narrative, convince him Musgrove will look like the bad guy for selling a fake bill of goods, maybe he'll bury the tape rather than risk the blowback—at least long enough for Linda's story to hit the news. It's a long shot, no doubt about it, but it's worth a try.

"Absolutely," she says calmly. "Kyle Porter, civic-minded private citizen, aiding the DEA in its effort to interdict a cartel money-laundering network."

"Excuse me?" Kane's shock is obvious.

"Come on, Kane. I know what you're saying. Porter in a room with two drug-dealer-looking types. Looks very bad. It's an odd conversation, admittedly, but it's obvious what's going down. I wouldn't have taken the risk myself, but Porter's a different breed. He really is one of those good guys. I know you have a hard time believing the type exists, being such an unrepentant prick yourself, but there it is in black-and-white, Porter laying it on the line to help his government fight the War on Drugs. Tell me you didn't feel just the tiniest bit of civic pride when you watched it."

"I have no idea what you're talking about Carnes. You gone mental on me? The stress getting to you? The tape I saw is pure unadulterated political death. Never seen purer, and I've seen a lot. One airing of this on the local news, and your guys drops into the teens, if that high. Might even go out with a fistful of pills and a bottle of whiskey."

"I'm sure you could cut it up to look bad, yeah." Mel sits on the edge of the bed, her jaw muscles aching. She knows she has to play this just right. *Keep cool, Carnes.* "It's definitely a shady-looking situation, I admit it, but seriously Kane? You think you can take our guy down on this? Some people might not like it, that I'm aware of, and I won't call Porter a hero, but it's not too far from the right word for it."

"You're fucking kidding me, right? Your guy makes a deal with a drug cartel to launder their coke cash, and you call him a hero?"

This is it, the critical moment. "That's what you saw?" Mel hits the perfect note of incredulity.

"Damn fuckin' straight that's what I saw. What'd you see?"

"Something much different than that."

"That's your spin? *Something much different than that*? Oboy, that's too goddamned much, Carnes. I thought *I* had balls."

1994

"No spin, asshole. Not this time. What I saw on the tape he gave me last week is my guy agreeing to participate in a DEA sting on a key money laundering route for the Columbian cartels. It's a shady setting, like I said—Porter is definitely concerned how it looks, so am I—but there's no ambiguity about it. Not in my mind. That's not spin, that's just the plain truth."

"You sure we're talking about the same tape here?" Mel notices that Kane's drawl is almost completely gone. She senses his doubt growing. She needs to keep him off-balance, get him to agree to watch her tape before he drops his on the press. She surges with confidence, warns herself not to get cocky.

"I only know of the one," she says.

There's a silence on the other end of the line. Mel lets Kane run through the possibilities for a few seconds.

"Why don't we meet somewhere," Mel says. "Bring our tapes? I'd love to see what you think you've got, and I'm sure you'd like to see for yourself what I'm talking about."

"You show me yours, I'll show you mine?" Kane says. "That what you're saying?"

"Couldn't hurt, right?" Mel can tell Kane likes the idea. He's known for being aggressive, but he won't take a calculated risk without being able to calculate, and to do that, he needs to know what Mel has up her sleeve.

They arrange to meet at a Motel 6 on I-71, midway between Cleveland and Columbus. Mel gets there first, pays for the room with cash, leaves the desk clerk with a description of Kane. "Send him up as soon as he gets here." He leers at Mel, sure he knows what kind of exchange is going down. If he knew the real reason, she thinks. It's a much better story to tell the night-shift guy than another truck-stop quickie with a high-class hooker. She wonders if she should hope the clerk thinks she's high-class, dismisses the thought immediately. *Stay focused,* she reminds herself. *This could be for all the marbles.*

Kane barges in with twice his usual confidence. It's clear he didn't spend the drive up here festering in doubt. He probably figures Mel is bluffing, buying time to think her way out of the mess. She makes sure she looks calm but not hiding-something calm, sure of her righteousness but just the tiniest bit worried. Kane might think there are two separate tapes, so she has to have entertained the same possibility.

They play Kane's tape first. Mel watches with a mixture of serious attention and mounting disbelief.

"That's it?" she says when it ends. "That's the whole thing? Everything you got?"

"Indeed it is. Pretty horrible, ain't it?"

"Then you're being played for a sucker, Dumbo." Mel ejects Kane's tape, tosses it dismissively on the bed. "Whoever gave you that atrocity butchered it to make my guy look bad. A hatchet job, plain and simple. Joke's on you."

"You expect me to believe that?" Kane crosses his arms over his chest, gives his best Henry Kissinger impersonation, but Mel can tell he's worried.

"I don't give a shit what you believe. Maybe you're the one who cut it up. How the hell would I know? What I *do* know is, you've only got part of the story. Watch." Mel slides her tape into the machine with supreme confidence.

Kane watches with exactly the disbelief Mel hoped for. He leans slowly forward in shock as the scene unfolds, a helpless coach watching his team blow a 20-point lead one touchdown at a time.

"What the fucking fuck," he says at one point.

Mel plays it cool, arms crossed over her chest and a thin smile on her lips, but she's roiling inside. Will he really believe it? Are the dialogue additions seamless enough, the conversational moves plausible? Do the actors look so close to the originals that Kane won't spot the difference? He's the toughest audience she'll ever have for this tape. If he buys it, she and Ernie really did pull it off. She keeps waiting for him to say, *What a pile of horseshit this is! That is* not *Kyle Porter!* The longer he doesn't say it, the more relaxed Mel becomes, but she's on guard as well. She wouldn't put it past Kane to fake getting taken in so he can trick her into confessing the truth.

"I don't goddamn believe it," he says when it's over, but it sounds like he does.

"You see what I'm talking about?" Mel tries not to sound too smug. "Someone at the DEA — I'm assuming that's where you got it, right? — someone handed you a cleverly edited sack of shit, and you bought it. Maybe you even paid good money for it. I almost feel sorry for you, getting all worked up like that. *Almost.*"

Kane sits in stunned silence.

"You're not gonna have a heart attack on me, are you? Or a stroke? You look like a prime candidate for a massively debilitating stroke." Kane says nothing, and Mel lets him ruminate for another long minute, trying not to seem too obviously gleeful. It's working, but there's still time to blow it.

1994

"Here's the thing, Kane. Maybe this is the first time you've seen what's on the whole tape, maybe not. How the hell do I know? Could be someone's playing you, could be you're a lying sack of shit. Whichever it is, if you leak your pile of crap, all I have to do is release mine, and it's obvious you assholes cut up the full record to make my guy look bad, when in fact he's the hero here. That hurts you way more than it hurts me."

"That's your play?" Kane says. "We both keep it in our pants because your pecker's bigger than my pecker?" He's got his drawl dialed up all the way again, seems to have his swagger back. Mel considers the possibility that he accepts her tape as genuine but figures it's worth a try releasing his anyway. He'll have the virtue of creating a negative first impression. They both know that a lot of people continue believing lies even when the truth is revealed to them immediately afterwards. People suck that way.

"Nice metaphor," Mel says. "But yes, that's what I'm saying. My pecker is bigger than yours. And it's uncircumcised to boot."

"I get that you've got some good-guy material there." Kane steeples his fingers, arches his eyebrows, the perfect imitation of a Bond villain. "What I don't get is why you'd try to talk me out of releasing my tape. If you're sure Porter comes out smelling like a rose, why try to talk me out of it?"

This is it, the crucial moment. Kane has to buy that she's not shining him somehow. She ignores his second question, focuses on the first. "It's potentially bad for both of us if this comes out," she says. "Might be that your version sticks in people's minds, might be that my version shows you up for being the scumbag you are and splashes blood on Musgrove. It's hard to say in advance which way it breaks, am I right?"

"That's true," Kane admits.

"So what I'm proposing is neither one of us risk it. Probabilistically speaking, it's an even bet for both of us, a jump ball. Mutually-assured destruction, if you prefer to think of it that way. I'd much rather fight this thing out the old-fashioned way—issues, character, blah blah blah—than get into a scandal fight. What about you? You convinced this won't hurt you more than me? Then go ahead and fire the first shot, and we'll find out which side of the coin lands up."

"You're mixing your metaphors, Carnes, but I see what you're saying." He stands up, grabs his tape from the bed. "I'll think it over. You guys keep climbing in the polls, that changes the calculus. Maybe it's a coin flip right now, but if the race gets too close, it could be a chance I'm willing to take."

"Fair enough," Mel says. Relief washes over her. She feels exhausted suddenly. "I hate that the choice is in your hands, but I get that there's nothing I can do about it. Can't say I wouldn't flip that coin myself, if I were in your shoes."

-32 TO ELECTION DAY

The Linda Musgrove story shows up in the *New York Times* and *Washington Post* but no locals. It's not the best timing or placement — Friday papers, near the back of the front section — and there aren't any of those hideous photos to drive it home. An unimpressive rollout, the *WaPo* article just six column inches, below a more compelling piece about the Ollie North-Chuck Robb campaign in Virginia, the *NY Times* story buried amid reports of G.O.P. progress towards capturing the House.

This is just the beginning, Mel tells herself. The feeding frenzy hasn't started yet, probably won't kick off in earnest until next week when the Ohio media has a shot at the story.

She calls a friendly producer in Columbus, learns he has Linda booked for Monday morning, *Good Day Columbus*, 7:30 A-bloc. Mel perks up. That's prime time for the gossip mill. By Monday afternoon, every PTA mom in the whole state will know Dick Musgrove for the battering scumbag he is.

Mel reminds herself not to seem too mirthful, to overplay her hand with the press. She doesn't need Porter's fingerprints all over this story, can't give Kane any ammunition to spin this off as a typical political attack. She can practically hear his obnoxious drawl, playing up the folksy Southern wisdom. *It's a tempest in a teapot, nothing more than negative campaigning from a candidate so desperate to win that he'll say or do anything.* The story has to grow organically, without her interference. Mel has a hard time with this part, letting a leaked story run its course on its own. Her instinct is always to guide and control. She tells herself to focus on what her job is. She looks over the crosstabs, tries to ballpark the bump they'll get. They could very well pull ahead by the end of next week.

Of course, there's the unknown of the DEA tape. If Kane drops it in response to a mounting domestic abuse scandal, all bets are off where the race goes from there. It *should* break her way, but politics doesn't always go the way it should. Mel tries to guess Kane's play here, wonders if he bought the logic that the two tapes side-by-side would make Musgrove look like the bad guy. It's a tough call. If she were in his place, she'd hold off on the tape, let the beating story run its course, even at a high cost, leak the tape in a few weeks—a late-October surprise—bet on gaining back lost ground by creating a negative impression of Porter that her version of the tape has a hard time budging. But that's her. Kane's known for being aggressive in the face of adversity. He loves to counterpunch right away, has to know that the Linda Musgrove story came fresh from Mel's hands however well she hid her tracks from the rest of the world.

She waits anxiously in her office all day, expecting the press to rain down on her with requests for comment on the alleged DEA surveillance tape apparently showing Kyle Porter agreeing to launder drug money. She thinks about the calls she knows Howard Kane must be fielding today, tries not to feel too much *schadenfreude*. It could be her next. It almost certainly will.

The calls never come, at least not the ones she fears. She gets a raft of requests for comment on the Linda Musgrove story—good to know that local reporters still pay close attention to the *Times* and *WaPo* —but she deflects them as much as possible. She's not about to let Porter become part of the story. "As a woman, I'm shocked and appalled," she tells Marvin Blakely at the *Akron Beacon-Journal*, "but that's off the record, my own personal opinion, not an official comment from the Porter campaign."

"We're following this like everyone else," she says to Chris Garvey at the *Columbus Dispatch*, "just hoping it's not true that Dick Musgrove was such a monster to his wife. It's hard to believe a man serving as our state's lieutenant governor could have a skeleton in his closet this big."

"This has nothing to do with Kyle Porter," she says to Jared Block. "The campaign has no position on this, and no, we won't be calling for him to withdraw from the race if it turns out to be true. That's entirely his choice. We're going to continue telling the people of Ohio why Kyle Porter is the man they want representing their interests in the U.S. Senate. Nothing more and nothing less."

When the dreaded call doesn't come by 7, Mel knows today's not the day. She's not surprised. Kane is old-school about news-cycle timing. He'd never leak something on Friday, not unless he wanted it buried. Saturday either, especially with a debate at Ohio State hogging the political coverage. They're safe until Sunday or Monday.

She checks in with Schooley down in Columbus doing debate prep with the candidate, then power walks to her hotel through a chilly drizzle, letting herself feel exuberant again. She checks her copies of the tape in the hotel safe, feels reassured by their presence, takes a quick shower before heading to the Gold Lantern for a much needed Scotch. "Make it a double, Sam." She loves how that sounds, loves even more that her cold has finally cleared out. The Scotch tastes like liquid equanimity, the cigarette she treats herself to the equivalent of an hour of meditation.

Thom Reynolds slides onto the barstool next to her not long after the second Scotch slides off Sam's fingers. She feels excellent and doesn't try to hide it.

"You must be overjoyed," he says. "I never would've pegged Musgrove for a beater, but there it is, huh?"

"I wouldn't say *overjoyed*. A woman's been victimized by a horrible, violent man. Hardly cause for celebration."

"OK, true. I'm sorry for sounding so callous."

"I appreciate you not saying *allegedly* victimized, even though that's technically the case."

"True. But something tells me this one's legit, not just a bunch of irresponsible mud-slinging cooked up by an opposing strategist. For example." Thom eyes Mel with mock suspicion.

She bats her eyes over-dramatically, pulls out a Scarlett O'Hara quote. "*I can't think about that right now. If I do, I'll go crazy. I'll think about that tomorrow.*"

"Seriously, though. This is pretty good for your guy. Obviously."

"I can't comment on that."

"Forgot to mention. We're off-the-record. Off the clock entirely. It's just Thom to Mel." He uses Mel's th-pronunciation of his name. Mel smiles at that. "I give Porter a 10-point bump on this. Whether it's sustainable is another matter, but it looks like we got ourselves a real horse race at last. So good for you."

Mel grinds out her cigarette, hopes she doesn't look too unfeminine doing so. "Let's not talk shop tonight, OK?"

Thom raises an eyebrow, Mel cocks her head towards the door, and they head to Mel's hotel without any further discussion.

Later—it was a perfectly lovely screw but nothing monumental— Mel flips through the channels, lingers on a panel of legal experts dissecting the O.J. Simpson case, discussing how important the racial and gender makeup of the jury could be for the final outcome.

—*Both sides are going to want a female-heavy panel, but for completely different reasons. The prosecution, of course, wants a jury that, underneath it all, is horrified by the brutal murder of a woman, any woman.*

—*That's absurd. The defense is going to want as many black men as possible, a true jury of his peers.*

"Can you believe how long this shit's dragging on?" Mel says. "And the trial hasn't even started yet. Jesus, how much can you say about jury selection?"

"It's exactly like the fucking political news," Thom replies. "Inside baseball endlessly hashed over for an audience that could give two shits but has nothing better to do than keep watching." He gets up, rummages the mini-bar, returns to bed with a Stoli for himself, a Clan Campbell for Mel.

"You're awfully sour sounding, Mr. Political Journalist."

Thom glugs his vodka into a plastic cup. "Don't tell me you don't get sick of it sometimes too." He sips, stares at the TV.

"Of course," she says. "It's an ugly game, and pointless to boot." Mel cracks open the tiny bottle. She's staring at the TV too, her and Thom's toes tickling the bottom of the screen. "All I do, year in and year out, is get these useless white men elected to high office, and I keep doing it, relentlessly, never stopping to think. Never stopping at all. Cause if I stopped to look around, to pay attention to what I've done, I'd realize I was doing exactly nothing. 0.0% impact on the world. And that's not something I care to know."

"Sounds to me like you're perfectly aware. And really, don't you think it might be more like 0.5%. Even 1%? You can't be doing absolutely no good at all."

"I'm gonna put that on my business card. Melissa Carnes. She's not doing absolutely no good at all."

"That'd be pretty funny. But seriously, why do you stick with it, if that's how you feel about it all? You strike me as a woman who could succeed in just about any field she wants. I bet you'd be a helluva sports agent, scooping in 10% on fat contracts and big-name endorsements. No mudslinging or depressing campaign rallies, five-star hotels and Palm Springs get-aways. Tell me I'm wrong."

Mel sips her Scotch, thinks it over for a few minutes. "I'm good at it," she finally says. "And it's challenging. That's a combo I like." She reaches for the night stand, taps out a Parliament. "What about you? You sound pretty sour about politics. Why don't you do something else."

"Seriously? This is the best job I could hope for. I'm lucky to've gotten this far, in *any* profession. In a more just world, I'd be a bartender in Athens, pouring Jaeger shots for drunk college kids. But you. We both know you could do way better, and there's plenty of challenges out there. So there's a little true-believerism in you, isn't there? That's at least part of what keeps you in it."

1994

Mel blows smoke rings, decides to let Thom's question float away unanswered. She does have a touch of TB, she has to admit. There's a hope, deep down somewhere, that electing Democrats is the best way she can contribute to making the world a better place. At one level, she knows it's bullshit—what have the Democrats really done for anybody lately?—but she also knows that letting the G.O.P. have its way is definitely not the answer. So she does her tiny part to keep the barbarians at bay. And she *is* good at it, a 5-1 record at this point. Even if she goes down to 5-2 on a Republican wave, it's impressive. That's 5 fewer asshole Republicans in office than there otherwise might've been.

"I do miss writing sports, though," Thom says. "Sometimes. At least it was honest." He sips his vodka, rolls on his side to face Mel. "That's how I remember it anyway. I'd probably be as disgusted with sports if I'd stayed with it. Fucking baseball strike. Again. Now a hockey lockout. Salary cap debates, draft and free agency analysis that makes O.J. coverage seem reasonable by comparison. I can barely watch ESPN anymore. It's hardly different from *Meet the Press* or *Nightline* sometimes."

Mel smokes placidly, tunes out Thom as he revs up his rant against the degraded condition of American sports and the sports-writing industry.

"Hey, you want to see a Browns game sometime?" he asks. Mel hears the question but doesn't know if it's a logical outgrowth of something Thom was saying or completely out of the blue. "I have season tickets."

"Of course you do," she says.

"Seeing a game live and unmediated is the only true sports experience left for me. Whaddya say? Bengals game in a couple of weeks? Big intrastate rivalry. Not that the Bengals are worth a damn this year."

Mel ponders. Is Thom asking her on a date? Does he realize that's what he's doing? Does she mind if he is, or does that break the strictures of campaign sex?

She pretends not to know the Browns' schedule by heart. "When is it? Next Sunday?"

"They're at Houston this Thursday. Fucking Thursday games. No, it's two weeks from tomorrow. The 23rd."

"We've got a big visit from Clinton 2 days later," Mel says, glad to have a ready excuse. "Could be kind of a crazy time. Can I get back to you on that?" Mel knows how much like a press secretary she sounds. It's a knee-jerk reaction.

Thom gets up, pulls on his pants. "Sure. No problem. Hey, thanks for the, you know, the campaign sex. Couldn't of done it without you. See you at the debate tomorrow, I assume." Mel lets him finish dressing and walk out without either of them saying anything else. It's uncomfortable and embarrassing, and she knows she handled it wrong, but she couldn't bring herself to spin away the awkward moment with a sarcastic remark or a movie quote. She doesn't even know if she wishes she had.

Porter Campaign
Internal Tracking Poll
Musgrove: 45%
Porter: 37%
Harris: 4%
Undecided: 14%

Mel couldn't have designed the schedule any better than this, a Saturday afternoon candidate forum at Ohio State sponsored by the League of Women Voters—they don't call it a debate, but that's what it is—while a domestic abuse story tarnishing Musgrove brews in the background.

Porter read the Friday clippings from the *Times* and *WaPo* that Mel gave him when she showed up in Columbus this morning. She noted that he'd already seen the latest piece in the *Columbus Dispatch*—still no photos but a lot more column inches, 20 in all with a 4-inch leader on the lower left of the front page. Below the fold, but a solid development. He said nothing about the story, and Mel mentioned it only once during their final prep session after lunch. "No need to comment on the Musgrove story. If anyone brings it up, just say you're grieved that terrible things like this happen, you'll do everything you can as a Senator to battle the horrors of domestic abuse—please make sure you say *horrors*—but you have no information about charges against your opponent, and you won't make a judgment before our system of criminal justice has a chance to make a determination about Mr. Musgrove's guilt. Don't say *guilt or innocence*, just *guilt*. Got it?"

Porter demonstrates for Mel. "I'm grieved that terrible things like this still happen in American households, and I promise that I'll do everything I can as a United States Senator to battle the horrors of domestic abuse." He pauses, looks undeniably statesmanlike, a master actor giving it all even in rehearsal. "At this time, I have no information about charges of domestic abuse against Lieutenant Governor Musgrove, and I won't make a judgment before our system of criminal justice weighs in on his guilt."

"Perfect," Mel says. She pats his shoulder, flashes her kindergarten teacher smile of approval, then moves on to run her guy through questions about equal pay, abortion, childcare tax deductions, etc. — the kind of issues they know they'll get from the LWV moderator, a left-leaning independent whose public friendliness with the Democratic Party may push her into being harder on Porter than she's otherwise inclined. At least Mel hopes it does. She wants a tough debate today, real substance. With the negative stuff chipping away at Musgrove from the outside, Porter can make this all about issues and empathy. Mel drives home the need to show a full measure of compassion for the problems and struggles of women, minorities, everybody but the rich white men like Musgrove and his ilk who've been in power too long.

That Porter himself is yet another one of these rich white men bothers Mel more this morning than she usually lets it. Will she ever have a chance to get a woman elected to high office? Or even a true Man of the People? She's generally resigned to just posting another win for the Dems, let someone else worry if they do anything or not while they're in Congress. Politics is a team sport — that's more than just a metaphor to Mel, it's an established truth, a given never to be questioned. She often likens it to football when rallying the troops — the candidate is the ball they're trying to get into the endzone, and she's the quarterback calling the plays and running the offense, but she needs a good offensive line to give her time in the pocket to survey the field, fast, sure-handed receivers to throw to, a good blocking tight end, a stout defense to keep the other team from scoring too much, etc. Everyone gets it, even the few who somehow never learned the basics of American football. When she's looking at her role in politics from a wider perspective, she tends to see politics as a relay-race. At this stage, she has the baton, and she needs to get it around the track faster than anyone else. If Porter gets elected — *when, when he gets elected* — she passes the baton to someone else — his chief of staff, someone with experience on the Hill, with legislative know-how and contacts everywhere — and it's that guy's job to try getting results at the policy level. She hates that Howard Kane's words come back to her, but he's right. *Doing good — that's what someone else does with your victories. That's why you bring them their victories, like a mother bird feeding her young. Without the nourishment of victory, the politician starves, and whatever good he might've done dies with him.* A different metaphor but the same basic idea. She has a specific job right here and right now, and that's to win the election. Nothing else matters. As soon as you start thinking about

January and beyond, you fumble the ball, or drop the baton, or whatever metaphor fits.

Mel tries to set these thoughts aside, focus on her note cards, but as she chain smokes and takes Porter through one last practice run—he's perfect, nails the Man of the People act exactly the way she wants, but he's still just an ersatz version, an actor playing a compassionate leader—she keeps returning to the same thought: Why didn't Mary Boyle win the nomination? If only she'd beaten out Porter, there's be no DEA tape looming over Mel's head, and maybe she'd be putting the next Patty Murray or Diane Feinstein into the Senate, helping further erode the male super-majority. Even if Boyle herself didn't get much done, ticking up the number of women in positions of power would be a good thing in itself. If only the ODP had pushed harder for Boyle, set her up with someone like Mel, a skilled strategist…Mel stops herself. *If only* has no place in her life right now — or ever. *Cut the crap, Carnes. We'd all like to be living in a better world. Fantasizing about it doesn't do anyone any good.*

She grinds out her cigarette, checks her watch, pastes a smile on her face and cuts off Porter in the middle of his bit on paid maternity leave. "That's good, Kyle. Perfect. You got it. No sense in overdoing the prep. There is such a thing as *too* prepared. We wouldn't want you to be unnatural out there. You're 100% ready." She straightens his tie, steps back, crosses her arms, appraises her candidate. "Very nice, Mr. Senator." She wants to leave it at that, but she can't stop herself from one last piece of advice. "Now just remember. When an issue calls for an emotional response, pause and allow yourself to feel the emotion before you answer. If you get a little choked up, so much the better. Don't overplay it, and for God's sake, don't try to fake it. But think for a second how hard some people have it, how legitimately hopeless they might feel, how tired they are after struggling day in and day out to make ends meet in an economy that's leaving them behind. Then imagine you're speaking to a gathering of those people, not a bunch of wealthy white women and a gaggle of media. Got it?"

"Thank you, Ms. Carnes. I believe I've been adequately pep-talked now."

Mel turns him over to Schooley to keep him company for the next 10 minutes and heads for the spin room. She lights a cigarette, paces like a man in a hospital waiting for news of his child's birth. Mercifully, she's alone, which is exactly what she needs right now. In 90 or so minutes, this room will be bustling with media and campaign surrogates tussling over how the debate is received. What's about to happen in front of 1,000 people is only the raw material for the more important struggle later—the fight to have themselves *declared* the winner by the bloviators and opinionators most people will hear about this from. Mel knows she ought to turn on the monitor and watch the debate so she's an informed commentator when the lions come rumbling in for their meat, but it hardly matters. She has her canned lines for the scribblers, sound-bites for TV and radio, the meat already ground, mixed, and flattened into patties. If anything untoward happens, Schooley has instructions to tell her immediately, and she'll figure out how to spin it on the fly. For now, she needs the meditative silence of the empty spin room to rejuvenate, get ready for the onslaught. She paces listlessly, smooches her cigarette, clears her mind of all thoughts—at least she tries to. She can't help replaying her meeting with Kane 2 days ago.

"Speak of the devil," she says automatically when Kane comes in a few minutes later. It sounds more collegial than she wants.

"You talking to your invisible friend again, Miz Carnes?" Kane pulls a cigarette pack from his pocket, shakes it without result, crumples it and shoves it back in his pocket. "Bum one from you?"

The last thing Mel wants to do is share a smoke with Howard Kane, but she's damned if she'll flee the scene, and it seems petty not to let him have one of her Parliaments. The honor code of smokers is supposed to trump any rivalry or animosity, especially on a campaign. She's bummed smokes from the other side plenty of times, shared them back when asked. Even a backstabbing mercenary prick deserves a butt and a light, is how the code operates. Mel wants to take a stand against precedent, draw the line at unrepentant rapist assholes, but the last thing she wants right now is to get into it with Kane a second time, force herself to listen to his smug denials. She shakes out a cancer stick, hopes this is the one that gives him emphysema—not that it works that way, of course—steps away without giving him a light, a small sop to her conscience. Kane pats his pockets, eventually comes up with a tattered book of matches.

He gestures at the inert TV in the corner. "You mind if I turn it on and watch?" It's a real question, Mel believes. Kane sounds genuinely cordial, as though there's nothing more between them than two pros from opposite sides trying to win an election. "I can go out front if you want the peace and quiet." He can sound really sincere and caring when he wants to, Mel thinks. It only makes her hate him more.

She drops to the couch. "Nah, go ahead. Peace and quiet's overrated anyway."

Before Kane can switch on the monitor, Carlton Schooley rushes in, a panicked look on his face. "Mel, there's some pissed-off pro-lifers here, Harris people I'd guess, and one of them yelled from the crowd, demanding that Musgrove and Porter both declare their position on abortion unequivocally."

"And?" Mel tries to remain calm. A nut-job pro-lifer should be Musgrove's headache, not theirs, but Schooley's alarm is contagious.

"Mr. Porter looked straight at her and said, *If you don't like abortion, don't have one.*"

"Oh, that's good," Kane says. "That one of your lines, Carnes, or'd he think that up all by himself?"

Kane flips on the TV, grins with pleasure as the screen comes alive to show Porter in close-up, looking genuinely distraught—not an empathetic listener, as Mel coached him, but pained—while an unseen audience member calls out, *Are you saying that pro-life advocates are intolerant of freedom?* The camera cuts to a 2-shot that shows Musgrove looking calm and dignified as Porter leans angrily into his podium.

"Oh, Jeez, it's gotten worse," Schooley says.

—I want an answer, Mr. Porter. Are you saying that someone such as myself, who knows in her heart that murder is committed every time an abortion is performed, is intolerant of other women's freedom? Freedom to murder is no freedom, and I'll never tolerate that! How dare you insinuate that that makes me anti-woman!

"Why the fuck isn't that bitch of a moderator doing anything about this?" Mel is almost screaming. The sweet smoky flavor of her Parliament turns to ash in her mouth. She flicks her cigarette at the TV, notices Kane's grin widening further and checks her impulse to yell more.

—*We have to build a bridge of tolerance across this great divide in our public, Porter says, more than a hint of desperation in his voice.*

"Just shut the fuck up," Mel mutters.

Musgrove interrupts, his voice steady, his brown eyes twinkling the kind of empathy Mel wants Porter to have.

—*Ladies. Mr. Porter's right. We have to be able to discuss our differences calmly. That's the only way we'll ever be able to find common ground on these crucial issues that face our great country and engage our most concerned citizens.* This elicits only tepid applause, but Musgrove nods like a statesman addressing an adoring throng.

Mel rubs her eyes, pulls out her cigarettes and lights a fresh one. "I gotta hand it to you, Kane. Musgrove is definitely rising to the moment, while my guy…" What the hell is she saying? Why would she ever give that asshole a compliment, even one that's deserved? She shakes her head, leans back, blows smoke rings at the ceiling.

Kane sits next to her, pats her knee.

"Do not pat my knee, you patronizing prick."

Kane holds up both hands. "Hey, I'm sorry. Just trying to show a little compassion here. I've been there, Carnes. No matter how well you prep 'em, sometimes the stupid motherfuckers just fall apart under pressure. Don't take it personally. I'm serious. You look way too wrapped up in this bullshit. You win some, you lose some. It's a cliché because it's true."

Mel holds herself back from explaining that it's not losing a race that bothers her so much as losing to *him*, to a rapist douchebag with the moral fiber of strained peas, and even worse, to that brutal monster Musgrove. Linda's horrifying pictures flash before her eyes. Mel struggles to clear her mind. She turns to the TV, smokes as placidly as she can through the next half hour, Schooley sitting tensely at her side, Kane pacing slowly back and forth, stroking his goatee with a distracting rustle. The room begins to fill up with more of Musgrove's people and the first of the media, a few scribblers bored with the main room looking to get early quotes. She wonders if Harris has anybody here to do spin, if he even knows what spin is, if he's savvy enough to have orchestrated that interruption earlier. Probably No on all counts. She just hopes he stays in the race all the way. He sure as hell isn't costing her guy any votes. Kane must be trying to come up with ways to push Harris out.

It occurs to Mel that Musgrove missed an opportunity with that pro-lifer attacking Porter. Musgrove made a perfectly statesmanlike plea for dialogue and understanding, a decent human response to a divisive issue, but not a very politically savvy move. He could've eviscerated Porter. She realizes how much Musgrove has been waffling on abortion—it's probably that fact more than Porter's predictable pro-choice position that drives those pro-lifers crazy—which is why Harris is still alive and kicking. He's been polling near 5 points, nothing like the percentage of voters who think abortion is murder. He's a slight thorn in Musgrove's side at this point, but that thorn could start to fester if the race tightens. Kane is obviously worried, and if Kane's worried, Mel should be trying to find ways to boost Harris further. When you're down as a Dem, a good third-party run from the right can only help.

Mel shoos away the journalists pestering her for early reactions, watches the monitor with exaggerated attention. She needs to focus. She's tired after a night of fitful sleep—she couldn't stop worrying about her future after Thom's hasty departure—but that's no excuse. She'll be tired for the next month, and she'll just have to suck it up and deal with it. She forces herself to pay close attention to the television, update her talking points as the debate unfolds the way any good strategist would. There might be something she can pick up on to highlight for the press, a scrap of weakness on Musgrove's part to amplify into a damning remark. It was pure laziness to think she could rely on pre-packaged material for post-debate spin, that she could spend the debate in blissful isolation, thinking God-knows-what while the fight raged on in the other room. She let herself believe Porter would glide through like he did the practice sessions, but that's idiocy. You can never relax—not 31 days out, that's for sure. She's not even 30 yet, and she's getting soft. Why else would she need a 90-minute break in the middle of a Saturday?

She perks up as Musgrove takes a question about campaign finance and swings it around to an attack on Porter for taking special-interest money. Porter looks like he's regained his composure, but she tenses. He whiffed on abortion. *Do not whiff this*, Mel says to herself, the closest she ever gets to prayerful.

Porter delivers his rebuttal exactly as they rehearsed it, turns the tables on Musgrove to prod him about his ties to the telecom industry, his troubles with the S.E.C. a few years back, his casual relationship with the Federal Elections Campaign Act. She silently cheers, breathes a literal sigh of relief.

Mel waits for the inevitable question about Musgrove's ex-wife, which she suspects the moderator won't raise until right at the end, after all the issues have been exhausted. She watches with glee as Musgrove lets himself get more huffy than she knows Kane told him to be.

—*Those are unsubstantiated and completely baseless charges intended solely to hurt my campaign. I won't dignify them with a response other than to say that they're categorically untrue.*

"You can't not dignify something with a response, and then give a response," Schooley says, a bit too loudly. "He's toast." He turns to Mel, remembers to whisper in the presence of the media. "Isn't he, Mel? Denying it that way makes him look seriously guilty, am I right?"

Mel shrugs her shoulders, lights another cigarette, checks her watch. Less than 5 minutes left until she has to let the scavengers start picking the carcass. She revs up her mind, gives herself a quick pep-talk, settles on a strategy for spinning this her way. Adversity is what tests a warrior. Porter slipped up once, took a bit of time to get his composure back, but otherwise he did a fine job. Not the kind of bell-to-bell performance she would've liked when Shep's tracking still has them 8 points down, but it shouldn't be hard to get the pundits to call this one a narrow win for Porter. It's a draw at the very worst, though a draw at this point in the campaign is problematic, a missed opportunity.

"Kyle Porter looked like a Senator out there today," she says to Jared Block 10 minutes later. She says about the same thing to all of them. "He showed Ohio that he's a man who can represent everyone in this state, fairly and cleanly. Musgrove looked like another Republican fat-cat with a lot to hide and rich people's interests at heart. I think the choice is fairly obvious."

That's more or less what she was always going to say — it turned out that watching didn't do her much good after all — but it's nice to know that what she said is pretty much the truth. There's a better chance the press will report it that way — a better chance, but no guarantee.

1994

Mel's hangover is ferocious. She grabs the alarm clock, groans at the blurry numbers: 10:42. Shit, she can't sleep in like this, even on Sunday. Especially on Sunday. What the hell are the Sunday morning talk shows saying? Is the Musgrove story gaining traction in the Sunday papers?

She licks her lips, drinks some water, reaches for the remote but tosses it across the room without turning on the TV. "Fuck it." She pulls the pillow over her head, goes back to sleep until the phone wakes her. She fumbles for the receiver. "What? Why are you calling me?"

"Hey, Mel." It's Carlton Schooley's voice. "We were expecting you for a strategy meeting at noon."

Mel looks at the clock—1:07. She rips the covers away, bolts upright. "Goddammit! And you waited this long to call? For fuck's sake, Schooley. If I'm late for a meeting, you give me maybe 5 minutes before you start checking up. Shit moves fast in a campaign. If I'm late for a good reason, I'm late for a good reason, but you need to find that out faster than an hour later. Got it?"

"I'm sorry." He sounds genuinely sorry.

"OK then." Mel tries to power down. She realizes her heart is racing, and it's not slowing. *What happens right before a heart attack?* she asks herself. She knows this is ridiculous. She's not about to have a heart attack. It's just a garden-variety hangover and the normal stress of a campaign.

"Mel?" Schooley prods after a long silence on the line.

"Yeah. I'm still here. I'll be in by 2. Keep everybody around, tell them it was unavoidable. We have a lot to talk about today."

"Fair warning." Schooley sounds worried. "Our new press secretary arrived today. Guy named Kline Braddock. He seems like a real dick." That's strong language from Schooley. He's either gone completely native over the past week or Braddock was pretty horrible. "I'm very sorry to have to tell you this," Schooley continues tentatively, "but he ran the meeting. That's why I'm so late calling you. He made us go around the table, introduce ourselves, tell him exactly what's going on. He ripped us a new one for what happened to Porter yesterday, but gently, you know. Laid out how we should've prepped Porter, which was almost exactly how we did it, but somehow he made us feel, I dunno, like idiots."

"And you just sat there and took it?"

"I know, I know, but he's very compelling. I feel like I was snake-charmed. That's good for us, though, right? You're always saying we need a top-notch press person up front. I think we've got our man."

Mel hopes it's true, but she's worried about having another power struggle on her hands. She knows Kline Braddock only by reputation. It's a good one, exactly what they need, but what if he's another one of these haughty know-it-all men who won't listen to a female boss no matter what? If she struggles to control him, she has only herself to blame. She hounded Tremont to hire a communications director and a press secretary. "We need a real com team, for fuck's sake. This isn't some city council race we're running here. You can't expect me to do *everything*."

Tremont demurred on the com director—he said Mel was more than enough of a leader to need another power center, which she thought was fairly keen—but he promised a press secretary. He interviewed a few obviously unacceptable applicants from the local gene pool then pretty much stopped trying, grumbled that Carlton Schooley would do for the time being.

"He's a smart kid, well spoken," Tremont said.

"Yeah, but he doesn't know shit about deflecting the media, staying on message. He's got TB, you dimwit. We can't have a truebie out there in front of the press. His instinct is to answer everything, straight up. I need a goddamned pro. You've got two days before I put Cliff Barker on it."

She kept her promise, called Barker on Thursday, and he kept *his* promise to get her someone top-notch as soon as possible. Barker must be feeling serious pressure from the top, to act so fast. She didn't expect him to dispatch someone so quickly. Braddock's not messing around either, showing up on a Sunday morning. If she wasn't there to greet him and put him in his place right off the bat, that's on her. She hates herself for screwing this up, for getting caught up in the stress so much that she just kept drinking and feeding the jukebox, yelling over the music to demand that Thom get her another whiskey.

Oh shit, she says to herself. She spins around, wishes she hadn't— the blood whirlpools around her head. She doesn't see any sign of Thom. He must've skulked out earlier, ashamed that he fucked someone so drunk. He had to be pretty drunk himself, matching her bourbon-for-bourbon, or so it seemed. She can't hold it against him, just hopes they used a condom. She drops to the floor, sees the Trojan wrapper tossed away by the radiator, breathes a sigh of relief, wishes she could remember more about last night.

"He thinks we need to step on the gas with this Linda Musgrove story," Schooley is saying. Mel realizes she still has the phone pressed to her ear. Schooley's been talking for a while, telling her god-knows-what. She needs to hang up, take a shower, drag her sorry ass into the office, fix the situation. If only her head didn't hurt so much. She tells herself to cut down on the booze, knows it's a futile resolution. There's a million reasons why pols drink so much during campaigns. She'll dry out over the winter, take her hazard pay for the mission and fly somewhere warm, read trash novels and lie in the sun all day, vow for a few weeks never to work a campaign again, then return to Washington with a ridiculous tan and start all over again. She knows almost no one in the game who doesn't promise to get out of politics as soon as the election cycle ends. It rarely takes.

"Okay, Schooley," she interrupts. "Just sit tight. Don't talk to Braddock anymore until I get there. Keep yourself busy. Go over the debate transcript again, look for something we can smash Musgrove with tomorrow, OK? I'll be there by 2, 2:30 at the latest."

# # # # #

Mel realizes right away that Braddock thinks of himself as a strategist as much as a press man. Great, the last thing she needs is someone second-guessing her directives, pushing the campaign in a different direction, following his *gut instinct* down a path to oblivion. Why do men think their instincts are so trustworthy?

"The way I see it," were the first words out of his mouth. Head pounding ferociously, Mel leans back in her chair and lets him hold forth to his heart's content. He's admittedly a very good-looking man, tall and well-built, lantern-jawed, black hair moussed to perfection. Keanu Reeves plays him in the movie, and people say *I knew Kline Braddock, and that's exactly what he looked like*. He's one of that rare breed of pols who clearly goes to the gym on a regular basis, and even when he's spewing obvious bullshit—Jesus, is he still talking?—he has a gentle smile that hides all sinister intent. If scientists could genetically engineer the perfect press secretary, Kline Braddock would be the result.

When he seems to be done, Mel sits forward, leans heavily into her forearms, lets Braddock see the full bloodshot of her eyes. "Great stuff there, Kline," she says as sarcastically as she can. "I'll take it under advisement, as they say. For now, here's what I need you to do. Our targeted issue attacks on Musgrove are working." She picks up a random folder from her desk, flutters it in the air. "Our latest tracks show him down 4 points after a week of new ads making it clear how bad his ideas are for working people. So we stay on message there — you mention NAFTA and the minimum wage as often as you can — and we keep going with the *Porter's a real human being who cares about the folks* line that's moving the needle with a few key groups. And most importantly, we stay out of this Linda Musgrove business entirely. We do not — I repeat, DO NOT — go negative on this. We stay above the fray, even sound slightly disbelieving. Shep's focus group report is very clear on this. The more we say things like *stunned* and *hard to believe*, the less the shit spatters us. We let the ugliness eat away at Musgrove's lead without any overt help from us. Got it?"

"I disagree," Braddock says. He listened to Mel with arms crossed and a patronizing look on his face, possibly didn't listen at all but just let Mel's mouth move until it stopped. "My feeling about a situation like this…"

"Enough!" Mel pounds the desk, stands slowly, menacingly. "Your gut tells you to go in for the kill — I heard you before — but I have about as much use for your guts right now as I have for a ten-gerbil enema. You're a mouthpiece, Braddock. I know you're a damned good one. That's why Cliff Barker recommended you. But you say what I tell you to say, in the way that only you can say it, and you don't — repeat DON'T! — dare tell me about strategy. You don't know shit — your guts don't know shit — so keep your untrained ideas to yourself and follow my directives down to the letter."

Braddock stands, stares hard at Mel. "Barker didn't just *recommend* me, Carnes. He took me off a key House race and *dispatched* me to help right this sinking ship. I'm not just a mouthpiece here. I'm a key part of the com team."

"I'll fire your ass before you have a chance to talk to a single reporter, you bloviating fuck face, unless I'm one-hundred percent certain you'll do things my way. You hear me?"

"You can't fire me," Braddock says. "I did my homework. Alex Tremont runs the show here. He's guy who signs the checks, and he's the guy who issues the pink slips. The org chart's pretty clear on that. "

"You think you're so smart, dumbass? Go. Talk to Tremont." Mel stabs her finger towards Tremont's office, empty for the moment. Her head is pounding ferociously, her heart racing, but she feels fantastic. She always gets jazzed by these power struggles, admits to herself, in those dark moments when she genuinely asks herself why the hell she stays in this ugly game, that the thrill of putting assholes like Kline Braddock in their place is half the fun of politics. She knows Braddock made a tactical error appealing to a boss he hasn't met yet. That's why he's a mouthpiece, not a strategist—he doesn't consider the entirety of the situation before taking a stand, thinks a cursory glance at an org chart is enough preparation to go into battle with a seasoned pro.

"I'm serious," she adds after a long moment. She sits down again, signaling how comfortable she is with the direction things have gone. "The last thing that lazy asshole wants is a douchebag press secretary on the premises. I had to force him to hire someone. Cliff Barker essentially *begged* him to take you on, then pulled rank and *demanded* it." Mel is making all this up, but it's essentially true. "You make the tiniest bit of stink, you turn *me* against you, and he'll can your flat ass faster than you can say *My gut instinct. Is that understood?"*

Braddock is silent, but his hands are balled into fists, his chest thrust out. He's every bit the gorilla, but Mel senses that he's a beta male, not an alpha. Well-dressed, good-looking, smooth-talking, self-aggrandizing, but essentially non-aggressive. He stares hard at Mel, face set in a mask of simian concentration. This is one of those times, she thinks, when it's advantageous to be obviously hungover. Her tangled hair and bloodshot eyes, the whiskey stink of her sweat even after a long shower—it signals to a beta like Braddock that here's a bitch who'll do what it takes to herd the pack.

"Look, Braddock." She softens her tone, sensing that Braddock is ripe for a lecture. She does, after all, have a superior reputation, and she's definitely right that Tremont will fire him with just the barest of cause, so there's no risk trying to win him over with logic. And she needs him, at least if he's pliable. She can't keep talking to the press all the time, not with everything else she has to do and her own weaknesses when it comes to keeping her emotions in check.

"Let's start again here, OK?" She rummages in her briefcase for cigarettes, talking while she searches. "You're a decent hitter, I'll give you that, but you've been languishing in the upper reaches of the minors. *Key House race*? Might sound impressive to a civilian, but I know exactly what that is. It triple-A ball—at best—no matter how swingy the district. You know it as well as I do. You're looking good these days, so you just got traded up to the majors. U.S. Senate. Majority control could very well hinge on this very campaign. So you're clearly getting your shot here, and I'm sure you deserve it, but you're a utility player, not the star hitter. Not yet." Mel lights her cigarette, aims a wan smile at Braddock.

"You help me win this, and you'll never do a House race again. It's Senate and governor from here on out, might even get to go presidential in '96, a primary run in 2000 at the outside. Who knows? But believe me, you have a lot to learn about strategy. You looked at the org chart, but what about the crosstabs? You even known what crosstabs are? Gut instinct used to work pretty well, but not anymore. It's a data game now. You listening to me, or is your crocodile brain snapping too loud?"

Braddock cracks. "All rightee," he says, trying to sound like he's humoring a crazy person, but Mel knows it signals submission. "She's the boss, as the great poet-warrior Mick Jagger once said." He shoves his hands in his pockets, leans against the doorframe, tries to appear unfazed, as though this is how he wanted things to turn out all along.

"*All rightee*?" Mel arches her eyebrows.

"You're the boss, and we'll do things your way," Braddock says.

"Good. Let's practice." She mimes holding a notebook, does her Jared Block impersonation. "Mr. Braddock, can you tell me the Porter campaign's position on the Linda Musgrove allegations?"

"We're stunned, obviously," Braddock says without the slightest hint of a sneer. He's good, Mel has to admit, the perfect actor for a role that demands it. "But Lieutenant Governor Musgrove, no less than any other citizen, has to be presumed innocent until proven guilty. That's fundamental to our system, gentlemen. Kyle Porter knows better than anyone how important these legal traditions are..."

"Let's try to avoid bringing up the fact that Porter's a lawyer," Mel interrupts gently. With Braddock put in his place, she can afford to treat him the same as she does her other underlings. "Shep thinks the negative perception of lawyers is one of the biggest things hurting us. He's issue-focused. That's the line we take here. Plus, try to avoid saying *innocent*. We don't want to pile on Musgrove too obviously, but it can't hurt to let the word *guilty* dominate the conversation. And try to slip in something about how horrible—no, *horrifying*—the whole thing is. Nothing too overt or direct, but get it in there. Dig?"

Braddock starts again without further prompting, a seasoned pro. "We're stunned, obviously, but it's our position that Lieutenant Governor Musgrove, no less than any other citizen, should receive a fair trial before being judged guilty. Frankly, it's hard to believe that he's involved in something so horrifying, but we'd really rather talk about the issues. That's what the voters of Ohio care about, and that's what Kyle Porter cares about."

"Nicely done." Mel allows herself a satisfied smile. "I knew Barker wouldn't let me down. Now, how about this one..."

1994

Mel gets to the office early Monday morning, sets up at her desk to watch *Good Day Columbus* on the satellite feed, sits in shock as Linda Musgrove calmly and firmly denies the stories of domestic abuse that appeared over the weekend.

—*I have no idea where such accusations could come from, Kelly. I know politics can be a hateful business, but this just seems so...so low. I'm as shocked and appalled as anybody.*

"What the fuck?" Mel massages her forehead, works it out pretty easily. *Goddammit!* She pounds the desk. Her chest tightens. She's been played. Perfectly and simply. *Jesus, Linda is good,* Mel thinks. Even though Mel is the victim here, she can't help but admire Linda for what she pulled off. She saw an opportunity for a payoff, planted a story she knew her ex-husband would want squashed, then negotiated a new divorce settlement more in line with Musgrove's current financial situation. She must've been prepared for years, since he ran for lieutenant governor probably, that folder of fake pictures stowed away at the back of her closet upstairs. That has to be it. There's no other explanation.

"It's goddamned brilliant, really," Mel says aloud to her empty office. *What an actress,* she thinks. And those pictures. So horrible but so fake. No wonder she squirreled them away so fast, wouldn't even talk about letting me have one.

So there goes her Musgrove scandal. If only it lingered for a few more days before getting blown up, some of the negative impression might've gotten imbedded. If only she'd moved more aggressively with the press...She hears the *if only* in her mind, reminds herself to stop, immediately. She has to live with the present reality, forever and always, and in the present, there's no Musgrove scandal, and Kane still has the DEA tape.

Carlton Schooley arrives with the morning papers half an hour later, sees Mel furiously typing on her computer, hair bunched on top of her head in a hastily assembled bun, *Good Day Columbus* still playing on the television. He stops in the doorway, waits for Mel to look up, listens to the hosts banter about the latest trend in youth birthday parties sweeping the area, magician-clowns who make balloon animal rabbits disappear and reappear to the delight of children across the state. He clears his throat loudly.

"What is it?" Mel says without looking up or slowing her typing.

"I know public polls are bullshit, boss." He advances cautiously to Mel's desk. "But the *Akron Beacon Journal* has us just 5 points down." He lays the Akron paper to the side of Mel's keyboard, points to a headline in the upper right corner of the front page. SENATE RACE TIGHTENS WITH FOUR WEEKS TO ELECTION DAY. The poll shows Musgrove down to 44% and Porter at 38%. Harris is up slightly at 6% with 12% undecided.

Mel glances at the numbers, resumes her typing. "We have new tracks from Shep?" she says sharply.

"I haven't talked to him yet. It's only 8:15."

Mel glares at Schooley. "*Only* 8:15? It's exactly 4 weeks and 1 day until the polls open, and our best bet for taking the lead just blew up in our faces." She stalks to the television, snaps it off with a fierce twist of the knob. She turns to Schooley, remembers that it's not his fault that she got played by that conniving…she won't let herself say the b-word, even in her mind. However manipulative, Linda is still a sister in the broader struggle, a woman who's been kept down by the patriarchy, her talents and intelligence obviously greater than the position she's attained — the woman is certainly fit for more than a secretary's desk — and now, by the looks of it, she'll get more of what she deserves. And after all, what did she do to get it? Made it harder for one privileged white male to win an election over another privileged white male. It shouldn't matter that Linda was false and underhanded to another woman. Mel's deeper loyalties to the women's rights cause stop her from judging Linda too harshly, even if it's merited. Men stick together when it's a matter of protecting male privilege. If women stuck together more, despite whatever else divided them, they might be further along in their struggle for equality.

Mel drops into one of the chairs facing her desk, realizes Schooley has been watching her with a mixture of curiosity and alarm. Did she mutter any of those thoughts? She brushes off the possibility, takes a deep breath to tamp down her rage. She pulls the fresh pile of newspapers into her lap, turns to the inside page of the *Beacon Journal* to see what Marvin Blakely has to say about the latest movement in the polls.

With pro-life independent candidate, Joe Harris, holding steady in the 4- to 6-point range for the past month, it would appear that Mr.

1994

Musgrove's largely non-committal stance on abortion has yet to hurt him significantly, though Mr. Harris's continued presence in the race could potentially cost Mr. Musgrove the election if he is unable to regain the voters he seems to have lost over the past several weeks.

"Shithead," Mel mutters. *Why didn't I think of that myself?* She's about to start beating herself up but remembers immediately what George Stephanopoulos said to her during the '92 primaries, when it was looking bad for Clinton over his claim that he smoked but didn't inhale marijuana. "It's hard to think straight when you're getting your ass kicked all the time." Mel tries to remember that whenever she gets angry for missing something obvious, or taking too long to figure out how to tackle a weakness in the crosstabs. She always comes up with something, even if it takes a while.

Schooley stands obediently, waiting for Mel to explain why she just said *Shithead*. He looks like he's sure Mel means him.

Mel jumps up, erases the whiteboard, starts scrawling notes. "Goddammit, Schooley, why haven't I been paying attention to abortion? Don't answer that." She keeps writing, the strategy flowing out of her. They need to move Porter up, there's no doubt about that, but breaking off more of Musgrove's base is equally important. For every point Musgrove comes down, they're that much closer to taking the lead, even if that point goes to Harris instead of them. She's been so focused on getting back Musgrove's share of traditional Democratic voters and cutting down the size of the undecided vote that she didn't think about putting the pro-lifers into play. She knew Harris was out there — she was glad for the conservative independent candidate as a distraction for Musgrove — but she didn't move to put Harris in play in any significant way. *Divide and conquer.* It's elemental. The question is, how to help Harris without making it look like they're helping Harris?

She's back at her computer, rewriting her strategy document for the week, when Kline Braddock shows up, dressed for combat in gray flannel slacks, starched white shirt with a dark blue tie, his newly installed *Porter for U.S. Senate* button pinned on a navy double-breasted jacket. He looks ready to jump on a yacht and sail to the French Riviera with some buddies from the Skull and Bones Club. "How's it hangin', boss lady?" Somehow he manages to make it sound both condescending and sincere at the same time.

Mel sees a small padded envelope dangling from the tips of his fingers, notes that he has a cat-that-ate-the-mouse smirk on his face.

"You see *Good Day Columbus* this morning, by any chance?" she says.

"Not personally, no, but I got a call from a friendly at the *Dispatch*. Guess we got all excited for nothing, huh?" He doesn't mention that she was right that they should stay out of it.

Braddock widens his smile, looks down at the envelope as though noticing for the first time that he's holding something. He tosses it to Mel without warning. She bobbles it awkwardly, ends up smacking it onto the floor back towards Braddock's feet. He plucks it from the ground, holds it out for Mel with a grotesque version of a chivalrous grin. He even says, "M'lady."

"Seriously, asshole? This is how you're treating me now? Try not acting like a douchebag for one second, would you."

Braddock looks like he's about to protest the name-calling, but he holds back, forces his smile even wider. "Just open it." He sounds like a kid on Mother's Day, certain he finally got mommy the exact thing she wants.

Mel flutters the envelope, hears a rattle that sounds like a cassette tape. "What's behind door number one?"

"Open it and find out. It's a kind of apology gift, courtesy of someone I know in the Musgrove campaign. A friend of a friend of a friend, really."

Mel eyes Braddock suspiciously, tears open the envelope as he sits and gracefully crosses his right leg over his left. He has the posture of a British duchess about to host a tea for the queen.

It is a cassette. Mel ejects her copy of *Tuesday Night Music Club* from the boom box on the shelf behind her desk, replaces it with Braddock's gift. She hesitates before pressing Play, notices that Braddock has leaned back to close the office door all the way. His leer tells her nothing.

"Don't worry. You'll enjoy it. I promise."

Mel sits on the edge of her desk, presses Play. The lead-in hisses loudly, followed by a click that sounds like a door closing softly. There's a scuffling or shuffling, papers possibly, or someone getting comfortable in a chair, a distant sound of multiple phones ringing, a soft burbling of office chatter, the words indistinguishable, everything slightly muted as though recorded from a concealed location, which Mel images must've been the case. She crosses her arms, waits patiently, feels Braddock's presence behind her.

A clicking again, clearly a door opening and closing, then Howard Kane's unmistakable Texas drawl.

—You wanted to see me, sir?

—*Sit down Howard*. Musgrove. No doubt about it. *We need to talk about this abortion memo*. There's a rattling of paper.

1994

Mel turns to Braddock, raises her eyebrows. He nods and flicks his finger off the tip of his nose. She never would've pegged him for an aficionado of *The Sting*. They're both tensely silent, as though they're actually eavesdropping on Kane and Musgrove.

—What about it? I thought it was completely clear. You know this is how we have to come at Harris. He's the only reason you're not completely burying Porter. We lock up the pro-life vote, nudge Harris out of the race, and it's game over.

—I'm just not comfortable saying these things. I know a lot of my constituents take a very strong stance against abortion, but I'm not convinced this is the right way to go. I'm a firm believer in small government…

Mel almost hoots with joy. She begins pacing behind her desk, hand on her forehead as Howard Kane interrupts his candidate.

—Not convinced? Who the fuck needs you to be convinced? You're running for the U.S. Senate, a seat held by Democrats at the moment. You say what you need to say to take it for our side.

—I know, but I…

Kane talks over Musgrove.

—*And then you don't do shit about it again, until and unless our oafish president appoints some pro-choice liberal to the High Court. Then you make a quick statement explaining your No vote for confirmation, and that's the end of it until you run for re-election, and we repeat the drill, exactly the same. You're not auditioning to play the role of God, so there's no need to wrastle with your conscience about it.*

—*I understand that, but couldn't I say something a bit more in line with how I really feel?*

—*And how is that, exactly?*

Mel can tell that Kane is on the verge of exploding. Her chest tightens slightly as she imagines sitting in Musgrove's chair, weathering that Mephistophelean glare. For the briefest of moments she admires Musgrove for even bringing this up. He has to know he's going to lose this argument, right? Mel forgets that she's listening to a tape that could potentially destroy her opponent, or at least tear off another 5 or 8 points and hand them to Harris, propelling Porter into the lead. With Harris strengthened, they could maybe pull this off. This is a gift from heaven, courtesy of Kline Braddock and some unknown mole in the Musgrove operation.

There's more shuffling of papers.

—*I took the liberty of writing up my own version of your statement.* There's a long silence with background office noise and the occasional guffaw from Kane, then the unmistakable sound of paper being balled up.

—*A man of conviction?* Kane says with dismissive scorn. *That's how you want to play this? Seriously?*

—*I thought it sounded pretty good, Howard. It shows that I've got moral fiber, that I'm not just a hack who coughs up the party line whenever it's convenient.*

—*Listen, Dick. That 'man of conviction' bullshit will reverberate for about 10 minutes, max, and then all any Republican voter will remember is that you're anti-life. That's exactly what they'll say in their beady little conservative-base brains. Anti-life. You got that? You wanna be the anti-life candidate, you go right ahead, but I may as well pack it up right now if you do, take one of these nice pieces of ass from the secretarial pool for a week in the Caribbean.*

—*Come on, Howard. It's not like…*

—*Don't 'Come on, Howard' me, you fucking boob.*

Mel raises her eyebrows, turns to Braddock with a genuinely gleeful look on her face.

"Holy shit, really?"

"Just wait. It gets better." Braddock and Mel are chummy now.

—*That asinine statement of yours is political death. Whoever told you you could think for yourself? I sure as shit never did. I know Haley Barbour never did. You don't get to have convictions, you stupid motherfucker. You hear me? You're a Republican. You have to act like one every second you're in public, and that means you're staunchly, unwaveringly pro-life until and unless we tell you otherwise. Got it?* There's a pause. *I said GOT IT?*

—*Jesus Christ, Howard. Calm down.*

There's a loud thumping, a fist on a desk most likely.

—*I will NOT CALM DOWN until you tell me you understand what I'm saying! You will read my statement to the press, and you will read it like you mean it.*

—*I just don't know if…*

—*You will read my statement,* Kane repeats with quiet intensity. *And you will answer questions as though you're personally convinced that every abortion, at whatever point in the pregnancy, is exactly and only the murder of a living human being with the right to life protected by our sacred motherfucking Constitution. If you can't do that, you may as well drop out of the race right now and practice telling your kids why daddy never made it past lieutenant governor.*

—*You're certain I can't play up the small-government angle?*

Mel can tell Musgrove is crumbling, but it hardly matters what else he says. The tape is pure campaign gold. She has to hand it to Braddock

1994

for this one. He knows how to make things happen. And what a coincidence. Mel doesn't believe in fate or kismet or whatever you call it, but this tape, arriving precisely when she realized how little they've capitalized on the Harris campaign to slice into Musgrove's support—whatever it is, it's perfect, one of those rare moments when you feel like everything is going your way. She has an answer to her question about how to help Harris, and what a beauty it is.

She huddles with Braddock for a few minutes to discuss how best to roll this out, whether to try moving it through the Harris people or leak it themselves. Mel is inclined to use Harris as a pass-through to distance Porter as much as possible. "Secrecy is key here," she tells Braddock. Even the least curious political hack is going to wonder where a tape like this came from, and there's a risk that its impact could be dampened if it looks like Porter is playing dirty politics.

"Negative works to a certain extent," Mel says. "Always has and always will, but the blowback is problematic, especially in an off-year. Americans hate ugly politics, at least they *say* they do. They respond to it all the time, but they're also turned off. In a mid-term cycle it's extra important not to give people a reason to stay home. We need excitement in our base. We need those undies to put us over the top. We get splattered with a reputation for playing dirty, we lose a lot of potential voters to low turnout."

"So we obviously have to pass this through the Harris people." Braddock sounds certain, but he looks unsure. So much for his so-called gut instincts.

"It's risky, though," Mel says. "They're complete amateurs. His wife's campaign manager. You should've seen her in the spin room after the debate. Horrible. He could have 10, 15 points if he knew what he was doing."

"He will, if we work this the right way."

Mel realizes that Tremont, for once, is the answer. "We need to run this past Tremont." She grabs the boom box. "He might know someone in the Harris campaign reliable enough to pass the tape to. One good thing about Alex. He knows everybody."

They march across the office and stand in front of Tremont's desk in identical poses—feet spread slightly apart, arms crossed over their chests—while he listens. Even Tremont has to grin when Kane begins yelling.

"Where'd you get this?"

"I have my sources," Braddock says.

"You've got a mole in Musgrove's camp?"

Mel can tell Braddock desperately wants to tell Tremont how he managed to infiltrate the opposition in such a short time, but he puts on his press secretary face and says, "It's not appropriate to discuss that at this time."

Mel suppresses a smile, realizes that Braddock is now fully her guy, this denial an obvious act of loyalty to her desire for secrecy on this matter.

"Look, Alex, it doesn't matter where we got it." Mel picks up the boom box, lets it swing gently at her side. "The only question is, what do we do with it? I'm inclined to drop it anonymously with the Harris people. You aware of anybody over there who'd know how to use it the right way?"

"No one. It's barely even a campaign in the traditional sense. His wife's running the show, and she's a complete amateur. President of the Ohio chapter of Operation Rescue. Good connections among the hard-core evangelicals, but it doesn't take much more than a newsletter endorsement to motivate that crowd. They've got no paid staff, zero media presence outside pro-life talk radio. It's mostly a word-of-mouth operation fueled by a bunch of volunteers with no idea what they're doing."

Mel lets herself be impressed by Tremont's knowledge of the Harris campaign. Apparently he's not just sitting here all day doing crosswords and directing traffic among the volunteers coming and going to knock on doors.

"So we have to do this ourselves," Mel says. "I don't like it, but if there's no other way."

"We could send it directly to Harris," Braddock suggests. "Include a typed note from a whistleblower type, someone working for Musgrove because she thought he was a pro-life Republican, then got disillusioned when she figured out he's soft on baby killers."

"Right, but how'd she make the tape if this is the conversation that clarified that for her? It stretches plausibility a bit far, don't you think?"

"You think Harris is going to put it together like that?" Braddock raises an eyebrow. "At worst, he does nothing, and we leak it ourselves next week."

"I'd rather not wait that long," Mel says. "With the Linda Musgrove story fizzling, we need to keep Kane off-balance. We hit him with this while he's still on the defensive, and it has a bigger impact. Let's use your whistleblower letter, but do a mass mailing to all the major Ohio papers. Somebody close enough to Musgrove and Kane to plant a tape-recorder like this would have the savvy to use their press list to get the word out."

1994

"Yeah, but aren't journies more likely to sniff out the lie than Harris?"

"True. So..." Mel puts down the boom box, pats her pockets for cigarettes. "We just send out copies of the tape, no cover letter, no explanation, nothing. We drive down to the Columbus suburbs for a postmark away from but relatively close to Musgrove HQ, and when the story hits in a couple of days, we go the same route we did on the Linda Musgrove story. Deny knowledge of the source, express shock at the vulgarity and political calculation of it, assure the public that we say what we mean and mean what we say, that the actual issues are important to us. Unlike, apparently, our opponent."

"I can work that angle," Braddock says.

# # # # #

The rest of Monday is a relatively quiet and somewhat normal day for a Senate campaign 4 weeks out. It's nonstop busy for everyone at Porter HQ, with phones ringing off the hook and critical planning functions running into unforeseen problems—the order for new lawn signs is late, the principal of a school where they're holding a rally calls to report a schedule conflict, etc.—but there's no actual crisis brewing and nobody seems to be on the verge of a complete freakout. Not unless you count Mel's constant worrying that Kane will drop the DEA tape at any moment now that the race is tightening, but she keeps that to herself.

Braddock brings Mel a banker's box filled with copies of the tapes, packaged neatly and addressed by hand by one of the secretaries. He's followed closely by Schooley delivering Mel's usual lunch, ham-and-cheese on wheat with mayo and lettuce, a bag of Lays potato chips, Diet Coke.

"Hang on, Schooley," Mel says. "You have a car, right?" He nods. "Nothing major going on this afternoon?"

"Not really, no. Why?"

Mel glances at Braddock.

"I'm not sure about this," Braddock says. "I can rent a car. I should really do this myself."

"Do what?" Schooley asks. He looks back and forth between Mel and Braddock.

"Nah," Mel says to Braddock. She pulls open the bag of Lays, crunches a chip, talks while she's chewing. "You've got a full afternoon drafting debate answers. We're scheduled to meet Porter at the mansion tonight at 6 sharp to start prepping him for Thursday. Plus, I trust Schooley here. You're completely reliable, right Number Two?" Mel knows Schooley is a *Star Trek: The Next Generation* fan, sees his chest puff out slightly at the reference to Commander Riker. She crunches another chip, pops open the Diet Coke.

"Whatever you need, Captain." He looks like he's suppressing a salute. His chest seems to puff out further.

"It's decided, then." Mel wants Schooley in on this for some reason. Maybe it's moral cover, or maybe she wants to see how he'll react to this little piece of *realpolitick* they're pulling off. She tells Braddock she'll ride with Schooley down to Columbus. She needs to get out of the office, get some air to help to reformulate their strategy in light of new developments. Schooley has a good ear to pour her ideas into. He's shaping up to be a decent deputy, asks good questions, listens, prods Mel to think more sharply.

Mel is unsurprised by the sensible car — '91 Toyota Tercel — but the musical selection throws her. "Really, Schooley? Sarah McLachlan?"

"That's my girlfriend," he says defensively. He ejects the tape and tosses it in the back seat as they pull onto Euclid Avenue. Mel notices how messy it is back there, a real shock. She wouldn't have bet on a car filled with loose cassettes, old newspapers, soda cans, crumpled fast-food bags, a box of *Porter for U.S. Senate* buttons rattling noisily amid the mess. Schooley is always so put together around the office. His car must be the place he lets loose. The front seat, at least, is relatively free of detritus, just a couple of unopened Gatorade bottles on the floor. She tosses the Gatorades in the back with everything else, settles her briefcase at her feet, wonders how the girlfriend feels about the backseat garbage dump.

"Whatcha want to hear?" Schooley turns around while he's driving, roots through the pile of cassettes, glancing back at the road just in time to see a stoplight.

"Jesus, just watch the road, OK?" Maybe this wasn't such a good idea. Mel braces herself against the dashboard as the car jolts to a halt. She pulls a copy of the Kane tape from her briefcase. "I've got something good right here." She slides the tape into the car radio. "Consider it part of your political education."

Schooley settles his hands at eight and four, glides onto the freeway as he listens to Kane berate Musgrove for his foolishness.

— *You're certain I can't play up the small-government angle?*

— *Look, Dick. I know principles are important to you. Seriously. But how much do you think you can do for the world from the Lieutenant Governor's office? You want your principles turned into reality, you want to reduce big* government, get people off welfare, scale back our overseas commitments, cut corporate taxes?

— Yes, of course I do.

— You gotta get that Senate seat, then.

— I've got a big lead, Howard. Why do I have to pander to these pro-life extremists when I'm already cruising to victory?

"Extremists?" Schooley says. "Did a Republican Senate candidate just call pro-lifers *extremists*?"

"Indeed he did," Mel says. "Keep listening."

...ever assume you're going to win, not til the last votes are counted. I've been doing this a lot longer than you have, dipshit. Your lead's already eroding. Hasselbeck told me this morning that he's got Porter up to 37 and us down to 46. That's too close for comfort. Way too close, when there's still 12% undecided and a month to go. You understand how tenuous your position is? Now that he woke up, Porter's starting to eat into our share of Reagan Democrats. We have to solidify our right flank, get Harris the fuck out of this race by nullifying the pro-life protest vote. Then we can start feeling secure.

Mel ejects the tape when it's over, watches Schooley processing what he heard as they race down I-71 at a bone-rattling 87mph—another surprise that Schooley's such a speed demon.

"What are you going to do with that tape?" he asks after almost 5 minutes. "And why are we going to Columbus to do it? We're not confronting Kane with this, are we?"

"Hell no. This is a surprise attack, all the way." Mel lays out the plan, watches Schooley closely to see how he reacts to his first experience with the underhanded side of politics. She tries to remember her first time. Was she ever as naive and idealistic as Schooley? Would this kind of thing have surprised her 22-year-old self? Probably not. Even before she graduated from college, she was fully prepped in the realities of modern politics. She can't remember being anything but overjoyed at the back room maneuvers she saw in her first position at the DNC, watching Paul Kirk and his lieutenants take the Senate with an 8-seat bump and expand the House majority to 258, then to 260. She wonders what Schooley's profs at Ohio State told him. If he never learned how polls really work, what the hell did they fill those kids' heads with? Civics nonsense? God, she hopes not.

Schooley gives no indication of what he's thinking, pulls off the highway at a desolate exit somewhere south of Mansfield, about halfway to Columbus. He screeches into a Duke-Duchess station, jumps out to pump gas, leans in the driver's side to ask Mel if she wants anything from the store. "This place has amazing creamed chicken sandwiches," he says. "Used to stop here every time I drove home from college. I'm getting one."

Mel accepts, can't believe how delicious it is, wonders why she never caught on to the great Ohio creamed chicken sandwich. "Goddamned amazing," is all she can say.

When they're done eating and the foil wrappers are thrown in the back seat with the rest of the garbage, the car flying south at 87mph again, Mel broaches the subject. "So, Number Two. What do you make of our plan?"

"I'd be worried that Kane might spin this back the other way," he says. Mel is impressed that he's thinking like a strategist, not a moralist.

"How?"

"I mean, the ugliness is mostly on Kane's part, right? Musgrove's actually trying to take a stand. He caves in the end, but he comes across as a genuine man of conviction. What if Kane spins it that way? He doesn't have many options, once this recording goes public. What else could he say? *It's a pack of damned lies. We never said those things. This tape has been faked. It's an outrage.*" Schooley does a decent impersonation of Kane.

"I doubt it," Mel admits. "Too risky." She thinks about her own fake tape.

"Then he's got no choice other than flying into the teeth of the thing. There's some decent sound bites for Musgrove in there. Man of conviction. Small government. *I'm not just a hack who coughs up the party line whenever it's convenient.* That's a great line."

"Damned sharp thinking there, Number Two." Mel is truly impressed. "You've got a future in this game. And what if Kane does go that way? How do we counter? Given, of course, that we're not the ones leaking this tape."

"I'm not sure how much it would help overall, but what if we take the morally outraged stand? Agitate for Kane's resignation. I know that doesn't directly hurt Musgrove, but it'd be a black eye. A shake-up like that at the top of the campaign, so close to the election, could be a mess for Musgrove, right? There's confusion, uncertainty, maybe a power struggle. If Musgrove's top aides think he's going to win, they'll all be angling for staff positions on the Hill. A 6-year term's forever. They'd be set, career-wise. So they'll fight to get made campaign manager as a sure ticket to chief of staff."

"Is that why you're working for Porter?" Mel asks. "You looking for a 6-year stint on the Hill?"

"Sure, why not?"

Mel continues to be impressed. She hadn't pegged Schooley for the ambitious type. He manages to seem like an idealistic doofus while he's actually planning a long-term career trajectory, getting in on the ground floor of a campaign that could take him to D.C. for life. *Not bad, Number Two*, she says to herself.

"But we're getting off-topic," he says. "I don't see, off the top of my head, anything better we could do if Kane goes that way. We try to use it as a wedge to create chaos in the Musgrove camp. Because honestly, Mel, as an average Ohio voter, I'm not that put off by what I heard Musgrove say."

"It's not the average Ohio voter we're looking at here. It's the pro-lifers. There's sure as shit more than 5 or 6 percent of the Ohio electorate who think *Roe v. Wade* was a travesty. If we can peel those people off Musgrove and hand them to Harris, keep that idiot in the race all the way to election day, we're in good shape. In a 2-way race, you need 50% plus one. That's a tall order for Porter—for any Democrat—in today's political climate. But in a 3-way race, you just need the most votes. You know what percentage Abraham Lincoln got in 1860?'

"Thirty-nine point eight," Schooley says without hesitation.

"And Bill Clinton in '92?"

"Forty-three on the nose."

"We could hold this Senate seat with a similar number if the other 60% is sufficiently fragmented. You heard what Musgrove said. *Pro-life extremists*. That's *our* sound bite. Forget *man of conviction*. Of course that's what Kane's going to play up. You're absolutely right about that. If he doesn't, he's slipping, and trust me, he's not slipping."

Mel remembers the DEA tape again. She obviously can't tell Schooley about that, but she wonders what he'd say. Kane's other obvious response to this leak is dropping the DEA tape and watching Porter sink even faster than his own guy. If that's how he plays it, is Mel really going to counter with her fake? She was so certain when she had Ernie make it that it was the only possible response, but she's been having doubts since then. Will Porter go for it? Will she have the guts to release it by herself if he doesn't? Will it even work? Maybe Tremont was right that there's no Hail Mary pass here. Maybe it's just better to go with a flat denial rather than pile fraud on top of scandal.

They're nearing the Columbus suburbs when a wall of brake lights appears out of nowhere over the crest of a hill. Schooley brakes hard, swerves into the shoulder to avoid rear-ending the car in his lane. The Tercel fishtails, skids to a halt in the gravel. Mel gets her hands up to the dashboard just in time to stop herself from smacking her head on the windshield.

"Jesus Christ!" She sees the car behind them shoot past and jam into the rear bumper of the car Schooley just evaded, a horrific screech of metal on metal, airbags exploding open. The rear car angles into the middle lane after impact, the corner of the rear bumper cutting off another car sliding to a halt, the car behind that plowing into its trunk. Glass shatters, more airbags deploy, another crashing sound somewhere Mel doesn't see. Horns blare and tires screech. Mel looks over her shoulder, sees the line of cars behind them stopping fast. Bumpers come perilously close to each other, but no more damage occurs.

Mel blinks at the cars next to them, less than an arm's length away. They're crumpled together into a hideous 8-door metal monster, the front end of the second car completely merged with the trunk of the lead car, the windshield spiderwebbed, the driver's head resting against the cracked side window. Mel's heart races and her hands shake as she realizes how much worse it would've been if they'd been in between, a double rear-end compacting the Tercel into a 2-person coffin.

Schooley jumps out of the car before Mel has a chance to think further. She unbuckles her seatbelt slowly, fumbles unsuccessfully with the door handle, suddenly remembers the box of tapes in the back seat. She turns to verify it's still there, undamaged, realizes what a disaster a car wreck could've been, her and Schooley in the hospital, Braddock's box of tapes in the hands of the state police. Her heart is still racing. She takes a deep breath to calm down, then another. Her hands are shaking worse now, but she manages to get the door open. It smacks into the car next to them, but it hardly matters. It's already totaled, the driver immobile, hands glued to the wheel.

Mel tries to focus on the current situation, scolds herself for worrying about politics rather than the lives of real human beings thrust into a sudden tragedy. She gets out carefully, peeks into the totaled Chevy, holding her breath and expecting a gruesome sight. She breaths again when she sees the driver let go of the wheel, put his hands over his cheeks, turn slowly to peer over at Mel. He's clearly in shock, but he's alive, seems to be unharmed. Mel steps around the front to survey the scene, a 6-car wreck that has the highway backed up for a half-mile down the hill. At least there's good visibility now—the cars approaching their wreck have plenty of time to slow and stop. She looks the other direction, sees the original problem, a tractor-trailer angled across two lanes about a quarter mile ahead, a Ford Escort on its side in the shoulder, the stoppage occurring at precisely the worst spot for cars speeding over the crest of a hill with no visibility to the accident ahead. It could've been a lot worse, almost certainly would've been if Schooley hadn't reacted so quickly to avoid slamming into the car stopped in his lane. At 85mph, she and Schooley could've been killed. Easily.

The headline pops automatically into Mel's mind. TWO DEAD IN SIX-CAR WRECK ON I-71. The story might run just below the latest Musgrove-Porter poll. DEMOCRAT NARROWS DEFICIT IN SENATE BID ONCE THOUGHT DOOMED. It wouldn't be until the next day that an item buried in Section 2 would announce her death. KYLE PORTER'S CHIEF STRATEGIST AMONG DEAD IN YESTERDAY'S SIX-CAR ACCIDENT.

She drops to the hood of the Tercel, hands shaking, knees trembling. This is her first near-death experience, the first time she's faced anything like mortality in the 15 years since her mother died. She can't help flashing back to the hospital, the tubes and machines, the hopelessly frail woman she couldn't imagine living without, her hand cool and smooth, lying weakly in Mel's as she tried to keep being a parent until the very end.

"Do something worthwhile with your life, poppet. Don't waste your one chance on Earth getting distracted by the shiny things. Make it count."

Nothing too heavy to lay on a 15 year-old—just the weight of the world. Not that Mel has ever blamed her mother. She had a few months to do all the rest of the parenting, to impart all the wisdom for a lifetime. She was just 40 herself, hardly a wizened sage, though she looked exactly that at the end, shrunken and pale, almost translucent, barely able to talk above a whisper, Mel leaning close to capture every word, stifling tears so she didn't miss anything.

"Please, sweetie. Just make your life count for something. Promise me you'll try your best."

Mel has done what she can not to let the memories harden into perfection, to avoid sanctifying her mother's every word and gesture from those final weeks, but it's hard not to feel that she lost the most amazing person who ever lived. The fact that Mel spent the next 15 years of her life pushing those pearls of wisdom out of her mind as soon as they showed up speaks to her own weakness, not any imperfection in her mother.

Mel begins to cry—nothing dramatic, no racking sobs of exaggerated grief, no teeth gnashing or pounding the hood with her fists, just hot tears dropping to her lap as she watches Schooley in full-on Boy Scout mode. He's been moving among the stopped vehicles, making sure everyone's alright. This is the Carlton Schooley she's come to know over the past 2 weeks, not the shrewd political calculator he just proved himself to be. He checks on the damaged cars, tells people not to move if they're hurt—thank God everyone's alive and conscious— dispatches someone to the closest emergency callbox, gets the flares out of his trunk to mark off the accident, finds a volunteer to direct traffic into the one lane still open, comes back to check on Mel.

"You OK, Mel? You're not hurt, are you?"

Mel wipes the tears with her sleeve, nods and sniffles. "Yeah, just a little freaked out, is all. I'm fine."

But not really.

Just make your life count for something.

And has she? Has she done something worthwhile? Could she face her mother and point with pride at what she's done, or has she been distracted by the shiny things? The dark things, is more like it, but distracted nonetheless...

TUESDAY, OCTOBER 11TH
-28 TO ELECTION DAY

Mel sits in Tremont's office hiding her hangover, slight nausea and a headache slicing from her left eye to the back of her skull, a pretty typical mid-October feeling. She calls its Political Morning Sickness, not to be confused with that other PMS, which she's also experiencing at the moment. Her rebellious body would be manageable—she's handled it in this state hundreds of times—if she didn't have to wrangle with Tremont over schedule changes at the same time.

"I don't give a fuck about the Cuyahoga Democrats or the Toledo Chamber of Commerce," she says. The scheduling bulletin board that normally hangs in her office lies on Tremont's desk like a custom board game, pushpins holding down 3x5 cards in a perfect grid, appearance locations, event details, contact info, all neatly penciled in Carlton Schooley's magna cum laude handwriting. She has PostIt notes over the entries for Wednesday, Thursday, and Friday mapping out a new agenda, a trip down the spine of steel and coal country—union hall speeches and meet-and-greets at shift-change time outside mines, mills, and factories, 2 1/2 days of good old-fashioned retail politics, the very thing Tremont was focused on when Mel arrived.

She normally favors a more population-intensive approach at this stage in the campaign, big speeches whenever possible, lots of press interfacing, a fresh set of ads every few days, but with the whistleblower tape, as Braddock calls it, about to hit the news, Mel wants Porter out of the spotlight for a few days. She realized last night, before the mini-bar took her away to unconsciousness, that a trip out east among the vulnerable working class was just the ticket to limit Porter's visibility until the next debate on Friday. She also has some ideas for new ads to shoot among miners and mill workers. Location shots and real voters are gold in spots like that.

"We have to get Porter out on the road," Mel explains to Tremont. "When that tape hits, we need to pump up the outrage but keep Porter himself above the fray as much as possible. Right Shep?"

Mel brought along Shep Blumenthal to provide backup. Shep never wavers when it comes to the perception of negative campaigning. "Every focus group I've done in the past decade," he said to her last week, "demonstrates the same point. Negative works, but only as long as people aren't consciously aware it's happening."

"Supporters and spokesmen can say nearly anything without major backlash," Shep says to Tremont, "as long as there's some kind of factual backing." He steeples his fingers, looks exactly the way Mel wants him to look, a wise man of politics. He's just the sort of older white male Tremont is conditioned to believe. "But as soon as the candidate himself says it, or the official campaign ads pile on, it turns people off in a major way, even if it's true. Musgrove's been investigated by the S.E.C.? Mel or Braddock points that out to the press, not Porter. I've seen a candidate drop 7 points practically overnight for calling his opponent a tax cheat, even when the proof-positive turned up a week later. You have his press secretary say it in a backwards way. *It's hard for us to believe Mr. So-and-So would cheat on his taxes, but...* And it's a bump instead of a dip."

Tremont seems singularly uninterested, sits worrying his toothpick.

Shep taps his forehead, fully in lecture-mode now. "It's basic psychology. Our brains evolved to detect immediate threats, so we're not equipped to make associations 2 or 3 steps away. You see a lion rushing at you across the savannah, you don't curse God for making it so flat and empty all around, for making the lion hungry and you look like dinner. You see that lion and you run, and when you make it to safety, you *thank* God that you're still alive. The lion takes all the heat, and God, the real culprit, comes out looking better than ever."

Mel has heard basically the same thing from every pollster she's worked with, and it's become an axiom of her strategy. When you go low, as you almost always have to do, keep the candidate up high. He's God in this scenario, reporters the lion. She's got Braddock prepping to deploy his quiet outrage as soon as the tape hits the news, at which point she'll be at Porter's side in some dead-end town with a steel mill at half capacity, a mine closed for a decade, double-digit unemployment and a lot of anger at a government that doesn't seem to care anymore, keeping him focused on the troubles of real Ohioans, not the scandal. The plan is, Mel will travel with the candidate for a few days—not something she normally likes to do, but necessary in this case—holding him at arm's length from reporters, offering "No comment" on the story roiling around Musgrove and Kane.

1994

"We can't cancel the Fairfield County Fair," Tremont says. "It's the last county fair of the season. That's an essential stop."

"Where is it?" Mel asks. She sounds testier than she intended. She knows she can bully Tremont into whatever she wants, but she'd rather get his buy-in, make this as smooth as possible.

"Lancaster, just southeast of Columbus."

"Fine," Mel says. She'll throw Tremont a bone. "We'll detour up there for 2 hours on Thursday morning, between shift changes, work the corndog stands and cow stalls—no speeches—then we're back down to the southeast until Friday afternoon." She scrawls a note on Thursday's PostIt.

"No way," Tremont says. "He has to do his stump speech, then stand there with the local slate. County commissioner. House candidate for the 15th. Mayoral candidate, too, I believe." He bends his head to read the notecard. "5pm. The Fairfield Democrats will be mightily pissed if he skips out."

"Tough titty, Alex. Let 'em be pissed until they can start bringing in more votes. Fairfield County's a total loss for us, a plus-20 for Bush in '92. It's bullshit we're even going there for 2 hours."

"There *are* some Democrats down there, Mel," Tremont fires back, uncharacteristically stubborn about this goddamned county fair. "Porter shows up, they get excited, we get an uptick in turnout."

"Enough with the turnout bullshit. Porter shows up, gives a slick speech, reminds Republicans how smooth and good-looking the devil is, they turnout *against* him. It's a wash at best, probably a net loss, and all in a county where something like 40 or 50 thousand votes will be cast, max. If we had better demographics down there, a decent-sized working-class base, I'd be fine with it, but it's a waste of time, and time is not something we have in abundance, in case you haven't noticed. Two hours working the midway, and that's my final offer."

"This isn't a horse trade, Carnes. I'm still running the show around here, if I'm not mistaken."

"And you'd still like to win, right? Who's the one who narrowed the gap from 18 to 5 points in just 2 weeks? If I say we skip the Fairfuck County Fuckfest, we oughta just skip it, no questions asked!"

"Jesus, Mel, calm down. You're gonna give yourself a heart attack."

Mel roots around in her briefcase for her Parliaments. "Look, Tremont. We need those votes down there south of New Philly. They're outside the major media markets, probably don't already have an opinion of Porter the lawyer we have to fight. He spends some Q.T. down there shaking and kissing, and we might have a fighting chance to actually win some of those Bush plus-5s like Gallia County, Morgan,

Washington, Muskingum. Just as key, we need to shore up support in all the Clinton plus-5s along that spine. Tuscarawas, Carroll, Guernsey. Noble was a dead split in '92."

"There's really a Guernsey County in Ohio?" Schooley says. He's been lurking behind Mel, watching and listening as instructed. He looks every bit the Mormon missionary today, unfazed by their brush with death, not the slightest hint that his car is a rolling garbage heap.

Mel scowls at him as she lights her cigarette. She reminds herself that Schooley's quick reaction may very well have saved her life, even if it was his insane speeding that put it in jeopardy in the first place. She has mixed feelings about the whole thing, residual shakes and an existential funk mixed with gratitude that she's still alive. She drank away the whole pile of messy emotions last night, but they're seeping back in as her hangover recedes.

"All right, Carnes." Tremont pushes the bulletin board away. "Have it your way. You've got it all figured out, as usual. You want my rubber stamp, here it is. Schooley, you call the Cuyahoga Democrats and the Toledo Chamber. Break the news, see if we can reschedule for next week. I'll have Cindy start booking hotels."

Shep comes back later in the morning, knocks on Mel's door and pokes his head in. She's huddled with Schooley, finalizing the details of the trip.

"You guys wanna see the latest tracks?" Shep eases inside, holds out his signature plastic-covered report. "It's decent news up and down the line. I have us within 2 points, 41-39." Mel flips quickly through the charts, looking for soft spots and rays of genuine good news. The data comes from a 4-day rolling call bank, which includes the 2 days when the Linda Musgrove story was beginning to brew, so she's not as excited as she might otherwise be. If only the abuse story had had more time to embed a negative impression of Musgrove before it got exploded. The fact is, most voters probably never heard the story, and Linda's denial yesterday ensured that anyone who did hear about it would get the idea that the whole thing was Porter slinging mud. But the data also tracks the Sunday and Monday reaction to Saturday's LWV debate, so there's bound to be something in there with legs.

Mel shoos Schooley out, sits at her desk and marks up the new crosstabs. She knows they tell an overly optimistic story, but it's a useful exercise nonetheless. Something moved the needle, and it wasn't just the Linda Musgrove story. She lets herself believe they're really reaching the people, though she notices right away that what's happening is more a decline for Musgrove than any real gain for them. They're only up 2 points over Friday's tracking numbers, while

Musgrove is down by 4. Harris picked up 3 of those 4 points, and the undies are about the same, down a click to a still-high 13.

That's fine. Musgrove comes down, they ease upwards, maybe Harris grabs some more of Musgrove's pro-lifers, and suddenly he's under 40%. Then it's a race to grab up the undies, which is where Tremont's get-out-the-vote effort could actually be the deciding factor.

Mel is particularly pleased about the way the black vote has moved up over the past week. They may end up giving back the suburban college-educated women who came over after the Linda Musgrove story first hit, but the uptick in African American support is more likely to stick. Last week's schedule was purely about solidifying the black vote. While she was in New York on Tuesday, Tremont took Porter through Cleveland's Glenville neighborhood, going door to door among businesses rebuilt only recently, after years of decay following the Glenville Riots of '68. She starts humming "The Revolution Will Not Be Televised" when she thinks about Porter walking down 105th Street, shaking hands and promising a brighter day.

> There will be no slow motion or still life of
> Roy Wilkens strolling through Watts
> In a red, black and green liberation jumpsuit
> that he had been saving for just the right occasion

On Wednesday, when she was in Chicago following her fool's errand with Linda Musgrove, Porter worked the Warren Sherman neighborhood in Toledo, visited a job-training center serving a predominantly African American clientele, ate fried chicken at Church's, finished with a speech at the Lucas County public library about tackling embedded poverty by expanding federal support for adult-literacy programs. Thursday they sent him down to Cincinnati to work Avondale and Bond Hill, decrying the policy of redlining and promising to push the Justice Department to fight more actively against de facto segregation. Friday morning, before he holed up in the Hilton Columbus for debate prep, he bounced through the Near East Side, working the more affluent African American neighborhoods that were starting to show a tendency to drift Republican. On Sunday, while Mel stayed in bed sleeping away her hangover, he sat through the services at the True Holiness Temple, an influential black church in Cleveland's Hough neighborhood, another area decimated by late-'60s race riots. She pictures Porter, trying not to look too self-congratulatory as Bishop Dixon pitches his candidacy with the circumspection of a minister barred from saying directly, *Vote for this man right here for*

United States Senate. She had the pleasure of watching Dixon do his thing for Bill Clinton in '92.

— We gather this morning in this holy place, bound by our faith in God, with genuine respect and love for the great democratic processes that give us a voice in the government of a just and mighty nation. We seek not to approximate the perfection of our all-powerful, all-knowing, all-loving God, but only to redirect our nation on a more humane, just, and peaceful course. No, we are not a perfect church, and we are not a perfect people. Yet, we are called to a perfect mission, as the Reverend Jesse Jackson reminded us in 1984. "Our mission," he said then, and it's even more relevant to us today. "Our mission: to feed the hungry. To clothe the naked. To house the homeless. To teach the illiterate. To provide jobs for the jobless." And so, when you go to exercise your God-given right to vote in a few weeks, keep in mind who supports this mission, and strives always to carry it out, and do your duty by God and country, and make the righteous choice.

"Even if these numbers hold," Mel says to Schooley when he comes in with her lunch, "we're still behind, and the easy pickups are dwindling. One-seventh undecided. That's what worries me. We're not making our case with these undies. Not in a way that's reducing uncertainty in any meaningful way." She pushes the sandwich aside, pulls out her Parliaments and lights up, gazes at the ceiling with a long sigh. "What the hell do they still need to know?"

"Maybe they're not paying attention yet."

"Baseball's on strike," she says, mostly to herself. "So's hockey. And basketball hasn't started yet. Football's only on Sunday. What the hell are they watching?"

"*Seinfeld*? *Roseanne*? I'm a big fan of the *X-Files*. It's got pretty good ratings."

Mel glares at Schooley. "I wasn't looking for a literal answer."

"Sorry. It sounded like you were."

"Jesus, Schooley." Mel clenches her teeth, softens when it's obvious Schooley is just being accommodating, like always. "Okay, magna cum laude. You've had a chance to dig through the numbers. You're a smart guy, and you're obviously catching on fast. Tell me what you think. Why aren't we doing better with these undies?"

Schooley unwraps Mel's sandwich, takes a bite. Is this some kind of power play he's pulling, Mel wonders. He takes his time chewing, a test for Mel's patience. She smokes as placidly as she can, pops open the Diet Coke.

"I think there's a lot of Democrats out there who might vote Republican," he finally says. He dabs his mouth with a napkin, delicately opens the bag of chips. "But they're afraid to say it to a pollster because they're, I dunno. Embarrassed? Ashamed? Not sure they'll actually do it?"

Mel snatches the Lays before Schooley can start eating her chips. "Reverse-halo effect? The lawyer thing still?"

"I think it's more of a social desirability bias. You're a lifelong Democrat. Everyone you know is a Democrat. Your wife, your parents, your co-workers. But you're fed up. You voted for Bill Clinton, but you're severely disappointed, didn't get what you paid for. Or maybe you voted for Ross Perot, a protest vote that went nowhere. Either way, you're not a Republican, but maybe you're ready to roll the dice, see where this Contract With America takes us. Only you can't really admit it. Not over the phone where your wife and kids can hear it. Probably not even to yourself. So you take the safe way out. Undecided. They don't know we call them undies, right? There's no shame in it. Far less shame than saying you're going to pull the lever for a Republican for the first time in your life. Or you *might*. Maybe you won't. Who knows? So you hedge."

"Fuck me, grasshopper. That's pretty good."

"Man who catch fly with chopstick accomplish anything." It's a fairly decent Mr. Miyagi, the first time Schooley has let fly with a timely quote. He's coming along nicely.

"Yeah," Mel says. She grinds out her cigarette, dumps the overflowing ashtray into the trashcan, pours some chips into her hand. "But how do we catch these sons-of-bitches?"

"To make honey." Schooley smirks. "Young bee need young flower, not old prune."

"All right Miyagi, that's enough. I'm being serious here. What's it gonna take to win over these goddamned undies? That's your assignment for this afternoon. Now get out and get to work." She pushes the chips into her mouth, crunches loudly as Schooley leaves. "And close the door behind you," she mumbles through a full mouth.

Mel spends the afternoon painting her whiteboard with ideas, doodles of hardhats and coal wagons mixed in with arrays of interlocking crosstab data and catchphrase ideas — *New Approach to Old Problems* and *Smarter Government, Not Smaller* — multi-headed arrows linking circled groups, tying together isolated ideas and clumped sets of numbers. This is how she thinks best, an untamed snarl of thought in all forms — visual, verbal, numerical, metaphorical — that eventually coalesces into a coherent whole, even if no one looking at the board would be able to detect it. No one but her. Her hangover is a distant memory, her existential funk as well, menstrual cramps tamped down with a handful of Advil, the strategy flowing out of her like rhymes from a rapper.

When daylight runs out, she power walks back to the hotel and holes up in her room with room service and the mini bar, writing TV ads and radio spots to support her plans, CNN on low volume across the room to keep her tied in to the day's events, mostly bad news for the Dems. Pretty typical these days. She's dimly aware of a Musgrove ad, wheels around to grab the remote off the bed, turns up the volume and watches with a cat-ate-the-mouse grin as Musgrove looks straight at the camera and delivers Kane's unequivocal pitch to the pro-lifers.

— *The life of every unborn American is as precious as any of our national treasures. As your United States Senator, I'll work tirelessly to guarantee that these lives are protected from the heartless liberals who condone the wholesale murder of innocent babies throughout our land.*

"You have no idea what's coming, do you?" she says quietly, smiles a Grinch-y smile at the TV.

She mutes the volume, takes a glug of Scotch, goes back to her notepad. She writes out a new line as neatly as she can, reads it in her best Kyle Porter impersonation. *"We spend 24 billion dollars a year for 150 different job training programs, most of which don't train people for the jobs that are actually out there in today's economy."* She switches to her deep narrator voice. *"Kyle Porter is a successful businessman, so he understands what it takes to get the economy growing. Training for real jobs. Support for struggling workers. Investment in small businesses. New approaches to the problems Americans face today."*

Mel nods, rubs her forehead, writes.

```
PORTER: I'll shut down the programs that don't work
and push for new ones that do. Washington should
spend our money on things that create real jobs and
real opportunities. What we need is smarter
government, not smaller.
```

She double underlines *real*, reads the line out loud. CNN catches the corner of her attention again, a bright blaze against a dark landscape, fire trucks, police, reporters. The ticker reads FIREBOMBING AT OHIO ABORTION CLINIC. She snatches the remote, unmutes the volume.

...have provided a few confirmed details. At around 9:30 PM today, an arsonist snuck onto the premises of this Lima, Ohio medical clinic, one of only two in Allen County that performs abortions, and set off what fire officials believe was an incendiary bomb that, as you can see, has now enveloped the entire building in a massive blaze. No one has yet claimed responsibility, but

a state police spokesman believes that a radical anti-abortion group is most likely behind the attack. We'll have more as this tragic story develops.

Mel drops to the bed, hatred coursing through her body. Goddamned anti-abortion radicals. Porter's misguided quip comes to her unbidden. *If you don't like abortion, don't have one.* That's not something a politician can say, but it's goddamned right. Killing abortion doctors, burning down clinics — in the name of protecting the lives of the unborn? Fucking hypocrites! Mel's passion stirs, a reminder of why she works so hard to beat callous assholes like Dick Musgrove and Newt Gingrich. They encourage this bullshit, beat the drum for these primitive fuckers who care so much about controlling women's lives that they're willing to firebomb a medical clinic to do it. She bunches her fists, jumps to her feet, paces a U-shaped path around the bed, back and forth, outrage and sadness battling for supremacy in her mind.

When women gain even the tiniest bit of independence, a little more control over their bodies, the forces of reaction come crashing down around them, the anti-progress parade led by a howling pack of so-called Christians. Where's the moral outrage over rape, over domestic abuse, over poverty and homelessness? If these conservative Christian assholes care so much about the message of Jesus Christ — the last shall be first, the meek shall inherit the earth — why aren't they fighting for those causes? Fucking sheep, is what they are, mindless motherfucking sheep! They think God will take care of the meek as long as we force kids to pray in public schools and don't ever make a move to curtail anyone's precious gun rights, as though Jesus Christ Himself founded the NRA and walks around Heaven with a pair of Colt-45s strapped to his belt. If J.C. has the backs of the innocent and the weak, Mel always wonders, how come there's still so much bad shit going on in the world? She clenches her teeth, remembers what she heard recently at a diner in Nebraska — a sentiment she's heard before in various forms — that God's punishing America with rising crime rates and broken homes, unemployment, dead soldiers in the Middle East, all to show His displeasure with our toleration of abortion. Yeah, *that* makes sense! It's *not* because we're shitty to our fellow human beings and let them suffer all around us without lifting a finger to do anything but write a check to pro-life assholes who countenance firebombing a goddamned medical clinic. That's your Christian conservative logic for you. Forget about the message of love and tolerance that's central to the New Testament, turning the other cheek and rendering unto Caesar. It's the angry tribal God of the Old Testament that gets the blood flowing, the firebombing of Sodom and Gomorrah, Abraham ready to sacrifice his firstborn to placate a God so insecure he has to play mind games like that. No wonder these Christians are so fucked up, with a Lord so twisted and unpredictable, his hippie son tortured to death, one of his calmer moments sending down the Flood—a real genocide if ever there was one, nice work there God.

Mel beats the pillows ferociously, like she's training for a fight with Apollo Creed. *God! Damn! Fuck! You! God! Damn! Fuck! You!* This goes on for nearly 5 minutes.

She drops facedown on the bed, panting from exertion. "I am going to take you down, you pandering piece of shit," she mutters through gasping breaths. She unflexes her fingers, rolls on her back trying to catch her breath, the hatred receding slowly as she blinks up at the blank ceiling, struggling to empty her mind of useless outrage. What's the point? She's not going to enlighten any of those idiots. The best she can do is keep them from taking over everything, use her genius to hold the line against the mercenary Rethuglicans who'll say anything to keep turning out the reliably righteous Christian vote, while doing pretty much everything Jesus was preaching *against*.

She gets up eventually, maybe 30 minutes later, grabs another Clan Campbell from the mini-bar, sits at the desk and looks over her notes. Her impulse is to scribble over everything and start fresh, but she stops herself, reminds herself to think calmly. *The best way to beat those bastards*, she says to herself, *is to stay focused on the best possible strategy. You've got it right here, Carnes. Don't be led astray by emotion.*

1994

-27
6:43AM

Most of what Mel wrote the night before holds up when she rereads it at the breakfast buffet. She sips her coffee, fights the urge to light another cigarette — she's had 6 this morning already, well above her usual quota.

She's reworking the ad she calls "New Approach" when Thom strolls up half an hour later, press badge dangling, notebook at the ready, dopey smile on his face and sensible shoes planted firmly on the carpet. It reminds her of the morning she first saw him in here. She counts in her head — it's just 12 days ago. Seems like 2 months at least.

"Thom Reynolds." She sticks with her th-pronunciation. "To what do I owe the pleasure? And so early on this beautiful Wednesday morning."

"I don't suppose you'd care to comment on that abortion-clinic bombing last night."

"Say what now?"

"It's all over the news. Tell me you haven't seen it?"

"Haven't been watching TV." Thom raises a disbelieving eyebrow. "I've been buried in work." Mel puts a loving hand on her pile of notepads and printouts, hopes the lie is somewhat convincing. She's not sure why she's lying to Thom about not seeing the story — protective instinct, probably. She didn't anticipate having to face the press so early, hasn't even finalized what she wants Braddock to say when he gets the inevitable calls this morning.

It's a tricky situation. They want Harris to eat into Musgrove's support, and this kind of thing plays badly for the pro-life candidate. His hard-core supporters won't have a problem with it, and at this point, all he's got are hard-core supporters. But his slice of the pie won't grow unless he can shave off some of the more moderate pro-lifers parked in Musgrove's camp for the time-being. Mel was hoping the whistleblower tape would accomplish that, but the firebombing changes the strategic situation. Kane is obviously going to pull those pro-life ads she saw yesterday, send Musgrove out to express nondenominational sympathy and ratchet up his usual rhetoric about law and order, try to make this about public safety, not abortion.

In this context, Mel's not sure if the whistleblower tape will even play to their advantage. It'll be easier for Kane to spin Musgrove as a man of conviction, a stronger play in this new environment. She almost wishes they could get those tapes back, but they're beyond Mel's control now. It won't hurt Porter, not directly — not as long as he keeps his foot out of his mouth — but it might help shore up Musgrove's sagging numbers, get him moving in the other direction again. What seemed like a brilliant jab yesterday could end up being a complete nothing, even a touch harmful.

"The campaign doesn't run itself, you know." Mel offers a pursed smile, pats the chair for Thom to sit.

"And the morning news isn't work for you?" Thom asks. He remains standing. "Come on Mel. Just say 'No comment,' if you want, but don't sit there and lie straight to my face."

"I'm serious." Mel decides to stick with the lie. "Shoot me for skipping CNN every once in a while. I've got a million balls in the air. So just tell me. What's got your panties all in a bunch?"

Thom recaps the story, watching closely for Mel's reaction. She sits stone-faced as he goes through the details known so far. The state police have identified a man and his two sons as the likely culprits, anti-abortion activists known for picketing the Lima clinic, throwing jars with preserved fetuses at the feet of young women trying to go inside, sending hate-filled screeds to the local newspaper.

"State police got a warrant based on that. Flimsy, if you ask me, but there it is. What judge is going to say *No* with all that national media covering every mote of the story? Anyway, they found bomb-making materials in their house. As of 6:30 this morning, they haven't located the guys yet, but they're hot on the trail. It can't be long before they're apprehended. They're not experienced criminals, just a bunch of misguided terrorists on the lam. Staties'll haul them in by noon, you watch."

"They calling them *terrorists* on TV."

"No. Course not. That's just me being me. If I used that in my article, the editor wouldn't even think twice before red-penning it."

"But they *are* terrorists, right? If they did the same thing to a government building, in protest against, I dunno, Desert Storm or NAFTA or some such, we'd have no problem calling them terrorists. Why do these anti-abortion radicals get a pass? They're terrorists. Let's call them terrorists." Mel realizes too late she's said too much, let her emotions get the better of her. She's lucky this is Thom, not Jared Block or Chris Garvey.

"Is that your official campaign statement?" Thom poises his pen above his notebook.

"Gimme a break, man." Mel grabs Thom's pen playfully, slides it behind her ear. "One-hundred percent off the record. In fact, you didn't even see me here. Call Kline Braddock for official comment. He gets in at 9."

# # # # #

Mel usually hates getting stuck chaperoning a candidate, but she's glad to be out of the office this morning. It'll do her some good to be on the road for a few days. She'll be forced to drink less, smoke less, watch what she says. Normally she hates all that, but she's looking forward to it this time. That brush with death, and now this abortion-clinic bombing—it's got her shaken up. Lashed to Porter's side for the next 3 days, she'll have to stay focused on what's right in front of her, a man of the people running for U.S. Senate, asking for votes from vulnerable, aggrieved workers with fraying loyalty to the Democratic Party.

Mel's hope for a quiet ride to Youngstown—they're going to hit a steel mill first, to shoot the footage for her "New Approach" spot—gets dashed when Porter's brother-in-law jumps in the van with him. Before the door is even closed, he informs her that he's coming along to observe, maybe offer some advice.

"This is Ronald," Porter says. "He's my wife's younger brother."

"Son of an ex-governor," Ronald adds quickly. "Been eating and breathing politics since the day I was born."

"And what day was that?" Mel lets slip.

"March 8th, 1970," he replies without hesitation.

Great, Mel thinks. *Another twenty-something dabbler.* She can tell by the look on Ronald's face that he has big plans to insert himself in the campaign. Why can't all these men just leave well enough alone and let her steer the ship? She knows the answer to that one. She wonders if she'll ever get to work a campaign with more women than men, without having to spend so much energy deflecting power grabs. Probably not.

Ronnie, as he insists on being called, asks Mel if she's seen Musgrove's latest TV ad.

"You mean the pro-life spot?"

"Not that one. It's new as of this morning, best I can tell. *How can you trust Kyle Porter? He's been repeatedly sued for false advertising, and his law firm has been sued for malpractice dozens of times. If he lied to his clients, why wouldn't he lie to the people of Ohio?"*

Mel didn't see that one. Kane must've had it in the can already and switched over as soon as the Lima bombing went down. He doesn't miss a trick, doesn't ever fall behind. The one bright spot with the whistleblower tape is that it could take The Shark out of the game. Braddock's ready with the appropriate outrage over the obviously mercenary advice Musgrove's getting, the best angle they could take given the dicey abortion situation. Getting Kane out of the way isn't exactly the victory Mel would've liked, but it's not a bad second choice. He leaves the campaign in disgrace, the rapist son-of-bitch, and whether or not Porter pulls out a surprise victory, Mel has some measure of vengeance. Plus, she'll rest easier for the next 4 weeks knowing Kane's out of the picture. He might even bury the DEA tape rather than pass it along to his replacement. Probably not, but Mel can hope.

"He's gone flat-out negative," Ronnie says. "Must be getting desperate. I saw Greg Blumenthal's numbers this morning. We're almost even, but there's a big chunk of undecideds out there. I have some ideas about mopping them up."

Great, he's got access to Shep's data too? Is he angling for her job, or Tremont's? Or does he just want to be senior advisor, wield power without responsibility, influence without risk? He dressed for the part, perfectly tailored charcoal pinstripe suit, light blue shirt, purple tie in a double-windsor, matching handkerchief in the outside jacket pocket. He checks his watch, solely, Mel thinks, to show her how expensive it is. "How long's the drive this morning?" he asks.

Ronnie seems completely different than when Mel saw him the first time. She wonders if he's a mild schizophrenic, whether he'll go whacko on her again, and if he does, when. If it's soon, she'll be able to ditch him. She wonders if it's risky to try provoking him? In front of Porter it is. She can't jeopardize her standing with the candidate by engaging in an obvious power struggle with a family member. So far Porter trusts her completely. If she loses that, she loses everything.

The drive is excruciating. Mel has to listen politely while Ronnie alternates between half-informed analysis of the crosstabs — at least he knows what they are, but he clearly doesn't know how to break them down effectively — and completely over-the-top ideas for a set of attack ads he thinks they should to start running ASAP. His attack lines do hit Musgrove's vulnerabilities, but he's entirely lacking in overarching strategy, doesn't listen when Mel tries gently to indicate the dangers of going negative so overtly.

1994

Mel checks on Porter before becoming more adamant. He's reading over the briefing report she prepared for the trip, studying his new part like a good actor, attention completely absorbed. Mel decides she can risk being more overtly dismissive of Ronnie's ideas. If Porter picks up some of it incidentally, that's fine — he could use to hear it too. She runs down Shep's pat argument about subtle negativity versus overt, uses his lion-chasing example, concludes her lecture by assuring Ronnie that they're already doing everything necessary to show the pubic Musgrove's ugly side.

"That's all fine and good," Ronnie says when she's done, "but Musgrove's clearly thrown all that wisdom out the window. The gloves are off, and I say we punch back. Hard."

Mel takes a deep breath, controls her urge to punch back in a more literal and immediate way. "See, here's the thing. If Musgrove's attacking us like this, it must mean he's at least a little desperate. His internal polling must indicate something that's not showing up in ours yet. Howard Kane — that's his campaign manager — Kane knows everything I just told you about the dangers of going negative. So if that's the way he's going, he must sense a vulnerability we don't see yet. This abortion-clinic bombing, for instance. That's potentially going to hurt him, no matter what he comes out and says officially. This is the kind of thing that riles up liberals, and that's a turnout boon for us, potentially gains us a chunk undies. That's undecided voters. Kane's preemptively trying to limit the bounce we'll get from this, hoping to bait us into sinking to their level so the usual disdain for mud slinging cuts equally both ways. I know how this guy thinks, believe me. We're not taking the bait. He goes low to draw us in, but we don't follow him there."

Ronnie narrows his eyes. He's clearly not buying it. Mel decides to throw him a bone. "For now, at least," she adds. "If it comes down to it, we can put together some ads like the ones you described, roll them out right before election day. If — and that's a big *if* — if the situation calls for it."

Mel has a chance to push Ronnie harder when they're at the steel mill to shoot the new ad. Porter is off getting his makeup done. She guides Ronnie to the catering table, picks up a bunch of grapes while he smears cream cheese on a bagel.

She leans in, makes it look like she's being conspiratorial. "Look, fuckwit," she says beneath her breath. She double checks that Porter is far out of earshot. "I don't know what you think you're doing on this trip, but your half-witted little brain doesn't know a tenth of what's going on, and I don't have the time or the inclination to catch you up.

You're a nuisance here, at best. A hungry little mouse sniffing around for crumbs of cheese. Only mice don't even eat cheese, you ignorant bed-wetter. They eat grain and nuts. People just think they eat cheese because of cartoons. That's what you know about politics—what you've seen in cartoons. That's what it's like for a kid watching his dad be governor—it's a cartoon. Pianos and anvils falling on people's heads, and everyone walks away with stars circling their heads. It's a lot messier and way more subtle than that. So take my advice and get the fuck out of my campaign before you embarrass yourself and lose this election for your brother-in-law. You think that's what your father or sister want? Huh? I'm talking to you, dipshit."

Ronnie's eye moistened as Mel spoke. He drops the bagel and stands stiffly, hands clasped in front of his penis in an unmistakable posture of weakness and fear. Mel has hit exactly the right note, her supposition that he's mildly schizophrenic right on the mark—or close enough to do the trick. Whatever he is, he's not 100% stable, not strong enough for hard-ball politics. He's a trailer park in tornado country. It looks like he might actually cry. This was all too easy, or so Mel thinks until Ronnie bounces the other way.

He grabs the grapes from her hand and hurls them across the room. "You fucking toady bitch," he yells. The crew turns to look. "Do you know who you're talking to?"

Mel stares him down, waits for the mania to subside.

"I'm a goddamned governor's son!"

"*Ex*-governor's *son*," Mel says quietly but intensely. "You've never won an election in your life, and you're not going to prove to daddy how smart you are if you fuck up this campaign. So back off, rent a car, and drive back to your mansion before I call your father and have him tell you this himself. You want that? Huh?"

Ronnie's gone by the time Porter's makeup is finished, a thin twig she snapped with ease. Not that it gives her any pleasure. She relishes her wins over men like Alex Tremont and Kline Braddock, but backing off a sniveling child like Ronnie Travis is hardly a prize. She feels a little dirty, even though she did the absolute right thing. Maybe she could've been a little more gentle and still gotten the job done. Mel starts to feel guilty, then stops herself. *Men don't feel guilty when they beat other men into submission*, she reminds herself. *Why should I?*

1994

Mel wakes before the alarm, reflexively grabs for the pack of Parliaments on the nightstand, scolds herself away from a first cigarette and suits up in her jogging shoes for a pre-dawn power walk. She's going to stick to her resolution to treat her body right while she's on the road with Porter, maybe catch the habit and carry it through for the rest of the month. It's not likely, but a girl can dream.

Zipping through the eastern part of Steubenville, she notes a lot of old brick houses that've seen better days, more than a few with FOR SALE BY OWNER signs, a church every couple of blocks, not much in the way of anything happening. Dean Martin was born here—that's the extent of Mel's Steubenville-specific knowledge, other than the basics, demographics and leanings, economic condition and political relevance. It's the seat of Jefferson County, which broke for Clinton 2-to-1 in '92, though that would've given him what? 20,000 votes? 30 at most. Not a big haul to be had around here—not in any of the counties this little stay-out-of-Cleveland tour is taking them through.

It's good for Porter, though, gets him out here among the struggling blue-collar families he's nominally the champion of, snagging some sympathetic coverage from the small press pool along for the ride. There's a van for the half-dozen pencil pushers and radio jocks, Dan Barnaby from the *Cincinnati Enquirer*, Marvin Blakely from the *Akron Beacon Journal*, Kate Winkler from the *Washington Post*, a guy from Ohio Public Radio whose name she always forgets—Clyde or Clive, something like that—and a local radio commentator from Youngstown, Biff Something, or Bill. Bill Byers, she thinks. Ever since Braddock came onboard, she's less scrupulous about keeping the reporters' names straight. There's also an Akron TV crew with its own van and nothing better to do, looking for a surprise scoop, she supposes, Porter punching a pro-life protestor, or marching into a courthouse somewhere to yell *I object!* and get the case dismissed on a technicality. What do they imagine they're going to see other than endless footage of the candidate shaking hands, saying, "I'm Kyle

Porter, running for U.S. Senate. I'd sure appreciate your vote"? Idiots. At least they're not obtrusive, don't try to shout questions at him, trick him into saying something embarrassing or substantive.

Mel arrives at the edge of the city, stops at the railroad tracks that run along the river, stares across the water at West Virginia. She stands with feet spread wide, panting from exertion, wonders what it's like over there, running Byrd's re-election campaign — it must be his 6th or 7th term. What a breeze. Someday, she'll get cherry jobs like that. But is that what she wants, a hayride, not even bothering to look at polls or focus groups, just keeping the candidate from making unforced errors on the way to a 30-point win? That's what Tremont wants, she's sure of that much. But what does *she* want? And why is she asking herself that damned question so much these days? Is it because her 30th birthday is fast approaching — only 3 weeks away now?

She grabs a handful of rocks, tosses them one by one into the river, tries to clear her mind, focus only on the slowly flowing water, the ripples from the rocks, the breeze rustling the trees on the opposite bank. She doesn't have time or energy for the big questions, not now, not for the next 3 1/2 weeks. She lights the first cigarette of the day, turns and plods back to the Red Lion, struggling against memories of her mother the whole way. The images are simple, pedestrian, but extra heart-breaking because of it — her mother pouring her a bowl of cereal while Mel studies the *New York Times* like the meaning of life is squirreled away inside somewhere, her mother carefully inking a sign for an anti-nuke protest she's headed to in Cleveland, her mother sitting on the front porch with her father, a bourbon in one hand, her other hand slashing the air as she makes a point, her face animated with passion, her eyes sparkling with the vision of a brighter future.

Crunching across the Red Lion parking lot, Mel feels a single tear drop to her cheek. She stops, turns away — what if one of the journalists sees her like this? — wipes away the tear, gives herself a brief pep talk. *Get it together, Carnes. You can't go into battle distracted like this.* She thinks of the Patton line from her rally-the-troops speech. *I want you to remember that no bastard ever won a war by dying for his country. He won it by making the other poor dumb bastard die for* his *country.* That one always makes her smile.

Entering the lobby, she sees Porter poking through the continental breakfast in a nearly empty dining room. He looks perfect — hair blow-dried, shirt pressed, tie knotted snugly against his collar, sleeves rolled to three-quarters like she showed him. He's ready for another day of pressing the flesh and keeping his composure. Mel loves Porter a bit more each time she's around him. He's a model candidate — handsome, pliable, always good-natured. Perfect, that is, other than the horrible skeleton in his closet. If it weren't for that, she'd be downright buoyant right now. As it is, she's anxious and sweaty all the time, expecting Kane to drop the bomb any second, especially now that the polls have tightened. What's he waiting for? Did he really buy her case that she's got the upper hand with her "full-version" tape? Doesn't he have contacts in the DEA to see if her story checks out? Why is he going negative over the air when he could just leak the tape and step back to watch Porter implode?

He must have his reasons, Mel tells herself, which only stresses her out even more. Maybe he wants the tape to drop as close to the election as possible so Mel doesn't have time to spin it away. Maybe. She's got nothing but maybes on that front.

What she does know for sure is Kane has a surprise coming to him, probably today, tomorrow at the latest. It adds to her stress that he'll deal with that as deftly as Schooley predicted. If that son-of-a-bitch weasels out of this one...she doesn't know what.

Mel grabs a yogurt and the least unripe banana available, fills a coffee cup and sits down with Porter, who's braving the scrambled eggs and sausage links like the working class hero he's pretending to be today.

"Morning, Mel," he says brightly, his politician smile erupting across his face. "Sleep well?"

"Not bad. I went for a walk this morning, did some thinking."

"That right? What about? You want me to do something different today? I thought it went pretty well yesterday at all those steel mills and factories. I'm feeling the love from Joe Lunchbucket."

"Please, don't ever use that term again, OK?"

Porter's smile drains away. "It's just us, Mel." He waves at the empty dining room. "I'd never say that in public."

Mel peels her banana. "I'm sorry. Of course you wouldn't. I shouldn't have snapped at you like that. You're a dream come true for a strategist, Kyle. I mean that. If you gave me a dozen more just like you, I'd secure a permanent Democratic majority in the Senate."

Mel wonders if that's going too far, if Porter realizes she's implying he's a commodity, not a person. But his smile returns, and Mel breathes again, cuts her banana into slices, stirs her yogurt. Why can't she just have a human moment with this person?

She looks around the room, verifies there's no press lurking anywhere.

"You know, Kyle. You've never said why you got into this race in the first place. It's a big leap, if you don't mind me saying so, from no political experience at all to running for U.S. Senate. Even for the son-in-law of a former governor."

"I don't mind at all." Porter worries the eggs around his plate with a contemplative look on his face. Mel wonders if this is genuine or another type of performance, the thoughtful Senator considering a tough question from a constituent. It's not something she coached him into, but it's a good one. She should remember this for the next press conference.

"It's a really good question, actually," he says eventually. "I got it all the time, in the primaries. I talked about the call to public service, wanting to leave the world a better place than I found it. The usual nonsense." He lifts his fork to his lips, holds it there, stares blankly for a second before eating the eggs. He chews slowly, still thinking.

"But you know. To be honest." He pauses, as though uncertain if he should actually be honest here. "To be honest," he repeats, "it was pretty much my wife's idea. It was about a year ago. She said to me over dinner—I remember it perfectly—she said, 'Kyle, I think you should run for Howard Metzenbaum's Senate seat when he retires next year. Daddy agrees.'"

"And *you* thought it was a good idea?" Mel can sense that Porter is being genuine here, and she's not sure she likes it. He's opening himself up, seems almost relieved to do it, like he's been carrying this horrible weight far too long and he's glad for a chance to offload it.

"I don't know if I did, but with her father's imprimatur, what could I say? Charlie's the ambitious one. I mean that. Me, I'd be happy as a simple country lawyer, maybe running for city attorney or county prosecutor someday. She pushed me into starting my chain of legal clinics, urged me to expand to other states, kept on me about growth, expansion, never letting up with the advertising. No one really knows it, but she's the power behind the throne." Porter stops, stabs a sausage, shoves it in his mouth, looks like he realizes he's revealing too much about his personal life.

Mel is on the verge of bringing up the DEA tape—*And neither one of you ever thought about that money-laundering problem?* — but she stops herself. She wouldn't know how to tell him about the contingency plan she worked up after Charlotte tipped her off. If and when the time comes, she'll have to sell him on releasing her tape. It's bound to be a tough ask, piling fraud on top of deceit—it's better to bring it up in the heat of crisis, not over a Red Lion breakfast buffet.

She wonders how Porter lives with himself every day on the campaign trail, knowing he got snared by the DEA. So what if he wiggled out of it with an entrapment defense, used his connections to bury the whole sordid affair? It's a political albatross, and rookie or not, he has to know it. Maybe he just doesn't think about it, managed to lock it away in the deepest dungeon of his memory, didn't take it into account when he decided to run. It's plausible. Mel knows a thing or two about denial.

The tension is thick at the table, a terrible reversal that makes Mel feel even worse than when Porter seemed like he was opening up. Melancholy weighs on her chest, slumps her shoulders. She scans the room again, sees that the dining room is coming to life, as much as it can on a Thursday morning in mid-October in Steubenville, Ohio. She spots Dan Barnaby getting off the elevator, excuses herself to make a phone call, tells Kyle not to talk to any press without her around. She cuts off Barnaby before he can get within earshot of Porter.

"Whatever you're planning to ask, no comment," Mel says. "And don't even think about approaching the candidate while he's communing with his breakfast. He's officially unavailable until our first stop at the…wherever the hell it is, I can't remember."

"Mingo Junction steel mill," Barnaby says.

"Right. The van leaves at 8:15 sharp. Enjoy your complimentary breakfast, but stay away from Porter. Got it?"

Mel uses the lobby phone, keeps an eye on Porter's table. She checks in with Schooley—he agreed to show up at the office at 7am while she's gone—learns the whistleblower tape finally hit the radio this morning, 6am for the early political talk shows, a 7am report on Ohio Public Radio. "Braddock called in not too long ago to let me know he heard from the *Plain Dealer* and a couple of other city papers that they're running the story this morning. He's working it masterfully." Schooley says this with undisguised admiration.

"Even if he does say so himself."

"I wouldn't be surprised if Kane's gone by tonight," Schooley adds.

"I would," Mel shoots back. "Kane's big game, Number Two. It'll take more than put-on outrage by Kline Braddock to get Musgrove to cut him loose. The pressure has to mount over a few days, and that's exactly how we want it to play out. We'll see them both in Dayton tomorrow for the debate. That's when we tighten the screws, let Porter deliver the final blow, questioning Musgrove's judgment in keeping on such an amoral political animal. That way we get rid of Kane *and* land a body blow on Musgrove. *If this is the kind of man you chose to run your campaign, what does that say about your judgment? Ohio deserves a better Senator than that, Mr. Musgrove. Wouldn't you agree?"*

"Nice, Mel. You're the man."

"The *man*, Schooley? Come on now."

"Sorry. You know what I mean. You're the best."

"*Better than any man*, is what I'm sure you meant to say. I'm welcome very much. OK, don't stray from the phone. I'll be checking in throughout the day. Keep an eye on Braddock, too, make sure he doesn't go off script."

"Aye aye."

Mel keeps the press at a distance all day, backs them up to watch Porter working the shift change in Mingo Junction, herds them into the press van before they can ask him any questions. She lets Chris Garvey ride along with her and Porter on the way to Lancaster, makes him get out in Martins Ferry to switch places with Dan Barnaby, switches the press again in Morristown, then Cambridge, then once more in Zanesville, gives everyone about the same face time with Porter, warns each in turn not to ask anything about the Musgrove campaign. "Mr. Porter won't be commenting on anything going on inside the Musgrove campaign today. You'll have to wait until the debate tomorrow for that. You break this rule, I roll you out the door, won't even have Frank slow the van."

They comply, ask generic questions about the economy, foreign aid, the deficit, taxes, the whole boring gamut of issues, and Porter paraphrases the relevant passages from his stump speech, never seems to grow bored, keeps beaming that you're-the-most-special-person-in-all-the-world smile at whichever reporter is back there with him until it's time for the changeover. Nobody's particularly pleased, but it's neither more nor less than the usual grind, so no one complains either. The tedium is one reason they all drink so much, in Mel's opinion, pols and reporters. She wonders what the candidates do to cope.

When they get to Lancaster, she walks with Porter through the Fairfield County Fairgrounds as he shakes hands, endures polite promises by obvious G.O.P. loyalists to consider voting for him, eats the requisite sausage, even wears a John Deere cap for a while. She curses herself for giving in to Tremont on this dog, but she looks over at one point and realizes Porter is having a grand time, suspects he'd make a better Republican and probably would've gone that way if his father-in-law wasn't already a powerful Democrat. He's a good enough actor, she knows perfectly well, to pull off either side of the political spectrum. She sours on Porter for the rest of the afternoon, feels increasingly depressed. She hates to think that all she's doing is getting another self-serving suit into high office, but isn't that pretty much what it comes down to? Is that all she's going to do with the rest of her life, getting these hollow men elected?

1994

Goddammit, Carnes! she yells at herself at a rest stop somewhere southeast of Athens, hovering above a cracked toilet seat in a roadside Exxon. *Stop analyzing your life until this fucking election is over, would you.* She needs to get back to the office so she can keep herself busy. This is why she hates going on the road — too much time to think, not enough to do. Not enough booze, either.

Internal Spot Poll
(n=720, +/- 4.5%)
Musgrove: 40%
Porter: 42%
Harris: 8%
Undecided: 10%

The dressing room at WHIO-Dayton is brutally cold, the air-conditioner running nonstop on a day that's below 60. Mel knows the lights make the studio hotter, but this is ridiculous. She's been in plenty of television studios, and this is way colder than normal. She makes sure Porter is well-tended by Carlton Schooley and Colin Burke, then heads outside for a smoke break. She needs some alone time after three days in the candidate's hip pocket.

Predictably, Howard Kane ambles up as soon as she settles in with her cigarette. She leans against the brick wall, smoking peacefully and staring at the clouds skittering past the station's bank of satellite dishes, studiously ignores him as he taps out a Marlboro and lights up.

"Smooth move with the bug." He exhales with relish. "I'm impressed. I didn't think you had that kind of moxie."

"I have no idea what you're talking about. Bug? What bug?"

"Cut the shit, Carnes. It's just the two of us out here." He flaps open his jacket, as though that proves he's not wearing a wire.

"Oh, you mean that whistleblower tape?" Mel flicks her butt into the parking lot, immediately lights another one, her 33rd of the day. "Nothing to do with me."

"Course not, course not. In any case, it's impressive how disciplined y'all are being, piling on me but keeping away from the candidate, holding your guy back from any comment whatsoever. Your boy Braddock, he's one slick little dick jock, ain't he? Y'all are handling this perfectly, in my humble, non-expert opinion."

Mel knows what he's fishing for, but she won't give him the satisfaction of hearing her say he played his response even better. It's true, though, whether she admits it out loud or not. She saw him on

TV last night on the Parkersburg NBC affiliate, interviewing via satellite from Columbus.

Elections can be an ugly business, Glenn, he said to Parkersburg media icon Glenn Wilson, who looked on from the split screen with his mustachioed mouth turned down in consternation. *I'll admit it, campaign managers can be mercenary and amoral sometimes. Ask around. It's not uncommon. But everything I was doing there, everything you heard on that tape you just played, was aimed at one thing and one thing only. Getting a highly decent man of conviction elected to the U.S. Senate. Even when he thinks no one's listening, he can't help acting with integrity.* Kane beamed triumphantly, like he'd just met Jesus Christ himself and personally been forgiven all his sins. Wilson nodded sagely, his mustache assuming a more sympathetic posture.

She heard from Schooley this morning that Kane hit every major TV market in the state, from Cincinnati to Youngstown, delivering the same basic message. Mel knows now they won't get any traction out of that damned tape she'd risked her life to mail secretly from the Westerville post office.

Kane is good, Mel has to admit, a fact that only enrages her that much more. She tries to keep her emotions out of it, but she has to beat her pillow mercilessly every morning before she can get out of bed, before she can even light her first cigarette of the day.

"You're one weasely son-of-a-bitch, I'll give you that much," is all the reaction Mel gives Kane, but it proves satisfying enough to him.

"Why thank you, Miz Carnes. And you are one cunt-faced bitch for thinking you could take me out. That mouthpiece of yours can beat the drum for my resignation all he wants. Never gonna happen."

"Why not? You got naked pictures of Musgrove fucking a prize hog? He'll cut you loose, all right. He's a politician, and you know what that means. Self-interest above all else."

"He might just do it, if we still had a big lead." Kane takes a long, contemplative drag, squints at Mel through the exhale. "But he's getting scared, truth be told. Ordered me to drop a bunch of attack ads we had in the can just in case. Nah. He won't put his precious campaign in the hands of some second-rate hack unless he's sure he's got a safe lead."

"Kind of a bind for him, then," Mel says. "He needs you 'cause the race is close, but maybe keeping you around is the reason it stays close, maybe even sinks him into second place. Our latest numbers look pretty bad for you guys. Yours look the same?"

"That's proprietary information." Kane tries to smirk, but he looks pained. Mel thinks she might be getting to him, wonders if his bravado is 100% bluff. Musgrove must be thinking about cutting him loose. The downside of Kane casting himself as the Faustian aide on all those TV shows is that it created a clear good-guy/bad-guy situation. That's good for the good guy, bad for the bad guy. Mel has a spark of admiration for Kane, risking his own position to safeguard his candidate. Unless he's running a different play. Maybe he *does* have some ugly hold over Musgrove. He certainly has something over Porter. Maybe that's all there is to it, that he told Musgrove he's got a secret weapon up his sleeve, and Dick has to agree not to fire him if he wants to use it.

Mel drops her cigarette, grinds it out with her toe. "See you in the spin room, cocksucker." It comes out more collegial than Mel intended. Maybe she's losing her hatred for Kane, just the tiniest bit. She tells herself to stop admitting he's a class-A pro all the time, keep remembering he's a rapist.

Mel peeks into the dressing room, sees that Porter looks perfect, that Schooley is going over his answers once more, that Kline Braddock also looks perfect. She heads straight for the spin room, prays that Howard Kane doesn't follow her again. She really does need the peace and quiet but can't keep herself away from the monitors. She expects fireworks tonight, knows she needs to pay close attention, take notes, be ready to prep Braddock to spin it their way, whatever happens. The race could be on the line tonight.

Mel lights #34 and watches Cheryl McHenry introduce the candidates. Mel pumps her fist at the TV screen. "You get him, Kyle. Win this one for me. Win it." She jerks her head around, certain someone came in and heard her, but the spin room is still empty. She sits on the couch, takes a deep drag, tries to relax her muscles as the moderator goes into her intro.

— *Before we get to the issues, let's first take a closer look at the candidates.*

The candidate bio segments are bland and overly long, WHIO's effort to seem neutral—Musgrove and Kane, like all Republicans, constantly complain about liberal media bias—pushing the station in such a vacuous direction that Mel wonders if there could possibly be any viewers left after the 2-minute intro segment. McHenry then spends an inordinate amount of time explaining and justifying Harris's absence from tonight's debate, and wastes even more outlining the rules, describing the issues the debate will cover—"Get on with it, would you!" Mel yells at the TV—and introducing the panel of journalists who will question the candidates. Mel looks at her watch. Five minutes in, and all the audience has seen of the candidates is their

1994

handshake. If the monitor weren't hardwired into the broadcast, even she would be surfing for a different channel already.

It doesn't matter who's watching right now, Mel reminds herself. It's all how the media talks about it tomorrow, how much each candidate gives the opposition to use against them. She's confident when she thinks about it in those terms. Porter's well-rehearsed on his talking points, knows exactly how to deliver them as perfectly sized sound bites, and Braddock's been drilling him all afternoon on how *not* to say something that could be taken out of context and spun in a damaging way. When it comes to performance chops, she knows Porter's top-notch. Plus, he looks so much more Senatorial than Musgrove. He's a full head taller, projects youthful energy and middle-aged gravitas at the same time, has a matinee-star jawline and the best goddamned politician's hair she's seen in a long time, maybe ever. Normally Mel would hate that about politics, how important personal appearance is, but it works to her advantage right now, so she's not complaining.

"Just don't blow it this time, OK," Mel mutters as Porter begins his opening statement. Visions of the League of Women Voter's hiccup, on a grander scale, flood her mind. She smokes ferociously, prays that Porter learned his lesson from that one. He's been completely disciplined ever since, hasn't shown a single crack in composure, though she finds that more worrisome than comforting, for some stupid reason. What if Porter's been holding it in too hard? Mel tells herself to stop stressing. She's done everything humanly possible to ensure her candidate is prepared for this.

And he doesn't blow it—not the opening statement at least, and not the first few questions. He's a master at sounding informed on foreign policy, breezes through the questions on health care and the economy. He starts slipping on crime, about 40 minutes into the 1-hour broadcast. Musgrove prods him for being a flip-flopper on gun control, then needles him for being a strip-mall lawyer without any real understanding of the criminal justice system, then outright accuses him of being a criminal himself.

Mel holds her breath. Don't tell me he's going to out the DEA tape right here and right now. That would be brutal. Brilliant, but brutal. Please, no.

She lets out her breath when it's just a rehash of the new ad pointing out Porter's many lawsuits for false advertising and legal malpractice. Porter should be prepared for this. He's been drilled on this exact attack line, knows how to float above it, duck back and let the blows glance off. They're all bullshit charges. Every doctor and lawyer in the country gets sued for malpractice all the time. It means nothing.

If that's what you think a criminal is, Porter should be saying, *you have a severe misunderstanding of the real crime problems our communities face.* Then he goes into his 5-point plan for decreasing recidivism, beefing up halfway house resources to transition ex-convicts more successfully into honest labor, et cetera. Only that's not what he's doing. Instead, he glowers in anger, starts jabbing his finger across the empty space between the podiums.

—How dare you…

"No no no!" Mel jumps up, launches her cigarette at the screen. She can't believe what she's seeing.

—How dare you attack me for these baseless, ridiculous charges, when everyone knows how much worse you've done.

"Do not," Mel pleads to the TV screen. "Back off. It's not too late."

But then it *is* too late. Porter goes into full-blown outrage mode. He takes a step away from his podium to advance on Musgrove like he's going to strangle him. His height works against him now, makes it look like he's physically menacing Musgrove, who stands his ground and remains calm, a brave nerd standing up to the bully on the playground. Musgrove doesn't even look too smug as he watches his opponent self-destruct.

—How dare you lecture me, or anyone else, about anything, you hypocrite!

"Do not do this," Mel says to the empty room, but it's a hopeless plea, quiet, resigned. She knows it's too late, the damage done. The attack ads write themselves, the unflattering news stories the media can run to disprove their liberal bias. Mel drops to the couch, lays against the arm as Porter notches another few degrees towards unhinged.

—I'm not the one who'll take whatever position is most convenient to get elected!

Musgrove interrupts gently, exactly as Howard Kane must've prepared him.

—I think everyone watching tonight knows that I'm not that kind of politician. I'm a man of conviction who…

Porter interrupts angrily.

—*That's a lie and you know it!*

Mel closes her eyes, listens as Cheryl McHenry finally steps in to end it, her prissy little face animated with joy, Mel just knows it from the tone of her voice.

1994

—Gentlemen, I believe we're out of time for our segment on crime. Thank you for a spirited exchange on the issues. We have one last commercial break before your closing statements. We'll be right back.

Mel checks her impulse to run into the studio and ask Porter what the fuck he thinks he's doing. It doesn't matter at this point, won't help salvage the situation. She tries not to blame herself for Porter's lack of self-control. He's a great actor, and he's been thoroughly prepped, drilled for exactly this situation. If he can't hold it together under battle conditions on live TV, that's not her fault. This must be the same trait that got him to say *Yes* to those DEA agents, a fundamental lack of discipline, deep down, easy to gloss over but impossible to root out.

It's cold comfort to Mel. She hates that Howard Kane's words pop into her mind. *No matter how well you prep 'em, sometimes the stupid motherfuckers just fall apart under pressure. Don't take it personally.*

And then there he is again, right on cue, waltzing smugly into the spin room with a coterie of journalists in tow. They must've been watching in the studio until now, or maybe wolfing down the catering in the green room. Jared Block has a smear of cream cheese on his chin.

Thom shoots her a sympathetic look, but it lasts only a second. He's busy scribbling down what Kane is saying.

"I think we saw clearly tonight, gentlemen, which one of the candidates is ready to take his seat in the United States Senate, and which one needs a bit more time to prepare himself for public service." Mel notices he's laying on the drawl particularly heavy at the moment. "Wouldn't you agree, Miz Carnes?"

Braddock slides around the slide of the pack, shakes his head *No* at Mel. She has the wherewithal to smile brightly. "I think it's clear from the issues," she says calmly, falling back on an old formula, "which of these candidates is in the best position to represent the needs and interests of the people of Ohio. That's an endeavor that requires the passion, commitment, and intensity you saw on display here tonight, but above all, it requires a clear-eyed assessment of what the people's needs and interests are, not the mercenary political calculation and empty rhetoric on offer from the Republican candidate."

Braddock steps in at that point, Mel's statement enough to let him know how he's supposed to play this, the quarterback calling an audible at the line, and the team shifting to a new formation. Mel says *Hut Hut Hike* in her mind and lights yet another cigarette to keep her mouth occupied. She's handed this one off to Braddock, and now she needs to keep silent. She wants to escape, but the spin room is filling up fast, everyone ignoring the candidates' closing statements playing on the monitor, the usual bromides drowned out by the noise of questions and chatter from the small group of people who will determine how this all gets processed and fed to the public.

—Kline, did you guys want Porter out there getting righteously angry? Was that the plan?

—Kline, Kline, you really want us to believe this is passion, not a lack of discipline?

Kane angles his way over to Mel, gloats that her guy just doesn't seem to have the discipline necessary to go the distance. "He's in over his head, Carnes. Not your fault. But why do I keep making excuses for you? You wanna blame yourself, go ahead. I don't give a shit. Just wanted you to know, you've got my sympathy. We've all been there."

"You know where you can shove your sympathy, Kane."

# # # # #

The Porter entourage retreats to Columbus for the night instead of going all the way back to Cleveland. Tremont has a busy schedule for the candidate tomorrow—fundraiser breakfast with the ODP, a round of leadership visits at the statehouse, foreign policy speech to a bunch of eggheads at O.S.U. Mel could go back to Cleveland if she wants, rent a car and peel herself away, give herself a well-deserved weekend off, or mostly off, have Schooley drag her computer to her hotel room and set her up to write memos and planning documents in the privacy of her suite.

That's normally the direction she'd go, especially after 3 days on the road in the candidate's hip pocket, a grueling exercise—she never knows how these guys do it, day after day, for 2 and 3 months at a time—but she decides to hang around the inner circle for another night. *Everything is going to be fine*, she tells herself. Porter had a moment of weakness that looked horrible on TV, but it's not the end of the world. It'll cost them a few points at most. The fact is, they're right on the issues, and Shep's data shows that they've been making that case successfully with the voting public.

Mel shoulders into her room, drops to the bed in exhaustion, tells herself not to drain the mini-bar tonight. She flings her shoes across the room, one of them bouncing off the TV screen. She's half-asleep, fully dressed on top of the covers, when there's a knock on the door.

She covers her head with a pillow, hears another round of insistent knocking, schlumps to the door and yanks it open to find Thom Reynolds looking mournful, as though he came to commiserate with Mel about her candidate's horrendous fuck-up.

Only he's got different news to break.

1994

"Howard Kane's in the hospital," he says gravely.

"What?" Mel knows she misheard. He must've said, *Howard Kane's in the lobby*, or something like that.

"They thought he was choking on his steak." Thom takes a step inside, looks like he wants to give Mel a hug. "But it was a massive coronary. He's only alive because the restaurant was just down the street from the hospital."

Mel turns away, drifts to the bed, flops face down. She wishes she didn't have such mixed emotions about this. The guy could be dying, and for more than just a fleeting second, she felt unmitigated pleasure at hearing the news. It morphed into a sense of justice being served — she even said to herself, *it couldn't have happened to a nicer guy* — before landing on guilt, but she's already talking herself out of that. Why should *she* feel guilty? She didn't put Kane in the hospital.

She remembers the last words he said to her. *You've got my sympathy*. Was Kane being an actual human being in that moment? Is she the monster for not feeling terrible that he's in the hospital, possibly dying at this very moment?

Thom rubs her back lightly, misreads her silence. "They said he's going to be fine." He's pure sympathy. "Just needs to rest. He'll probably quit the campaign — seems like a good time to get out — go back to Texas after he's released from the hospital. Should be a few days, a week at the most."

Mel rolls over slowly, groans to a sitting position. "Jesus. You wanna know what I'm thinking right now?" Should she say it? She decides to say it. "I'm thinking, *good riddance*. Get the fuck out. Die, you worthless piece of shit."

"Jesus, Mel."

"You know that Howard Kane raped a friend of mine? I'm sure she wasn't the only one. No, of course you don't. That's not in his press briefings." Mel stands, puts her hands on her hips, shoots Thom a challenging look, as though he's bound to come to Kane's defense, say *allegedly raped* like the apologists always do. "He's the lowest form of scum on the earth, Thom." She forgets to use her usual th-pronunciation. "He deserves to die. I know I'm a cold-hearted bitch for saying it, but that's how I feel. No guilt. No shame. That pile of human garbage deserves to die, and I, for one, am glad he's finally getting around to it. Almost makes me believe there really is a God."

Thom looks horrified. Mel can't tell if it's her revelation about Kane, or her brutal callousness to his condition. "That's a lot of information right there," he says. It's still unclear to Mel where he stands.

"I want to see him," Mel says. "Is he taking visitors?"

"I doubt it. He's in the I.C.U. Probably just family can get in, if even. It's late."

Mel picks up the phone. "What hospital did you say? I'm gonna find out. I need to see him before he dies. Spit in that motherfucker's face."

"Jesus, Mel. You're a hard case," Thom says quietly. He leaves Mel jabbing at the phone, trying to get an outside line. She doesn't notice him go.

-24
6:00AM

Mel flips on the TV first thing to see how the debate is being portrayed. She lights a cigarette right there in bed, calls down for a room service omelet, wonders if Kane's condition will get any coverage. She doesn't have to wait long to find out. CBS opens with a teaser about the debate report, then leads with the story about Kane, typical asshole TV move.

— *Last night's Senate debate in Dayton kicked up a few sparks towards the end. But before we go to full coverage of that event from CBS-10's own Marla Hoffmeister, we've got Ben Wheeler, coming to us live from the O.S.U. Medical Center, where Howard Kane, campaign manager to Republican Senate candidate Richard Musgrove, was hospitalized overnight after suffering a heart attack yesterday evening. Ben.*

The screen cuts to Ben Wheeler standing with one of Kane's press aides, the prototypical press operative in a Republican version of Kline Braddock's uniform, dark-grey slacks, black single-breasted blazer, white shirt, red-and-blue striped tie.

— *Thank you, Michele.* Ben must realize he seems too chipper for a hospital piece, recomposes himself to look more appropriately grave. *The Musgrove campaign announced early this morning that Mr. Kane has officially resigned from his position, citing health reasons. I'm here at the O.S.U. Medical Center with Dave Parker, one of Mr. Kane's aides, to repeat that official statement.*

That's some hard-hitting news, Mel says to herself, getting a campaign flak to repeat an official statement on live television. "Nice work, Ben Wheeler." All Mel can think about while Parker is saying his piece — memorized verbatim, she notices — is Kane's media-release habits. He only drops things on Saturday that he wants to bury, and this isn't just Saturday, it's pre-dawn, for fuck's sake. It strikes her as she's listening that Kane could be faking it to give himself a reason to get out of Musgrove's hair without having to admit wrongdoing. It's a perfect play, if that's what he's doing. Mel wouldn't put it past Kane to fake a heart attack and actually spend the night in a hospital, all to wiggle his way out of an awkward situation.

She clicks off the TV without waiting for the debate coverage. Braddock and Schooley can fill her in later. She needs to see Kane as soon as possible, though she's not exactly sure why she feels this sense of urgency. She dresses quickly but thoughtfully, puts the finishing touches on her cover story while she does her make-up, tries but fails not to imagine her impending confrontation with Kane. However hard she works at it, her version of Kane's dialogue is too self-reflective, too easily apologetic.

—You know, Carnes, I realize what an asshole I've been to you. To all women. I know it's no excuse, but there haven't been enough people to call me on my bullshit. I could've used someone like you in my life 30 years ago.

Yeah, there's about 0.1% chance he'll say anything remotely like that.

On the cab ride over, Mel forces herself to focus on the radio banter, weather, the Buckeye's game that day, a splash of human interest, hears the first 20 seconds of *Secret* before she jumps out at the hospital, the lyrics ridiculously apt at the moment, though not in the way Madonna intended — *Things haven't been the same, since you came into my life. You found a way to touch my soul.* She massively over-tips the driver, as though she can assuage her guilt in advance by rewarding some anonymous blue-collar guy who said all of 2 words to her the entire drive, "Where to?" It's not like she's headed inside to snuff out Kane with a pillow, though it's fun to picture for a second.

Mel lies to the nurse, tells her she's Kane's niece, a graduate student in journalism at O.S.U., shows her the Mary Baker credential — "I'm really just an intern, but my uncle got me this press badge so I could go along with him sometimes" — insists she has to see her uncle as soon as possible, she's so worried after seeing on the news this morning that he might be dying.

Mel fakes a sniffle, scrunches up her face like she's just barely holding it together. In truth, the smell of the hospital brings her back 15 years, chokes her up more than she wants to admit. The last time she stepped inside a hospital, her father put his hand on her shoulder and said, "She's gone, Boo Boo. She slipped away in her sleep." Mel still hasn't forgiven him for how relieved he sounded. She remembers balling up her fists, controlling the urge to punch his stupid, sympathetic face. Her chest tightens at the memory, her fingers curling reflexively.

Mel didn't realize how hard this would be, didn't count on the memory the smell would conjure, obviously didn't think this through as thoroughly as she should've. What if Kane really is dying? Is she actually going to feel good about that?

"Nobody told you last night?" the nurse says. Her brown eyes remind Mel of Bambi. Jesus, she needs to stop with the dead mother references.

"I was out all night." Mel notices she's using just the slightest fake drawl, more South Carolina than Texas. "And I didn't check my messages this morning. I saw it on CBS. Can I see him now, or do I have to wait? I'm just so worried. I hope he's alright."

The nurse puts her hand on Mel's shoulder. "Don't worry, sweetie. He's doing fine this morning. It was a fairly minor cardiac episode. He could be released as early as this afternoon."

"Really?" *Ah hah!* Mel almost breaks character. "That's fantastic news," she says brightly. "Just simply the best news." Her accent is getting a bit too thick, she notices. Better reign it in.

Dave Parker is sitting outside the door. He knows who Mel is but doesn't blow her cover with the nurse. Does he have instructions to let Mel in if she shows up? Mel can't help feeling she's getting drawn into a sinister plot, forgets for a second that she's the one lying her ass off here.

Kane's watching CNN when Mel enters. He looks pretty pale, Mel admits, has wires stuck to his chest, an IV in his arm, a machine reading his heartbeat peeping steadily, all legit as far as she can tell, but it also looks exactly like a hospital scene in a movie. Then again, so did her mother's room. She remembers thinking that all the time, remembers also how she berated her 15-year-old self for returning to that idiotic observation, but she couldn't get over it. If you wanted to shoot a mother-daughter cancer scene, that's exactly how you'd set it up. The thought was a defense-mechanism, Mel later realized, a subconscious attempt to deny the reality of the situation.

Mel stands back while the nurse fusses with Kane, writes something on his chart, none of which seems necessary or does anything to make the scene appear less cinematic. *Come on, Mel, don't be a dick*, she tells herself. *This guy legitimately had a heart attack, minor or not. Stop looking for spin all the time. It's a bad habit.* She reminds herself that the only thing in here that's fake is "Mary Baker."

"Take as much time as you need, Miss Baker," the nurse says. She touches Mel's shoulder again in passing as she leaves.

Kane smirks, turns his head slowly. *"Miss Baker?* You lie your way in here, Carnes?" Mel holds up the Mary Baker credential. "Not bad. You come in here to unplug my life support, put yourself out of my misery?"

"*I took the mission,*" Mel says in her Martin Sheen voice, remembers she used this quote on Cliff Barker not too long ago. She didn't realize at the time there'd be a bona fide Colonel Kurtz waiting up that river. "*What the hell else was I gonna do? But I really didn't know what I'd do when I found him.*"

"*Apocalypse Now,*" Kane says. "Great movie. So you *are* here to kill me?"

"It's what you want, isn't it?" Mel makes a ridiculous finger-gun. "*I felt like he was up there, waiting for me to take away his pain. He just wanted to go out like a soldier. Hell, even the jungle wanted him dead.*" Mel smirks back at Kane, glad the mood is lightening. What the fuck is she doing here, and why is she being so collegial all of the sudden? She drops to a chair. "I suppose I can't smoke in here."

"Dammit, Carnes, why'd you mention cigarettes? I'm dying for a smoke, but it's off limits. All I've got is CNN and some kind of synthetic opioid." Kane rattles the IV tube. "Not bad stuff, though. A fella could grow to like it. Only they tell me it makes you constipated. Is that more than you wanted to hear?" He makes a strained face, grunts. "Old Howard Kane can't shit anymore. Cosmic justice for all the crap he's spread around the world in his day?"

Mel couldn't have put it better herself. She shrugs, turns her attention to the TV, sees Bernard Calb talking with Gwen Ifill on *Reliable Sources.*

—*It's just that we, and the American public, have to be smart enough to make the distinction between fact and opinion,* Ifill says with her signature earnestness.

"Bunch of horseshit," Kane says. "Pundits talking about punditry. People blame *us* for the sad state of American political discourse, when it's these jackasses who spout the *real* bullshit. A goddamned cable TV show analyzing the way the news media covers politics. It's no wonder people hate us all. *I* hate us all most of the time."

Mel almost says, *Me too,* but holds back. Whatever drew her here, she didn't come for a panel discussion on the idiocies of their shared trade.

"I saw you're quitting the campaign," she says. She itches for a cigarette, notices Kane has a pack of gum on his nightstand.

"Yup," Kane says. He flicks off the TV. "Health reasons."

"That's what your flak out there said."

"It has the virtue of being true."

"It's not the *whole* truth, though, is it?"

Kane narrows his eyes at Mel. "Jesus H. Christ, Carnes. Let it go. I had a heart attack, simple as that. I'm going back to Texas as soon as they let me out of here. Not everything is spin."

"For people like us it is."

"No. Not always." Kane sounds sincere. Maybe he's had a genuine shock here, a come-to-Jesus moment, as Kline Braddock likes to say.

"I'm going to tell you something straight here, Carnes. OK, we *do* spin everything. Of course we do. That's our game. It's a necessity, at least from our narrow-minded little viewpoint. But sometimes, very rarely, it serves an actual greater good. Whatever's going on up there." Kane gestures dismissively at the dead screen of the TV. "Deep down in the American psyche, where it counts, there's an honest-to-God Republican revolution coming."

"*Republican revolution*? You're telling me that's not spin to make this wave election seem more consequential than it is?"

"It's way more than a wave election, Carnes. It's a seismic shift. I mean that. I've been in politics a long time, over 40 years. I actually remember the last time we had a Republican Congress. I was a staffer on the Hill, Bruce Alger's office. Only Republican in the Texas delegation. You don't remember when Texas was solid Democrat, do you? This is Lyndon Johnson and Sam Rayburn days. It was Eisenhower's first term, Republican majorities in the House and Senate with a Republican president for the first time since Hoover. It lasted all of 2 years, haven't had it since."

Kane unwraps a stick of gum, shoves it in his mouth. He looks passionate and wistful at the same time. He really is going through something, Mel thinks. She lets him continue without interruption, forces herself not to argue back. She wants to know where this is going, actually enjoys the personal history lesson. She knows all this, of course, but it's interesting to hear it from Kane's perspective, from an old white Southerner who lived through it, helped make some of it happen. Maybe this is why she came, some kind of twisted urge to give Kane a chance to explain himself.

"You guys have had 6 decades in the driver's seat," Kane continues. "Unified government at least half the time since '32. Some good's come out of it, some not-so-good, some genuine bad. I'm not praising or blaming. That's just life — the good, the bad, and the ugly."

Mel reflexively mouths the Ennio Morricone theme. "*Wa wa wa.*"

"Exactly. But your era is finished. The Cold War's over. The New Deal's run its course. The American people want a government that's run like a business, not a charity. It's time for fiscal responsibility, trimming the fat—and there's plenty of it—getting back to first principles."

Kane pauses, gives Mel a chance to make her expected rebuttal. She opens her mouth, ready to argue, closes it again, purses her lips and raises her eyebrows. The last thing she wants right now is a debate about politics.

"You don't believe it," Kane goes on. "Or more precisely, you don't *want* to believe it. But it's true. I'm serious, Carnes. I've been out among the people for a long time. Bending their minds my way when I can. Manipulating the public, if that's how you want to put it. Sure, that's my job. That's *our* job. Difference this year is, they're *running* to us, begging for the Contract with America, not just voting for us out of fear or stupidity like they usually do. *Running*. They *want* the Republican promised land. A return to individualism and an end to whining and government handouts. We're not just gonna win this election. We're gonna have a long-term Republican majority in Congress, a Republican president next. Clinton's got one-termer written all over him, another Jimmy Carter. We're looking at 3, maybe 4 decades of unified government—on *our* terms. It's the dawning of a new age, as your hippie friends once thought, only it's not the Age of Aquarius. Oh no, baby, it's the age of responsible small government and genuine personal freedom. Put that in your hash pipe and smoke it, you hippie fucks."

Kane stops, looks angrily at Mel like it's Jane Fonda sitting there, his eyes burning with something Mel has never seen there before. He looks like a crazy Biblical prophet, or the guru for a new cult. Mel feels the pull of his passion, the power of conviction underlying the bitterness and tribal hatred. He practically glows, despite the tubes and machines and sterile hospital walls. The moment is heavy with possibility, one of those turning points in life you look back on and recognize for its importance. *And that's the day I became a Republican.* Jesus, God, no. Is Kane trying to win her over here? Convert her to the Dark Side?

Mel practically shudders, almost lets fly with an *Empire Strikes Back* quote, says instead, "You really believe all that?" It's actually a question, not a challenge. "You think that's what the American people really want?" Now it sounds like a challenge. Mel can't help it. She's amazed that after all these years, Kane might actually buy into all that Republican bullshit about small government and pulling yourself up by your bootstraps.

The moment passes, the zeal draining from Kane's face. He unwraps another stick of gum, tosses the pack to Mel, a couple of hardcore smokers stuck in a hospital room talking shit, nothing more consequential than that.

"Nah, you're right." Kane licks his lips, his face sagging in resignation, like Mel just talked him out of a stupid idea. "Politics is bullshit. Business is bullshit. The deficit? Who gives a fuck! NAFTA? Iraq? Lobbyists, pundits, whistleblowers, spin doctors? Just a bunch of assholes. We all die, Carnes. That's the only reality of human life. So I say, *Fuck it*. Do what makes you happy. I've been a miserable prick for 40 years, and this is where it landed me." He sweeps his arms around the room. "Call it spin if you want, but I quit for health reasons, that's the God's honest and 100% complete truth. Maybe I'll come back, maybe I won't — who knows? — but if I do, it'll be different. I don't need the money anymore. Hell, I haven't needed the money in 20 years. This time…" He stops, turns away from Mel, grabs his goatee, mashes the hair in his meaty fingers. Mel expects him to say, *This time it'll all be different.* The moment draws out, Kane thinking God-knows-what.

Eventually he turns to Mel, eyes blank. He says nothing, seems to've forgotten his train of thought. He looks old to Mel for the first time. He must be mid- to late-60s if he was a Hill staffer in 1953. That's a lot older than Mel ever thought. She figured him for a perpetual 51, old enough for battle scars but nowhere near retirement age. She senses the chasm of time separating them, a full 3-plus decades, an entire political era.

"You know," she says. "I actually thought you might've faked the heart attack to get out of a tough spot."

"Seriously?" Kane looks genuinely affronted. "You think I'd fake a heart attack to get out of a minor campaign flap?"

"I don't know what you would or wouldn't do, you fucking reptile." Mel wishes she didn't sound so bitter, but she can't help it. Seeing Kane looking frail but otherwise healthy, buying into the Republican brand of bullshit — it sets her on edge.

"Maybe you're projecting here, Carnes. Is there anything *you* wouldn't do to win?"

"Don't make this about me, old man."

"I'm serious. You seem like a gloves-are-always-off kinda gal, if you want the truth. I respect that. I really do. Hell, I *admire* it. There's not a lot of women like you out there. But maybe it bothers *you*?" Kane narrows his eyes. "Just a little? I'm the one who's supposed to be soul-searching here, little lady, but maybe it's time join me? Huh? Am I right?"

# # # # #

Mel lets Thom give her a ride back to Cleveland. Fraternizing with the press like this would normally be out-of-bounds—it's one thing to sleep to with a reporter after hours, another thing entirely to spend 2-plus hours in a car with one unless there's a candidate in tow—but Mel gives herself a pass this time. She's shaken up by Kane, even more than she was by her brush with death. How many days ago was that now? Four? Five? Jesus, what a week it's been.

"I've had a real bear of a week," Mel says after 20 minutes of silent freeway driving. Thom is being marvelously understanding of her mood. Maybe too understanding. This is boyfriend-level understanding if Mel has ever seen it. Not that she has much experience. Her boyfriends tend not to last—10 months at the most so far. Her glimpses of unconditional support have been few and far between.

Her last boyfriend started off with all the promise of every new relationship. Up-and-comer on the Hill, assistant chief of staff to the majority whip, smart, knew everything going on in D.C., but funny too, seemed not to take himself too seriously. That's what initially attracted Mel, his irreverence. They met at a DNC happy hour, free drinks and a spread of meat, cheese, and celery, half the crowd unpaid interns making this both lunch and dinner, everyone drinking as fast as possible before the open bar shut down at 7.

"Salami?" he said to Mel as she jabbed a square of white cheese with a toothpick.

"Excuse me?" She was on guard, these events always a meat market, especially as 7 neared. Mel wasn't there for the snacks or the men. Her boss on the Sam Farr campaign sent her to recruit young talent from the Hill for the race, with the promise of plum staff positions if and when he won. So far, she wasn't having any luck. No one with decent chops was willing to risk it for an uncertain future with some no-name California state assemblyman who only had a 5-point lead in the polls in a left-leaning South Bay district.

Mel knew Tyler by sight and by reputation, knew he wasn't going to leave Bonior, but he might be able to give her a tip on likely recruits.

"Salami," Tyler repeated, only this time it sounded like a statement. He lifted a floppy, graying slice with the tips of his fingers. "Dinner of champions." He opened his mouth, pretended to toss it in but threw it over his shoulder. "That's it," he said. "That's my pick-up line. Whaddya think? Needs work, doesn't it?"

Mel laughed despite herself, and she wasn't even that drunk yet. She agreed to let him "buy" her a G-and-T, as he put it, using full-on air quotes. He was smooth and awkward at the same time, told Mel exactly what he thought of President Clinton. "He looks like a cracker in a suit and tie, but the problem is, he's actually too smart for his own good. The next president'll be a C student, you watch." He admitted he was courted by the College Republicans when he was at Georgetown. "I went with the Democrats because everyone knows liberal women are looser."

"Did you really just say, *Liberal women are looser?*"

"Oops, sorry. I meant to say, *more loose*. No, wait, it's *more looser*, isn't it? I suck at grammar."

Thinking back on it now, Mel can't imagine why things went any further than that, but she was bored and lonely in her perfect little Dupont Circle apartment, doing early leg work for a campaign that wouldn't tax her energy in a meaningful way for another couple of months. She needed a distraction until it was time to head for California and lose herself in the tornado of a June special election. Thus Tyler and his cavalier attitude toward politics.

"It's a game, kid." He called Mel *kid* even though she was older by 18 months. He seemed to enjoy masquerading as the cynical old hand. "You can't whip a vote unless that's how you see it. You start getting attached to a policy detail, some super-important rider that's the lynchpin for the whole thing—the program is a twisted wreck without it, right?—you start thinking that way, you'll go crazy in 10 minutes 'cause it's always the first thing on the chopping block when the horse trading heats up."

Mel was attracted to his detachment, his track record as a caucus wrangler, his obvious disdain for everything but NCAA basketball—"purest competitive endeavor in the known universe"—and some weird idea known as string theory that Mel had never heard of and hasn't heard mentioned since. But then, of course, that was exactly what started driving her away—his lack of a moral center, his non-stop derision of everyone and everything, his crowing over how he was nailing his Final Four bracket. Maybe it was too much of a reminder of her own shortcomings, or maybe he was just a genuine asshole. Whatever it was, it resembled in its general contours the sporadic parade of boyfriends who'd come and gone before, 8 months for Tyler, 10 for Malcolm, 5 for Greg, 7 for Fritz, 2 for a guy she only ever called "Doogie" whose real name she never bothered to find out. It was like a demented version of "The Twelve Days of Christmas."

In the first 29 years of life
No true love came for me
Just eight months of Tyler
Ten months of Fritz
Fiiiive months of Greg

"So, are we doing something real here," Thom says, "or is this just campaign sex?" They just whizzed passed the spot where Schooley nearly killed her, a bad time for Thom to break the silence with a question like this.

"It's, uh…" What to say? It seems to have gone beyond campaign sex, but it doesn't seem to be a real relationship either—not yet anyway. She's never seen Thom's apartment, doesn't know his middle name, hasn't watched him stirring a pan of pasta in his underwear.

"Yeah," Mel says after an awkward silence. "It's a thing all right. Something. A thing-a-ma-bob."

"Very articulate." Thom looks studiously forward, hands at 10 and 2, exactly 4 mph over the speed limit.

"Well excuse me, Mr. Writer." Mel is pissed for some reason.

"Wait a minute. Are we about to fight?"

"Fuck you, Thom." She uses the hard-T.

"If we're fighting, this must be a real relationship." Thom smirks.

"You baited me." Mel punches Thom's shoulder, her anger receding as quickly as it came. "You fucking baited me."

"I'll fucking *bait* you, Carnes." Thom checks the mirror quickly, yanks the wheel, cuts sharply across the empty slow lane to exit the highway at the last second. He screeches into an empty parking lot that turns out to be a porn store for truckers—the massive sign, visible for a mile in both directions, reads only ADULT— unbuckles his seat belt and levers himself onto Mel's lap.

"Let's do this thing," he says.

Mel can't help breaking the moment with a non sequitur movie quote, her best mood-killing Scarface. *"First you get the money. Then you get the power.* Then *you get the woman."*

Thom leans backs against the dash, looks like he's wondering if this is a brush-off, a not-so-subtle way of telling him to get the fuck off her lap. He clearly has no money and precious little power.

"Nah, the hell with it," Mel says. "You can have the woman anyway."

SUNDAY, OCTOBER 16TH

Mel enters consciousness to a muddle of indistinct noises, echoes at the end of a long tunnel is what it sounds like. Her head throbs, her eyes piercing dots of pain, like someone drove railroad spikes into her skull exactly where her eye sockets used to be. It's a familiar feeling, more intense than usual but almost comforting in its well-remembered contours. Hangover extraordinaire. She keeps her eyes closed, thinks of the old Frank Sinatra line. *I feel bad for people who don't drink. When they wake up in the morning, that's as good as they're going to feel all day.*

She rolls on her back slowly, trying—but not too hard—to remember what sliced her down this time. The night is a giant blank. The last thing she remembers with perfect clarity is heading to the Gold Lantern with Thom after an aerobic bout of something-more-than-campaign sex, the elated feeling of a body drained by exertion and orgasm, finally allowing herself to admit that she has no problem with what happened to Howard Kane, that it's OK to bask in the ouster of her nemesis, the comeuppance of a scumbag rapist with delusions of Republican grandeur. Howard Kane, gone trubie—that's almost the best vengeance she could hope for.

Flash forward to two of Kane's pretty boy press aides, showing up with Chris Garvey from the *Columbus Dispatch*. "What the fuck are you goons doing here?" she remembers saying, very loudly, already decently drunk by that point, Thom at her elbow just as drunk, if not more. They were celebrating something they wouldn't admit out loud, buying each other shots of Jack Daniels—"If it's good enough for Keith Richards," Thom said every time they clinked glasses—engaging in a downward spiral of PDA, to the point where Sam the bartender had to give them a warning that he'd 86 them if they didn't cut the crap.

It comes back to Mel, slowly, her head throbbing harder as she reconstructs the night. The Kane boys ignored her, headed to the other end of the bar.

"Why are those Musgrove dickweeds in Cleveland at all, much less *my* goddamned bar?" she remembers slurring to Thom. He offered some kind of explanation, signaled for another round, had the bartender send a round of JDs to the enemy camp down there pointedly ignoring him and Mel.

They sent the drinks back, Sam showing up at their end of the bar with the three shots. "They said they don't take drinks from baby killers."

"Fine. Fuck 'em," Mel said. "Fuck you, you douchebag trubies!" she yelled down the bar. She was treacherously drunk at that point, but she grabbed one of the shots, lifted it high, yelled even louder, "This one's for Howard The Rapist Kane. May his soul rot in Hell with the all the Republican scumbags he ever worked for." She shot the drink back, slammed it on the bar, took a second glass and sipped contentedly, the demon temporarily exorcised. Thom added the third shot to his collection of glasses—they wouldn't let Sam take the empties away because they were using the glasses to form an outline of Ohio on the bar in the front of them—clinked Mel's glass lightly, sipped the whiskey with grim determination, his eyes gone pretty glassy by that point.

The rest of the night is pure blackness.

"MELISSA CARNES!"

A clanking, a rattling. Mel opens her eyes slowly, sees an institutional green ceiling with an intricate pattern of cracked paint, intuits she's in a drunk tank somewhere. She hopes to hell it's the Cuyahoga County lockup, not somewhere more distant like Detroit or Chicago, but anything's possible.

The lady officer watches with arms crossed and brow crinkled as Mel groans out of the cot. She squints—one of the most painful things she's ever done—scans the cell for her glasses, slides them on with an another groan.

"OK, Carnes. Let's move it," the officer says. "Some good-looking hunk of meat showed up to bail you out."

Thom looks like he's pretty roughed-up himself, but he's clean shaven and casually dressed, jeans with blown-out knees and an old Cleveland Cavaliers t-shirt, Nike sneakers she's never seen instead of his trademark brown shoes.

"Jesus Christ, Mel. You bit a guy."

"Fuck. Really?"

"Really."

"Is that why I'm in here?" She pushes her glasses to her forehead, rubs her eyes. "Oh, Christ, my head."

"Drunk and disorderly was the official charge. That Musgrove guy you bit decided for some reason not to press charges for battery. Maybe 'cause Chris Garvey's planning to write it up for tomorrow's *Dispatch*.

1994

Porter Aide Bites Musgrove Staffer in Drunken Rage. Probably all the punishment he thinks you need."

"Fuck me. Porter's gonna have a fit. Barker too. Can't say I'd blame 'em. I really *bit* a guy?"

Thom lifts Mel's forearm, places his teeth gently on the meaty part up near the elbow. "Right here. I don't know how hard. You didn't draw blood or anything. Come to think of it, that's probably why the guy didn't press charges. A love nip is all it was."

"How'd it happen?" Mel asks. "No, wait." She flutters her hand. "I don't wanna know. If I can't remember, that's my brain's way of telling me I *shouldn't* remember."

"It's pretty fuzzy to me as well," Thom says. "Couldn't say I'd be a very reliable eye-witness if I had to testify. We were both stupendously drunk. Quite a celebration." Mel smiles at Thom's use of the word *celebration*. So he feels the same way she does, that something happened between them yesterday that was worthy of a party, even if she ended up in jail after biting a guy.

A wave of nausea hits her. She slouches onto a wooden bench, spreads her legs in front of her, feet bowed out in a very unladylike pose. "I bit a kid in kindergarten," she says. Thom stands over her protectively, looks down with nothing but kindness on his face. It might even pass for something like love. What a guy. He bails her out of the drunk tank, and now she's admitting to a history of biting, and instead of ripping into her for being astoundingly irresponsible, all he can do is smile at her with a puppy dog look on his face.

"My father was apeshit mad, but my mother just laughed it off. *Sometimes you gotta bite people*, she said. At least that's how I remember it. I can't imagine she actually said that. *Sometimes you gotta bite people*. Maybe she really did, though. She was a scrapper. That's what my dad always says. Plus it's a true thing. Sometimes you *do* gotta bite people.'"

"I'm not sure you had to bite that guy last night. I honestly don't remember what they said, but it couldn't've been worth the risk of an aggravated assault charge. We're Democrats, Mel. Liberals. We're supposed to rise above."

"Fuck rising above. If I did it, I'm sure I had to."

"You were drunk. Stupendously drunk."

"In vino veritas."

"You also said you shouldn't be fucking me. I remember that."

"I don't, but it's true. I *shouldn't* be fucking you. Not that it's gonna stop me, but it's true. I'm campaign, you're press. This is off-limits fraternization of the most irresponsible sort. Campaign sex is supposed to be confined to *campaign* people. You can fuck someone on the other side, but you're supposed to keep the press out of it."

"I never knew the code was so clear-cut." Thom sits next to Mel, lays his hand on her thigh. Is he commiserating, or signaling possession? "What's the rule on biting the opposition?"

"Never had to look that one up before."

Schooley bustles in, looking even more ready for church than usual. Mel wonders if that's where he's coming from. He looks around like a Saint Bernard on safety patrol, spots Mel and Thom, rushes over. "Jesus Christ, Mel," he says before she can ask how he knew she was here.

"That's exactly what Thom said."

"Well it's exactly true. *Jesus Christ*. What the hell did you do?"

"Apparently I bit a guy."

"You look like absolute hell."

"I just spent the night in jail." She turns to Thom. "Which reminds me, why didn't you bail me out last night instead of this morning?"

"The cops told me to go sleep it off or they'd haul me in too. Some bullshit about accessory to the crime or whatnot. I'm sure it was complete crap, but I was pretty drunk, so I guess I bought it. I'm sorry. I should've made a stand. Never let you leave my side without a fight."

Mel takes Thom's hand, gives it a light squeeze. This suddenly feels like a scene from *Sid and Nancy*, and it turns out that's romantic to her. "*AAGGHH!*" she says with her best Chloe Webb. "*I look like fuckin' Stevie Nicks in hippie clothes!*" It's barely apropos, but it's the only line she remembers right now.

"What?" Thom says.

"*Sid and Nancy*. You know, Sid Vicious, Nancy Spungen. If you haven't seen it, we have to rent it sometime. It's the most awful, beautiful love story you could possibly imagine."

"Sounds great. Let's watch it tonight."

"Is that a date you're asking me out for?"

"Ahem!" Schooley says. "Let's focus here, Captain. You guys can play lovey-dovey later, if you want. Right now we have to deal with the fact that the chief strategist to Kyle Porter, Democratic candidate for the United States Senate—remember him?—she just spent the night in jail for, apparently, biting someone. Anything else I should know?"

"It was a guy from the Musgrove campaign," Thom says.

"No goddamned way." Strong language for Schooley. "Mel, is that true?"

"Technically, I was arrested for being drunk and disorderly. According to our intrepid reporter here. The biting charge was never formally entered into the record."

"Don't get technical with me right now." Schooley looks every bit the disappointed father. "You bit a guy from the Musgrove campaign, and you spent the night in jail."

"Oh, yeah," Thom says. "And there was a reporter there. Besides me, that is. Chris Garvey, *Columbus Dispatch*."

Schooley is speechless at this extra piece of information.

"Fuck," Mel says. "Does somebody have an Excedrin?"

"In my car," Schooley says. "Speaking of which, that's why I'm here. Tremont called a meeting. All com staff." Schooley checks his watch. "Five minutes ago."

Even through her hangover, Mel recognizes how unusual that is. "Tremont? Really? A com-staff meeting? On a Sunday?"

"She appears to be picking up signals," Thom says to Schooley.

Mel punches his shoulder. "Very funny, asshole. Mock a woman with a hangover, and you don't get your treat later. Capiche?"

Thom holds up his hands, does a decent Eddie Murphy. *"Wadn't me."*

"Look, Mel," Schooley says. "I'd love to banter some more with you guys, but we really should get going. Mr. Tremont very specifically said not to be late, and we already are."

"Not to be late? On a Sunday? What the hell lit the fire under his saggy old ass?"

It turns out Tremont's not even at the meeting. "Got called to the Porter place," Braddock informs them. He's sitting in a chair next to Mel's TV and VCR, a video cassette in his lap. Colin Burke paces in front of the whiteboard, Shep sitting to the side with his legs politely crossed, wearing a light blue cardigan and looking exactly like Mr. Rogers about to tell everyone to be good to each other.

Mel drops to the floor and sits cross-legged. "First he calls a com staff meeting." She massages her scalp. "Which he's never done before. Then he goes to the candidate's house on a Sunday morning. What the fuck is going on around here?"

"I have no idea," Braddock says. "But I do have a tape." He shakes the video cassette. The nausea rolls through Mel, partly from the hangover, mostly from dread that this is the moment the skeleton tumbles out of the closet.

"Musgrove's latest attack ad," Braddock says, sliding the tape into the VCR. "Running right here in Cleveland on the Sunday morning talk shows. Kane may be gone, but the Kane machine grinds on. Watch."

Mel breathes again but braces herself for something fairly bad, if Tremont wants them all to see it before Monday morning. Just as she predicted, the new spot features Kyle Porter at Friday's debate, jabbing his finger and looking like a maniac.

—How dare you?

Freeze frame on Porter's angry face.

—Richard Musgrove dares to be a man of conviction in a world of self-serving politicians who'll say anything to get elected.

—How dare you attack me.

Freeze frame on Porter looking deeply offended.

—Richard Musgrove dares to stand up to the special interests that have donated over a million dollars to Kyle Porter's campaign fund, and who knows how much else to him personally.

—How dare you lecture me.

Freeze frame on Porter's mouth in an O-shape.

—Richard Musgrove dares because the lives of 11 million Ohioans matters more to him than ruffling a few feathers. What matters to Kyle Porter? More of the same old hot air.

—That's a lie and you know it!

Freeze frame on Porter's most simian expression, then a slow crossfade to a benign head shot of Musgrove at a desk, flanked by the American and Ohio flags. It looks to Mel like his official lieutenant governor photo.

—On November 8th, vote Richard Musgrove for United States Senate.

"Or Kyle Porter will rampage through your town, raping and pillaging and accusing you of hypocrisy." Mel would shake her head, but it still hurts too much.

Braddock stops the tape.

"When they say *the attack ads write themselves*," Colin Burke puts in, "this is exactly what they're talking about, isn't it?"

"That's fine, though, right?" Schooley says. "It shows how desperate they are. For 58 out of 60 minutes, our guy killed it on the issues. He was informed, empathetic, eloquent without being too eloquent. The perfect Senator. So what if he had one bad moment?"

"And if you drew a tiny little Hitler mustache on the Mona Lisa, would anybody say, *Yeah, but it's still 98% perfect*?" Mel raises her eyebrows, which only hurts a little.

Schooley drops to a chair. "Point taken. But this shows they're desperate, right? They've gone full-on negative, and that's bound to turn people off. That's what you're always saying, Shep. Why would this be any different?"

"It'll hurt him, some," Shep admits, "but it probably hurts us more. This is Musgrove going low, but he's got our guy dead to rights. The ugly stuff comes straight out of *Porter's* mouth. The fact that it's a Musgrove ad blows back a little on them, but that's minimal. He loses a couple of points with the holier-than-thou crowd. If he shears off 5 or 6 from us, it's a net gain."

"What are we going to do?" Colin Burke sounds despondent.

Mel rubs her eyes. "I don't know what else we *can* do but keep putting him out there the way he is 99.9% of the time and hope the passion defense carries us through to the next debate. Shep, what'd your Saturday focus groups say?"

"The passion plea worked OK, just like last time, but I picked up on some serious character doubts creeping in. More of a general trend than anything Porter-specific, but it could definitely hurt us. The electorate's looking for an antidote to Clintonian charisma this cycle. I've seen this before. I call it the Character Pendulum. People were moved by Clinton because he's charismatic, emotional, thoroughly human—the exact opposite of Bush—but then they get a couple of years of that, and the economy still isn't great, and healthcare didn't happen, and crime still seems to be getting worse, and they start thinking they need a crop of boring H & R Blockheads like our friend Dick Musgrove, and that'll make everything right. This is where Porter's good looks and natural charm could hurt instead of help."

"So what do we do?" Braddock asks. "Try to tone down Porter, make him nerdier and less charismatic?" His sarcasm is obvious. "I say we play up the passion, not hide it. Musgrove may be a calm in a storm, but he's as uninspiring as a goddamn case of herpes."

"The thing is," Shep says, "we've already *got* those people, the ones who like Porter's enthusiasm and verve—not that I would advise ever using those words—and we're not going to lose *them* over some little debate kerfuffle. It's the undecideds we need to worry about. That's who Kane's playing to with these new ads, or whoever's taking over for Kane. Same difference. They'll keep running his playbook as long as it works."

"That's our advantage, then," Mel says. She has an idea. "With Kane out of the picture, they'll coast on momentum for a while, keep going with whatever plan he set in motion before he left. They keep going negative, and we tear a page out of Clinton's '92 playbook and use the negative spots against them. You remember that one, Shep? There was this attack ad against Clinton, and Carville just flat-out picks it up, puts it in *his* ad?"

Shep shakes his head. "Doesn't ring a bell."

"Maybe I dreamt it," Mel says. "In any case, it goes like this. Open with a clip of that ad we just saw, then have the camera pull back to show it's playing on a TV in some nice, normal suburban living room, a disturbed-looking blue collar dude watching, the sound of kids playing, pots clanking on the stove as the volume of the ad fades down." Mel holds up her hands to frame the shot, shifts to her baritone narrator voice. *"What's Dick Musgrove so afraid of?"* She drops her hands. "And then something, I dunno. That's all I've got." She looks to Schooley for help, her head pounding, her throat dry. She should've grabbed one of the Gatorades rolling around the floor of his car.

"I like it," Schooley says. "What's Dick Musgrove so afraid of? Is he scared of being called a hypocrite? Does it hurt his feelings to get called a liar? What else, Colin?"

Burke looks between Schooley and Mel, unsure how to join their riff.

"No, I dunno," Mel says. "Maybe we just go pure issue ads."

"Yeah right." Braddock snorts. "Foreign policy, healthcare, 5-point crime plan, the same boring old bullshit. We could double down with the humble roots and worker empathy spots too." He crosses his arms, glares at Mel with open disgust. He looks ready to take command, mutiny against his hungover captain. This is the moment he's been waiting for, Mel realizes.

She licks her lips, starts to say something, but Braddock, nostrils flaring, beats her too it. "That's a losing strategy. If this is what Musgrove's decided to go with." He jabs a finger at the TV. "Why not attack him for it? Go low but make it look like we're going high. Make Musgrove look like the asshole here. It'll work. I know exactly how we can do it. We…"

"Maybe that works, maybe it doesn't." Mel interrupts. She hates herself for putting it this way, for even uttering the word *maybe*. Braddock's making a power play, and she's equivocating, granting that he might have a point rather than squashing him at the outset. "But why risk it? The *same old boring bullshit*, as you put it, it's been getting the job done. Extremely well."

"The numbers bear out Mel's approach," Shep puts in, addressing Braddock directly, calm and reasonable as always. "We've come up from 31 to 42 on a steady diet of what-we're-for/what-we're against/who-we-are. I'd wait to change course at least until we have some 4- and 5-day tracks on these new Musgrove ads. Ride it out til the end of the week, re-evaluate then."

"With only 3 weeks left?" Braddock says. "We can't wait a few days."

Mel remembers saying the same thing to Tremont on her first day. She knows exactly what Braddock's up to here. He's never been comfortable with Mel as his boss and has only been going along to wait for a moment like this, when she's weak and the campaign looks like it's in disarray. It's exactly how she would've played it in his shoes.

The only difference is, she was right and he's wrong. She feels the power rushing through her veins again, the fighting instinct back in action.

"Yes we can," Mel says. "We've still got the lead, as far as we know. We keep on keeping on until Shep's data tells us otherwise."

Braddock starts to say something, but Mel holds up her hand. "Listen, Braddock, and maybe you'll learn something." She turns to Schooley. "Number Two, start working on some ideas along those other lines, just in case we do start slipping. You and Burke write me some scripts by tomorrow, first thing, 15- and 30-second spots. Bring in Braddock on it too." Why not throw him a bone, use his idea as a backup plan? But more importantly, exert her authority, order him to work under the guy working under *her*, spend the rest of his Sunday playing JV instead of challenging her for starting quarterback.

She lights a cigarette, glares Braddock into silence, continues instructing Schooley. "Think Cinci and Columbus media markets, not Toledo and Cleveland. We're solid along the lake. We need the heartlanders to make this a win. Now if that's all, gentlemen, I have to go throw up and sleep until tomorrow morning. Maybe call a lawyer first. I bit a guy last night, in case you hadn't heard. You can read about it in the *Dispatch* if you're interested."

# # # # #

Instead of a lawyer, Mel calls Thom, tells him to come by her suite around 6 with a video.

She power walks back to the hotel, the air doing her a world of good, throws back a couple-three Excedrin and starts a bath, but she has to deal with a visitation before she can sink into the cleansing waters, the Ghost of Christmas Past in the form of a telephone call from Ronnie Travis.

"Miz Carnes," he says with condescending formality. "It's Ronald Travis. Kyle Porter's brother-in-law."

"Yeah, I know who you are, Ronnie. Can't say I've missed you these past few days."

"I'm in the lobby of your hotel. I have to come up and talk to you for a few minutes."

"Not a chance." He's downstairs? What the fuck? "Why are you bothering me?"

"I need to talk to you about a certain. Ahem. Tape." Oh fuck, *he* knows? Ronnie lowers his voice. "It's better done in private, I'm sure you'd agree."

"I don't know what you know—or what you *think* you know—but it's handled. Just stay out of it, OK?"

"There's a new wrinkle," he says. "Charlie asked me to reach out."

Mel pauses. It seems unlikely the ice queen would trust her whack-job brother with something important like this, but it could be true. Maybe Ronnie has something on Charlie—an infidelity? couldn't be incest, could it?—or maybe she has a ridiculous younger-brother soft spot, wants this loose canon of a sibling to feel useful somehow. Mel realizes she has to play this carefully.

"I have a hard time believing that," she says at last.

"I'm not asking you to believe me. Whatever you may think of me, Miz Carnes, I have my sister and brother-in-law's best interests at heart. And I have important news on that certain front. Insider info from a source in a certain government agency. I just got the call a few minutes ago."

"I thought you said your sister asked you to reach out."

"Uh, yes, of course she did. After I told her about the call. She said I should get in touch with you right away, apprise you of the situation in person."

Now Mel knows he's full of shit. Oh, Christ. This is some kind of spy-novel fantasy Ronnie's got going. He must know something about the tape—eavesdropping around that creepy mansion, no doubt—and he's concocted an intricate conspiracy to insert himself in the story. He really is crazy—not just bored rich kid nuts but actually mentally ill.

"I'm coming up," he says when Mel doesn't respond.

"You do, and I'll have security throw you out. You want that? You think that'll help your brother-in-law? What the fuck did you learn from your father, anyway?" Mel realizes too late she should play this more carefully, handle the dippy kid with a softer touch, but she's riled up and let her anger get ahead of her strategy. "Look, whatever you have to say, say it on the phone and go away. You shouldn't even be in the lobby of my hotel. If you ever have to call me again, call me from a pay phone, OK?" Dammit, that was a mistake, feeding the delusion. What if she has to spend the next 3 weeks getting odd-hours phone calls from all over the city?

"No, you're right. Obviously." Ronnie speaks in a strained whisper now. "Sorry, my mistake. Won't happen again."

Mel only half pays attention to him spinning his tale as she tries to figure out how to handle this. Will the curve-balls never end? What the hell else could this shit-eating campaign throw at her? At one point, she lays the phone on the pillow to adjust the temperature of her bath water, picks it up again to hear Ronnie off on a tangent about deep state conspiracies against the Clinton administration. She pictures him down there in the lobby, sounding like a maniac, realizes she can't postpone action on this front. What happens if Ronnie shows up at a rally acting like this, buttonholes a reporter and gives out just enough to put someone on the trail. She imagines Jared Block hearing Ronnie's crazy story. He'd know it for what it was, but his instinct is sharp enough that he'd follow up anyway, in case there's a kernel of truth to it, which of course there is. How the hell did Charlotte let her nutjob brother find out about the tape? Mel decides to call Charlotte as soon as she can get Ronnie off the phone, tell her to bury him in a clinic for the duration of the campaign or they're all sunk.

"OK, look," she says when it seems like Ronnie's done rambling. She lowers her voice to match Ronnie's conspiratorial whisper. "Head home and wait there until I figure out what to do. It won't be long. I'll reach you through your sister. Don't tell anyone else what you told me, not even Kyle, and don't take instructions from anyone but her. Got it?"

Mel wants to slam down the phone, but she controls herself and hangs up gently. She decides to distance herself from the damage control, so she calls Tremont at home and gives him a précis of what just went down, dispatches him to the mansion for the second time that day to put a lid on the whacko brother-in-law.

"I'm getting too old for this shit," she mutters at herself. The faces looking back at her from the infinite depths of the three-sided mirror don't disagree. She gives herself the finger, dry swallows two more Excedrin, and sinks into the bath, her skin going immediately red in the scalding water.

Why is everything such a goddamned struggle, she says to herself, her mind flooded with the problems she faces. Ronnie's handled — for now — but the DEA tape still looms, and there's Porter's unpredictability to worry about, not to mention Braddock's misguided ambition, Tremont's old-fashioned tendencies, the recalcitrant undecideds, Musgrove's negative ads, the press circling like sharks now that the race is close, and who-knows-what betrayals and misfortunes right around the corner, not to mention Newt Gingrich grinning smugly in the background the whole time with his fucking Republican Revolution. Mel wants to let it all go, clear her mind and float in a bath of blissful ignorance for a while, but her fists clench when she considers everything she has to contend with. Kane's ashen face appears before her mind's-eye. *You seem like a gloves-are-always-off kinda gal. Maybe it bothers you?*

Maybe it does. What the hell has she been fighting so desperately for all these years? It strikes her that she's been running as fast as she can away from something. Away from herself. Away from her mother's legacy. Away from a reckoning with her deepest beliefs. She hates that there's a streak of true-believerism buried deep in her soul, but maybe that's the only thing that's kept her going all this time…

She's still in the bath — the water tepid by now — when Thom shows up with *Groundhog Day*, an excellent choice to end the batshit weekend she's had. She's glad he didn't go with *Sid and Nancy*.

"Okay, campers," he calls from the bedroom, "rise and shine. And don't forget your booties, 'cause it's cooooold out there today."

Thom pokes his head around the corner with a smirk, waggles a grease-stained paper bag. "I brought cheeseburgers and fries. Chocolate shakes too. Just the medicine, I hope."

"You are a god."

They spread out a towel on the bed and eat the feast while they watch, make quick, semi-desperate love while the credits roll, and Mel's asleep by 8:30, all thoughts of the campaign temporarily banished.

1994

-22
5:43AM

Mel wakes before the alarm, fully restored. Thom, once again, has slipped out unnoticed, but this time it strikes her as odd. Is this turning into a real relationship? She lights a cigarette, puts the thought out of her mind. She feels amazing. No sense wasting it with awkward questions.

She suits up in jogging clothes and takes a 45-minute power walk through the pre-dawn quiet, counts her steps up to 100 then starts again to keep her mind focused and quiet. She takes a half-hour bath, scalding hot — she manages to keep her mind empty there too, counting in and out breaths — then lingers over breakfast with the *USA Today* Sports section for distraction. It almost makes her feel like she's a normal person, tagging along with her husband on a business trip while her dad watches the kids back home. The imagined husband is, as always, facing away from Mel, one of the suits at the breakfast buffet piling scrambled eggs on his plate. She gives up the fantasy and returns to the paper before one of the suits turns around. It's a dumb fantasy anyway. What so-called "normal" woman would go to Cleveland with her husband for a getaway? Only a pol or a hired killer.

It's pouring rain by the time she heads out at 8:50 — she'll get to the office after everyone else for a change — so she hails a cab, realizes she hasn't been using anything close to her $95 per diem except when she buys drinks for everyone.

She decides to do a one-man focus group, asks the driver — African American male, 35-45 years old — who he's voting for in the Senate race.

"Voinovich," he says after a long pause. He's clearly reluctant to engage.

"That's governor," Mel says. "What about Senate? Musgrove or Porter? Who's your guy?"

"Never heard of 'em."

"Really? You're a cabbie in downtown Cleveland, and you never heard of the two men running for U.S. Senate?"

"I try to keep to myself, lady. It's better that way for a black man drivin' a cab in this day and age." With that pronouncement, he clams up entirely, spins the dial on the radio to a classical station he must think Mel listens to and cranks the volume.

Mel eases back in her seat, tries to imagine how nice it must be not to know everything happening in American politics all the time, and not caring—in fact, actually being happy about it. It sounds great and it sounds horrible at the same time.

Porter HQ is buzzing when she arrives, a palpable jump in excitement now that the race is getting serious. She sees some staffers and volunteers smile at her admiringly as she passes through the bullpen, feels the power of what she's done here in the past three weeks, reviving a moribund campaign, giving hope to the hopeless. She wonders if they've heard yet about her Saturday night arrest. Maybe that's why they're smiling. *Is that a good thing or bad thing?* Mel asks herself. She admits she can come off as kind of a nut job sometimes, which isn't necessarily a terrible reputation for a strategist to have. The face of Chevy Chase in *Caddyshack* bobs before her mind's eye. *Be the ball, Danny.* She's been the ball alright. She just needs to keep being the ball for another 3 weeks, and 2 years from now she could be Clinton's chief strategist, younger and more famous even than that little pudwacker Stephanopoulos.

Schooley's waiting in her office with a thick file folder—the requested scripts, no doubt—and the morning papers. He holds out the *Dayton Daily News* triumphantly, showing Mel the front-page story.

Senate Race in Dead Heat
By Anita Washington

DAYTON, Ohio, October 17—A U.S. Senate race that once looked like a sure win for Republican candidate Richard Musgrove has tightened substantially over the past two weeks, the latest Dayton Daily News/WHIO-TV poll shows. The race is currently tied at 40%, with independent candidate Joe Harris showing 11% support, and 9% undecided (based on 925 respondents to a telephone survey conducted over the weekend, +/- 4.5%).

This represents significant progress for Democrat Kyle Porter, who trailed by 6% in the most recent public poll, released last Monday by the *Akron Beacon Journal*. That poll showed Mr. Musgrove leading 44 to 38% (+/- 5%).

One campaign official attributed the movement to Mr. Porter's obvious passion for the people of Ohio. "He's passionate about the issues that matter to the people of Ohio," said campaign spokesman

Kline Braddock. "He's passionate about making people's lives better, and that's regular people, not rich people and corporations."

Mel loves it. It reads like a press release. She moves Anita Washington into the friendly column, makes a mental note to have Braddock give her a 10-minute sit-down with Porter next time she covers an event. Thom Reynolds says roughly the same thing in a piece noting Porter's surprising momentum as election day nears. Without fresh *Plain Dealer* polling to back up what he says, it's classic friendly reporting, naked optimism for the Democrat backed only by quotes from people attending Porter rallies and more of Braddock's post-debate spin.

> "Kyle Porter is most definitely passionate," said Kline Braddock, Mr. Porter's press secretary, after the debate in Dayton on Friday night revealed the Democratic candidate's combative side. "He's an enthusiastic booster for the causes that matter to working-class Ohioans, and he'll bring that energy to Washington."

She wonders if Thom is letting his dick do the writing here. If he is, so's Marvin Blakely at the *Akron Beacon-Journal* and Kate Winkler at the *Washington Post*, who writes, "Despite a moment of pointless aggression at Saturday's televised debate, Kyle Porter appears to have found his legs in a race most pundits had written off only three weeks ago."

"I talked to Shep on the phone this morning," Mel tells Braddock at their regular 10am sit-down. "He ran another focus group yesterday, test-drove the passion plea again. He says we should keep using the word *passionate* as much as possible. Try to avoid *enthusiastic*, *ardent*, and *energetic*. Says they come across too cold."

"You ever think of getting out of politics?" Braddock says. He brushes imaginary lint from his signature grey flannel slacks, makes a minute adjustment to the lay of his blue-and-gold striped tie.

"Sure," Mel says. "Then I wake up sober, and I know I never will. Where's this coming from?"

"I don't know. You seem pretty unhappy most of the time."

Mel wonders what's up with Braddock. Is he trying to unbalance her with negative psychology, or does he actually care?

"I'd make a lousy civilian," Mel says, ducking the accusation. Does she really seem unhappy?

"That's not a real reason."

"What about you?" Mel asks. "You dying to get out? Thinking about it?"

"I'm not unhappy like you are."

"That's not the same as being happy. Besides, who says I'm unhappy?"

"You're not?"

"I'm good at what I do," Mel says firmly, "and that's more than most people can say. Politics is bullshit most of the time, sure, but we have to make it as hard as we can for those asshole Republicans. They don't make *you* unhappy? They make *me* unhappy, and that's putting it mildly."

"It's only going to get worse," Braddock says philosophically. "Just watch what they do with their new majority. That New Gingrich—he's a piece of work."

"Vicious prick, is how I'd put it."

"Agreed. I wouldn't be surprised if he holds the budget hostage for welfare cuts, Social Security reform, probably some draconian crime bill. Telecoms, banks, mining companies—it's all gonna get deregulated. Someday, people will look back and hanker for the civility and good governance of the '80s and early-90s. Mark my words."

"You think *you'd* ever run for office?" Mel asks. Braddock is the perfect candidate. He already looks more like a Senator than either Porter or Musgrove.

"Can't. I smoked pot in college. Made out with a guy once. My parents are a mess—like get filmed on *Cops* kind of mess—and I've never had a girlfriend more than 6 months. Oh yeah, and I've got a DUI to my name. Any one of those, I might be okay to run for state legislature, maybe even House in a safe district if I could fake some kind of come-to-Jesus moment, but that's as high as I'd ever go, and only by wading through a swamp of dogshit. Nah. I'd rather say behind the podium, run interference for the assholes who think they're bulletproof. What about you? We could use more women running for office. A lot more."

"I wouldn't have expected you to say that." Mel is genuinely surprised. Sometimes she forgets that Braddock's a Democrat like she is, therefore one of the good guys. He comes across as such a classic male prick a lot of the time that it's hard to remember he probably considers himself a feminist. "The part about needing more women. You really think that?"

1994

"Sure, why not? Women are 51% of the population, nearly 55% of the electorate most years. They oughta make up more than 10% of Congress. What's stopping them?"

"Two words. Double. Standard." Mel roots around in her briefcase for her Parliaments, talks into it, mostly to herself. "If a woman had gone out there and sniped at Musgrove even half as hard as Porter did, there'd be no spinning it her way, no calling her *passionate*. She'd be a bitch on wheels for the rest of her life, and that's that." Mel flicks her lighter, blows smoke at Braddock. "You think I'm unhappy now? Imagine me out front of the cameras, spouting platitudes and trying to act so perfect no one could touch me. And they still would. They'd say I was *too* perfect, not human enough, not a real woman. Fuck me with a tree trunk, Braddock. Not in a million years."

TUESDAY, OCTOBER 18TH
3 WEEKS TO ELECTION DAY

After fretting all day Monday about a sneak attack, Mel starts to let herself believe Kane's resignation is the end of the DEA tape. By Tuesday afternoon, she's cautiously optimistic that they're in the clear, that Musgrove's new attack ads that landed Sunday and Monday are as bad as it'll get, but she forgets to consider Kane's distaste for Friday through Monday news drops, somehow ignores the likelihood that he'd orchestrate a Tuesday release to give the story maximum impact.

And that's exactly how it happens. The local news that evening leads with it, Kyle Porter's stupid mop of hair in full fish-eye lens right there before Mel's eyes. She watches in stunned paralysis as the *Channel 3 News* intros with a quick snippet of background before playing the last 2 minutes of the tape uninterrupted. Mel's been dreading this so long, it's almost anticlimactic. It feels unreal, until her phone starts ringing. The segment isn't even over yet. She lets it ring itself out.

She composes herself, takes three deep breaths, shakes out her shoulders. *Suit up, soldier*, she tells herself. *This is it.* She wonders briefly if she should do what she's planning, or duck calls until she can talk to Porter.

When the phone rings next, all of 45 seconds later, she makes a snap decision to risk it. If Porter doesn't like the plan, she can walk this back later. For right now, it's important to get out in front of this shitstorm, try to get their counter-narrative circulating as quickly as possible. She takes another deep breath, snatches up the receiver, goes into full outraged mode as soon as she hears the request for comment. There's no way to overplay the outrage here, the more histrionic the better. Mel vents the past 2 weeks' stress in a pure flow of anger.

"This is the most irresponsible, vicious, immoral attack I've ever seen!" she yells at the phone. "I've never seen the truth distorted so mercilessly. Dick Musgrove and his campaign staff oughta be ashamed of themselves."

"So you're saying the tape's not genuine?" the caller asks. She forgets who it is, *Cincinnati Enquirer* she thinks. "That's your official response?"

"The tape is genuine all right," Mel says, seething. "It's just so hideously cut up and taken out of context, I don't even know where to start correcting the record."

"Out of context? I've seen the whole tape, Ms. Carnes. Dave Parker had it messengered over an hour ago. I've been calling around. The whole pool got a copy. I don't see how there's anything out of context here."

Schooley peeks into the office, mimes to Mel that she's got other calls. He holds up seven fingers. Mel shoots him back just the one, pumps it three times for emphasis. "All I know is what I just saw on the goddamned evening news," she yells, "and I didn't see anything I know that's on that tape that might provide context. It's a hatchet job, plain and simple."

"So you're saying we got an incomplete tape? Edited by the Musgrove campaign? Seriously?"

"That's absolutely what I'm saying. I have a copy of the original. The *complete* original, right here in my office."

"You do?"

"Of course I do."

"And? Your tape shows what?"

"My tape shows the whole truth, not this astoundingly butchered monstrosity Howard Kane fed you gullible pieces of shit."

"You mean Dave Parker? Kane resigned, if you haven't heard already. I'm surprised you haven't."

"Whatever. Whoever. The point is, this is the height of irresponsibility. I can hardly believe this went on the air without anybody checking with me first."

"Not my call, Carnes. That's your TV pricks for you. No principles. I won't write about it until I know your side. That's why I'm calling. To clarify the record before we go to press."

"Don't write anything tonight," Mel says. She tries not to sound pleading, but she's losing her nerve, worries suddenly that it wasn't smart to speak so definitively about a full tape. "I'm calling a press conference, tomorrow morning, first thing, 7am. Right here at HQ. If you can't make it, we'll conference you in. I know you have a deadline tonight, but it's just one day. Your story hits the streets first thing Thursday morning, I promise."

She slams down the phone before waiting for an answer, strides to the door. "Schooley! Start calling the press pool. You, Cindy, and you, whatever the fuck your name is, help him out. Press conference, here, tomorrow, 7am. Simultaneous conference call for anyone who can't make it in person. You got that? Abby. Call over to the mansion. Tell Porter I'm on my way. If he's not there, find out where he is, radio the location to Frank."

Mel is about to rush out when she notices how quiet the room has grown beneath the incessant ringing of telephones, none of which are being answered for the moment. Everyone looks at her, 2 dozen pairs of eyes that saw exactly what she saw a few minutes ago, the 3 TVs in the bullpen still showing the local news channels, the volume muted now. The sense of anguish, of betrayal, is overwhelming. Mel knows she has to rally the troops, right now, prop up morale for the coming battle. This is a make-or-break moment for her as a leader.

"OK, attention everybody." This is hardly necessary. Everyone is already staring at her. She puts her hands on her hips, scans the room, waits a couple of beats. "We've got a bona fide campaign emergency on our hands," she says. "As I'm sure you all just saw, the media has acquired a video tape of our candidate in what looks like a very compromising situation. It *looks* bad. Very bad." She crosses her arms over her chest, wrinkles her brow. "I won't lie to you. It *is* bad. The media coverage is what I'm talking about, the damage it can do to our campaign. I can't tell you much more at this point, not until I talk to Mr. Porter. What I will tell you is, our guy's not that guy." Mel jabs her finger at the TVs, an odd gesture given that none of them is currently showing Kyle Porter. In fact, they're all on commercial break, cars and jeans and beer getting their share of screen time.

"The way they made it look, it *looks* really bad. I'm sure you're all thinking that. But." Mel pauses, knows she has to be careful here. She doesn't want to say too much in case Porter doesn't approve her plan. Not that it matters what she says to this roomful of loyalists, but this is a good practice run for the phone calls she'll have to make later tonight, and for tomorrow's presser. Circumspection is the order of the day, even if her instinct is to play the counter-move as strongly as possible, the way she just did with whoever it was who got her on the phone a few minutes ago.

"But, there's a perfectly logical explanation, and we're going to be very measured, yet very firm, in making sure the media gets this story absolutely right. What I need right now, what Kyle Porter needs right now from everybody in this room, is calm and strength."

Mel looks around, sees heads nodding, a few tears being wiped discretely from the corner of the eye. She tells them not to confirm or deny anything, to relay only the specific details of tomorrow's presser, nothing more, no glimmer of a personal reaction, no comment on the state of morale at HQ. She dredges up her George C. Scott voice, decides against an exact quote.

"I know I can count on everybody," she says with her gravelly Patton. "You've proven yourself over the past three weeks to be the best campaign staff I've ever worked with." Her voice catches in her throat, the emotion of the moment almost too much. She swallows hard, fights back the tears of frustration and worry. "Right now is when you need to show that professionalism more than ever. Thank you so much for everything you've done and everything you will do. We'll get through this. Together."

# # # # #

As Frank maneuvers the van up the curved drive of Porter's mansion, Mel thinks about the one other time she was here, precisely 2 weeks ago. She wonders if she'll have to deal with Ronnie the nutball, if Charlotte will make an appearance, and if so, what she'll say. How will she feel about the radical way Mel decided to deal with the tape? How will Porter take it? Mel prepares her pitch, knows it's a long shot Porter will go for it. She's asking him to sign on for flat-out fraud. What's her backup if and when he rejects it? She doesn't know, hasn't gamed out that conversation yet, an oversight that's forgivable only because of how frenetic everything has been since Charlotte handed her that damned timebomb.

A maid answers the door this time. She escorts Mel into the study.

Tremont is there already, reading *The Evening Leader*, the St. Mary's local daily. Mel has no idea how she knows what this newspaper is, even less idea why Tremont has a copy. She sees the headline, SCH. BD. PASSES BOND LEVY BEFORE ELECTION, wonders involuntarily what's going on with school board politics in St. Mary's and how that plays into the Senate race. Is that what Tremont's doing, advance work for an appearance in St. Mary's? It's always good prep for a candidate to know the local issues, be able to address voters about problems no Senator can do anything about. *Will you make sure our property taxes don't go up? Teachers already make more than I do, so why do they need more money? How come they haven't gotten around to repaving our stretch of the interstate yet?*

What's in St. Mary's? Then Mel remembers—Porter's home town. Is Tremont thinking like a strategist for once, planning to send Porter in front of a supportive home-town crowd to address the scandal? It's a pretty good idea. She tries to remember exactly where St. Mary's is, how far the drive is, whether it's in a deep-red county or not. It sounds pretty rural, generally unfriendly territory for a Democrat in today's world. Mel hopes Porter's parents still have their haberdashery.

She pictures the event in precise detail. Porter steps out of the shop after visiting his parents, no press allowed inside. The old couple flanks him supportively as he makes a folksy, mildly angry statement.

—*I find it distasteful, as I know a lot of voters do as well, how negative the Musgrove campaign has become over the past week. This latest incident is just more evidence that my Republican opponent will say or do almost anything to win this election. It's been particularly difficult for my family. My parents, who worked so hard, as so many parents do, to put me through school. My wife and children, who've been my rock during the rigors of this campaign. It's difficult for them to sit idly by and watch a man they know and love be mercilessly attacked. But that's politics, I know. If you can't take the heat, get out of the kitchen. Well, Dick Musgrove and his attack machine can turn up the heat all they want, because I'm in this kitchen for the people of Ohio. To fight for the causes and issues that matter to them. To make their lives better, the way they deserve.*

The home-town crowd cheers appreciatively.

It could seem desperate to some people—it is, in fact, *extremely* desperate—but it'll play to the mid-brain emotions of most voters, what's known colloquially as the *heart strings*. That's a misnomer, Mel knows. She dated a neuroscience researcher for about 8 months, just out of college, when she still occasionally socialized outside politics. "When people say something *tugs at their heart strings*," he explained once, "they're generally referring to a reaction from the amygdala, the same place the fight-or-flight mechanism resides." Mel hated his professorial side—his penchant for these kinds of explanations was one reason it didn't work long-term—but she often has cause in her job to make use of mid-brain emotional reactions, so she remembers this ex more often than the others. She wonders for a brief second where he is right now, what he's doing, if he's still such a pedantic prick.

Focus, Carnes, she tells herself. She spots the bar cart discretely tucked in the corner, pads quietly over the Oriental rug to pour herself a Scotch, wonders if it's kosher to smoke in here.

Tremont notices Mel at last, the clank of ice dropping into her glass startling him from his paper. He folds it neatly, taking his time. "Porter fires me tonight," he says at last. "You watch. He'd fire you too, but you're on the DNC payroll. He might lock you out of the building, though. Give Schooley your office. Maybe, maybe not. You charmed him from the start, so you might get to stay. But me, I'm fired for sure.

Someone has to take the fall for a fuck-up of this magnitude. That's how it works."

Mel tries to convince him not to give up so easily. If Porter cleans house, it's tantamount to admitting he did something wrong. She reminds him about her tape, their best hope for turning this scandal into a net positive. "We have to stay on the offensive here, and we need to stick together. Convince Porter to go in there tomorrow, quietly outraged that Musgrove would be so underhanded." Mel is thinking about the presser she's scheduled, her St. Mary's fantasy already forgotten. It's too obviously desperate. They need to play this more as a matter of routine, cleaning up the messy untruths perpetuated by a ratings-crazed media, not going into damage control mode. Making a drastic play to curtail the scandal practically proves it's a real thing. They stay in Columbus, hold a simple presser to get her tape out there, give Porter something like the statement she just imagined, let him take a few questions even—though that might get dicey if he can't keep Mel's new storyline straight on only a few hours practice.

"He'll never go for it," Tremont says. "I know this guy pretty well by now. He'd rather go down in flames than sign on with a lie as big as the one you've got."

"Then we have to convince him. Together. We hammer home that there's only one option here. The other fork leads straight to defeat. I'm serious, Tremont. It's united-we-stand time."

"That's a helluva speech, Carnes. You ever consider running for office yourself sometime?"

"Why do people keep asking me that?"

The door opens quietly and Charlotte enters. "Ms. Carnes. Mr. Tremont. My husband will be down shortly." She sits across from Tremont, crosses her legs, drops into an eerie silence, her sang froid almost frightening.

Mel freshens her drink, nearly offers one to Charlotte before realizing it's Charlotte's own booze she's serving herself, without having asked or been offered. She sits next to Tremont, trying for the physical manifestation of United We Stand. Tremont picks up *The Evening Leader* again, pretends to read the front page.

Porter races in a few minutes later, no jacket, tie undone, sleeves rolled to three-quarters. He looks ready for a union hall rally, or like he just came from one. Mel wonders where he's been, why it's taken so long for this little assembly to coalesce.

"Ms. Carnes. Alex. We'll get started in just a few minutes. Mr. Braddock has kindly agreed to join us. He should be arriving any minute."

Mel catches the use of *Ms. Carnes* instead of *Mel*. The formality adds to her stress level, already redlined. She also takes note of Porter inviting Braddock on his own initiative. Mel already called Braddock to tell him what's up and order him to sit tight in his hotel room and await further instructions about tomorrow's presser. Porter's desire for Braddock signals distrust in her judgment, though it could also play to her advantage. Braddock's always advising a more aggressive approach. He could be the voice that convinces Porter to give her plan a shot.

"*The Evening Leader*," Porter says, noticing Tremont's paper. "I haven't read one of those in a long time. Why on earth do you have an *Evening Leader*, Alex?"

"I'm thinking about a St. Mary's appearance. Tomorrow, late-morning. It's a 3-hour drive, I know, but that'll give you plenty of time to practice your statement. I have Colin Burke working on it right now." This is news to Mel. It worries her that the com staff is being engaged without her knowledge, but she's pleased to see Tremont thinking strategically, getting out ahead of this. He must not be as apathetic as she thought, not as resigned to being fired as he made it sound.

"The next 24 to 48 hours is critical," Tremont continues. He's calm and clinical, his usual detachment, but he looks Porter straight in the eyes, firmly, clearly knows he's making a pitch here as much as he's offering an explanation. "I've been through scandals before. If we handle this calmly at the outset, move deftly to set the voters' concerns at ease, we'll be in good shape. Otherwise..." Tremont lets the word float off, leaving it to Porter's imagination how bad it could get.

Mel can tell that the word *scandal* jolted Porter. Did he really expect to get through the campaign without this coming to light? Could he be in denial that it's really happening?

Mel almost can't believe it herself. She's been worried about this for 2 weeks, day and night, then she lets her guard down, and that's exactly when Kane delivers the blow. She knows this was his plan, his timeline and stagecraft. The negative ads on Sunday and Monday were an aerial assault to soften up the enemy for the next day's invasion. It's classic Dessert Storm politics, a favored tactic of Kane's school of thought even before anyone knew where Iraq was. Kane probably had this planned out weeks ago. Dave Parker is merely pushing the buttons in his absence.

"Sir," Mel says. She's not about to call him *Kyle* now that he's *Ms. Carnes*'d her. "If you would, I have a contingency plan already in place." She glances at Tremont. He grins dumbly, which Mel takes for cautious approval.

"How could you have a contingency plan, Ms. Carnes? Wait. You knew about this before today?"

"I gave her a copy of the tape, Kyle," Charlotte says flatly. She remains still as a statue, as though none of this has anything to do with her.

"You what now?"

"Kyle, if you'll allow me." Mel decides to risk a collegial *Kyle*, reassert her trusted advisor status. "Your wife simply wanted me to be aware of a potential problem for the campaign, so I could be prepared in the unlikely event that it came to light. Which it has. And it's a good thing, too, because I have the perfect response."

"Perfect response?" Porter drops to the couch. "You saw that tape, Ms. Carnes. What response could be in any way perfect, other than dropping immediately out of the race?"

"Do you have a television and video recorder handy?" she asks. "I'll show you."

Charlotte rises, slides back a bookshelf to reveal a tastefully hidden media center, three televisions, a VCR, a laser disc player, a high-end stereo sound system. It's like a scene from a James Bond movie, Charlotte the villain in her high-tech lair. Mel pulls the tape out of her briefcase, sees her pack of Parliaments, itches for a smoke.

The four of them watch the beginning of Mel's tape, no mention of waiting for Braddock.

"What the hell is this?" Porter mutters about a minute in, after one of Ernie's actors has just filled in "Kyle Porter" on the DEA's need for an outsider to help them infiltrate cartel money-laundering networks.

Mel stands, pauses the tape, explains her plan. Braddock enters near the beginning, unnoticed by everyone but Mel. He drifts to the bar cart to listen, pours himself a Scotch, neat, sips reflectively as Mel talks, nodding in agreement.

"Stop right there, Ms. Carnes," Porter says before Mel can finish. He's so obviously stunned by all this that he can't even seem appalled.

"Just hear her out," Charlotte says sharply.

"I will not hear her out, Charlie. I'm not going to participate in a criminal conspiracy just to win an election. To *maybe* win."

Mel knows it's done. He'll never go for her plan. He seems relieved, in fact. She remembers Steubenville, wonders if he's been secretly hoping for this tragic endgame all along.

"You need to at least deny it's you on the tape," Braddock says, stepping from the shadows. He sips his Scotch, as though that's the gesture that establishes his authority to make such a pronouncement.

"He's right, Kyle," Tremont says. "Otherwise you're completely sunk."

"Maybe I *deserve* to be completely sunk," Porter shouts. He gives Charlotte an angry glower.

"We can't just throw in the towel, Kyle," she replies with pure ice in her tone.

"At least let *us*." Mel swirls her hand to include herself, Tremont, and Braddock. "Refuse to confirm it's you on the tape."

"*Refuse to confirm?*" Porter says. "That's rather Orwellian, wouldn't you say, Ms. Carnes? I'm on that tape. I was in that hotel room. Not the one on that horrible fraud there. The *real* hotel room, where I really did, God forgive me, agree to an illegal business arrangement. I regret that decision, but I have to live with it. I have to quit the race, effective immediately."

"All due respect," Braddock says, "but you can't do that." He looks to Tremont, as though that's the correct direction to make an appeal. "There are a lot of people relying on you. Think of all your supporters."

"They've been supporting a fraud," Porter says. He drops to the couch, leans into his hands. "A complete fraud."

"If you're not comfortable with a denial," Mel says, realizing the angle she should take. Porter's lawyer side, his genuine love of justice—that's the best appeal. "At the very least we need to express outrage over this illegal leak. You were cleared of all charges, let's not forget that. A clear case of entrapment, the evidence sealed by a federal judge to prevent the DEA's illegal actions from tarnishing your reputation. And now your privacy has been violated. Egregiously. That injustice is only compounded by quitting the race. You can't give in to this underhanded maneuver. If you do, you're admitting that two wrongs does make a right."

"I can do outrage," Braddock says. "Easily. The press eats that up. But that's just a start. We need something along the lines of a denial, if you're not comfortable with an outright denial."

"*Along the lines of a denial?*" Porter shakes his head in disgust.

"That's right," Mel says. "Create some reasonable doubt that it's you on that tape. Anything short of that, we're doomed."

"I talked to Shep before I came over," Braddock adds. "He says we'll drop 10 points overnight, no matter what. What we're looking at is cauterizing the wound as fast as possible, then finding a way to get back in it. There's still 3 weeks til election day. We can do it."

Ronnie bursts in. "What'd I miss?"

"Sit the fuck down, Ronnie," Porter snarls. It's the first time Mel has heard Porter use foul language. The stress is obviously getting to him.

"Look, Kyle, this is total bullshit." Ronnie waves his hands randomly. "That's not you on the tape. It's as simple as that. It *looks* like you, but no one ever says your name, and the footage is grainy enough to make it doubtful."

"How do you know all this?" Porter asks. "They only showed a small clip on the news."

Ronnie glances at Charlotte. "I've seen the whole tape. *Before* this. Charlie showed me. Who else in here's seen it already?" He looks at Tremont, then Braddock, gives Mel a lingering smirk.

"We've been through all this already, fucktard," Mel says. Porter shoots her a look. They've both revealed hidden vulgarity in the past minute. Porter seems unfazed. Even with Mel's fraudulent tape and her Orwellian suggestions, both of which he clearly finds objectionable, he doesn't seem on the verge of tossing her out. Not that it matters. Without a radical way to beat back this scandal, all the strategy in the world isn't going to win this race.

In the end, Porter agrees to a St. Mary's appearance, tomorrow at noon—"a High Noon showdown," Ronnie says unhelpfully—his statement coordinated with Braddock going on the attack against Musgrove for the leak and against the media for its irresponsible scandal-mongering. No further mention of Mel's tape by anyone, least of all her. She's secretly relieved that she didn't have to go down that dark alley. It's enough that she thought it up and brought it to fruition.

Frank takes Mel, Tremont, and Braddock back to town in the campaign van.

"Are we completely fucked?" Braddock asks when they're out of the driveway.

"Absolutely," Mel says. "Which will only make it that much more epic when we pull off a win."

Tremont looks unconvinced. "Keep dreaming, Carnes."

"I refuse to give up," Mel says, and she means it. She's fired up. Despite Porter vetoing her original strategy, they have a decently aggressive avenue to pursue, a narrow but not unrealistic path to success. "You think Bill Clinton would've been half as impressive without the Jennifer Flowers scandal? It strengthened him, made legends of Carville and Stephanopoulos for getting him through it. It's our turn to prove that Democrats can deal with scandals as well as Republicans do. If we fuck Howard Kane and Dick Musgrove on this one, we're legends in our own time."

THURSDAY, OCTOBER 20TH

Mel power walks to HQ through a pre-dawn mist of acid rain, arms pumping fiercely, her new trenchcoat flapping behind her like an errant sail on a storm-tossed ship. The 10-minute walk nearly destroys her uncaffeinated body, and she pants and wheezes as she unlocks the front door. She's completely let herself go over the past 3 weeks, smoking and drinking far beyond her usual limits, even for a late-stage campaign. Now that the campaign is unraveling—Wednesday's effort to head off the scandal at the pass was a complete disaster on all fronts—she needs to start taking better care of herself. She feels another cold coming on, hacks up a blob of phlegm and spits it onto the sidewalk before pushing through the door into the empty bullpen. At least she's not hungover this morning, a rare beginning to her day lately.

She stands in the middle of the quiet room, turns slowly to take it all in, as though this is the last day she'll be here instead of the 19th-to-last. It seems like the election should be much closer, 4 or 5 days at the most, just a weekend instead of 2 1/2 weeks separating her from the catastrophe the voters seem prepared to hand her and her party. It's not just Porter who's sinking—the Senate map looks increasingly desperate, the House flip a foregone conclusion. Last night on Ted Koppel, Newt Gingrich was downright ebullient, talking about the *opportunity society* as though he actually gave a single goddamn about the American people.

Mel drops to a chair at a random desk, sits there until her breathing returns to normal, then lights her 1st Parliament, wonders what the hell she's going to do with the next 20 days of her life until she can go back to D.C., a thought that leads naturally to the bigger, gnarlier question: what the hell is she going to do with the next 20 *years* of her life? She's an 8-year veteran of high politics—10 if you start the clock with her junior internship at the DNC—and already it seems as though this career has run its course. But is she really ready to give it all up and start over? Will she be able to accept going out on a loss? Does it even matter?

1994

She sits there staring into space, chain smoking, until the first of the volunteers arrive at 7. The three young women are startled by Mel's presence—she's often the first to arrive, but she never sits in the bullpen with the lights off—one of them reaching into her briefcase, probably for her pepper spray, before realizing who it is. They apologize for frightening Mel, making a ridiculous fuss—it's Mel who scared them—and driving Mel to retreat into her office. It's too bad. She might've stayed with them for a few minutes, talking about their experience working for the campaign, sympathizing with their worries about the future under a Republican Congress. These kids came of age during the Reagan-Bush years and got just the tiniest taste of unified Democratic government before facing a Republican tsunami. Or is Mel just projecting here? Maybe these young women, working at the lowest rungs of the Porter campaign, aren't as politically concerned as she assumes. They certainly seemed light-hearted, pushing through the main door with smiles on their faces, chattering about something frivolous Mel didn't catch, maybe even gossiping about which men in the office are the best husband material.

Mel admits to herself that she has no idea how the typical twenty-something woman sees the world of 1994. Are they as worried about the stalled progress of feminism as she is? Do they even identify themselves as feminists? Could they possibly think that gender equality has more or less been achieved, as she's heard a lot of men—all Democrats—imply over the past few years? Mel needs to get Shep to run a focus group on these questions, use up the polling budget for something she can take with her beyond this doomed campaign.

She erases the whiteboard in her office, stares at the blank surface for a full minute, refocusing her attention on the problem she faces today. To even call it a *problem* is absurd—as though it's solvable. What could she possibly write? What Hail Mary can rescue them from this sinkhole? Yesterday's *Cincinnati Enquirer* poll has them down by 14 points again, 45-31. Shep's latest tracks are less horrible—they're only trailing 44-33—but he said the bleeding hasn't fully registered yet. "I wouldn't be surprised if we're south of 30 by the weekend," he said yesterday when he delivered his mid-week report. "In fact, I'd be surprised if we aren't."

"GODDAMMIT!" Mel spikes the marker against the carpet. They were finally ahead, even if their lead was well within the margin of error. There were plenty of undies to vacuum up, a clear path to doing it, the time nearing when Tremont's vaunted get-out-the-vote operation would come into play. Just 3 days ago, she actually believed they could win this thing. Now it's clearly over, Porter's appearance in

St. Mary's turning quickly into an ugly media feeding frenzy, Braddock's attempts to pump up the anti-Musgrove outrage a complete fizzle.

She's relieved, in a way, that Porter decided not to go with her video. She'd be shitting bricks right now, and for the rest of the campaign, if they'd released it, but at least they'd be in the running, the adrenaline flowing, every day a challenge to be all you can be, as the Army says. At this point, it's a matter of climbing back out of another hole, only with much less time and a bigger anchor attached to them, and Mel knows that everybody, including Porter, thinks it's impossible.

She's on the verge of quitting herself but hasn't made the leap. It's not in her DNA to give up, even on a lost cause. She reminds herself for the 50th time in the past 2 days how her parents reacted to her suspension in 6th grade for the safety patrol strike, what her mother said when it was all over. *A short-term loss means nothing as long as you never give up.* Sure, this is about a million times worse than that, but if she admits defeat, she's basically telling her mother to fuck off. Her dead mother. You can't argue with a dead woman's advice—not her canonized mother, not quite yet.

Mel picks up the marker, chews the end to keep herself from lighting the day's 7th cigarette, consults the schedule on the bulletin board. There are two bright spots, two chances to turn it around. Clinton's coming to town next Tuesday to speak at a big rally downtown—if he doesn't cancel, that is. He's supposed to stump for Porter along with the Democratic House incumbent, Louis Stokes, and the Democratic gubernatorial candidate, Rob Burch. If she were Clinton's White House strategist, she'd advise the president against standing next to a guy who said *Yes* to drug lords in a video that's all over the national news. Burch is already toast, running consistently 30 to 35 points down against a massively popular incumbent, and Stokes is cruising to an easy victory in the heavily Democratic 11th district, so there's no real loss to the party if Clinton backs out.

There's also the final debate 2 days later, no cancellation possible there. Broadcast live on every FOX affiliate in the state, it's their last chance to make their case—to tear down Musgrove, is more like it. Porter's stuck in the mud, so their only hope is to get Musgrove down there too, rip away his soft support, hope Harris can climb into double digits on the shit flying between the two principals and the undies mostly break their way at the last minute. It's a slim hope, but it's not nothing. The only question is, how to drag Musgrove down? Her Linda Musgrove bullet got deflected, ditto the whistleblower tape. Kane played that off as deftly as anyone could, exited stage left with grace and a time bomb that would assure his guy's victory. He probably got a resignation bonus to boot, the fucking rapist.

Mel sits at her computer, starts rewriting Porter's stump speech, a pointless exercise, but it keeps her busy.

Schooley arrives at exactly 7:30 with his daily delivery of newspapers. The *Columbus Dispatch* has a nasty and misleading headline — DRUG-RUNNING DEM IN BIG TROUBLE WITH VOTERS — over a flash poll from Wednesday, sample of 752 likely voters, +/- 5% margin of error. Mel lays her head on her desk after glancing at the graph showing Musgrove with an 18-point lead, 48-30, almost exactly where they were a month ago when Barker sent her on this kamikaze mission. They've got Harris at 10 and undecided at 12. Mel tries to take solace in those numbers. Musgrove is up only 8 points from his pre-tape 40%, so he hasn't picked up all of the voters Porter lost. A decent chunk are parking in undecided for now, waiting to see how it plays out. If she can think of some way to minimize the damage, they might get those undies back...

Braddock pokes his head in at 9:30. "Any genius ideas, boss lady?" He looks and sounds like they have a comfortable lead. Mel throws the whiteboard marker at him. He swats it away like a cornerback knocking down a wobbly pass, flashes Mel a plastic smile, closes the door.

Shep comes in at 10:30 with his spot poll from last night. "I've got us down by 16, 45-29, with undecided at a 2-month high of 18."

"That's a lot of undies," Mel says, the hope evident in her voice.

"I wouldn't count on them breaking for us in any meaningful way," Shep says. "The tape is still a fresh wound, plenty of time for reaction to sink in, and as it does, it's not likely to get better for Porter. The die-hard Dems will hold their nose and stick with us, but the blue-collar social conservatives we sometimes get will definitely go with Musgrove. My bet is that a lot of those undecideds are simply going to stay home in disgust, or leave Senate blank on their ballot. I've seen it before. When undecided runs this high in mid-October, turnout is even lower than usual. The factors line up. The governor's race is a blow-out, there's nothing compelling in the ballot measures. I wouldn't be surprised if we see turnout below 25%, and that would be pretty bad for us under any circumstances, scandal or no scandal."

Mel still can't believe that's the word — *scandal*. It's kind of unreal, the whole situation. She realizes she didn't let herself fully believe it would happen until the tape actually hit the news. Up to that exact moment, it was always just a strategic factor — something to worry about, plan for, spin away if possible. It was a McGuffin driving the side plot between her and Kane, not something that would actually impact the race between Porter and Musgrove. She thinks back to her motel showdown with Kane, remembers it almost like a movie she saw years ago, some noir political thriller — her own personal *Manchurian Candidate* — slashes of light from the blinds striping Kane's chest as he says, *You show me yours, I'll show you mine, huh Carnes? Is that what you've got in mind?*

Mel mouths her line, a sardonic smile curling her lips. *Couldn't hurt, right?*

She must've thought, deep down, that it couldn't, that there'd be no real-world consequences. Now that everyone in Ohio knows what a stupid greedy fuck Porter is, now that he broke down in St. Mary's and admitted straight up that, despite the entrapment, yes, he was the man on that tape agreeing to launder money for drug lords — now that there's no amount of denial or subterfuge that can hide that fact, and no one doesn't hear the giant sucking sound pulling Porter into the ground, it's still hard for Mel to accept that this is the reality she faces. She wishes she could've seen Cliff Barker's face when he heard the news.

Mel goes back to staring at the blank whiteboard, hoping for an inspiration. She's in something like a trance when she gets a call from the West Wing an hour later, Clinton's event planner confirming the expected cancellation. Mel sits with it for a minute — it wasn't a matter of *if*, just *when* — then puts in a call to David Wilhelm, just to hear the rationalization from him personally. He confides that he's not sure how much the president is helping anyone in any case, given his sagging approval rating.

"He dropped from 44% approval last month to 41 in the latest Gallup." Wilhelm sounds angry. "He's at 40 with independents and only 68 with Democrats. Did you hear that? Just two-thirds of all Democrats approve of a Democratic president 21 months into his term. That blows for the whole party, Carnes."

"So it's over, then?" Mel says. "For us, I mean."

"We've taken you off the board," Wilhelm says flatly. "Calling it a Republican pickup."

"This soon?" Mel knows she sounds pathetic. "We've still got 19 days to make our case."

"And a 16-point deficit, Shep tells me. You're not the only one we're writing off, if that makes you feel any better. We're throwing in the towel on Oklahoma, Maine, and Arizona too. And forget about the House. It's pretty obvious at this point that's going to be a bloodbath.

We're bracing to lose as many as 5 dozen seats, so it's not just the majority, it's anything even close. We're focused entirely on holding the Senate. With 4 definite write-offs at this point, we're clinging to Wisconsin, Michigan, Pennsylvania, and Virginia. We're sweating it in New Jersey. Ditto Pennsylvania. We've got a Democratic governor refusing to endorse our guy, if you can believe it. We were feeling good about Tennessee for a while, but that's turning sour. We have 2 possible pickups, Minnesota and Vermont, but I'm not confident. It's possible we don't pick up a single seat, which means we can lose 6 at most and still have Gore for the tie-breaker, but fuck me if it's not looking like we might lose 9 or 10 overall. And that's not even worst-case. Feinstein could go down in California. And there's that Chuck Robb bullshit. If we lose a seat to Oliver Fucking North, I swear to God, I might go postal. I'm not boring you, am I Carnes?"

The truth is, Mel was barely listening. She put Wilhelm on speakerphone, lit a cigarette, and stared blankly at her whiteboard, crisscrossed with doomed ideas, barely legible in any case.

"No, I get it, David," she says. "You need to vent. You're on the razor's edge. Not much to vent about out here. Porter's a turkey, and there's nothing we can do about it."

"You've got almost 3 weeks, Carnes. Maybe something happens, a juicy scandal in the other direction, or Musgrove flips out and starts punching reporters at a presser."

"I'm not holding my breath."

"Yeah, well." There's silence on the line. Mel lets it draw out. She can hear chatter in the background, pictures Wilhelm in his war room, maps and charts and a thick haze of cigarette smoke, the room swampy with the smell of desperation B.O., HQ for a losing cause. She heard the election called a Republican Revolution for the first time last night on CNN, hates that Howard Kane might've been right to use that term.

"Yeah, well," Mel echoes a minute later. She's pretty sure Wilhelm doesn't even remember he's on a call. "We can always hope. Good luck, David. I mean that. I wish I could do more."

"Yeah, uh, you too, Carnes." The line goes dead.

Mel listens to the dial tone, lets it drone on as she crosses the room and erases the whiteboard, Wilhelm's words slowly sinking in, jarring her from her funk. *Maybe something happens, a juicy scandal in the other direction, or Musgrove flips out and starts punching reporters at a presser.* She yanks open the door, yells for Schooley, an idea suddenly hitting her. There *is* one more Hail Mary she can throw.

# # # # #

Mel flies to Chicago that night, gets a hotel at the airport under a fake name, spends the night watching everything but the news. She drains the mini-bar by midnight, but she gets up at first light, takes a 20 minute shower, lays out her Mary Baker outfit—navy pinstripe interview suit and white silk blouse—drinks the in-room pot of coffee sitting at the desk in her hotel robe. She stares out the window at the airplanes taking off and landing, imagining all the different places she could be right now. Instead of flying to Chicago, she could've quit the campaign and jetted off to the Caribbean, or Fiji, or Paris. It would be mid-afternoon in Paris. She could be sitting at a cafe, reading Simone De Beauvoir and sipping wine instead of drinking tepid hotel coffee and dreading the day ahead. She has the money, doesn't need to work again for at least a year, probably more like 2 or 3 if she's careful. She has the freedom and means to do whatever she wants.

This is the point where you say you're going to quit politics and write a searing novel about your experience, Mel chides herself. This idle fantasizing has to stop. It's not doing her any good, doesn't reduce her stress like it used to sometimes. *Calgon, take me away*. It doesn't take her away these days, only makes her feel worse for trapping herself in a life that alternates between frenzy and boredom, the frenzy entirely in the service of middle-aged white men who so far have done precious little to make her and her fellow women's lives any better. She remembers the title of the psychiatrist's book in *What About Bob*—*Baby Steps*. They take baby steps, and sometimes not even that.

She gets up from the desk, paces the tiny room, does a Richard Dreyfus impersonation for herself. *"So the real question is, what is the crisis Bob? What is it you're truly afraid of?"* It's a joke movie, but it's a real question. What *is* she truly afraid of?

She drops to the bed. Why is she asking herself this? Melancholy sweeps over her, a tear at the corner of her eye as she pictures her mother, pale and defeated, the beeping of infernal hospital machines competing with a voice grown weak from disease. "Do something worthwhile with your life, poppet."

Mel addresses the sprinkler in the ceiling. "All right, Carnes," she says aloud. "Enough bullshit. Stop feeling sorry for yourself. Right now! Get up, get dressed, and fix this shit."

She's annoyed to notice how much of the morning she let slip away with her self-flagellation. It's past 8:30am when she steps into the cab, 9:15 by the time she reaches Linda Musgrove's duplex.

1994

She gets a brief feeling of *déjà vu* as she raises her hand to push the doorbell. She thinks back — it's been 2 weeks and a day since she was last here, hardly any time at all in a straight life, but a lifetime in this horrendous campaign.

When the door opens, Linda Musgrove tries to look casual, but Mel can tell she's surprised. "Yes, uh." She's wearing a silk kimono and wool leggings, no make-up, a mug of coffee held loosely in her hand. There's no indication that she's getting ready for work. "Can I help you?"

"You mind if I come in? There's a few things we have to talk about."

Linda says nothing, stares at Mel for a few seconds, then turns and leads her to the kitchen. She sits at the table, sips her coffee, doesn't offer Mel anything.

Mel waits a beat, lets Linda look deep into her eyes to know how serious she is, then slides a photostat of a brokerage statement across the table. "You've had quite the windfall there, Mrs. Musgrove." Mel emphasizes the *Mrs.*, expects Linda to flinch and insist on being called Ms., as she's listed on the statement.

"I'm not sure, Miss Baker, how this is any business of the *Wall Street Journal.* Unless you're looking for investment tips, that is. I've had a good run of it. Not that I'm prepared to share my secrets with your readers, if you don't mind."

Mel lays her official campaign credential on top of the statement. "OK, I'll start by cutting the bullshit. My name isn't Mary Baker, and I'm not a reporter. I'm the chief strategist for Kyle Porter's Senate campaign. Mel Carnes." She holds out her hand, but the other woman stares it back into her lap.

"What do you want, *Miz* Carnes? I believe I made it perfectly clear on *Good Day Columbus* exactly how I feel about those irresponsible allegations made against my husband."

"I agree they were irresponsible." Mel pushes her glasses up her nose. "I just don't think the public knows quite yet the original source of that irresponsibility."

"You can't prove anything."

"No?" Mel reaches into her bag, slaps a photograph in front of Linda. It shows her with a badly beaten face, a decent reproduction of the photos Linda flashed to Mel the last time she was here.

"That's obviously a fake," Linda says. She flips the photograph over so she doesn't have to see herself looking so abused.

"Indeed it is," Mel says with a smirk. "Just like the ones you showed me. You didn't realize I slid one into my briefcase when you weren't looking, did you?"

"There's no way," Linda says. "That's not the…" She stops herself, realizes the trap Mel laid.

"Not the same as the photos you showed me that day? Admittedly, no. I had to use a still from the *Good Day Columbus* tape, and naturally, my guy didn't recreate the same bruising pattern your guy used. He might've gone a little over the top, in my opinion, but it's awfully realistic, wouldn't you say." She flips the photograph right side up so Linda has to look at it.

"What, exactly, are you saying?"

Mel can tell Linda's getting nervous. Linda glances down at the photograph, flips it upside down again.

Mel takes her time lighting a cigarette. "You don't mind if I smoke, do you?" she asks, blowing smoke past Linda's shoulder. Linda says nothing. "You're figuring out what I'm up to, aren't you? You told your story, and now I'm prepared to tell mine. How you contacted my office at Porter HQ, lured me to Chicago with a tawdry story, showed me those horrible pictures, promised a sensational scandal for my candidate's opponent, gave me a sample of your work to prove it."

"I never…"

"Your word against mine, and I've got the photograph right here to back up my story. This is a copy, of course, so tearing it up won't do any good."

"It's bullshit, is what it is."

"And just why would I manufacture such a thing? You, on the other hand, obviously had a motive for doing so, as evidenced by this sudden infusion of cash." Mel taps the brokerage statement. "So you see where I'm going with this, right?"

Mel lays out how Linda could be charged with blackmailing her ex-husband, publicly shamed for manufacturing a domestic abuse story and bringing it to the enemy camp to force him into a difficult situation he'd obviously be interested in buying his way out of. "That's exactly what you did, isn't it?" Mel gets up, runs the end of her cigarette under the kitchen tap. "I don't expect you to admit it. Of course not. I'd be disappointed if you did. But we both know that's how it went down, and I'm *extremely* confident that I could make the charges stick." She flips the photograph over again, hovers over Linda's shoulder. "Yeah, my photo is fake, but *who* faked it? If I had, why wouldn't I release it to the press when the story was hot, when it could do the most good for my guy?"

"What do you want me to do? Go back on TV, say I lied before? That Richard really is a monster? Who would believe me?"

Mel sits, folds her hands on the table, gives Linda her most sympathetic look, head nodding slightly, eyes crinkled, lips pursed. "No, I get it. It's pretty embarrassing, admitting you lied, but honestly, it's the most natural thing in the world for a woman who's been abused. Covering for her abuser. Lying to herself, even. It's an easy sell, especially for someone with your obvious acting ability. Why don't you practice it for me. Imagine I'm Kelly Hastings." Mel flashes a vapid smile. "*Mrs. Musgrove, why don't you tell our viewers why you've come back on our program this morning?*"

"I won't do it. You're bluffing. You can't charge me with blackmail."

"No, not personally, but I *can* accuse you publicly of lying, and I can easily envision Dick coming after you once he's won the election."

"That's such bullshit. He'd never do that. He'd have to admit he paid me off, and what would that get him?"

Mel does her Geraldo Rivera impersonation. "Senator Musgrove, I have evidence here that you transferred a large sum of money to your ex-wife right before she went on television and denied that you ever abused her, as the newspapers were beginning to report at the time. Why would you do that, sir? You already had a divorce settlement, years ago. What were you covering up?"

Mel lights another cigarette, lets it sink in how this whole thing could play out, then makes it explicit for Linda. "He's got one option. He admits he paid you off, says he had to do it, not because he ever beat you but because you were blackmailing him. It would've destroyed his political career — needlessly — if he didn't get you to tell the truth. So he gave you a financial incentive to be honest, the very incentive you were asking him for. He's got the truth on his side, you see, because that's exactly how it happened, isn't it?"

"That's not…"

"Plus," Mel presses on, "he's in for much worse if he denies it and the story keeps growing. It's the drip-drip-drip that kills politicians, not the big bombshells. But if he tells the truth — and seriously, it's a simple truth — then he's the victim and you're the villain, a blackmailer, gold digger, the worst kind of opportunist. You'll be crucified in the media. It'll be ugly. Truly ugly. And that's even before the trial starts." Mel blows smoke rings at the ceiling, let's Linda writhe.

"But that's not how it has to go. You go back on TV, tell the real story, how you finally worked up the courage to tell the truth, but then he got to you. He went crazy, threatened your life, then his campaign manager offered you money to deny everything, so that's what you did. They scared and cajoled you into covering it all up again." Mel takes Linda's mug, sips the coffee, grown cold by now. "That's a much better outcome for you. Instead of being a blackmailer, you're a terrorized victim whose rich ex-husband and unscrupulous campaign manager thought they could shut up with an avalanche of hush-money."

"But it's not true. He never beat me. I can't go on TV and say he did. He'll sue me for defamation of character."

"So I guess it's a good thing you've got enough money to hire the best lawyers. Do you know how hard it is for a public figure to collect libel or slander damages? Practically impossible since the Sullivan standard. Ask your lawyer about it. I'm serious." Mel takes out a pen, writes *New York Times v. Sullivan* in the margin of the brokerage statement, adds the name of her hotel and the room number. "I'll be there until tomorrow morning. Call me tonight, once you've had a chance to talk to an attorney and think it over. You seem like a shrewd woman, Linda. I'm confident you'll do the one thing here that makes the most sense for you."

# # # # #

Mel goes to the observation deck of the Sears Tower, looks down at the ant-like cars crawling through downtown, tries to imagine what it feels like to be a god, to be truly amoral and unconcerned like the ancient Greek gods must've been. She's not sure how she feels about what she just did. On the one hand, it's horrible to manipulate a fellow woman like that, just to win an election — *maybe* win an election. It's still a longshot that Musgrove won't win anyway. He is running against a guy caught on tape agreeing to launder money for drug lords. Between a beater and a crook, it's a tough call who loses fewer votes.

On the other hand, Linda started it, and she is, in fact, a blackmailer. That's the only reason Mel could talk herself into doing it. Politics is an ugly business, but she didn't drag Linda into this. On the contrary, she got played by a manipulative gold digger. Mel almost hopes Linda refuses so she can watch Geraldo and his ilk tear her to pieces.

Yet it gives her no joy to ruin someone's life, even if she could make the case to herself that Linda deserves it. So maybe it really is time to get out of politics, where the need to ruin someone's life for a minor nudge in the polls is always a possibility. This is Mel's first time manipulating someone with such blatant callousness, but she knows it won't be her last — not if she keeps doing this job.

She cuts off this line of thought, turns from her godlike view of Chicago and heads for the elevators, itching for a cigarette. She's not quitting anything until November 9th at the earliest, so it's not doing

1994

anybody any good to consider a life outside politics. Not for another 18 days.

Mel walks the streets of downtown Chicago, trying to think what she'll do if Linda doesn't call, how she can possibly rescue the campaign from its present morass without a counter-scandal to drag down Musgrove. She has exactly zero ideas, eventually gives up and finds a theater showing *Pulp Fiction*. She's been meaning to see it since it was released a few weeks ago but hasn't had a chance to get away from the campaign, even for 2 hours. *Pretty soon, I'll have plenty of time to go to the movies as much as I want,* she says to herself. That sounds amazing at the moment — unstructured afternoons, one after the other, sitting in a darkened theater, subsisting on popcorn and red vines, ducking out for cigarettes — though she also remembers the horrible emptiness of the slack season, the feeling she has as soon as she emerges from a movie that there's no point in doing anything, no point to life at all. Often she turns around and goes right back in, watches 2 and 3 movies in a day, sometimes runs into a streak of total crap but occasionally hits a vein of pure gold, like that day in '92, a few weeks after Clinton won the White House, when she saw *The Crying Game*, *Glengarry Glen Ross*, and *A Few Good Men* right in a row, starting with the 2pm matinee and ending just before midnight with Jack Nicholson's voice ringing in her head, *You can't handle the truth!* Nope, it's true. And neither can anybody else.

The violence and wit of *Pulp Fiction* sweep Mel away, make her yearn to be as bad-ass as possible, to face the abyss with aplomb and a full awareness of the absurdity of humans' futile striving to build a comfortable nest for themselves. She emerges from the darkened theater to a piercingly bright Chicago afternoon, cures her sense of disorientation by immediately ducking into the nearest bar for a whiskey. She quotes the movie to lock in some of her favorites, to practice getting the voice right. It's one of the reasons she can recite movie lines on the fly so easily. Practice.

"Uncomfortable silences," she says to the bartender. "Why do we feel it's necessary to yak about bullshit in order to be comfortable?" The bartender stares, comfortable with uncomfortable silences, Mel surmises. "That's when you know you've found somebody special. When you can just shut the fuck up for a minute and comfortably enjoy the silence."

When he comes back to see if Mel wants another drink, she says, "Get it straight buster. I'm not here to say please, I'm here to tell you what to do, and if self-preservation is an instinct you possess, you'd better fucking do it and do it quick."

"You just saw *Pulp Fiction* across the street, didn't you?" He wipes a non-existent spot from the bar and drifts away before Mel can think of a good line to shoot back. It bums her out a little that he didn't even try to flirt. She must look like hell. She trots off to the women's room to confirm—yup, absolutely downtrodden face—thinks about leaving but goes back to the bar.

She returns to the hotel after 3 drinks, checks for a message from Linda, waits in her room watching ESPN until 1am. Linda never calls. Not that Mel can blame her. She'll take her chances with the tabloids and the blackmail charge rather than risk compounding it with defamation. Sensible advice, if that's what her lawyer told her. *Sullivan* makes it hard for a politician to collect damages but not impossible, not when you have evidence to prove malicious intent and reckless disregard for the truth. That's a tough standard, but Linda has to know that there's ample evidence for Musgrove to prove that in her case. Mel could be subpoenaed, questioned about her role in bringing the domestic abuse charges back into the news, forced into admitting her intention to bring down Musgrove—a classic case of libel. The blackmail charge might be almost as hard for Linda to fight, but she's probably betting that Mel won't follow through on the threat to turn her over to the lions, and it turns out she's right. Mel didn't know she was bluffing at the time—she convinced herself flying here that she wasn't—but now that Linda has called her on it, she realizes it *was* a bluff. She just can't do it. However hard-core she considers herself, she's not about to destroy someone's life, even a gold digger, just to grab a few votes in a Senate race that's probably been doomed from the start anyway.

"You see, mom," she says to the ceiling of her airport hotel room. "I'm not such a bad person after all."

Sure, Boo boo, comes the imagined response, *but are you doing something worthwhile with your life?*

PART 3
BLOWOUT

MEL GOES TO THE BROWNS-BENGALS GAME after all. Clinton's cancellation and Linda Musgrove's decision to stick with her story leaves her without much to do, so she decides to take off the entire weekend for the first time in her campaign career. She calls Thom on Saturday morning from a pay phone in O'Hare, says she's in for the game if the offer is still on the table. She holds her breath as he thinks it over, expecting a flat *No* followed by a dial tone. She avoided him all week, too engulfed by the scandal to deal with her personal life, too freaked out by the possibility of something real developing between her and Thom, so she simply never called him, ignored the two messages he left with Schooley, one on Tuesday, one on Thursday.

"Still on the table," he says laconically.

"What about dinner tonight? On me. Someplace pols never go. Maybe a nice dark joint in Little Italy?" He agrees to that as well.

Mel goes straight from Hopkins airport to her hotel, doesn't even check in with Schooley, takes a long, hot bath, then watches *Midnight Run* on cable, followed by *Broadcast News*, fills the rest of the afternoon before her date reading the sports section of *The Plain Dealer* and repainting her fingernails.

They gorge themselves on pasta primavera and veal scaloppini, tiramisu for dessert, then head to Mel's room afterwards. They stay up late doing everything but talking politics. They avoid the subject of their relationship too, don't say much of anything in fact, working off the blizzard of calories through a purely physical expression of whatever is on their minds.

Shep calls her Sunday morning at her room, offers to give her a peak at the latest tracks, admits it looks pretty hopeless. "We bounced back to 32, so maybe the worst of it is over, but Musgrove's double-digit lead is holding, and undecided is back down to 11." Mel demurs on having Shep deliver the full print-out. What will the crosstabs tell her that the bare total doesn't?

"I'm going to the Browns game today," she tells Shep, adds that Thom Reynolds is taking her. Thom, listening from the pillow next to her, raises his eyebrows at the admission. "Seems kind of pointless not to mix business and pleasure at this point, huh Shep?"

"Just don't get arrested again, OK Bubala?"

Mel smiles at Shep's endearment. "I'll try my best. No guarantees if the game's tight. Those Bengals' fans can be real dicks."

They have a half-decent brunch at the Gold Lantern—Mel's avoided the Eggs Benedict for a month, wishes she'd discovered it sooner—then head to a pub near the stadium to warm up for kickoff. Mel drinks fast but sticks to beer, so it doesn't take her down like whiskey would. She manages to avoid talking politics until early in the fourth quarter.

It's a tight game until then, the Bengals clawing to a 13-10 halftime lead, and most of the third quarter a nail-biting defensive battle, the kind of Browns-Bengals grudge match everyone hopes for. Then it all goes the Browns' way in a 4-minute spurt of special teams magic. Late in the third, the Browns recover a fumbled punt, kick a field goal off the turnover, force a three-and-out on the Bengals' next possession, then block that punt and return it for a touchdown. Eric Metcalf returns the next punt 73 yards for another touchdown, and suddenly the Browns have a 14 point lead after a ridiculous 17-point tear. Mel's voice is hoarse from yelling so hard—her and 77,000 other people.

She's had 6 beers by then, courtesy of Thom, and she's feeling reflective about the race. She starts with a football metaphor, obviously.

"It's fourth and long for Porter, second half of the fourth quarter, and he's two scores down. Does Coach Mel go for it, or punt it away?" Thom knows better than to answer. "She goes for it, of course. Flies to Chicago for a long-shot trick play." Thom raises an eyebrow at that, and Mel, tipsy as she is, realizes she's venturing into dangerous territory.

"What's in Chicago?" Thom asks. Mel watches his journalistic instincts kick in.

"Nothing." Mel takes a long swig of beer. "Forget I said anything. GO BROWNS!"

Thom doesn't press it, and they watch the rest of the game without any mention of the election. The Browns add another 10 points to their lead to go to 7-1, a full game ahead of the 6-2 Steelers atop the AFC Central. Mel lets herself be happy about that and ignores everything else on her mind—for the moment.

Thom takes her back to his apartment after the game, her first visit. Normally she would pay close attention to every detail, check the fridge and the medicine cabinet, look for mismatched socks and dust bunnies in the corners, but she falls asleep on the couch watching the 49ers blow out the Buccaneers while Thom makes a few calls from the kitchen. She wakes up spooned with Thom, who must've wriggled in close while she was sleeping. He snores lightly, hanging treacherously at the edge of the cushions. Mel playfully dumps him on the floor, flops on top of him and begins kissing his neck.

"What's the score?" he says reflexively, cranes his neck to see the screen but gets a Bud Light commercial. "I miss Spuds MacKenzie."

"I miss my innocence," Mel says. She pushes herself up, sits in an easy chair with her back to the TV.

"Oboy. Is it time for a deep conversation, or would you rather I ignore that?" Thom groans his way onto the couch. "Seriously, we can talk about it if you want. Did something happen in Chicago?"

Goddamned journalists never forget anything you say.

"Other than 850 murders last year?" Mel says, the stat popping into her head like this is a press conference and she's talking about Porter's 5-point crime plan.

"You know what I mean. If you need to unload something, Mel, I'm the guy. Seriously. Journalistic confidentiality."

"What about spousal?" Mel says through a smirk. "We could fly to Vegas right now, get hitched. Do the 5th Amendment thing til death do us part."

"You're not serious?" Thom looks genuinely worried.

"No, just kidding. You don't need to look so scared, buddy boy. We might've gone beyond campaign sex here, but it's not *that* serious."

"You'll be back in D.C. in a couple of weeks anyway," Thom says. When Mel doesn't take the bait, he adds, "You want a beer?" He goes to the kitchen without waiting for an answer. It's clear to Mel that he hopes she'll say she's at least thinking about staying in Cleveland after the election.

She *has* thought about it, but everybody in campaign vows to give up politics as soon as the next election is over. Mel doesn't know a single one who hasn't come back after a few months on the beach reading spy novels that eventually give way to the occasional *New York Times,* and then it's not long before the familiar itch returns full force. A few days later, they're sitting on an airplane with a week's worth of *Washington Posts*, wondering what they fuck they were thinking when they decided to quit politics.

But what if she does it a different way, makes a real plan instead of flushing politics for a Caribbean halfway house? A budding relationship here gives her a reason to set up shop as a consultant in-state. She can afford to take a pay cut, easily. She already makes way more money than she has time to spend, figures she's sitting on enough savings to ride out 2 full years without making another cent and still not be completely impoverished. Why not take a step back, rebuild from a position of financial security?

She could get a place in one of the newly redeveloped parts of town, take 6 months off to watch basketball and read that Simone de Beauvoir book she's been lugging around for a decade, then start building an Ohio operation for Clinton '96, purely on spec, sell it to the DNC for a nice profit when the time comes. Or just work cut-rate state assembly races, consult for city council candidates, play in the low-stakes world of state and local. She can imagine what her colleagues in D.C. would say — *You can't give up The Show for state and local, Mel. It's crazy* — but why should she care?

Even if the thing with Thom exploded in a month, which it very well could without the campaign to glue them together, it's not a bad plan. She thinks about getting out of politics all the time but knows she can't go cold turkey. Maybe a backwards move to Ohio is exactly the right step, phase one to kicking her addiction someday. Live somewhere real, hang around with people who don't eat and sleep politics day and night, maybe get a dog, start doing aerobics, join a book club, ease her way into a normal life, with or without Thom Reynolds in it.

Thom hands her a beer, turns up the volume on the TV, loses himself in the fourth quarter of the Raiders-Falcons game.

Mel appreciates that he can sense her need for time to think. He's the best boyfriend she's had in a long time, maybe ever. Athlete turned sportswriter turned political journalist — pretty good trajectory for someone with a shot to keep her interest beyond a few months. They have a common language but different experiences, a solid basis for a connection that extends beyond sex. She thinks about her mother and father, the grassroots liberal activist and the middle-of-the-road history professor, just the right amount of overlap with enough tension to keep the strings in tune. Maybe she and Thom have a similar combination, the pol and the political journalist, downscale Cleveland power couple.

She glances at him, engrossed in the game, sipping his beer every few seconds. He gets up for another one, lifts Mel's can and shakes it to see if she needs one too. Mel flushes with warmth at that small unconscious gesture of consideration, but then her Devil's advocate voice pipes in. Thom may be a successful professional in one sense, but he's the kind of boy-man she can't imagine herself in a lasting relationship with. He bailed her out of jail when she bit that guy, sure, a very mature thing to do, but he was right there with her, shot for shot, when the shit came down, and he clearly wasn't the voice of reason to prevent her from getting out of control.

Mel always imagined the man she'll eventually end up with is the one who can file the edges off her wild side, financially successful without seeming to try, probably conservative—a price she's willing to pay, or so she thinks. He's completely stable, totally loyal to her, someone who could take away her need to prove herself to the world, make it OK to stay home with the kids, use her time and energy to volunteer. Clearly that's not Thom Reynolds. But is that what she really wants, or simply what she always expected, a fear rather than a dream?

Some day I'll leap over the cliff, she's said to herself more than once, imagining how life is likely to go in her 30s, but there'll be this boring, secure guy there to catch me while I'm falling, prevent me from breaking my skull open, and I'll stay with him for the rest of my life out of pure gratitude. Not exactly inspiring—more of a horror story than a fair tale. When she sees women whose lives have gone that way, wearing expensive clothes, drinking rose at 10am, doing charity fundraisers and pestering the headmaster to add new extracurriculars, she thinks of defeat, not victory.

If she wants to avoid that fate, she has to take control of her life, stop running towards that cliff at such breakneck speed, use her genius for strategy to map out a life campaign with a better chance of success. Quitting the DNC and moving to Cleveland doesn't seem like such a bad idea.

A WEEK FROM THE SCANDAL BREAKING, the campaign has found a new rhythm—it's an old rhythm, actually, a return to what was going on when Mel showed up. They're back to basic retail politics, shaking hands in shopping malls and grocery stores, holding rallies in high-school gymnasia and labor halls. Porter is torpid, his smile patently fake as he shakes hands with the meager crowds, his thumbs-up as pro forma as they get. He's dead and he knows it, only keeps going because Tremont keeps scheduling appearances, the calendar more full than ever, like they're actually making a sprint for the finish line here.

It's a hair shirt for all of them, Mel most of all. She knows she could stay behind at HQ, write useless strategy memos, edit and re-edit the next round of TV and radio spots, but she deserves the punishment as much as any of them, so she forces herself to ride along in the campaign van, sits up front with laconic Frank, reads the *New York Times* to pass the hours as Porter and Schooley sit silently in the back, staring out opposite windows at the countryside flying past. She strides alongside Porter in desolate A&Ps from Defiance to Marietta, pestering customers as they compare the price of Maxwell House and Chock Full O' Nuts. "Kyle Porter. I'm running for U.S. Senate. I'd sure appreciate your vote."

No one seems excited to be meeting a man running for such a high office. Either they think this guy with his white dress shirt, sleeves rolled to three-quarter length, blue-and-red diagonal striped tie slightly unknotted, is about to sell them a condo timeshare in Florida, or they know perfectly well who he is, and they eye him suspiciously, concerned the neighbors will see them fraternizing with a guy who launders money for drug dealers. It's beyond depressing, though it's nothing like the fresh hell greeting them at the small-town rallies Tremont packs onto the calendar, joint appearances with local Dems so desperate to avoid electoral slaughter that they agree to appear with the Democratic Senate candidate, a man whose face is at least somewhat familiar to a lot of the voters, even if it's for all the wrong reasons.

1994

They're at one today in Apple Creek, home town of John Emerson, a Democratic county commissioner running for re-election in deep red Wayne County. This isn't far from Mel's hometown of Wooster, the county seat about 15 miles away, so she's intimately familiar with the local politics, at least in its general outlines. She wonders how a Democrat got elected here in the first place, knows without any polling that Emerson is going to get swept away in the Republican wave.

Porter banters glumly with Emerson, a super-intense dairy farmer with the biggest hands Mel has ever seen. His handshake envelopes her, crushes her fingers. He seems at ease, though. "I'm fucked," Mel hears him confide quietly to Schooley. "Voted to raise taxes last month. We need it to pay for the new prison, but I should've waited until after the election. I see that now. Goddamn Fred Cannon's eating my lunch over it. It's pretty much all he says. That and how high-holy Republican he is. That's his whole platform, pretty much. *I'm a Republican.* It's all they need to hear. I have no idea why I ever got into politics in the first place. It's a goddamned mess."

Schooley glances at Mel with desperation. *Get me out of this*, he seems to be saying. Even Schooley, the nicest guy Mel knows, can't take it.

The speeches are pure torture. The 20 or so people gathered know it's all bullshit. Mel smokes fiercely to keep herself from yelling, "Shut the fuck up!" every five seconds. The whole exercise is pure masochism, but what's coming next may be even worse. Her father lives just 20 minutes down the road, so she can hardly avoid meeting him when they're done here. She called ahead this morning before they left Cleveland, told him they had a last-minute schedule change, and she'd be in Wayne County that afternoon. It's hardly last-minute—they booked this sad outing last week as a substitute for Clinton's cancelled speech at the Cleveland Hilton, an event that was supposed to propel them across the finish line. Mel saw on CNN this morning that Clinton's in Michigan and Minnesota today, Wisconsin tomorrow, trying like hell to hold the Senate. Good luck, Big Bill.

She railed at the Republicans on the phone with her father, kept chattering about the blood bath they were looking at across the entire map in order to keep him from asking any disquieting questions, like why it's so last-minute, and how come she's not staying the night, and how come it took her so long to get around to visiting home when she's been living in a hotel an hour away for nearly a month.

They sit on the front porch with jelly jars of Maker's Mark, the mid-autumn weather simply perfect—pure blue sky, sun warming their faces, red and orange leaves floating past in a light breeze, the temperature just below 60. Her father looks like a caricature of a college history professor, tan corduroy jacket with honest-to-God elbow patches, blue shirt open at the collar, grey v-neck sweater, dark green pants, shiny brown penny loafers. Mel has on her road uniform, black tights, blue wool skirt, off-white silk blouse buttoned close to the throat, topped by one of her mother's old cable-knit wool cardigans to keep her warm. She dug it out of a trunk in the basement, the last of her mother's things, pushed back by the furnace and forgotten by her father, who remarried a local airhead less than 2 years after her mother died and immediately began acting as though he'd never had a first wife.

Luckily for Mel, Nancy is out of town for the day, doing something her father mentioned but she forgot as soon as he said it. Mel could give a shit what Nancy is up to, whether it's organizing a food drive or raising money for breast cancer research—whatever highly mainstream cause Nancy's into at the moment. Mel's just glad she's not here. She can never relax around that horrible vapid woman who muscled her way into her father's life when Mel was still coming to terms with her mother's death. Mel knows—it hardly took a therapist to make her aware—that no other woman, however amazing, would've had a chance to compete with her sainted mother, but it didn't help that her father moved on so quickly. He told her that's the way her mother wanted it. "She didn't want me to linger in grief," he's claimed more than once, though Mel had never heard anything of that sort herself. "She said not to waste the rest of my life pining for her. This is what she *wanted*, Boo boo. I wish you wouldn't be so mad at me for it."

Mel listens to her father talk about his classes, complain about how uninterested undergraduates are in history, how know-it-all yet politically apathetic they are, the familiar complaints of middle-aged white male professors everywhere. It's oddly soothing to Mel that her father has remained essentially unchanged over the years. Every once in a while she even finds it in her heart to be thankful that he still lives in the same brick house on Pearl Street where she was born and raised, that Nancy didn't talk him into moving out of town to some horrible new-construction McMansion on five acres with a creek and a salt lick for the deer. Mel comes home only rarely— maybe a dozen times in the 8 years since she graduated from college—but she's glad her father is so averse to change, at least on the housing front.

1994

"So, how's the campaign going?" he asks after returning with refilled jars of Maker's.

"Come on, dad. You know we're getting destroyed since that DEA story broke. It was a real horse race there for about a week, though. I thought we actually had shot at keeping the seat."

"Don't beat yourself up over it, Boo boo. It's not your fault that Kyle Porter's a crook."

Mel fights the impulse to push back over that label. It's just her dad here, not the press. She doesn't need to point out that all charges were dropped because of entrapment, that the court records and all evidence were ordered sealed, that the only reason anybody even knows about it is illegal meddling by rogue elements in the DEA. She's tired of saying these things. She takes a long sip of her drink. "I thought, for just a second there, that he might've been one of the good ones. But there aren't any goods ones. Not politicians. There aren't even very many good people, period."

"That's an awfully dark assessment of humanity. I remember when you used to be so idealistic. Just like your mother."

"Politics is where idealism goes to die, dad." Mel ignores the reference to her mother. "But you knew that already, didn't you?"

"I had illusions once, just like everybody else. But, yes. They were long gone by the time you were born." He sips his bourbon, the clinking of the ice cubes tightening Mel's chest, as always — the sound of her childhood. Before her mother died, her parents would sit on this very porch, in these very chairs, and drink together, talk about life, history, politics, the future they wanted for their precious daughter, Mel inside with a book, pretending to read but listening to every word.

There's really nothing else to say. Mel knows she should tell her father she forgives him for marrying Nancy so quickly, for moving on at all, but the words stick in her throat. She dredges up a quote from *The Deer Hunter*, one of her and her father's favorites, her De Niro impersonation as sharp as it always is. "*You know, Nicky, you're the only guy I go hunting with. I like a guy with quick moves and speed. I ain't gonna hunt with no assholes.*"

Her father smiles. "*The Deer Hunter*. Best movie ever made."

"*Apocalypse Now*," Mel says. It's an old dispute, one they maintain cordially. Mel prefers the surreal, gliding slowly up the river to do something horrible but necessary version of the war-is-hell theme over the heart wrenching home-front one. She loves *The Deer Hunter* too but finds the decaying steel town version of the Vietnam hangover a touch too depressing, even for her.

They drink for a while more, then Frank pulls up with the campaign van, and it's time to introduce her father to Porter, fresh from working the shops on Liberty Street after a sit-down with the editors of the *Wooster Daily Record*, every second a complete waste of time in this staunchly conservative town. She suggested a rally at the College of Wooster where her father teaches—the students and faculty are predictably liberal—but Tremont said the turnout rate for college students was too low, and Mel, knowing it doesn't matter anyway, didn't push it.

"I'm sure you're quite proud of your daughter," Porter says as he shakes her father's hand. He looks like he's ready to get back to Cleveland for the night, get in the van again tomorrow to head west and south to do it all again, the pointlessness no excuse for not doing it.

Mel smiles falsely, her cheekbones aching from doing this for days on end. She worries that her father is going to say something like, *I would be, if she were doing something worthwhile with her life.* Naturally he doesn't. That's a line for her mother's ghost.

"She is amazing at what she does," is what her father says, the backhanded compliment obvious, especially when he adds, "But yes, of course. Very proud."

1994

THE FINAL DEBATE IS PREDICTABLY UGLY. Down by 15 points in their internal tracking poll, 51-36, with undecided reduced to 5% — this time Mel tells Porter where he sits before sending him out to the podium — Porter behaves much as anybody else in his position would. He delivers his opening statement with his usual actor's skill — a wide-ranging attack on Musgrove's policies and the negative campaign he's running, on the relentless scandal-mongering of the media, with a brief mention of his own policy agenda once he gets to the Senate — but as soon as Musgrove starts prodding him, he comes unwound. Porter leaves his podium again at one point, stalks all the way to Musgrove's side, looms over him with anger twisting his face. It's almost comical, a Monty Python skit mocking American politics.

Mel sits in the spin room, chain smoking and shaking her head. They're dead, and she knows it. Everyone knows it. She has to admire Porter for fighting on with such gusto, but it's wasted energy. You can't beat a scandal with passion or policy. You have to destroy it like a vampire, with garlic and silver bullets and a stake through the heart. She provided them with the silver bullet, but Porter wouldn't use it, so here they are, pretending outrage when they should be preparing their closing argument.

Musgrove lets himself get more emotional than he should — a sign that Dave Parker doesn't have the kind of control over his candidate that Howard Kane did — but he never loses his cool in the dramatic way they need to spark another comeback. Even if he had a full-on meltdown, it probably wouldn't be enough to turn the tide against him — not with a double-digit lead and only 11 days left and the undecided vote evaporating fast. Mel keeps a sharp eye on Musgrove's every move nonetheless, looking for a sound bite she can put in an attack ad, something to make it look like Musgrove is the maniac here.

It may be pointless, but she still has a job to do. If nothing else, a nice sharp attack ad will be good for her portfolio. She has to think past this turkey of a race. So what if she gets creamed? Nobody could've done better, not with a candidate as flawed as Porter turned out to be. If only one of his primary opponents had turned up that

DEA tape, the DNC might be in a position to keep this goddamned seat. Mel tries not to think about *what ifs*, but she can't help it. The runner-up in the Democratic primary was Mary Boyle, a popular Cuyahoga County Commissioner the Ohio party leaders had lined up for the nomination. Maybe Mel would've gotten the nod from Barker for her campaign too, had a chance to get a woman into the Senate, help start an upsurge in female power politics. Mel grinds out her cigarette, shoves aside this bunch of unhelpful *maybes*...

The spin room afterwards is unlively in the extreme. Dave Parker lays out his case in a nasally monotone while Kline Braddock reprises the passion plea to the small group of scribblers who even bother to talk to him. Most of the high-quality journalists have moved on to other stories rather than wasting their time picking over the corpse with the locals, Jared Block and Kate Winkler gone for a week now, focusing on the 6th District horse race, where Ted Strickland is making a good run at keeping Ohio from being an all-out drubbing. Mel stands to the side and smokes silently, watches Braddock, Schooley next to her in loyal readiness to do whatever she asks.

"Kind of a farce, isn't it?" he says. There's more sadness in his tone than cynicism, but Mel catches a note of the weary old hand. Schooley is the quickest study in politics she's ever seen. Maybe she could bring him on to help her start something here in Cleveland, the Carnes and Schooley guns for hire. His mother's connections could probably get them all the work they'd ever want, give Schooley a chance to learn things from the local side before taking another shot at D.C. with a new Democratic Senate candidate in '98. "Makes me want to go back in time and major in physics or something," he adds.

"God bless America," is all Mel can say.

Four days later, she's standing in the same pose, only now she's dressed as Amelia Earhart, a childhood hero of hers, attending – she has no idea why – a charity fundraiser organized by Porter's wife. Charlotte circulates merrily, as though everyone in the room doesn't know she's married to a crook, wearing, of all things, a Hillary Clinton costume. Porter arrives late from some absurd Halloween Night rally Tremont insisted on, dressed as...really? Did he actually decide to come to this thing as an astronaut, as though he's some kind of John Glenn knockoff? He should be wearing a Richard Nixon mask, going around saying, "*I'm not a crook!*"

Mel waves it off, heads to the bar, orders a double Manhattan, dry. It hardly matters what Porter wears tonight, or any night for the next week. If they weren't already dead in the water, she would've consulted with him about his costume, gotten him to go as Lincoln maybe, another tall lawyer, or possibly Andrew Jackson, the fiery man of the people.

She takes big sips of her drink and circles the room slowly, sticking to the outer edges, ducking the boozy leers of old men used to getting exactly what they want. She tries not to think about the race but can't help it. The latest public poll released that morning by the *Columbus Dispatch* has Musgrove's lead down to 10 points, 51-41, with Harris at an improbably low 2% and undecided still at 6, the sample size small enough that the margin of error is +/-5%.

"Yes," she admitted to Schooley when he brought the *Dispatch* into her office this morning, "it's technically possible that the 5-point margin of error means we're actually tied, but we all know that's a statistical possibility only, not anything like reality." Just to make sure, she called Shep to see how their internal tracks were looking, and he had it almost exactly the same for the principals, 52-40, but Harris and undie reversed, Harris at 6 and undecided down to 2. She asked him for a prediction of final results based on recent trendlines.

"The way Porter hovered in the high-30s, low-40s when we were at our best, I'd say as a rough guess, we'll get 38 to 40, max. Musgrove pulls a solid majority, 52 or 53, maybe at high as 56, depending on how many Harris people defect back to their natural resting place with the G.O.P. Harris will probably hang on, though. I'd give him 6, maybe 7. It's easier to cast a protest vote when you're pretty sure your second choice is cruising to victory."

"So it's a blowout," Mel said flatly.

"Looks like it," Shep agreed. He held on the line for a half minute of silence, then hung up when it was obvious Mel didn't have anything else to say.

Mel lets herself drink faster than she normally would at a quasi-work event. The cake is baked at this point. Even if she bites someone again and gets tossed in jail, no harm will come of it—not for Porter, at least. She might get a psych recommendation for recidivist biting, but how bad would that be? Maybe she could use a professional evaluation, an objective observer telling her she needs to get out of politics before she hurts someone for real. She considers calling her old therapist when she gets back to D.C. Why not? It never did her much good in the past, but it's something to do once a week in the slack season. She can't spend all her time watching movies and reading books.

She continues to circulate, a shark unable to stop moving or it'll die, sipping her Manhattan steadily. She briefly ponders the idea of leaving politics to go into charity fund-raising, use her savvy to get rich fuckers like this to write big checks for good causes. She can see herself as the wife of somebody wealthy like Porter, dedicating herself to do-gooder stuff, but she suspects Charlotte is completely miserable underneath it all and doubts she'd be any happier. Plus, the politics of it probably isn't any less obnoxious than the politics of what she already does.

At one point, Charlotte corners Mel, thanks her with what sounds like genuine sincerity for trying to salvage the situation. "Your fake tape was brilliant, Ms. Carnes. I watched the whole thing after you left that night. Extremely well put together. It might've done the job if my husband weren't such a prude about the law." She chuckles in a disturbing way, beams a smile at Mel that's rimmed with vodka. Mel looks into Charlotte's sparking eyes, knows she's good and drunk—they both are.

"If only *you* were on the ballot," Mel says out of nowhere. "We'd have a 10-point lead over that pencil-neck Musgrove." She's talking too loud, her cadence uneven, classic drunk bullshit, only she means what she says—*in vino veritas*. "You ever decide to run for office, Mrs. Porter, I'll be right there to help you win. Just say the word."

"Travis-Porter," Charlotte corrects her. "But you can call me Charlie."

"No, you gotta drop that hyphenated bullshit. Stand on your own, 'specially now, with the Porter name splattered in shit." She glugs her drink. "I know some good divorce lawyers here in town," Mel adds, because the liquor makes her not care. "Big donors to your husband's campaign, for an added touch of irony. Fucking men."

Mel expects a sharp rebuke, maybe even a slap, but Charlie grins, puts her hand on Mel's shoulder, says reflectively, "You don't think it's hard enough for a woman to run for office in this country already? We've got two strikes coming out of the gate. Divorce is three-strikes-you're-out, Melanie. Men, those bastards, they can get divorced and remarried a dozen times—even fucking Republicans, the hypocrites. Let a woman even separate, or decide not to have kids, or not smile enough, or smile too much, or anything, and she's doomed. How many women in the Senate right now?"

Before Mel can answer—it's only 7, an all-time high—an oily state assemblyman slides over, draws Charlie away to talk to somebody he says is *super important*, leaves Mel to drain her glass and return to the bar.

She spots a good-looking guy dressed as Luke Skywalker, puts together an opening gambit—"*You underestimate the power of the Dark Side, my son*"—before she remembers Thom. *Christ, Carnes*, she says to herself, reflexively sipping her Manhattan, *you* are *a hard case. You ever gonna settle down and get a real life?*

Later, she makes an unsuccessful booty call to Thom. His phone rings and rings, the answering machine either broken or switched off.

She decides to walk the 20 blocks back to her hotel, tottering on unfamiliar heels and too much booze, even for her. She sits down on a bus bench at one point, drops her head to her knees, wishes she could puke out everything she's said and done for the past...what? 8 years, since she got into campaign? 15 years, since her mother died? 20 years, since she got her first taste of insurgent politics? Her whole life maybe?

She puts a finger tentatively down her throat, retches a little, spits bile onto the sidewalk but nothing more.

"Hey lady, you OK?"

Mel looks up, smirks drunkenly. It's a fucking cop, of all people. Or is it someone from the party dressed as a cop? She starts singing. *"I woke up in a Soho doorway, a policeman knew my name. He said you can go sleep at home tonight, if you can get up and walk away. Whoooooo, are you? Who-who, who-who."*

She pushes herself up. "Goddamned Pete Townsend, huh?"

She expects another trip to the drunk tank, but the cop lets her go with an apathetic, "Just be careful, wouldja." Maybe it is just a guy in costume.

When she gets into the office the next morning at 9:15—her hangover more manageable than she would've predicted—Shep is already there, drawing some kind of complex Gaussian blur on the whiteboard. He has the latest spot poll from Monday night.

"I've got Musgrove up by an even 20, 55-35, but I wouldn't take it too seriously. Halloween is a terrible day to poll. Only got 385 responses, so we're looking at a pretty big margin of error. I only did it because we've got a decent chunk of money left in the polling budget, and the kids at my call center could use the cash. Tremont green lighted it, if you're wondering."

"I could give a shit about the budget at this point." Mel drops to her chair, lights a Parliament, massages the top of her head. "There's no ad blitz that's going to save us now, so no reason to tighten the belt in other places. Even with a less flawed candidate, I think we'd be fucked this cycle. You seen the latest RNC spot? It's running in a coupla dozen states. They're even using it here, God knows why. Probably one or two of the House races aren't a big enough blowout for their comfort."

"No, haven't seen it."

Mel mimics the announcer, her voice conspiratorial, a woman clearly afraid of what's going on in Washington. *"It's a matter of trust. Clinton and the Democrats attack and distort Republican plans. But behind closed doors, the Clinton White House discusses cuts in Social Security and Medicare, and billions more in tax increases. A secret White House memo details a national sales tax, tax on health benefits, even a tax on Medicare and Social Security benefits. Fed up with the Democrat double-talk and hypocrisy on taxes and spending? This November 8th, send the Clinton Congress home."*

"That's pretty good."

"Even if it is a bunch of transparent lies. A tax on Social Security benefits? Even Clinton's not that much of an idiot. The DNC spots are pretty sharp too, for all the good they'll do." Mel switches to a deep voice, gravelly, on the verge of outrage. *"The Republicans just met in Washington to sign a contract for America's future, but it's really an echo of a failed past. Huge tax cuts for the wealthy, billions in defense increase, and gigantic new job-killing deficits.* Truth. For all the good it'll do."

"I saw Clinton on CNN last night, up in Michigan I think it was." Shep tries a Clinton impersonation, doesn't get enough drawl in it, sounds more like a Harvard professor to Mel. *"Don't let a frustrated electorate wind up votin' for what you're against, and against what you're for. That's what they want. Look what they say they're for. They say they're for a new plan that will give a huge tax cut to the wealthy, increase defense spending, and balance the budget, all at the same time. That sound familiar to you?"*

"Yeah, well." Mel exhales sharply. "We may hold Wisconsin, but we're not getting Minnesota, and Michigan looks like it's slipping away. We're not just dead here in Ohio. It looks bad in Pennsylvania too. How the hell are the Republicans winning *anything* in the Rust Belt, much less pretty much everything? Tell me that, Mr. Pollster."

"It's a wave, Mel. You haven't seen one before, but I have. '80 and '82 were back-to-back waves, Republican then Democrat. Were you even in high school at the time?"

"I graduated in '82, you old fart. I remember Reagan's first campaign like it was yesterday. That fuckwit Carter blew it with all his talk of malaise. What a major bummer that guy was. He couldn't have beaten Barry Goldwater with that shit, much less Bonzo goes to Washington. Clinton's no Carter. Our new prez knows how to give a speech."

"Come on, Mel, you sound like a civilian, talking like that. You know perfectly well what a climb the first mid-term is for a president.

1994

Any president. Reagan knew how to give a speech too. About all he knew how to do. He lost 26 seats in the House in '82."

"We should be so lucky to lose that few."

"Damned right," Shep replies. "The fact is, Clinton blew it on health care, wasted his time on gays in the military, caved on the crime bill, and now he's trying to cut defense spending and out deficit-hawk the Republicans with all that talk of balancing the budget. He really think we wouldn't get eviscerated this cycle? *New Democrat* isn't a term any responsible pollster would try to sell. May as well call yourself *Republican Light*. If your only choice is a real Republican or an ersatz one, what do you think people are gonna go for?"

Mel lights another cigarette, turns to her computer, stares at the blank screen, considers leaving it inert for the day. What's the point of slogging on like there's hope? Shep turns back to the whiteboard, erases what he drew and starts over with a more complex multivariate distribution curve, if Mel recognizes it correctly.

"So we're dead in the water here," she says, reaching for the On button. "Twenty points down or 10, it hardly matters. What do we do for the next 6 days?"

"Start thinking about the future."

"I became a strategist so I wouldn't have to think about the future," Mel shoots back, fully aware of the irony. It may be ironic, but it's true. She likes the close time horizon of a campaign, the need to focus myopically on a single goal only a few months or weeks ahead, all the incentives lined up to get everyone thinking in purely short-term and instrumental ways—looking for soft spots in the crosstabs, getting a nudge in the polls from a new ad, spinning an exogenous factor like the abortion-clinic bombing, prepping the candidate to say and do whatever suits the moment. She's never been in a blowout like this, never had to kill an entire week til election day with essentially no way to deny the looming emptiness of the near-term future. It's pretty horrible.

Mel leans back as the computer whirs and beeps, as purposeful sounding as always, the stupid machine. She smokes placidly as Shep erases the board again, removes every stray pen mark, then draws a giant and perfect question mark. "There's one thing the data's never going to tell us." He tosses the marker to Mel. "What's the meaning of it all. Politics, life, anything. We add the meaning ourselves, in a blind leap of faith. That's the hard part, Bubala." He drifts to the door, watches Mel watching him. He puts his hand on the knob, looks like he's thinking something over. "I don't see you doing this much longer."

Mel blows smoke rings at the ceiling, stares blankly at Shep, her face empty of all emotion. She's 95% convinced he's 100% correct.

"That's just one opinion," he adds. "A single data point. But I've been around a while. I've got 2 daughters myself. It would kill me to see one of them like this." His face softens into what Mel takes for genuine sympathy. He seems like he wants to say more, his eyes imploring Mel to ask for elaboration, to let him be the one-man focus group for her future. She remains statue-still, unblinking, the smoke curling up from her fingers in tight spiral. Shep shrugs, says quietly, "Just one opinion," then heads out, closing the door quietly behind him.

Mel instantly regrets letting him go without a reply. Shep is the perfect person to open up to about her doubts and fears, the non-judgmental pollster/father figure, the ideal sounding board. She flicks her cigarette at the whiteboard, hits the question mark dead center. "Fucking life," she says to the empty room. She hears it as more resigned than angry, but anger is what she feels rising up inside her. She curls her fingers, pounds the desk with both fists, tears of frustration welling behind her eyes. "GOD! DAMMIT!"

THE THURSDAY BEFORE THE ELECTION is Mel's 30th birthday. She has no interest in making a big deal of it, keeps it from everybody on the staff, but Thom remembers—he's a good boyfriend, if that's what he is these days. He must recall her saying once she was born the day LBJ stomped Goldwater. Despite the obvious cooling between them since the Browns' game, he talks her into going out for a fancy dinner.

Mel skips the office all day, tells Schooley she's got food poisoning, which he probably thinks is a euphemism for a hangover—for once it isn't—and spends the day shopping for a dress to wear. She hasn't gone shopping in Cleveland since her mother brought her to the big city to get her a dress for the 8th grade dance. That was just before her mother was diagnosed, practically the last normal thing Mel did with her—maybe the last normal thing she's done since, period.

She decides to do it right, heads to the newly redeveloped part of town, wanders Tower City Center looking to buy everything new, from shoes to dress, underwear included. She goes for a new bra first. She's been battering the ones she has for nearly 2 years, and they're war fatigued, barely up to the job for a normal workday, completely unfit for special-occasion duty. The bra lady immediately feels her up—"Oh honey, you're got lovely breasts, but you're wearing the wrong cup size. We can't have that now, can we?"—spends an hour running Mel through the entire inventory of 36Ds, ends up selling her two black lace bras—"Excellent support and so very sexy at the same time"—for $150 apiece, but Mel happily pays it. Who cares? She's got the money, more than enough. She never has time to spend what she earns. She vows to let herself go completely crazy today, spend $2,000 if she wants, if she even can. She drops another $250 on new underwear and a pair of silk stockings with garters, tries on dresses in the $1,200-$1,500 range, as though she's shopping for the prom or something.

It feels ridiculously good to be so frivolous, to spend money like it's meaningless, to treat herself to the best for once. *Happy birthday, Mel*, she says to herself every time she makes a purchase. In the end, she drops over $2,000 on the dress and underthings, another $225 on shoes, plus $50 for lunch—she only has one martini, doesn't want to get sloppy before the big date—calculates that she's still well below her unused per diem money even with the sudden extravagance.

"Holy shit," Thom says when he sees her. "We going to the Oscars or something?"

Mel smiles brightly, twirls like the female character in a romantic comedy. Her dress does look like something out of Hollywood, a sparkly silver floor-length gown with spaghetti straps and a slit up the side to mid-thigh, shiny silver tassels that fly out from her waist as she spins around. She sees it as a kind of a hula girl meets flapper on the red carpet look.

She notes with slight disappointment that Thom is wearing scuffed black wingtips, a charcoal pin-stripe suit, a dizzying paisley tie. They're a mismatched couple, Mel the picture of expensive elegance, Thom looking like he borrowed a suit and tie from his dad. She tells herself to shut the fuck up, stop being critical, just have a good time tonight and relish the fact that she's not spending her 30th birthday alone, the way she always expected.

That's the first surprise in a night full of surprises. The next surprise is that Thom brought a limousine—*Now it does seem like the prom*, she stops herself from saying out loud—the third surprise that the limo blows a tire halfway to the restaurant, the fourth that they get mugged when they decide to walk the rest of the way instead of waiting for the driver to install the spare.

Mel felt it coming, heard the echo of shoes behind them as they got midway down an empty, mostly dark side street in one of the pockets of downtown that hasn't been redeveloped yet. She takes Thom's elbow, hears the footsteps behind them speeding up, feels Thom turn suddenly when the perp yells, "HEY!" He looks homeless, menaces a kitchen knife at them from 5 or 6 feet away, frightened jabs in the direction of Thom's pelvis. "Gimme all your money. Right now!"

Thom is paralyzed.

Mel thrusts out her purse. "Here, take it." The mugger takes a tentative step towards Mel, looks like he suspects a trick, flashes his eyes wide when she pulls the purse back and says, "Let me just keep my cigarettes, OK? Just one. You can have the rest." She rummages in her purse.

"Mel, I, uh…'"

"Your wallet, man. Hand it over. NOW!"

Thom flinches as Mel finds what she's looking for, pulls out her can of mace, sprays the mugger's eyes while his attention is on Thom.

He screams, drops the knife, his hands clawing at his face. "FUCK FUCK FUCK!"

Mel kicks the knife away, breaks a heel in the process, knees the guy in the balls, Ninja-like reflexes she didn't know she picked up from that self-defense class she took a few years ago. Thom grabs her wrist, and they dash to the corner streetlight while the mugger spins, blinded, howling like a wounded animal. "FUCKING FUCK!"

They see a group of four people up ahead, crossing at the next block. They speed walk towards them, Mel hobbling on her broken heel. There aren't any footsteps behind them, just the distant sound of the mugger still screaming in rage and pain.

"Jesus Christ, Mel. You fucked that guy up." Thom sounds appalled rather than awed.

"That's pretty much what you said when you bailed me out of jail that time. Same tone and everything."

"What's that supposed to mean?"

"I just saved us from a mugging, Thom." She uses the standard hard-t pronunciation. "You might at least be a little impressed."

"You saved us — what? A couple hundred bucks? Some calls to our credit card companies? A wait at the DMV for a new license? We could've been stabbed." Thom sounds panicked, like the mugging is still in progress.

"Only we weren't stabbed, now were we? I stopped us from being victimized."

"*Victimized*? It was just some poor homeless guy. We didn't have anything to worry about if we just gave him our money."

"*We didn't have anything to worry about*," Mel hisses. "Easy for a privileged white male to say. You're never in any real danger of any kind."

"This doesn't need to become a feminist rant, does it?"

"*Feminist rant?* You son-of-a-bitch." Mel pushes Thom away. "You pansy-ass piece of shit. I took action in a highly uncertain situation. Sure, maybe he was just some starving homeless guy who wouldn't have hurt us, but I had an instinctual reaction to danger, and I did something about it. You don't know what it's like to feel vulnerable, do you?" Mel glares at Thom. "Do you?"

"Come on, Mel. I just didn't think we *were* in danger."

"Said the privileged white male again."

"Cut the shit. That's got nothing to do with it."

"You don't think it does, because you can't see all the privilege and immunity you get because of your white skin and your goddamned penis. It's invisible to you. The fish doesn't know it swims in the water, either. Doesn't mean it's not real."

They walk on in silence, Mel doing her best not to hobble too much so Thom won't offer to carry her or some stupid chauvinistic crap like that.

Despite the mugging and the fight, they do their best to enjoy dinner, order double cocktails as soon as they're seated, gamely try talking about anything but politics or what just happened. The liquor does its job, softens Mel. They manage to relax and laugh, break the ice by making up fake biographies for the diners around them, largely an older crowd in expensive clothes.

"That guy in the gold tie's a retired car-dealership owner," Thom offers. "Franchises, ten of 'em. Used to do his own commercials. *I'm Marvin Ridgeway, owner of Chevy City. I don't wanna make money. I just loooove selling cars.*"

"No, he's a superior court judge under indictment for soliciting a prostitute. No, wait. Male prostitute, truck stop bathroom, only the hooker's an undercover agent dedicated to cracking down on the rampage of gay sex."

It seems like they've put the mugging and the fight behind them. The final surprise of the night comes when Thom asks Mel to move in with him after the election. He has enough cinematic savvy to wait until dessert arrives before popping the question.

Mel responds reflexively with a Molly Ringwald quote, Sixteen Candles, perfectly apropos. *"When you don't have anything, you don't have anything to lose. Right?"*

Miraculously, Thom knows the next line, fires it right back. *"That's a cheerful thought."* Or maybe he doesn't know the line, and it's just a natural rejoinder. Did he really watch and remember *Sixteen Candles*? She can hardly believe she enjoyed it herself, as a 20 or 21-year-old college student. She's always been a vacuum for movies, figures she's seen maybe 2,000 in her short life. She's able to quote accurately from as many as 200 to 300 at a moment's notice, in perfectly appropriate ways, but she draws a blank on what her next line should be. Maybe a warning shot from *Working Girl*? —*I am not steak. You can't just order me.* That might be a good one.

Thom must be able to tell Mel's mind is wandering. He reaches across the table, takes her hand, just like whatever movie gave him this idea. What would it be? *When Harry Met Sally*? *He Said, She Said*? *Singles*? Mel looks down at his fingers, the strong hand of a baseball player turned writer, uses her other hand to sip the last of her wine, lingers as she drains the glass to give herself time to ponder, but the only thing that comes to mind is how she wishes she'd used a different *Sixteen Candles* quote — *I have a dance to go to. At school. It's a very important dance. We're being graded on it. For gym.* That would've been better. She could've made a graceful exit, Thom's final memory watching her hobble away on a broken heel after quoting Molly Ringwald. Shazam.

Instead she's stuck here at this fancy restaurant with Thom gazing into her eyes, waiting hopefully for a *Yes*. She *wants* to want this, but Thom's response to the mugger ruined everything — his flaccid response, then his attack on her feminism, his failure to see even the barest outlines of his white male privilege, his man-boy response to the whole thing, brushing it off as quickly as possible. It's all too much for Mel.

She checks herself before saying *No*, wants to make sure she's not rationalizing her way out of something that's scary. Nope, what's she's doing is recognizing before it's too late that Thom simply isn't the right guy for her. She's actually glad for the mugging — it saves her the time and heartache of learning those weaknesses later, when she's more deeply involved, when it would hurt more to break things off.

"Yeah. I'd say *I have to think about it*, only I don't. Doesn't seem like the right move." She pats Thom's hand, realizes how horribly grandmotherly that is, leans across the table and kisses him on the lips. "I'm not saying I won't stay in Cleveland after the election," she adds, not untruthfully. "I'm leaning that way. For real. I just don't think going from my hotel to your apartment is the right move. For either of us."

It sounds perfectly sensible. Thom nods agreement, waves for the check, doesn't struggle too much when Mel insists on paying.

Porter Campaign
Internal Tracking Poll
Musgrove: 55%
Porter: 38%
Harris: 6%
Undecided: 1%

MEL SLEEPS IN ON ELECTION DAY, orders a ridiculous room service breakfast—Denver omelet with extra toast, pancakes, fruit and yogurt, a bagel with cream cheese—spreads it out on the bed and takes a bite of everything in rotation until she's gorged. When she's done, she picks up the copy of Grisham's *The Chamber* she bought at O'Hare flying back from Chicago that last time, lays against the pillows, forces herself to avoid turning on CNN. She knows it's bad out there. She'll find out how bad tomorrow.

When she gets tired of reading, she turns on ESPN, tries to imagine Thom back in his sportswriter days, wonders what it would be like to do something completely different. Why not? What's keeping her in politics? Hatred of Republicans can only carry you so far. With Newt Gingrich coming to the helm, it's the perfect time to get out. Move to a small town somewhere, or maybe California. New York. Austin. Madison. Athens. Portland. She could go anywhere, do anything, find a husband and have kids, learn Mandarin or Arabic, run for PTA president and see if that goes anywhere. That's what Madeline Albright did, and now she's ambassador to the U.N. The world needs more women in diplomacy.

Mel flips off the TV, starts to run a bath, sits on the edge of the tub with the water rising up her ankles like the truth coming up to drown her. *I'm never quitting politics*, she says to herself. It hurts to admit it for some reason, but it's not such a horrible realization. There are far worse fields to be in. She could be a lawyer for a mining company, working to strip native peoples of what little they have left, or an investment banker, turning money into more money with no goal other than churning up as much profit as possible for the firm. Politics doesn't seem so bad compared to jobs like that, but Mel runs out of steam thinking up worse occupations, admits to herself she must be pretty desperate for a rationalization to set what she does against a mining-company lawyer.

The phone rings in the other room. She steps out of the tub, out of the rising tide of truth, picks up the phone and says, "Whoever you are, do not talk about the election, or I'll hang up immediately."

"Appreciate the warning." It's Thom. "Actually, I was calling to see if you wanted to go to the Cavs game tonight. It's the home opener, christening for the new Gund arena, should be quite a show. I tried you at the office, but Schooley said you're not planning to come in until late-afternoon. He says you left him to write the first draft of Porter's concession speech. That's quite a piece of delegation. I thought you strategists loved writing these election-day speeches, win or lose. Kind of the capstone for the whole horrific spectacle of running a campaign."

"No election talk, remember? I'm on the verge of hanging up here."

"OK. I haven't said anything about the actual election. So, you in? Cavs game tonight? I have an honest-to-god feeling they're poised for a playoff year. Something tells me Hot Rod Williams earns his millions this season."

"Sounds delightful," Mel says. *Delightful*? Why the Mary Poppins act? "You doing anything right now? I was about to get into the bath, but I'd be happy to put it off til you could get here." Mel braces for the inevitable rejection. Her job on this campaign may be all but done, but today is the Big Day for political reporters. She can't expect Thom to drop everything and waste his time playing with her, especially now that she's made it clear to him they have no future. They're back to campaign sex, the clock on that ticking down fast. The fact that he's inviting her to a basketball game tonight, when he should probably be in Columbus covering Musgrove's victory speech, is a bit strange — either sweet or desperate, Mel can't tell. Well, it *is* the home opener, the first pro game ever played at the new arena, bound to be much more fun than a Republican victory party. There's more to life than politics, even on election day.

"Shit, I'm in Columbus." Thom sounds genuinely bummed. "I could be there by 1, if you can hold off til then?"

"Nah, the Cavs game is soon enough. I should just shower now anyway, suck it up and go in one last time and write that damned speech. It's a big ask to put Schooley on it. Not that he probably doesn't already have something brilliant."

Mel drags herself to the office by 12:30, tries to hold her head high as she walks through the bullpen. No one else is holding their heads up. They've got CNN on all three TVs, the Republican Revolution unfolding as prognosticated, reporters not even waiting for the official release of exit polls to start drawing conclusions. She stops, watches Bernard Shaw interview a reporter outside a polling station in Newt Gingrich's district, a low brick fire station with a line running down the block.

—*Republican enthusiasm is running high today, Bernard. Obviously, here in the district of the man who will soon be the Speaker of the House, if all goes according to plan. And that's exactly what we've been hearing from Gingrich headquarters throughout the late morning and into this afternoon, that today is, indeed, going as planned.*

—*That's the same thing we've been hearing from around the country, Mike.* Shaw emits a pained grin. *Republican enthusiasm, exceptionally high turnout in heavily Republican precincts, contrasted with depressed turnout in Democrat-leaning locations.* We go now to Debbie Brooks, in one of those Democratic enclaves.

Mel ducks into her office before the screen can cut to Debbie, piling on about how bad Democratic turnout is looking today. She picks up the phone to call Shep, the atmosphere of Porter HQ infecting her for a moment with the need to know, to strategize, to do something. This is exactly why she didn't want to come in today. There's nothing to do, but the feeling of needing to do it anyway is palpable inside these walls. She hangs up the phone, pushes her files onto the floor—in resignation, not anger—lays on top of the desk and lights a cigarette, stares at the ceiling smoking placidly, clearing her mind of all thoughts.

Schooley interrupts her a few minutes later, jars her from a genuinely meditative state. "Hey, Captain. Cindy told me she saw you come in. Everything OK?"

Mel taps her granny ash onto the carpet—won't be here come tomorrow anyway, so why bother taking care of the place?—groans to a sitting position, crosses her legs and stretches down to the floor for her briefcase. "Yeah, sure. What wouldn't be OK for me right now?"

"It's perfectly understandable to be mad. Or sad. Or confused. Even afraid."

"Thanks for the lesson in basic emotions, Number Two, but I'm genuinely OK." She sings a snatch of Sheryl Crow. "*All I wanna do, is have some fun. I got a feeling, I'm not the only one.*" Mel lights another cigarette, plasters an obviously fake grin on her face. "See? Perfectly OK. Need any help with that concession speech?"

1994

Schooley hands her a folder, sits with his hands folded on his lap, an eager student awaiting praise from the teacher.

"Mel, I've got something to tell you." He sounds strangely somber, old beyond his years. Mel narrows her eyes, sees an oncologist preparing to deliver bad news.

"I don't like the sound of that, Number Two."

"Yeah, you're not going to like what I have to say either. I'm genuinely sorry. I want you to know that before I say anything. I'm really, really sorry."

"What the fuck, Schooley? You're freaking me out. You're not dying, are you?"

"I'm a mole." He fidgets, unfolds and refolds his hands. "For Kane. I've been a plant the whole time."

Mel stares, uncomprehending. "No!" She nearly flicks her cigarette at Schooley's chest, grinds it out right on the desk instead. "No, goddammit! You are not a fucking mole!"

Schooley nods, looks even more like a doctor giving out a death sentence. He starts to say something but thinks better of it.

Rage tightens Mel's chest, but she takes a deep breath, stretches out her face muscles. "Tell me this is a joke. Some kind of election day prank you and Braddock cooked up. Ha ha, Schooley. Really fucking funny."

"It's not a joke." He explains everything, his mission to report back to Kane with schedules and ad copy, strategies and internal polls, whatever he could get his hands on.

Mel listens with clinical detachment, as though Schooley's story is about someone else. She should feel like a complete fool — taking this kid under her wing, thinking him so green and innocent, proud of how quickly he seemed to be learning — but it leaves her oddly unmoved. Sure, maybe Schooley's intel gave Musgrove an edge he otherwise wouldn't have had, but it's obviously not the decisive factor in the race. With or without this spy, Musgrove was going to win.

"I really am magna cum laude from Ohio State, double major, like I said. Class of '91, though, not '94. And my mother really is co-chair of the Medina County Democratic Party, if you can believe it. She doesn't know about this, of course, but I did use her name to get the job."

"And all the rest?" Mel tries to remember Schooley's cover story — a legislative internship, working for a lobbyist maybe, a statewide campaign? — but it's too long ago to recall precise details, too many other facts pushed into her brain over the past 6 weeks.

"Complete bullshit. I went to George Washington, like you. Graduate School of Political Management, M.A. '93. Top of my class. That's where Kane recruited me. I worked the Virginia gubernatorial election with him, deputy assistant campaign manager."

"George Allen," Mel says automatically. "Big win for you fuckers, if I remember correctly."

"Uh huh. We started 29 points down, ended up with a 17-point win. Pretty tremendous experience for my first campaign. There's nobody like Howard Kane. Sorry."

"And whose idea was this spy bullshit?"

"Mine, actually. We had a plant in the Terry campaign, gave us some useful if somewhat limited insights. I suggested we try it again, see if we couldn't get better intel this time around. I volunteered for the job, figured I could use my mother's connections to get a decent position. I never expected to get elevated so high, though, to have access to everything going on at the top. Prime intel."

"And Kane's heart attack? Was that a lie too?"

"Yup. Total 100% fake. Kane's been running things from his ranch in West Texas since leaving the hospital."

"That son-of-a-bitch! Really? He really faked a heart attack? Then laid all that soul-searching bullshit on me?"

"'Fraid so." Schooley sounds awfully glib, but he looks genuinely apologetic. Pretty amazing actor, Mel says to herself. We even went to the same school, lived in the same city, and he never once let anything slip. Impressive.

"Like I said, I'm really, really sorry. You're an amazing woman, Mel. I mean that. I have nothing but the utmost respect for you."

"*Utmost respect*? So much respect that you could lie to my face every day for 6 fucking weeks."

"I know. It's pretty terrible. Last time I'm ever gonna do this, I promise."

"I honestly don't know what to do here." Mel stops herself from adding, *Number Two*. Jesus, she even had a flattering nickname for him. "I feel like I oughta be able to kill you, right here in my office. Claim self-defense, or *posse comitatus* or some shit." A smile cracks Mel's face, the absurdity of the whole thing too much to take. Fucking Howard Kane planted a mole in her operation, and she took the kid under her wing, her first mentee. Who would ever believe it?

"I've learned a tremendous amount over the past 6 weeks. I'm not kidding. This has been a really great experience for me, except for…"

"Except for the spying part. Jesus Christ, Schooley. Now I've seen it all. I really goddamned have."

1994

Mel realizes she's been holding Schooley's folder the whole time. She helicopters it across the room, the papers fluttering in all directions.

"I can't fucking believe you, Schooley. A plant! Goddamn Howard Kane. Goddamn all you Republican pieces of shit." The words are angry, but Mel's tone is light. She can't dredge up the necessary sense of betrayal. It's simply too ridiculous. Her rage at Howard Kane should be off the charts — a rapist and a spymaster, what a complete asshole! — yet she feels only embarrassment, a sense of relief even, for some stupid reason.

Schooley gathers up the spray of papers. "You've been an amazing mentor, Mel. Seriously. I've learned so much from you over the past 6 weeks. And Porter was never gonna win this. You know that, right?"

"Yeah, I know." Mel has an urge to tell Schooley about her fake tape — it's the one thing he doesn't know about, the one slim hope they had to win the race — but that's a piece of strategic genius she decides to keep to herself, legend be damned.

Schooley drops his hand on Mel's shoulder. He suddenly seems like the older and wiser one here, the mentor consoling the mentee for a rookie mistake. "No hard feelings, I hope. It's just politics, after all."

Mel remembers Kane saying the same exact thing, more than once. She wishes she could fully accept that, but after this asinine up-and-down campaign, she knows she can't. Does that mean it's time to get out of the game? Probably. It was a mistake all along to believe she had an honest-to-God mission to preserve a Democratic Senate, even worse to make it a personal fight against Kane.

"There's nothing worse than True Believerism, right?" The capital letters are obvious in her tone of voice.

Schooley nods knowingly, hands her the folder. "I really did write a concession speech. I actually think it's pretty good. Take a look."

Mel reads what he has out loud, stops a few times to point out phrases that aren't quite right. Schooley takes notes, heads back to his desk to finish out his ersatz services by polishing the speech into final form. Not that it matters. It's not like Porter has any future in politics anyway. The graceful, optimistic concession speech is for candidates who'll live to fight another day. Porter's a different breed entirely, a Gary Hart, not a Bill Clinton. Mel tries not to feel bitter about it but doesn't succeed very well. *At least no one can blame me for Porter getting shellacked,* she tells herself. *Even if he goes down by 20 points, the DNC's not going to cast me into the wilderness.*

No, but she might go there of her own accord. She still hasn't decided, hates herself for being so irresolute, wishes Thom had turned out to be Mr. Wonderful so her decision would be easier. Or would it? Does she really want a man to be the reason she moves to Cleveland? Or stays in D.C.? Or does anything? Of course not. So, logically, it's a good thing Thom turned out to be campaign sex with a twist, not a real thing, or she'd be sitting here second-guessing her choice to stay in Cleveland, wondering if she was doing it for herself or making choices based on men. That's logically. Emotionally — well, maybe she should ask Schooley what she is and isn't allowed to feel about the slow implosion of her relationship, about her indecision, about this whole frustrating, messy, ultimately meaningless endeavor called life. He's a pretty smart kid even if he is a shameless liar.

OK, Carnes, don't go plunging into an existential funk here. Just light yourself another cigarette and focus on what's right in front of you, not the infinite abyss of a meaningless universe.

It doesn't work — there's nothing else to focus on anyway. The election is lost, her relationship too. She has no friends or hobbies, doesn't even want any. Just the word *hobbies* annoys her. What would she do? Paint watercolor landscapes? Collect stamps? Learn to knit? Jesus, the thought of it makes her shudder.

The only problem is, there's nothing to distract her from the abyss. In moments like these, all she's left with are the ghosts she normally outruns by staying busy with work, by drinking, by...well, that's pretty much it.

The first ghost to appear is Jimmy Carter, of all people, her mind flashing back to April 25th, 1980. She remembers the date exactly, one of those tragic milestones people like her simply know by heart, like November 22nd, April 4th, October 23rd, February 26th. On April 25th, she watched President Carter, weary and distracted, announce the failure of the Iranian hostage rescue mission, watched again later that day as Walter Cronkite offered his analysis, his basset-hound face and grave tone expressing the nation's sense of tragedy far better than the beleaguered president did. She sat up late that night as her father drank whiskey and pontificated about the colossal fuck-up and what it said about America's decline. It hit Mel hard, the death of those 8 servicemen she never knew, drawing tears on her pillow that night, tears she hadn't yet shed for her own mother, gone for 5 months at that point. She got up at dawn the next day, hiked across town before school to visit her mother's grave, sat on the wet ground off to the side, the grass over the fresh mound of dirt just starting to sprout. She stared at the gravestone until the engraving was burned into her eyes.

ELEANOR TRUMAN CARNES
BELOVED WIFE AND MOTHER
JUNE 22, 1939 TO NOVEMBER 28, 1979
"Make It Count"

She thought back to the funeral, remembered how she wouldn't let herself cry, felt bad suddenly that her first cry of the past half year was over the death of anonymous soldiers in a far-off desert—senseless deaths, yes, but remote, unconnected to her life except in the most abstract way. Why could she cry for them but not for her own mother? Why wouldn't she *let herself* cry for her mother? That was the real question.

"Make it count," she read out loud from the gravestone. She forced her voice to be steady, scrunched her eyes to forestall the tears. Crying over her mother wouldn't do anyone any good, wouldn't help her live a life that counted for something.

Or would it? What was she walling herself off from? Was the energy she used to build that wall draining her for other pursuits? Was she killing her mother's memory more surely than the cancer had killed her body?

The pain seized her chest suddenly, melted every muscle in her body. Mel crumpled face down on the mound above her mother's casket, parted her lips, welcoming cool clods of dirt in her mouth, one of her mother's dying admonitions echoing in her mind. *Do something worthwhile with your life, poppet. Don't waste your one chance on Earth getting distracted by the shiny things. Make it count.*

She vowed ferociously to remember, to honor her mother's memory with every deed, but as soon as she felt the tears coming, she shot up, brushed the dirt from her front. *Crying won't help anybody*, she told herself, blinking back the tears. It was her first piece of advice to herself, nothing that either of her parents had ever said or would ever say—though of course she'd never seen them cry either. It seemed like a message her mother would approve. *Actions, not words or tears—that's what makes the world a better place.*

She said it out loud—"*Crying* won't help anybody"—then repeated her new dictum as she strode purposefully from the cemetery, emphasizing a different word each time. "Crying won't help *anybody*. Crying won't *help* anybody. Crying *won't* help anybody."

She's cried since then — of course, she's not a robot — but it never lasts long. She won't let it last. Whether or not her mother would be disappointed by the life she's led, it's still and always true: crying *won't* help anybody.

Yet here she is, age 30, feeling the urge to cry over her dead mother, over her wasted youth, over the sad state of the world and her inability to do anything about it — everybody's inability to do anything about it. The Republicans are about to take over, crime is at an all-time high, the ozone layer is melting, the human population growing to unsustainable levels, and on and on.

Oh for fuck's sake, Carnes. Get your shit together!

She has to do something to beat back this idiotic tide of anxiety.

You're too young for a midlife crisis, she says to herself, but she's unconvinced. Why not? Or maybe it's a *mid-youth crisis*. She still has a decade before she's middle-aged. Is she going to use the rest of her youth the same way she's used it so far? *Use*? It's more like *waste*.

Do something worthwhile with your life, poppet.

Oh for fuck's sake, shut up! Mel pounds the desk with both fists, feels the tears coming again — from frustration and rage, not sadness. The voice in her head won't stop asking, *Have you lived up to your mother's dying admonition?*

She doesn't know. She honestly doesn't. Objectively, it seems like she hasn't done much — gotten a few Democrats elected, pushed the boundaries on women in politics a few millimeters maybe. What else? Or is that enough? Is that as much as anyone could hope for, inching towards a better world? Is she being too hard on herself? Or too easy?

She knows she can't see the matter objectively. She's always been extremely hard on herself, always washed up on the shores of disappointment when the slack time gives her mind too much room to run with the big questions. It's an occupational hazard of campaign, no time for yourself followed by too much time — way too much time. It strikes Mel that her angst might simply be a form of bad sportsmanship. Is all this anxiety simply because she's losing some stupid campaign? This is only her second time facing defeat. It feels like shit even though she knows not to blame herself. Or is it deeper than that — because she's facing the predictable ruin of yet another short-term relationship? Will she ever be satisfied with a man, or is she doomed to brushing aside every possibility for nitpicky reasons?

1994

Or is it deeper still? A growing certainty that she's betrayed her mother's legacy with every decision she's made since she rose from that mound of dirt in 1980 and told herself not to cry. Who can she ask if she's lived up to her mother's dictum? Mel drops her cigarette in the ashtray, rests her forehead on the desk. There's only one person, and she knows it. She turns slowly to contemplate the telephone, blinks at the inert plastic blob. She's been avoiding this phone call forever, never even seriously contemplated having the conversation she knows she needs to have.

Come on, Carnes. Stop dancing around the edges of your life. Pick up the goddamned phone.

She bolts upright, resolved, snatches up the receiver and punches in the numbers quickly. She stares unfocused at the whiteboard as the ringtone repeats, three, four, five times.

"Hello."

Mel's breath catches at the sound of her father's voice. She's paralyzed. She licks her lips, her mind racing. She can't figure out what to say.

"Hello?"

"Dad. It's me. Mel." Please don't say something to make me feel guilty. Please!

"Boo boo, what's the matter? You sound strange. Are you OK?"

"I don't know, dad. I don't think I am." This is the first time she's ever admitted something like this to her father. She used to confess her doubts and fears to her mother, admit her abiding sadness and let herself be soothed, but that all died on November 28th, 1979 — 15 long years ago.

"What's the matter, sweetie? It's not this stupid election, I hope."

"No." Mel sniffles. She feels the tears coming, and for once she doesn't fight it. "Have I been a good person?" The tears flow hotly over Mel's cheeks, the questions flowing with them. "Have I lived up to mom's expectations? Have I made a difference? Have I done anything worthwhile with my life?"

"Of course you have, Mel. Of course." There's not an ounce of doubt or hedging in his voice. He sounds genuinely supportive for once. "Where's this coming from?"

"I dunno." Mel sniffles, wipes her nose. "I just think if mom were still alive, she'd be pretty disappointed in how her daughter turned out. Do you think she'd be disappointed in me? I've done…questionable things."

"You mother was no saint, Mel. She was an amazing woman, but she was human like the rest of us. She had her flaws."

"Like what? Name one flaw." Mel feels the defiance tighten her chest. She squeezes the receiver tightly, fights the urge to bang it against the desk.

"You don't want to get into this, sweetie. I promise."

"What the hell is that supposed to mean? What are you hiding from me?"

"Nothing." There's a long pause. Mel can hear the ice clanking in her father's glass. She senses his hesitation, imagines him wrestling with himself over how to proceed. She notices she's holding her breath, forces herself to let it out, to breathe deeply through her nose, in with the good air, out with the bad.

"Your mother was human, like everybody else," he says at last. "Let's just leave it at that."

"I can't leave it at that. I really can't. I've been living with mom's ghost hovering over me for half my life. I need to start facing up to what that's done to me. I need to know who she *really* was so I can put it all in perspective. I really do need this, dad."

"It's nothing major, sweetie. She drank too much. Me too." Another pause, more ice clanking, the sound of her father sipping something, as though to demonstrate his point. "She cheated on me a few times," he adds ruefully.

"What?" Mel pounds the desk, shoots to her feet. "What the fuck did you just say?"

"Jesus, Mel. Calm down. I told you, you don't need to hear any of this. I cheated on her too, if that makes it any better. It was the '70s. Everybody cheated. Didn't mean you didn't have a good marriage. We were all just so…so restless, I guess."

Mel wants to hurl the phone across the room. She asked, though. She realizes this is the conversation she and her father have been avoiding all these years. Maybe it was smart. Denial does have its function.

"Is that why you remarried so fast? Because you and mom were already on the rocks."

"It wasn't like that. Our marriage *wasn't* on the rocks. We loved each other. Deeply. I still love her, just as much. Probably more. Hardly a day goes by I don't think about her, even still. And I ask myself that same question all the time—the one you just asked me. Would Eleanor be disappointed in me? I started asking that practically as soon as we met. I always wanted her to be proud of me, and even though she agreed to marry me, and bore me a child, I always knew I fell short. *Way* short. That's a hard feeling to live with, Mel."

1994

Another pause, another sip. Mel takes a deep breath again, then one more, waits for her father to continue.

"I don't know how it happened, but at some point we both started looking for something outside the marriage. There was always some man way more impressive than me, an activist or a politician, a movement leader, somebody for your mother to admire unreservedly for once, to feel inspired by. I was fine with it. We had you, so I didn't worry she'd leave me. She wasn't that kind of person. She valued our family and our home, and she loved me. I always knew that. But I knew she also needed to feel like she was living at a higher level for a while—a few hours, a few days, a few weeks at most. And me…sometimes I needed somebody down at my level, somebody who didn't make me feel like a useless lump in the middle of the road, teaching my stupid classes about the past and watching the future go to shit without doing anything about it. You see what I mean? We were just human beings. That's all any of us are. Flawed. Limited. Pretty lame creatures by almost any measure. But there it is. The human condition. Inescapable."

Mel can tell her father expects her to say something, to agree or disagree, to support her position as though he's just given his students a discussion prompt, and he's waiting patiently to get the back-and-forth going. She hesitates to take up the challenge. This isn't the conversation she wanted to have. Or is it? Maybe it's time.

"Mel, honey. You OK?"

Mel's crying loudly now, a sobbing sound that hasn't come out of her in over half a lifetime.

"I'm sorry to lay all that heavy crap on you when you're obviously feeling pretty down."

"No, I'm fine." She wipes away a tear. "It's just that I miss her so much."

"Me too. But you can't let her memory hang over your head. Trust me. I've done it too, but it's never done me any good. She was an amazing person. She lived a great life, flaws and all, but she's gone now, and we have to live our own lives now, make our own judgments about ourselves and the world. It's hard, I know, but it doesn't do anyone any good to live in someone else's shadow. You're just as amazing as your mother, but in different ways. In your own way. I know it's trite, but you have to be yourself."

"I just wish I knew what that was."

"Yeah, that is the tricky part."

Mel realizes she's stopping crying—naturally, not because she forced herself. She feels wrung out, but it's a good feeling, the constructive kind, not the kind of wrung out she feels after a long day of strategy and a long night of drinking.

The silence on the line lengthens, but Mel feels no urge to speak — or hang up. It's nice knowing her father is there, listening and waiting, 100% on her side. She's never felt that kind of unconditional love and support from him, almost feels guilty for realizing it's been there all along, she just never noticed it. *Almost* feels guilty. She doesn't think she needs to let guilt cloud her relationship with her father anymore — at least she hopes she doesn't.

"Thanks for saying all that, dad. I really needed to hear it. I'm sorry if I've been a bad daughter all these years. Distant, standoffish, critical. I really am sorry."

"It's all right, Boo boo. Neither one of us has done a very good job of this."

The nickname almost makes Mel start crying again, but she smiles instead. She realizes she's forced herself to think like an orphan all these years. It's good to know she actually has one parent left, and he might be exactly the one she needs right now — philosophical, forgiving, realistic.

"So what am I going to do with the rest of my life? Other than *be myself*, that is. I don't think I can stay in politics anymore, but if not *that*, then what? It's all I know."

"You can always come live with me while you figure it out. It'd be nice to have you around for more than a few hours."

"Thanks, I appreciate it, but I need to go back to D.C. and be in my own place, figure it out there. I can always call and talk it over, right?"

"Absolutely. Day or night. And I promise I won't joke about you being in jail if you do. I get a sense you never really appreciated that one."

"I never knew you were joking. It never *seemed* like you were joking."

They linger on the phone a while, and Mel confesses in a lighthearted way about her latest stint in jail, unworried that her father will judge her for it. They laugh over the kindergarten biting incident, and her father confirms that her mother really did say, *Sometimes you gotta bite people.*

"That's exactly who she was, sweetie. It's a pretty crazy thing for someone to say to her 6-year-old daughter, if you really think about it. Crazy but human. 100% human."

Mel takes another deep breath after she hangs up. She's never felt so buoyant, so free, so filled with a sense of possibility. She rises and erases the whiteboard, steps back and crosses her arms, considers the blank canvas that represents the rest of her life. If she's going to reinvent herself, she'll to do it the way she devises strategy, free-associating, building ideas and connections from whatever bubbles out of her.

She picks up the pen and begins painting the whiteboard, a smile creeping onto her lips, as though she's about to share a particularly revealing secret with the world, and in a way she is—she's about to share herself, her true self, for the very first time...

THE END

Made in the USA
Middletown, DE
12 July 2022